MW01003046

IN THE NAME OF

A KATE HOLLAND SUSPENSE: BOOK 2 IN THE HIDDEN VALOR MILITARY VETERANS SUSPENSE SERIES

CANDACE IRVING

BLIND EDGE

DEDICATION

For Don Curtis,
a true friend.

ACKNOWLEDGMENTS

My ideas tend to fall well outside the range of my expertise. I'd like to thank the following folks for loaning me theirs. The cool stuff belongs to them; the mistakes are all mine.

I'd like to offer my profound thanks to Dr. Patricia Resick, Ph.D. Dr. Resick is the creator of Cognitive Processing Therapy for PTSD. I can't thank Dr. Resick enough for her incredible direction as I crafted Kate's CPT therapy content, timeline & results.

A huge shout-out to Don Curtis & Special Agent Mike Keleher, NCIS Retired. Thanks for all the brilliant insider cop & agent info!

My deepest thanks also go to my editor, Sue Davison, for her outstanding skills & savvy suggestions. I'd also like to thank my critique partner, Amy McKinley, for her fantastic input, as well as my Beta readers/ARC team in the Goat Locker. Finally, I'd like to thank the wonderfully talented Ivan Zanchetta for yet another amazing cover.

You're all fantastic!

PROLOGUE

He woke to screaming.

Azizah?

He flung the quilt from his body as he jumped off the bed, only to trip over the skateboard sticking out from beneath and crash into the wooden chair at his desk. Confusion overrode the sleep still fogging his brain as he gained his balance—for another piercing scream had rent the air. His sister was definitely in danger.

He could hear his uncle shouting in Persian as he stumbled out of his bedroom and down the hall toward the main part of the house.

The garage. The bellows and screams—and now his sister's violent sobbing—they were all coming from out there.

Whore?

Why would his uncle—

He reached the door to the garage. Through the embedded square of glass, he saw his uncle's thick fist swing up, then down, smashing into his sister's cheek, the heavy ring on *Amoo*'s middle finger splitting the flesh wide as she fell to her knees.

"Azizah!" He wrenched the door open and vaulted out onto

the icy cement, sliding to a halt as the soles of his feet landed amid a slick of old oil.

Before he could right himself, his uncle's fist had bashed into his sister's bruised and bloodied face again.

"*Amoo*, no!" He lunged at his uncle, only to come to a jarring halt as another determined hand gripped his arm from behind and jerked him around.

"*Baba*?"

Like his uncle, his father's face was nearly purple with rage as he spat onto the concrete near the chest freezer beside them. "Azizah has brought dishonor upon the family. She must suffer the consequences."

Dishonor? His sweet, gentle, *always* subservient sister? What could she have possibly done to invite this horror upon herself?

Reza.

Oh, no. He grabbed at his father's shirt. "*Baba*, no! Reza wishes to marry—"

His father's knuckles cracked into his jaw, knocking the rest of his words back down his throat before they could escape. "You *knew* she was shaming us with that boy? And you told me nothing?"

Another crack to his jaw. This blow carried such force, it spun him around and sent him stumbling into the echoing garage. He lurched into his sister's kneeling body. Her arms lashed about his waist, her frantic fingers digging into his back, her face pressed into his front as she buried her sobs in the gray sweats she'd given him from her new college.

His uncle closed in on them. The man raised his thickened fist yet again—only this time, the ivory handle of his grandfather's cherished dagger was clenched within, the curved blade slicing ominously down.

He gripped Azizah tighter, turning them both to shield her more fully as he flung himself over the top of her *hijab*, the pale blue silk of the headscarf already stained with the splatter of her blood. *Amoo* had struck her, yes. But surely he would not—

He grunted in stunned agony as the dagger plunged into his upper back.

A moment later, the dagger was slicing out, grinding against shrieking nerves and violated bone until it was free.

He was still clinging to Azizah, gasping for air as his father's fingers clamped about his arms to haul him off his sister. His father flipped him onto his spine and held him there as the blade sliced down once more, this time piercing his exposed belly.

"*Baba*!"

His father ignored his scream, those hot, stunted breaths beating into his eyes and cheeks as the man pinned him to that ancient slick of oil amid the concrete.

Terror, pain and disbelief battered together, somehow enhancing his vision as time itself seemed to slow. He could see each curl and flourish carved into the curved steel of the blade that his uncle had smuggled out of Iran as it came down to slice into his flesh—again and again.

Eventually, the dagger that both *Amoo* and *Baba* treasured ceased those excruciating arcs. But he still couldn't move, or even look away from the satisfaction hardening his father's face, as he felt the warmth of his blood spilling out from his abdomen. The fabric of Azizah's final *Eid al-Fitr* gift to him was soaked with it.

He grew cold. More confused.

Why?

Why stab him? And why had his uncle stopped?

He caught his sister's shallow gasp and found the strength to turn his head.

Azizah's split and swollen lips moved ever so slightly as she whispered his name. Their grandfather's blade. He knew why it wasn't slicing into him anymore. It was buried to its now tainted ivory hilt—in Azizah's chest. Her lashes fluttered once, then stilled. Those beautiful dark eyes he adored were now sightless and glassy.

The only person who had ever truly loved him was dead.

1

In the past week, how much were you bothered by: repeated, disturbing and unwanted memories of the stressful experience?

Kate Holland shifted her focus to the columns at the right of the post-traumatic stress assessment attached to the clipboard on her lap. The numerical ratings on the PTSD symptoms checklist spanned from 0 to 4, with the corresponding qualifiers at the top ranging from *Not at all*; to *A little bit*; *Moderately*; *Quite a bit*; and *Extremely*.

So...getting sucked so deeply into the memory of Max losing his head that she could see, hear and smell the bastard wielding that gleaming sword four years later and seven thousand miles away? And remaining trapped within the horror for so long that all three of her remaining fellow Braxton PD deputies—*and* the sheriff—had not only noticed, but had crowded in around her desk at the police station before she'd found the strength and presence of mind to snap out of it?

Yeah, that definitely fell under *Extremely*.

She circled the 4 in the column beneath and moved on to the second question on the sheet. Was she bothered by: *repeated, disturbing dreams of the stressful experience?*

Let's see...being woken from a sweat-soaked nightmare at least twice a night this past week by an increasingly worried and seriously stressed-out German Shepherd jabbing his nose into her neck so frantically that he'd begun to leave bruises?

Yet another shoo-in for the *Extremely* column.

Kate circled her second 4 out of a possible 4 and moved on to the third question. By the time she'd pushed through all twenty queries—including *Feeling distant or cut off from other people?* and the ever-incriminating *Feeling jumpy or easily startled?*—she was contemplating dumping the clipboard on the waiting room's deserted check-in counter and escaping this emotional sinkhole of a dilapidated VA hospital tasked with juggling the state's surfeit of screwed-up veterans. Permanently.

The temptation to bolt intensified as Kate noted the succession of fours she'd circled down the front and back of the questionnaire.

When she'd signed the contract agreeing to attend no less than twelve weekly, soul-shredding sessions of cognitive processing therapy, Dr. Manning had informed her that a baseline total of thirty-three on this very assessment pointed to a probable PTSD diagnosis in all its raging glory. She didn't need a calculator to know she'd blown past that sum with the first ten questions alone; she could feel the reality of her deepening deficiencies ricocheting along every jagged line of her seriously cracked psyche.

It was barely noon on a lazy Saturday in early December. The parking lot outside the main doors to Fort Leaves had been all but deserted upon her arrival, leaving her to commandeer the first slot. If she bailed now, she could be back inside her Durango with the engine fired up and the bulk of Little Rock in her rearview mirror within two to three minutes. Less than thirty later, she'd be back in Braxton, pulling into the drive of the split-log home she'd inherited from her father, returning one of

Ruger's humblingly ecstatic greetings and a slew of his more sedate, balming hugs as she and the Shepherd escaped to the couch for the remainder of the weekend.

Even better, she wouldn't have to explain the skyrocketing scores on her weekly questionnaire, let alone the reason behind them.

And what she planned to do about it.

Heck, she wouldn't even have to explain her decision to Liz. As a newly baptized shrink herself, not to mention her best friend from high school, Liz would definitely have had something to say about it, too. But Liz was out of town for training and wouldn't be back for two more weeks. Long enough for Kate to strengthen herself against the coming disappointment.

That decided it.

Kate stood...only to hear the soft snick of the inner door across the waiting room as it opened.

Dr. Manning's deceptively placid blue stare eased into the waiting room, pinning her in place as the remainder of the shrink's lanky, sixty-something form followed. "Good afternoon, Deputy Holland. I see you found the PTSD assessment I left for you. Excellent." He opened the door wider and waved her into his lair. "Please, come in."

Trapped, Kate tightened her grip on the clipboard and abandoned the row of rust-colored chairs, taking care to keep her sights locked on the shrink's shoulder-length strands of silver—and not the collection of cobalt blue pottery looming along the floating shelf to her right as she moved deeper into the waiting room.

It took thirteen steps to clear her first landmine of the afternoon. Five more had her safely through the doorway, but flush with the second.

Unfortunately, short of closing her eyes, there was no escaping the three-by-five-foot, tattered Islamic flag on the wall above the faux leather couch as she paused between the matching armchairs located on her side of the coffee table.

Manning had offered to have the flag and pottery removed. At least until she'd gotten through her first few sessions. While she appreciated the gesture, she'd passed. What was the point? It wasn't as though she needed the sight of those bowls and jugs—or even that singed scrap of white on green—to trigger her own private hell anymore.

It was there. Twenty-four hours a day now.

Whether she closed her eyes or not.

"May I take your coat?"

"Thank you." Kate set the clipboard on the seat of her usual chair and slipped off her Braxton PD jacket. The jacket she'd deliberately donned before leaving her house, along with the long-sleeved department polo beneath, and her police utility belt and trousers—despite the fact that she didn't have duty until Monday.

What better way to obscure the real reason for her shoulder holster and the loaded 9mm inside? The 9mm she still couldn't leave the house without.

Where her clawing need to remain armed twenty-four/seven would leave her once her boss figured out the rest, she had no idea. But it would help now with the exceptionally sharp VA psychiatrist turning away from the brass coat tree beside his desk to approach the pair of wingback chairs.

Or not.

That sharp blue stare hadn't zeroed in on her Glock. Or the clipboard she'd retrieved with her right hand. The stare was fused to her left—or, rather, her wrist.

Max's dive watch.

Crap.

She'd meant to remove it before she bailed out of her SUV. If only because she and the shrink had agreed that she wouldn't wear it for the duration of her therapy.

Correction—Manning had pressed his position with that quiet, insidious logic of his. Something about how he'd noticed that she tended to use the watch she'd yanked off the wrist of the terrorist who'd beheaded Max as an instinctive grounding technique. And that, while grounding techniques were generally a good thing—and that he did encourage keeping the watch near so that she had something to touch when stressed—he'd also noticed that she tended to carry the twisting and scraping of the oversized band around her wrist to the point of self-harm and avoidance.

So she'd removed it.

She'd made it twelve days with the watch in her pocket—until the sheriff had stopped her on her way out of the station late Thursday afternoon. The moment Lou had dropped the governor's bombshell on her, her wrist had begun to itch worse than it had since she'd stumbled across Joe's betrayal four weeks earlier.

Hell, worse than it had itched since she'd woken up in that quiet room at the Craig Joint Theatre Hospital at Bagram, Afghanistan, four years ago.

Like it was itching now.

Somehow, she managed to ignore the sensation as she dumped the clipboard onto the chair next to the shrink. She turned her wrist, popped the stainless-steel clasp and slipped the oversized, orange-faced Doxa into the pocket of her uniform trousers—and sat.

The comforting bulk and weight at her upper right thigh should have helped to calm the itch as Manning retrieved the clipboard from the opposite armchair and settled himself within—but it didn't.

If anything, the itching increased.

He finished reading the assessment she'd filled out in the waiting room, then moved on to the homework he'd assigned the previous week. Flipping through the worksheets, he studied her comments. Even if she hadn't placed the sheets beneath the assessment in the order in which she'd completed them, she'd have known when he'd reached the one he was looking for.

Shrinks weren't the only ones adept at reading expressions. Cops could too.

Even shitty ones, like her.

Manning finished the final worksheet and looked up.

She nearly squirmed in her chair. That laser focus of his she could deal with. But the insidious compassion that replaced it?

It was so much worse.

The itching had become so intense, her forearm shook with the force of resisting it—until she couldn't. Against her will, the fingers of her right hand slipped across her lap to rub at the bracelet of scratches and older, fine white scars that she'd been adding to since Thursday afternoon.

The uppermost layer of skin had darkened from an irritated pink to livid scarlet a mere hour earlier, shortly before she'd left the house.

Right around the time she'd screwed up the courage to fill out the trio of blocks on that final worksheet.

But instead of addressing the content of those blocks, the shrink shifted his attention to her wrist. She was still rubbing it. He didn't need to repeat his earlier, clinical assessment. It was thrumming through the air between them.

Avoidance. She was practicing it again. Without the watch this time.

Lovely.

She tugged her fingers from her wrist—and anchored them beneath her right thigh. "Sorry."

Manning's soft sigh filled the room. "Kate?"

"Yes?"

"You were in a relatively good place when you left this office last Saturday. You had accepted that PTSD is normal after a severe trauma. We spoke about natural emotions like anger and fear, and manufactured emotions like guilt. We also talked about the importance of allowing yourself to experience the natural emotions connected to the trauma you experienced in Afghanistan, and the importance of not—" That insidious compassion shifted to the band of raw flesh. "—avoiding them. We even discussed the likelihood that your scores, and the symptoms behind them, would increase over the next few weeks —because you now remember your trauma in its entirety. *But* that embracing these connected emotions is what will allow their intensity to lessen and burn out, much like a fire that's lost its source of fuel."

He waited for her guilty nod, then flipped through the stack of papers on the clipboard to remove that final, damning worksheet and set it on top. "Last week, you also composed a statement on why you believe your trauma occurred and how it has affected your life. In it, you admitted that you hated the Silver Star that was awarded as a result of your POW experience and the eleven terrorists you were forced to kill during your escape —and that you felt responsible for the beheading of your friend, Max."

She had. But since he'd begun last week's session with a similar review of their initial one, she bit her tongue and waited for the rest.

Not to mention an actual question for her to respond to.

The shrink glanced at the sheaf of papers. "Last Saturday, we discussed the concept of stuck points as well. That is—problem areas in thinking that interfere with the recovery process, thereby keeping a person 'stuck' in PTSD. We found several of yours and began with the one regarding the beheading: *I should have protected Max*. We worked through this stuck point together with your first ABC worksheet and discussed it at length. You agreed that the crime scene investigation conducted by your former Army CID colleagues proved there was nothing you could have done to save Max. You told me you were going to reread the reports and review the video recording that the terrorists made of the beheading this past week. Were you able to do that?"

Though it had damned near killed her to read and watch and listen to it all again, "Yes."

"And do you still agree that, given the circumstances that day, there was nothing you could have done to save Max's life?"

That *she* could have done? "Yes."

He must have been satisfied with the honesty behind that silently split hair, because he nodded. "Then perhaps we should discuss this." Manning tapped his index finger over the initial block of the worksheet she'd forced herself to fill out that morning. The one that spelled out the first—and final—task that she'd be performing as Deputy Holland when she reached the police station come Monday morning.

"What happened?"

Kate shrugged. "It's right there." She tipped her head toward the label above that first block, the one that read: *Something happens*. "I'm turning in my badge."

"Why?"

Well, hell, that answer was right there on the worksheet too. Scratched out in the next square over, directly beneath: *I tell myself something*. She pushed forth another shrug as she gave voice to the supposed stuck point she'd written in the block—though, admittedly, this shrug was stiffer than her first. "My judgment can't be trusted."

Manning nodded as he retrieved the pen from its slot at the top of the clipboard. "*My judgment can't be trusted* is a stuck point.

However, while *turning in my badge* may be what is *about* to happen—and we'll discuss that possibility in a moment—it is not the activating event. So..." He used the pen to cross out *I'm turning in my badge* and sat back, once again trapping her within that cloying web of compassion. "Let's start with the *real* activating event, shall we? What happened this week that led you to fill out this sheet?"

What the hell. "Have you heard of the Diamond Award?"

The slight uptick of the shrink's brows suggested yes.

She nodded and pushed deeper into the muck that had been simmering deep inside her gut for four-plus years now. "The governor's decided to hitch his tattered coat-tails to our lowly department. Lou and the rest of the guys are scheduled to get attaboys from the state police, and I'm supposed to get slapped with that."

Another uptick in that silvery brow. "From what I understand, the Diamond is the state's highest award. It's—"

"Bullshit."

"I was going to say *natural.* As in, following a heinous and high-profile case like the one you recently solved, it's natural for awards to follow. Expected even."

Yeah, well, she didn't need another award fêting her and her so-called skills. Let alone one with Joe's, Grant's *and* Burke's names attached to it.

And there was the rest.

"Kate?"

She sighed. "According to Lou, the thing's supposed to be presented by the Secretary of State. But, no, Mr. 'Look At Me, And Not My Declining Poll Numbers' finagled a way to steal the stage—by dragging the battle-scarred war hero up onto the dais with him. The governor decided the entire farce should go down at the capitol after the legislature reopens. And then he expects me to trot over to the governor's mansion with him, arm in arm, for a black-tie reception. Be his grisly-faced guest of *honor*."

Sure, the rest of the department would be there. But so would the press. Taking photos. Adding to the fraud and spreading it around the entire state—and beyond.

She wasn't sure which was worse.

All she knew for certain was, "I can't do it."

"Can't? Or won't?"

She refused to touch that one.

Unfortunately, Manning was undeterred. The doc simply returned the pen to the top of the clipboard and settled into his chair. "What about the rest of the department? Do the sheriff and your fellow deputies share your feelings about the circumstances surrounding their respective awards and the reception to follow?"

Lou's beaming face slipped into view—along with Owen's and Drake's. She pushed all three aside. She had to.

"No."

"And what happens if you turn down the Diamond Award? Am I correct in assuming that the entire event would be canceled—including the awards for the other officers who worked the Garbage Man case?"

"Yes." Talk about blackmail.

Then again, they were dealing with a career politician. They didn't come any more self-serving than that in her book.

"Hence your decision to turn in your badge."

"Why not?" With her out of the way, Lou, Owen and Drake—and, yes, even Seth—would still get the recognition they deserved. The recognition she *didn't*.

"Are you certain—"

"*Yes*. I've made up my mind. I told you; I never should've accepted that Silver Star. I won't add to the lie."

"Lie?"

"That I'm some super cop—military or civilian." The assessment was so far off it should've been funny. But it wasn't. Nothing about this was. "It's *my* fault Max is dead."

"Kate, should we review the circumstances surrounding Max's death again? And why you feel—"

She shook her head. "I'm not talking about that bastard with the sword. I agree with you there; there was nothing I could've done then that would've stopped Max from losing his head. But someone else could've. I told you last week. My dad was right; I wasn't cut out to be CID. If I hadn't enlisted, Max would've brought another agent along on that convoy, and he'd have confided his suspicions about Joe to that agent—a *good* agent. If he had, that ambush probably wouldn't have even happened."

"Why?"

"Because another agent would've realized Joe was dirty long before the ambush, and he or she would've taken Joe down."

"Because this other agent would have been a good agent?"

She ignored the renewed itching at her wrist and nodded. "Yes."

"And you are not a good agent—or cop?"

"Nope."

"And you believe this because of Joe Cordoba?"

"And Grant, and Burke."

The trifecta of fuck-ups. And they were all on her.

She hadn't realized that her former fellow CID agent and so-called buddy, Joe, was up to his lying lips in a monstrous scheme that had left countless soldiers and veterans alike dead and diced up, with their respective organs and body parts sold off to the highest bidder on the black market. And there was Grant, her former lover—who'd been performing the dicing. And last, but not least: Burke. The soldier who'd tipped Max off to the entire scheme four years earlier, leading Joe to arrange the ambush that had taken out their convoy and had led directly to Max's beheading.

And, then, there was yours truly. Not only one of CID's supposed finest, but a glorified war hero.

Except she hadn't been able to wedge a single piece of the entire twisted puzzle into place until Burke had murdered four members of the organ harvesting racket—including Grant—and left their sectioned body parts in tidy rows of crisp brown paper bags along the backroads of Braxton...as a pointed *get your shit together* message to her.

Three other members of the racket had died as well, before she'd regained her memories of Max's final moments and figured out enough to track Burke down.

And Burke?

Damn it, she'd *liked* him.

Admittedly, the IED and traumatic brain injury that had stolen the staff sergeant's legs had also severely damaged the moral center of Burke's brain—but she should've noticed something, right? Especially since Burke had been using another soldier's identity?

She pointed to the clipboard on the doc's lap. "Like I wrote on that sheet, my judgment can't be trusted."

Manning retrieved the pen and circled the statement. "You are right in that *my judgment can't be trusted* is a stuck point. But the correct, corresponding activating event is...?"

They might not have been doing this for long, but she'd gotten the hang of what Manning wanted, so she gave it to him. "Joe, Grant and Burke were involved in the organ harvesting and those murders."

Manning passed the pen and clipboard to her.

What the hell. She added the statement she'd just voiced out loud to the first block, then stared at the trio of words blaring up at her from the final square. That morning, beneath *I feel something*, she'd written *shame*, *disgust* and *fear*.

She still did—and it was all directed at herself.

"Kate, let's go back to this hypothetical good agent of yours. How would he or she have known that Joe was involved with the organ harvesting?"

"He would've picked up on something that I didn't. Something I missed."

"Like what?"

"I don't know."

"Is it possible that you didn't miss anything?"

"I must have. I was fooled, wasn't I? By all of them." The guilt she'd been battling for weeks burrowed in that much deeper. She dropped her attention to the band of scarlet on her wrist, fighting the urge to give in to the temptation to rub.

"As I was."

Surprised by the shrink's confession, she glanced up.

Manning nodded. "Grant was involved in my Thursday night therapy group. Burke volunteered here at the hospital. Burke's TBI notwithstanding, I, too, knew both men while they were doing what they were doing, and I didn't realize what was happening either. In fact, no one here at Fort Leaves knew that Grant and the other three VA employees were involved in murdering veterans for their organs. So...does that make the hospital's entire staff incompetent? Is our judgment untrustworthy, as well?"

"No."

"But we produced the same purportedly glaring fail as you."

She shook her head as she passed the clipboard back to Manning. "None of you are supposed to be trained investigators."

"But we did know Grant and the others. Worked with them. And many of us who did are therapists—hence, also trained observers of human behavior. Surely we should have realized that something was off."

"But you're not cops. You're doctors, nurses, caregivers. Most people who show up on a hospital doorstep want to be helped. Grant and the others didn't."

Hence, Grant and every one of his murdering cohorts would have done their damnedest to keep hints of the truth from bleeding through.

The shrink leaned closer. "Ah....then what about Joe? He spent time at the crime scenes and worked the investigation with your sheriff and your fellow Braxton deputies. Did your boss or the other officers in your department—or even the FBI/BAU agent who arrived with Joe to assist in the investigation —did any of them realize that Joe was dirty?"

She knew what Manning was doing. The same thing the doc had done the week before when he'd managed to chip away at her belief that there was something she could've done in that mud brick hovel back in Afghanistan to prevent Max from losing his head. Manning was employing his own charming brand of relentless Socratic questioning, flipping her arguments back onto herself and forcing her to pick them apart and think through them.

Defend them.

Lousy cop or not, she was still a seasoned interrogator. Did he think he could lead her through her own professional dance and not have her recognize the steps?

But damned if it wasn't working. Because she was beginning to doubt herself...again.

"Kate?"

"No."

"No...?"

She knew what he wanted there too. The full statement. Spouting from her mouth, not his. *Fine.* "No. No one at the

Braxton PD, much less Agent Walker, realized Joe was dirty until I figured it out and informed them."

But why would they?

She allowed her frustration to spill out as she raked her fingers through her hair, disturbing the short ponytail she'd fashioned that morning. Socratic questioning or not, the doc just didn't get it. Because he didn't want to. "Don't you see? Lou, Agent Walker and the other deputies in my department—they all knew Joe for less than forty-eight hours. They hadn't worked side by side with the man for years. Shared investigations with him. As I did—*while* Joe was dirty."

That earned her a nod—but not one of agreement. "I can tell you feel strongly about this stuck point." Manning thumbed through the sheets on the clipboard, then looked up. "I see you've entered it into your log. That's good. We'll be coming back to it in later sessions. But right now, I'd like to take a few moments to discuss your decision to surrender your badge. From your comments earlier, it sounds as though your resolve to quit the force is a direct reaction to your pending award. Is this correct?"

Score one for the shrink's own interrogating skills.

She nodded.

"And when is the ceremony and the reception?"

"January eighteenth."

"So, it's over six weeks—and six more of our sessions—away. We'll be working through a lot in the coming month and a half. And that work will change you—for the better. I suspect you'll feel differently about the award and the reception by then."

"I doubt it."

"But it is possible, yes?"

Sure. And Joe would be breaking out of Fort Leavenworth that afternoon—to rousing cheers from the families of all those soldiers and vets he'd murdered.

"Kate?"

"Theoretically, yes. It's *possible*."

"If that's the case...what would be the harm in waiting a few more weeks—two, at the very least—to see if your feelings change?"

"About the ceremony?"

"And turning in your badge. You've already begun therapy." He pressed his tented fingertips into the stack of worksheets. "You're putting in the work. Very solid work, too. Do you think that perhaps you owe it to yourself to postpone the decision to resign? To make absolutely certain you're basing a serious career move on your desires and not your fears?"

As much as she hated to admit it, the man had a point.

Not to mention, before that horrific slew of Garbage Man murders, there'd been but two homicides in her jurisdiction in the previous decade and a half.

What could be the harm in waiting fourteen more days?

Because there was the added fact that they were already down two deputies in Braxton—or about to be.

Besides Lou, they were supposed to have five additional officers in the department. Bob Feathers had retired a few weeks before Burke had left that first row of sacks on a deserted gravel road on the outskirts of town. The department's next senior-most deputy, Seth Armstrong, had turned in his notice this Wednesday morning. The easygoing, until-now unflappable bubba had held up against the sight of those crisp sacks and the shrink-wrapped body parts that had been inside, only to fold upon confronting a rusted barrel brimming with the remnants of countless murdered vets awaiting disposal when he, Lou and the others had executed the warrant on the pet crematorium.

Lou was still reeling from the fallout of this latest pending loss and scrambling to find the talent to fill not only Feathers' slot, but now Seth's as well.

It was the only reason she hadn't bailed on Lou on the spot when he'd told her about that asinine award.

"Kate?"

"Fine." The delay would give Lou a bit of a breather before he had to hire someone to fill her position too. "Do I need to sign another contract?"

The shrink's laser stare returned. "Do you need to?"

Well, the last one hadn't kept Max's watch off her wrist, had it?

She flushed at the depth of her weakness. Shook her head. Then gave the doc the verbal commitment she knew he wanted. "I'll hang onto my badge for at least two weeks—and I won't turn it in without telling you first. You have my word."

The added offer to discuss it with him first got her off the hook with the watch, at least for the moment, because the man nodded, then leaned over the arm of his chair to retrieve a stack of ABC worksheets from the coffee table. They were identical to the ones on his lap—except these were blank. Manning set the virgin sheets atop the others and used his pen to scrawl several words inside the middle square of the uppermost one.

He leaned forward to pass the entire fresh batch to her. "This week's homework is more of the same. Consult your stuck point log and choose at least one a day to work through—including the one I just wrote out for you."

Even before she glanced down, she knew what he'd written. She was about to respond when the far-right pouch on her utility belt vibrated.

Her phone.

Manning sat back in his chair and tipped his head toward the pouch. "Go ahead; I can see that you're on duty today."

Her flush returned—with a vengeance. But she slid her phone from its slot as she stood. Short of copping to the implicit façade her department polo, utility belt and 9mm presented—and worse—what choice did she have?

Either way, it was a good decision. Lou's name flashed onto the screen.

She headed for the corner of the office for privacy as she accepted the sheriff's call—just in case. "What's up, boss?"

"Afternoon, Kato. I just swung by your place, but only saw Ruger."

"I'm in Little Rock. I had something to take care of this morning." Something she'd deliberately left out of her recent conversations with the sheriff—even though Lou was more akin to honorary uncle than boss, and had been for over a decade and a half.

And, no, she did not feel guilty.

Kate glanced back at Manning, ignoring that pointed, silver brow and the silent *tsk* that came with it.

Damn it, she *didn't*.

"You 'bout done with that errand?"

Oh, Lord. This was more than one of the "I was in the area" drop-ins that Lou had taken to making these past four weeks to not-so-subtly check up on her following Grant's murder and Joe's arrest. She could hear it in the rasping stress of his tobacco-roughened voice.

She set the homework sheets on the corner of the shrink's desk so she could tug Max's watch from her pocket. No wonder Manning had retrieved the homework blanks. They'd chewed through the session's allotted time a minute ago.

She returned the watch to her pocket. "I'm wrapping things up now. I can be back in Braxton in half an hour. What's wrong?"

"We got a body. It's lyin' in Parson Weaver's current crop of winter wheat. No idea what poor soul it belonged to though."

She closed her eyes—and prayed.

It'd been barely a month. That was just enough time to rouse the psychos out there. *Please* don't let this be a copycat.

Lou must have sent up the same prayer when he'd gotten the word, because his telling sigh filled the line. "No, it's got its head —and all the important parts. Least ways, I think so. Cain't say for sure...'cause damned near every inch of what is here has been burned to an unholy crisp."

She kept her eyes shut. It was the only way to fight the urge to slide down to the carpet beneath her boots and curl into a quivering ball.

The only thing stronger was that damned itch. The one that'd taken up residence once again in and around her left wrist.

She slipped the fingers of her right hand back into her pocket and anchored them to Max's watch, holding on to the Doxa's solid face with her last remaining shred of sanity as she forced herself to open her eyes. To stare at the stack of work-sheets she'd set on the corner of Manning's desk.

My judgment can't be trusted pulsed up at her.

Somehow, those five simple words were that much more real in the shrink's handwriting. That much more decisive.

"Kato?"

Despite that stark, written statement—and all the muck that had been churned up with it—the distinct edge of fear in Lou's voice managed to slice deep into her gut and anchor in. Her fingers were clenched around the watch so tightly now, they hurt.

She blew out her breath anyway—and nodded.

"I'll be right there."

2

Thanks to the portable cherry atop her Durango and the heavy boot she'd applied to the gas, it took Kate twenty-two minutes to reach the outskirts of Braxton. Another three had her abandoning the interstate off-ramp and swinging around the backside of town to turn onto the gravel road that twisted through the outer rolling hills of her jurisdiction to reach the Weaver farm. It wasn't until the Durango was headed up the lane that she realized that Jakob Miller's wooded property—and the dump site for the first line of brown paper bags that Staff Sergeant Burke had left around town—was just beyond the vast spread of thriving winter wheat to her right.

Kate shook off the eerie coincidence as she parked her Durango behind the sheriff's sedan.

Other than Lou's official wheels, the medical examiner's wagon and Nash Weaver's gleaming-white, extended-cab Ram 3500 and older, significantly more beat-up gray Chevy pickup, there were no other vehicles within the driveway's doublewide spread of gravel. Nor did the two cars slotted in with the farming equipment along the side of the barn to her left appear out of place.

Lou and Nash stood on the covered porch that ran the length of the two-story clapboard house to her right, talking. Her former high school classmate acknowledged her arrival with a half-hearted wave, then headed into his house as her boss turned around to descend the wooden steps and cross the lawn.

Kate hauled her stainless-steel crime scene kit from the rear hatch of the Durango. She was setting it on the gravel as the sheriff's stocky girth reached her side. Lou didn't even bat an eye at the sight of her matching police uniform on an off day.

Odd.

Almost as much as the dearth of official vehicles in the drive.

She glanced around, noting the distinct lack of Braxton PD personnel as well. They were light on deputies at the moment—but not this light.

"Where are Drake and Owen?"

The sheriff shook the thick crop of gray that insulated his scalp. "They're both still 'bout two hours out. I promised I'd hold down the fort this weekend. Owen and his girlfriend were headed to Fayetteville for the last game of the season. Drake's a closet LSU fan, so they got him a ticket too—so's they could watch him squirm."

Yeah, she wasn't too sure about that. Given that the Tigers were having a great year, and the Razorbacks a crappy one, Drake might've been the one chortling and rubbing it in on the drive home—had Lou not made that call.

As it was, she and Lou would be the ones squirming.

Hell, she already was.

The wind had shifted as she'd reached back into the Durango's rear hatch to grab the sack of evidence markers. The odor now wafting in on the chilly early afternoon breeze? The multi-layered stench of burnt human flesh.

Kate pushed aside far too many memories as she and Lou turned in tandem, instinctively keeping the breeze—and that nauseating smell—to their backs for as long as possible. "So, what have we got, boss?"

Lou used an already gloved hand to lower the SUV's hatch for her. "Not much. Weaver's been on a pastor's retreat for a solid week."

"Was his absence publicized?"

"Yep. In the church bulletin and on the website."

Meaning whoever'd torched the body had probably known he or she had time and privacy on their side. Worse, with the damp weather they'd been experiencing? Anyone spotting smoke from this side of Braxton would've assumed a neighbor had fired up the burn barrel—but they'd have been too far away to pinpoint *which* neighbor, much less offer a timeline on that distinctive smell.

Lou's thoughts must've traveled down the same dead-end lane as hers, because he sighed as he tugged a spare set of latex gloves from his trouser pocket and passed them to her. "Yep, we got bupkis for witnesses. And that ain't all. Weaver's *Goin' Prayin'* notice went up on the website a full two months back. They been repostin' it in the church bulletin almost as long. The man got home 'bout an hour and a half ago. The wind hadn't shifted yet, so he didn't notice the smell when he drove up. Since he'd just picked up his lab from the kid who was watchin' him, he brought the dog straight in to feed him. Once the lab finished, he let him out to do his business—and saw the body. Well, he didn't know it was a body 'til he got closer."

Kate set the bag of markers down on the gravel beside her crime kit so she could don the gloves the sheriff had provided. "Did Nash touch it?"

"Nope. Got nowhere near close enough. He swears he stopped when he reached the base of the hill. That puts him a good ten, twelve yards shy of the body. What with how he was still shakin' like a meth head comin' down off the chalk when I drove up, I'm inclined to believe him."

So was she, and not because Nash had taken up the pulpit since her return to town. She'd been Nash's partner way back in Mr. Barring's tenth grade anatomy class. Two weeks into the syllabus, she'd ended up with a front row seat—and smell—to a then sixteen-year-old Nash's introduction to their furry, four-legged dissection subject and the formaldehyde it'd been preserved within.

Hopefully, the thirty-one-year-old man Nash had grown into hadn't been enjoying a meal of his own while he'd been waiting on his dog. "Did he see anything else? Notice anything out of the ordinary in the garage, house or his barns?"

Lou shook his head. "Nope. I made a point to walk him through all of 'em while we were waitin' for you, too."

"What about phone calls? Email? Snail mail?"

Though Nash's church had a hundred regulars at best, she couldn't ignore the religious fire-and-brimstone angle. Not with a charred body waiting on her...and the fact that the congregation's previous home had gone up in flames the year before.

The frown marring Lou's craggy features deepened. "You think it's connected to last August?"

While the town fire chief had leaned toward accidental in his final report, he hadn't been able to rule out arson, had he? "I don't know, boss—do you?"

"Christ, I hope not. That's all we'd need after that shitstorm we just waded through with all them bags. Not that we need any more dead bodies in town, no matter what the cause."

"Amen." And then there was the rest.

Kate glanced over Lou's shoulder as he reached into his shirt pocket to retrieve his chew. Jakob Miller's treeline loomed closer than it ever had when she and Nash were teenagers as Lou dug out a heathy pinch of tobacco from the tin and shoved it into the side of his mouth. Two murders in the past decade plus. Then those endless lines of sacks.

And now this?

Dumped on the next property over?

The ominous feeling she'd had while driving up the lane returned.

The sheriff followed her stare to Miller's demarcating thicket of mixed pines and balder, deciduous trees. "Yep. It's all stickin' in my craw, too."

Kate shook off the feeling as best as she could as she leaned down to scoop her crime kit and the bag of evidence markers off the gravel. "All right, then." Gut-churning odor or not, "We'd best get to it."

The distinctive stench of burnt human intensified as she followed Lou across the dormant front lawn and around to the back of the house.

The blackened source of that smell lay directly below and roughly thirty feet out from the base of the hill upon which the home had been built, and—as Lou had stated on the phone—just inside Nash's current crop of sprouted and already thriving winter wheat.

Several feet further to the right of the charred corpse lay an oversized heavy duty plastic body bag, already zipped open and waiting. Between the two, Braxton's dark-blue flannel and denim-clad medical examiner.

The afternoon winter sun glinted off Tonga's sleek ebony scalp as he turned away from his own crime kit to kneel beside the body.

Kate glanced at Lou as they headed down the hill. "Where's Nester?"

While she hadn't seen their forensic guru's van in the drive or parked beside the barn, Lou had been known to swing by Nester's place and grab him on occasion, leaving one of the department's part-time crime scene techs to bring up the rear with the official wheels and gear.

The sheriff had phoned her a good half an hour ago.

So where was Nester?

Lou shook his head as they reached the base of the hill and breached the crop line. "He'll be an hour behind Owen and Drake. Nester stopped in late yesterday to let me know he was takin' his crew to his cabin in the Ozarks for some fishin' 'n' forgettin', now that the forensic hustle of the last case has settled down."

Great. Talk about timing. While she understood the deep-seated need to decompress, that left them with just Seth. Only from Lou's sheepish shrug, they didn't have Deputy Armstrong and his dwindling days with the department either.

"I didn't have the heart to make Seth smell what's out here. Not after what he found in that damned crematorium. I told him to head to the station and hang out there in case we needed anythin'."

It was just her, Lou and Tonga for the duration then.

Given the pinched features of the medical examiner's face as they reached the body, they were in danger of losing him too. And it wouldn't be in another year and to Tonga's well-earned retirement. It would be in less than thirty seconds and to the appalling close-up view that went with the smell the ME was currently leaning over.

Lou had been right about the setting, wrong on the description of the corpse. The body hadn't been reduced to an unholy crisp. Though not for lack of some bastard trying.

Somehow, that made it worse.

The mass of cooked flesh lying amid a haphazard pile of ash, mostly burnt tree branches and scorched wheat appeared all too human. Though the right side of the body was deeply charred—including the eyeless head, torso and abdomen—parts of the victim's thighs, lower legs and the outermost portion of the upper left arm were still fleshy and almost...normal. Both arms also displayed the characteristic triple flexion or "pugilists' pose" Kate had noted on far too many burnt corpses in Afghanistan and Iraq—military and civilian.

And the *stench*.

Even if she hadn't spotted the dehydrated curve of what remained of the victim's left breast, along with the strands of singed hair that were caught up at the base of a nearby shriveled stalk of wheat, she'd have been able to hazard a guess as to gender from the overpowering odors of sulfur dioxide and hydrogen sulfide that were still being churned up with each breeze. "It's a woman."

The intensity of the expended sulfur trapped within the damp Arkansas air pointed to one with a serious amount of hair too.

Tonga nodded as he came to his feet. "Agreed. I have Vick's Vapor Rub in my bag for the smell, but—" A resigned sigh escaped. "—it won't help."

He was right. As putrid as those sulfur byproducts were, Kate could make out the disconcerting scent of grilled meat that clung to the layers of charred muscle and fat—along with the metallic tang of cooked blood, and more, from what appeared to be a still pink kidney bursting from within the split of blackened abdominal flesh.

But that wasn't the worst of it. It was the latest memory that had seared in with the sight of that blackened split and the rest of the harrowing odors that came with it.

Corporal Babin and Sergeant Gault.

Babin had been driving the Humvee in Afghanistan that fateful day. Gault had been teasing Babin about how she'd finally be able to impress her dad with her chauffeur skills when they returned home. Max had been smiling and jabbing his elbow into Kate's ribs and winking, because he was certain she was going to have to pay up on the bet they'd placed over the romance that had been budding between the younger soldiers in the preceding months.

A split second later—that earth-shattering blast.

Flipping upside down in the blink of an eye and hanging there, suspended amid melting rubber and splintered steel—and the overpowering stench of Babin's burning hair and bubbling skin. The searing agony in her own shredded face. Struggling to breathe through the thickening smoke, a crushed clavicle and fractured ribs.

And then, as she'd identified the source of the coppery warmth dripping into her eyes, her shattered heart.

"Kato?"

She flinched—and jerked her fingers from the thick scars knotted along the upper ridge of her right collarbone beneath her jacket. She could still see Max. *Feel* him standing beside her. For a full second, nearly two, she could've sworn that his welcoming arms had been wrapped about her, bracing her.

Kate swallowed the knot of grief clogging her throat and nodded as the sheriff's face replaced her friend's. Lou looked as green and rattled as she felt.

"You okay?"

She nodded numbly.

"You sure? Thought I'd lost you for a moment there."

He had. And they both knew it.

She faked a smile and tacked on a pretty lie for good measure. "It's all good."

She set her crime kit and the bag of markers down between two rows of sprouted wheat before Lou could follow up the pity dulling the soft brown in his eyes.

Tonga's too.

"So, boss, what do we know about her?"

Lou took the hint and turned to aim a stream of tobacco juice at the three-inch tower of mud built up around a fresh crawdad hole several feet away. Kate made a mental note to mark the tower for crime scene exclusion as the man shrugged.

"Other than that she's a she? Not a busted thing. What about you? You see anythin' yet?"

It was more what she didn't see. "There are no visible signs of a struggle." And with the remnants of those carefully arranged tree branches amid the surrounding virgin blades of wheat and loosened dirt, there would be. "I'm also pretty sure I smell a petroleum-based accelerant, but I can't be positive." The stench of the sulfur byproducts was too strong; they'd have to wait for confirmation in the chemical analysis.

Either way, she was all but certain that this was not their primary crime scene. "Unless the woman was unconscious, she had to have been killed elsewhere. As to how?" Kate shook her head. "Not a clue."

Unless Tonga saw something she'd missed, they'd be waiting on the autopsy to confirm that too.

Kate pointed toward the tip of the metal strip poking out from between the woman's relatively intact upper left arm and remaining breast. "And there's that."

Lou bent closer. "Is that a piece of wire?"

She nodded. "Manufacturers weave them into the cups of bras for added support. The substantial diameter of that one suggests her cups were on the larger size."

"Our victim was probably well-endowed then."

"Yup." The underwire's presence revealed something else, as well. "She was also at least partially clothed when she was set on fire." If they were lucky, the chemical analysis would provide specific information as to the type of fabric the woman had been wearing. Though Kate doubted it would do them much good.

Both Lou and Tonga moved deeper into the field as she

retrieved her smartphone from her utility belt. She opened the camera app and snapped a slew of wide-angle shots of the body and the dump site in general, then moved in for a series of close-ups.

Since Lou had been first on the scene, he'd have already taken the official photos. But he wouldn't mind if she followed up his efforts with duplicates of her own. Ever since the department had lost a set of accident photos due to a digital camera glitch six years earlier, he actively encouraged it.

As she returned her phone to its pouch, Tonga skirted around the right side of the corpse and crouched beside the remains of a scorched branch to better examine that protruding kidney.

She knelt beside him. "What have you got?"

The ME shook his head. "Not much more than you. The body has already cooled. It's equal to the surrounding temperature, in fact."

That meant the humid air alone was responsible for zealously trapping that godawful smell. It also meant they were looking at a crime timeline of twenty-four hours or more.

Time of death was going to come down to the insects.

Kate stifled the urge to push Tonga for speculation. She'd worked enough accidents and natural causes deaths with the man to know he wouldn't be weighing in on larval activity until he'd finished collecting his samples and had brought them all back to the lab and examined them at length.

"Cooper! Get back here!"

Kate glanced over her shoulder in time to see her old classmate-turned-preacher grab the collar of his energetic yellow lab and nudge the dog through the slider.

She stiffened as Nash turned to wave an apology down at them.

Shit.

Jackknifing to her feet, she whirled around to stand motionless as the suspicion simmered in. It bubbled into a full-blown boil as she judged the line of sight from where she, Lou and Tonga were standing and up to the view from the deck.

If the body behind them hadn't been lying precisely where it was—

"Kato? What is it?"

She spun back to Lou. "He wanted us to find her. Today. The moment Nash returned."

"The killer?"

"Yes."

"How can you be so sure?"

She turned around again and pointed to the upward slope of the clapboard's back lawn. "Like Tonga said, the body's cold. It's been lying out in this field for a day at least, possibly longer. You also said Nash *just* got back; that folks knew he'd be gone. Whoever gathered up these branches and used them to set this woman on fire, did so knowing that too. But he also placed the body exactly here, so that when Nash returned and let his dog out, he'd see her."

"Shit. I been standin' here prayin' some jealous asshole decided his woman done him wrong and lashed out in his rage, then tried to cover it up." Another stream of spittle hit that tower of mud. "But that ain't it, is it? This ain't a one-off, so-called crime a passion."

"I don't think so." In fact, she was beginning to suspect far worse.

Burnt corpses didn't bear any resemblance to bloodless, shrink-wrapped body parts. But that ominous feeling she'd been getting had returned, and it was growing. Twisting. And she did not like the path it was taking. Because this entire crime scene was starting to feel familiar. *Planned.*

Her wrist began to itch.

She forced herself to ignore it. To focus on the case.

This case.

For some reason, the bastard who'd killed the woman at her feet hadn't wanted the charred remains to rot away, unnoticed.

Nor had the killer set this woman on fire solely to obscure her identity—if that outcome had entered his twisted agenda at all.

Too much thought had gone into this dump. Too much effort. Not only had Nash's house been vacant, the body had been laid out just past the first row of wheat. Given that the only boot prints in the field belonged to her, Tonga and Lou, the reason was obvious: the killer had been intent on concealing evidence of his own footprints. Someone that meticulous and determined would've known to add an old mattress or a good half a cord of kindling instead of a nest of two-inch branches beneath the body to ensure that it burned consistently and completely. Nor would a killer that smart have left the remains where some small-town preacher would be able to spot it within minutes of his return home—unless he'd wanted just that outcome.

Were they looking at a fire and brimstone connection, after all?

"Sheriff? Deputy? I'm ready to move her."

"I got it." Lou stepped in front of her, using his girth to cut her off before she could argue.

Despite the fresh wave of pity washing his frown, she was grateful. Not only was the itch clawing at her resolve, it had spread around her entire wrist, completely encircling it.

Lord only knew what would've happened if she'd had to physically handle the source of that smell.

Kate caved into the need and slipped her fingers beneath the cuff of her jacket, discreetly rubbing at the band of abraded flesh that'd barely begun to heal over as she headed for her forensic gear. By the time she'd bent down to retrieve several evidence markers from their bag, the itch had calmed enough for her to concentrate on the job at hand.

Namely, the singed hairs she'd spotted upon her arrival.

She slipped the markers into her jacket pocket and unlocked her crime kit to select a pair of tweezers and several collection envelopes from within. She deposited the first tented number beside the crawdad tower Lou had been targeting to tag the man's tobacco spittle for exclusion, then approached the strands of inky hair that had gotten caught up at the base of that nearby stalk of wheat.

Placing a second tented marker down beside the strands, she snapped several photos, then used her tweezers to transfer the hair to one of the envelopes.

She was still kneeling as the men lifted the body.

Was it her imagination, or had something white fallen from the corpse?

Curious, she waited until Lou and Tonga had carried their burden over to the body bag and gently set it within, then closed in on the dump site. The dirt where the body had lain was scorched, the branches that'd been used to jumpstart the fire completely reduced to ash...except for a single stone gleaming up at her.

She added another evidence marker and snapped a photo, then bent to snag the rock.

Lou reached her side as she stood, using his own gloved fingers to shield his view from the glare of the winter sun behind her. "Whatcha got, Kato?"

"A stone." She flipped it over. It was roughly an inch and a half in diameter, and blackened on the opposite side like the dirt in front of her.

Had it gotten hung up within the seam of the woman's legs while the killer was preparing to torch her? Or had the stone come from the primary crime scene? The one they'd yet to locate?

Lou squinted down at her palm. "That there's a milky quartz. Had a rock collection as a kid. Was even into lapidary for a couple a years. Those stones are pretty, but they ain't worth squat. Won't help our case neither. Quartz is the most common mineral on the planet. Pieces get smoothed out and polished up over time from all the runnin' water in streams and the like." The sheriff shrugged as he straightened. "There's probably a hundred others just like that one in this field alone."

He was right, about all of it. Especially since Braxton and its entire, outlying acreage had once been subject to the ebb and flow of the Arkansas River.

But this stone? Something about it didn't sit quite right with her. For one, it was too round. Too polished. Too...perfect.

And wasn't there something in the Bible about women and stoning?

She'd have asked Lou, but he'd attended church even less often than she and her dad. Seth, however, would've been able to spout chapter and verse.

She'd have to drop by the station on her way home.

Until then, the rock had been wedged into a crevice created by their victim while she was on fire. That meant it was going to the lab.

Lou's phone pinged as she used a second envelope to bag the quartz.

Kate caught the sheriff's scowl as he closed his text app. "What's wrong?"

He shot another stream of tobacco at that marked crawdad tower. "Weaver was frettin' about his congregation earlier, and with good cause. He mentioned a phone tree, so I gave the go ahead to fire it up and see if all his folks were accounted for."

"And are they?"

"Yep." Lou's scowl deepened as he shoved his phone into his pocket. "Don't get me wrong; I'm head over heels they're all okay. It's just—" He waved a hand at the corpse nestled inside the unzipped bag. "With those prints of hers charred off, identifyin' that poor woman's gonna be a task and a half."

Kate nodded. And then some.

While there was enough viable flesh to obtain DNA, a closely related genetic profile would need to be waiting in the database for the computer to cough up an instant match to the woman or a traceable family member.

That left dental work. But since there was no centralized dental X-ray database in the country, or even the state, that was going to take time and legwork. Nor would they be guaranteed a match there either. Especially since the bastard they were after had proven himself sharp enough to have disposed of the body far from where he'd killed—and possibly farther yet from where the victim's former dentist worked.

The only thing they had going for them was the dump site itself. Since Nash's farm was in the middle of nowhere, even by Braxton standards, the odds were good the killer had a personal connection to this specific field and/or the person who owned it.

But if not?

She didn't even want to consider that possibility.

Kate sighed as Tonga finished packing up his ME's kit. From the slump to the man's shoulders, the depressing reality of the coming autopsy was already setting in as he gently pulled the bag's plastic flap over the victim and began to zip it.

He finished sealing the bag and retrieved his kit. "I'll be back shortly."

Kate returned Tonga's nod as he headed across the field and up the sloped lawn to prepare the back of his wagon for its coming cargo.

She faced her own crime kit and tucked the pair of sealed

envelopes within. As she regained her feet, she spotted a pinpoint of light glittering from a nearby stalk of wheat. Intrigued, she made a beeline for the plant.

The glitter had disappeared the moment she'd moved. She maintained her focus and kept walking. Since her target stalk was a good three rows of wheat beyond the section of scorched earth and deeper into the field, her coming prize was bound to be another specimen of milky quartz. That, or a plowed-up shard of old glass.

Or...nothing.

She couldn't see anything but green as she bent to study the stalk. The plant in question was as crisp and upright as the ones surrounding it. So what had caught her eye? She bent lower, grasping the blades and gently spreading them apart, frowning as something red slid deeper into the plant.

"Whatcha got now, Kato?"

No idea. Yet. "Can you grab my tweezers? I left them in my kit."

"Sure thing."

While she was waiting, she pulled another evidence marker from her jacket pocket and set it down next to the stalk in question, then snapped several photographs, just in case whatever she'd spotted was connected to their case after all.

Lou rejoined her as she finished the photos, tweezers in hand, along with a fresh collection envelope.

She glanced up. "I thought I saw something glitter."

"Probably another bit of quartz."

"Probably." Except she'd swear the flash had been red. She accepted the tweezers, carefully slipping the tips down between the blades of the plant to grip something small and solid.

Lou's whistle drifted between them as she sat upright. "I'll be damned. It's an earring."

Kate nodded as she deposited the crusted stud into the envelope he was holding open, then stood. Definitely an earring. But as to whether the gem crowning the top of the gold post was real or not, that was for someone else to determine.

Jewelry was not her thing. She'd rarely come across it in eight years as an Army cop, even these last three and a half as a civilian deputy.

As to how this piece had landed this far from the body, that she understood. The fat inside burning flesh tended to spit and pop as it cooked off. The blackened bit of skin clinging to the base of the stud suggested its volatile point of origin.

DNA would confirm it.

Lou peered inside the envelope for several moments before tipping his head toward the tweezers in her hand. "Can I borrow those?"

"Sure."

He used the tips to grip the base of the stud, an honest-to-God curve overtaking the man's lips as he held the gem up toward the afternoon sun.

Why, she had no idea. Bit of blackened skin and childhood rock collection or not, she did not want to think about why that particular stone was tinted with that particular shade.

Lou's smile actually deepened as he slipped the stone back into the envelope. "This here's a diamond, Kato—a *pink* one. I'll bet my pension on it."

That explained his lack of nausea over the shade...and his beaming expression. Overpriced chips of ice weren't just some mythical girl's best friend. Cops of both sexes had been known to buddy up to them too. Especially if the chip in question had been found at a crime scene.

Diamonds tended to come with a microscopic serial number inscribed on the girdle of the stone.

And with that number came a registered *owner*.

But would this tinted chip come with one?

Based on the certified grin that overtook Lou's face as he sealed the flap to the collection envelope, he believed so. "The heck with quartz—*this* is a rock worth finding. We're lookin' at IDing that poor woman in days now, not weeks. Ya done it again, Kato."

She shook her head as she accepted the envelope so she could label it. "Nester and his team would've found it."

"Maybe. But what with how far that stone was launched durin' the burnin'? And where it landed?" The sheriff shook his head. "I doubt it."

She finished labeling the envelope and held it back out to the sheriff.

Lou didn't take it. Worse, his smile had bled down to a deep, dark frown.

As she followed his line of sight, she realized why. The cuffs to both sleeves of her Braxton PD jacket had ridden up her forearms while she'd been bent over, rooting through that stalk of wheat. But it was the band of skin now visible around her left wrist that had captured her boss' attention.

It was tinted several shades darker than that diamond she'd bagged, and definitely due to smeared, freshly dried blood. Hers.

For a moment, she was afraid Lou would demand to know what had caused the abrasions. The fear mutated to terror—because he didn't. There was no need.

He already knew.

The urge to grab Max's watch from her pocket nearly felled her. And then the itch set in.

Make that clawed.

She forced herself to slide her left hand in front of her abdomen and held it there, strangling her wrist with the concealing fingers of her right as she kicked herself for not listening to Dr. Manning. The shrink had cornered her after she'd hung up from Lou's call and before she'd been able to escape his office. Manning had politely read her the riot act again about grounding techniques taken to the point of self-harm.

It didn't matter that the shrink was right; she'd still been pissed.

But the doc had also had a solution.

Manning had suggested that she stop on the way here and pick up a tube of ointment and an ace bandage. He thought that, with her wrist wrapped even after it was healed, she'd be able to wear the watch, since the twisting sensation would be dulled enough to keep her from using the accompanying pain to tune out.

It would've been a quick stop to make too.

But with each gas station she'd passed upon leaving Fort Leaves, the reality of an already dwindling shortened winter day had bucked up against the ironclad experience of just how long it took to canvass an outdoor crime scene and scour it for evidence.

She wished she'd taken the time to stop now. Because Lou was still staring.

Like the shrink, the sheriff knew what she'd been doing to her wrist, all right—and why. It was in the murky depths of his eyes. They'd begun to glisten. His attention finally shifted to the sealed black bag several feet away.

His hoarse whisper followed. "I am *so* sorry."

What? "Why?" She released her wrist and stepped closer. "Boss, I'm the one—"

"No. You ain't at fault here, Kato. It's all on me." The glistening strengthened as Lou took his own step forward, his entire craggy face now brimming with guilt. "I knew you was havin' trouble. A lot longer than Seth, too. I'd wonder what the hell I was thinkin' sendin' him to the station and bringin' you here—

but there's no need. 'Cause I *wasn't* thinkin'. Didn't want to. Don't get me wrong; I like Seth. I respect the hell outta that boy. But I need you. And now—" That damp remorse slipped over to the body bag. "—I done made it all worse by makin' you stand here and look at what we put in there. Smell it. Feel that goddamned *shit* you went through over there all over again."

The irony of it.

She managed a smile. Sort of. "That's exactly what I'm supposed to be doing."

Confusion clouded over the guilt.

She nodded. "Remembering. Feeling." Burning through all those charmingly horrific, *natural* emotions that her brain had been actively avoiding for four years now.

"This advice coming from your shrink?"

She tensed. For a split second, she suspected that her boss had followed her to Fort Leaves. But no. This was Lou. He'd never violate her trust like that. The man was simply that good at reading her. Understanding. Far better than her own father had ever been. Not for the first time did she wonder why.

"Kato?"

She met that muddy pain. It was threatening to spill over, intent on bringing a flood of guilt down with it. Enough to drown Lou on the spot. That, she couldn't allow. "How'd you find out?"

"That you was seein' someone?"

She nodded.

"Did the math." Pink tinged the man's jowls as he shrugged. "I stopped by your place two Saturdays ago, followin' the funerals, to see if you were up for a spur o' the moment lunch, but you were out. Stopped by last weekend, too. Same time. Then again today. Different reason today, o'course. But still—three Saturdays in a row? And there's your phone." The pink in those jowls deepened to scarlet. "You'd set it on your desk last week to help

Owen with that drunk and disorderly. There was somethin' about an impact statement on the screen. I was pretty desperate, so I picked it up. When I realized that what I was readin' was private as hell, I turned off the phone and put it back. But it was kinda too late. I'm sorry."

Oh, God. It was bad enough that Manning knew what was in that statement. But now, so did Lou. Namely, how she really felt about that Silver Star and the entire, truly fucked up chain of events that had spawned it.

How she felt about herself.

Lou was her boss, for crying out loud. The man who'd issued her the service weapon currently tucked inside her holster. The man who could revoke her right to carry that weapon at any time—and prevent her from carrying another.

And Lou now had a doozy of a reason to support either. Typed out by her own betraying fingers, no less.

The only silver lining in this entire rotten cluster of blackened clouds that'd become her life was that the drunk and disorderly she'd assisted with had gone down on Monday. Even if Lou had read the accompanying stuck points log that she'd been adding to ever since she'd downloaded the CPT app so she could work on her therapy assignments away from home, he wouldn't have read that she planned on quitting—because she hadn't added her decision into the software yet.

But from the dread still torturing his stare—and the raw confession that Lou had offered earlier about Seth—he'd figured that out as well. Lou knew she was on the verge of following the department's senior-most deputy out the door.

Sixteen years of leaning on the man standing in front of her in lieu of her own father had her wishing she could put his mind at ease.

She even got her mouth to open. But the words wouldn't come out.

Yeah, she'd promised Manning two more weeks of purgatory. But she'd been hanging on by a thread ever since she'd turned into Nash's drive. And with each whiff of those nauseating sulfur byproducts still tainting the air, it was fraying that much further. There was no telling when it was going to snap.

But she could soothe another fear. Though this one was more akin to terror.

"Lou?"

He flinched.

She wasn't surprised. She rarely called him by his first name. At least, not to his face. Not even when he'd insisted on the practice after she'd come home from the Army. It had seemed disrespectful somehow. Especially after she'd accepted this job. But she needed the man's absolute attention now. So he'd know that what she was about to say was the truth.

She stepped closer and looked straight into his eyes. Made certain he was looking into hers. "I am not going to eat my gun. *Ever*."

Those muddy eyes turned even glassier than they had before. The jaw beneath began to tremble and work amid the silence that followed, until a hoarse whisper finally escaped. "*Promise*?"

She could feel her own eyes filling up as she nodded. "On Ruger's life."

Oh, there'd been a moment or two before she'd stumbled across the German Shepherd out behind her spare cabin as a pup three years earlier, bleeding out from some heinous hunter's bullet, when she wouldn't have been able to make that vow, but Lou did not need to know that. Not now. Given the strength of that fresh wave of tears spilling down to swamp the crevices of his face, probably not ever.

More tears followed. His thick shoulders shook with the force of them—until his entire body was shaking.

She reached out a split second before he could, wrapping her arms around his stocky chest just as tightly as he was wrapping his around her.

She held on until the quaking ebbed, then pulled back to use her latex-covered fingers to wipe at the moisture still drenching his cheeks. She'd just have to swap out the compromised gloves for a sterile set later.

"I been so damned scared for you, Kato."

Her nod came out a wobble. "I know. Me too. But you're right. I am seeing someone. He's a shrink with the VA."

Lou's nod was steadier than hers, though not by much. "Is he helpin'?"

Yes. No.

She pushed forth a shrug as she stepped back a bit, opening up the space between them again. That tenuous thread of trust. "I don't know."

"You want him to?"

Ruger's gorgeous, furry face flashed through her mind's eye. The Shepherd's absolute joy at simply being with her. Living his life alongside hers.

She'd do anything to keep that dragon's tail of his flapping about indefinitely.

Anything.

She rubbed the burning from her eyes and nodded. "Yeah, I do."

Lou's own gloved palms came up to cup her face—the smooth and the shredded sides. The nod that followed was firm. Resolute. "Then this shrink *will* help. You just need to hang in there. Do what it takes to get where you need to be. 'Cause this town—me? We need you. You're too blessed good to crawl in a dark, deep hole somewhere and give up. You cain't let them bastards win. I meant what I said about Seth. He's top-notch. But you're better. Better than the whole dang department put together, me included. Even with half your wits tied behind your back."

She opened her mouth to argue, then closed it again.

What was the point? It was that stupid Silver Star. No one could get past it. Not even Lou. Despite what he'd found in that app on her phone.

His flush returned. "I'm truly sorry I read your private thoughts."

"It's okay."

He shook his head. "Nah, it ain't. But you been fadin in 'n' out these past few weeks. More than when you first come back. And I—" It wasn't until he broke off and glanced past her shoulder that she realized Tonga was headed down the hill.

It was time to move the body.

She braced herself as she turned—only to pause as Lou touched her arm.

"I got this. Geraldine Oakley passed late last night. Her daughter claims her pacemaker failed. Tonga had already started the autopsy when I called to tell him about this. He'll need to finish Geraldine, then open up this poor soul first thing tomorrow. We both know this crime scene's as clear cut as they get. Not much left to do." Lou checked his watch. "Drake and Owen will be pullin' up soon enough. Nester and his boys will be showin' soon afterwards. I'll stay. You go home. Spend the evenin' with Ruger. If we find anythin' else—and I doubt it—I'll let you know."

She thought about arguing. But why?

There was nothing left for her to do case-wise except decide if she had the strength to withstand the silent plea suffusing the sheriff's features. The one begging her to come back to work in the morning.

Don't leave him to work this mess alone.

She ignored the sludge that had been bubbling up in her gut

since the moment she'd taken that call in Manning's office. "Okay. But I'll stop by the station first. Log the stone and hairs into evidence." She held up the envelope containing the earring. "Get Seth started on tracing the number engraved into this."

Kate turned away from the relief that was blistering through Lou's entire body—because she could see the hope churning up in its wake. Hope that was as false as the man's faith in her and her skills.

Tomorrow.

She'd deal with quitting tomorrow.

After the autopsy. Just as soon as Seth was able to make an ID from that diamond. She'd call Manning. Given the nature of this case, surely the shrink would understand.

Hopefully, so would Lou.

She gathered her shredded nerves along with her crime kit and headed for the base of the hill, reaching out to give Tonga's arm a silent squeeze as they passed.

Before she knew it, she'd breached the crest, then the gravel drive.

Kate stowed her stainless-steel case in the rear of the Durango and climbed into the driver's seat. She was about to lay the evidence envelopes on the passenger seat when she spotted the homework Manning had handed her hours earlier. On the uppermost sheet, blaring at her in bold ink even more loudly than it had in the shrink's office: the stuck point Manning had insisted she work on this week.

My judgment can't be trusted.

She drew her breath in deep as she worked to quell the fresh mix of panic and guilt that seared in with those five simple words.

It didn't help.

Her wrist had already begun to itch.

She dumped the envelopes on top of the worksheets, staring directly into the SUV's rearview mirror as she straightened.

The mishmash of mottled scars and pockmarks that had made up most of the right side of her face and neck for the last four years stared back.

Manning had asked if they bothered her.

She'd told him the truth. She welcomed her rearranged features in all their repulsive glory. They kept her honest about what lay beneath.

Turning in her badge was for the best.

For her and for Lou. Hell, for the entire town—especially that horrifically charred woman whose body was headed for the morgue.

She was simply not the cop Lou or Dr. Manning believed her to be. Nor would working through a thousand worksheets make it so.

She'd misjudged Joe Cordoba, Grant Parish *and* Staff Sergeant Burke. In doing so, she'd failed to prevent the murders of countless fellow soldiers and homeless veterans, as well as the monsters who'd been preying upon them.

If she caved into Lou's pleas and Manning's demand to stay on the force to work this case—how many more men and women would die because of her?

3

She woke to screaming.

Hers.

Kate bolted upright, choking on that distinctive blend of melted rubber, singed hair and crackling skin. It took half a dozen panicked breaths to accept that the ghostly flames, belching smoke and noxious fumes were searing through her mind, and not her lungs. She was *not* in Afghanistan, hanging upside down in that shattered Humvee. She was in Braxton, in the split-log home she'd inherited from her father.

But she was not in bed.

Somehow, she'd made her way out of her room and into the far corner of the darkened, double car garage, where she was huddled up against the tightly packed row of firewood she'd split and stacked earlier that fall—and she could hear barking.

No, make that full-on howling.

Ruger.

The German Shepherd was inside the house, frantically clawing at the opposite side of the door that led into the kitchen. And, Lord, was Ruger pissed.

"I hear you, buddy! I'm coming!"

Kate dusted the dirt and chips of wood from her Braxton PD sweatpants as she stood. At least, she tried. Her matching gray tee was so drenched with the vestiges of her latest night terror that the smaller splinters of wood remained stuck to the fabric.

She gave up, padding along the icy cement of the garage until she'd skirted around her Durango and crossed the empty, spare slot to reach the door to the kitchen. She could hear Ruger shuffling backward to give her room.

She pushed the door open. A split second later, ninety-plus pounds of sinewy Shepherd launched into her, nearly knocking her back into the garage.

Ruger growled, whined and huffed his continued displeasure, even as his frantic tongue bathed every square inch of her face.

Kate wrapped her arms around his solid warmth, hugging the Shepherd close as she slid down the left door jamb all the way to the wooden floor, burying her face in the comforting fur of his neck. She could feel Ruger's heart pounding in his chest as he continued to whimper and chuff at her.

"I know, buddy; I know. I'm so sorry. I did it again, didn't I?"

She'd abandoned her bed while still sound asleep seven times now since Joe had been arrested. But during the previous six, she'd woken on the floor of her bedroom closet with Ruger's soothing bulk curled protectively around her. This time she'd made it all the way into the garage without him in tow.

She must've shut the door in his face. No wonder he was so stressed.

Just how long had she been out there?

Hell, she didn't even know what time it was. Thanks to Manning's latest lecture, Max's dive watch was sitting on the nightstand beside her bed next to her Glock.

She couldn't blame her latest zombie jaunt on her sessions with the shrink though. She usually woke to the soul-shredding image of Max's severed head hitting the floor of that mud brick hovel and rolling across the dirt to her feet.

This latest foray down nightmare lane was a result of Braxton's most recent crime scene. Of that poor woman's charred and blistered body—and the sickening stench that a solid half hour spent in a steaming shower hadn't been able to purge from her lungs.

Both her and Ruger's nerves finally soothed, Kate clambered to her feet, closing the door that led to the garage and padding across the distressed wooden slats of the kitchen with Ruger stuck to her heels.

The cuckoo clock she and her mother had purchased during a mother-daughter trip to the Harz mountains dutifully provided the time as they passed.

0649.

Given that she'd finally managed to drop off well after one a.m., she could do with another hour or two of shuteye. But why bother? Not only would she not be able to fall asleep after that nightmare, she had a job to do. A case to work.

For now, anyway.

She settled for unlocking the front door and letting Ruger out to do his own morning job. He'd calmed enough to bound off the porch and across the front lawn without her, the hitch to his gait from that hunter's bullet more pronounced than usual as he galloped into the mixed pine and naked hardwood trees that enveloped the house.

Minutes later, the Shepherd was breaching the treeline again, this time to lope back across the lawn, up onto the porch and straight into the living room.

She doubted he'd taken the time to sniff before he'd squatted.

Kate closed the door and cut a path back around through to

the kitchen to fill Ruger's stainless-steel food bowl with kibble and refresh his water.

Guilt bit in as she finished. She'd taken to stopping for a pair of Saturday afternoon burgers on her way back to town to celebrate surviving another session with Manning. One for her; the other for her four-legged, stalwart champion.

Upon leaving Nash's farm, she'd considered Ruger's drooping disappointment for all of two seconds and driven right past the drive-thru.

There was just no way she'd have been able to consume meat last night. Any kind.

Ruger had taken one whiff of her uniform as she'd peeled it off to dump it inside the quarantine barrel in the garage and had seemed to understand.

Kate assuaged the remaining pangs of her conscience this morning, as she had last night—with an extra slice of cheddar from the oversized tub in the fridge.

With Ruger's belly reasonably content, she filled the coffee pot and set it to brew, then padded down the hall to turn on the shower.

Twenty minutes later, she was clean, dressed in a fresh deputy uniform and seated in her spot at the kitchen table with a steaming cup of coffee in hand.

She opened her laptop and checked her department email. She already knew from the text Lou had sent last night that Nester and his boys hadn't found anything else out of place at the crime scene. Nor had any new forensic reports been added to the electronic case file during the night by Tonga or one of the department's dwindling deputies.

It didn't matter.

She'd made up her mind during the drive home last night. And, this time, her decision was final. Waking up cowering beside her woodpile only confirmed the wisdom behind it. As soon as she ID'd this woman, she'd be quitting. Unlike Seth, she wouldn't be offering to work out her two weeks' notice, either. Not unless Lou agreed to let her handle traffic patrol and the department's pissant calls.

And *only* those calls.

Manning and all his platitudes rattled in, but they didn't matter, much less help. There was just too much riding on this case. Too much she could screw up. Too much she could miss. And probably would, if she stayed on.

Just like with Grant, Burke and Joe.

Drake might be new to law enforcement, but Owen wasn't. They'd managed to steal Owen from Conway's much larger police department two years ago. Though he was almost a decade younger, the deputy was nearly as experienced as Seth. Nor was Owen burdened with the baggage that both she and Seth were lugging around.

Owen would do just fine.

Yes, she'd promised to phone the shrink, and she still planned on doing so.

After. When it was too late to talk her out of it.

Her mood and stress level lighter than it had been in weeks, Kate stood and headed deeper into the kitchen to refill her coffee mug and pop a blueberry muffin from the fridge into the microwave. Within minutes, she'd reclaimed her seat at the table and was clicking out of the department's Jane Doe case file and entering the National Missing and Unidentified Persons System.

The only parameters they had to go on at the moment were female, possibly well-endowed, with a copious amount of black hair. The strands she'd collected had been bone straight. But since the color and lack of curl could be the result of chemical processing and/or a simple flat-iron, she widened her hair search to all colors, styles and types.

The cuckoo clock chirped out nine o'clock as she exited

NamUS with her list of potential matches. Unfortunately, her gut was leaning against all of them.

Most were too old. Not in age, but in how long the missing persons entry had been sitting in the system. Plus, according to Lou, their Jane Doe had been wearing diamond earrings. None of the potential matches mentioned diamonds, let alone the rarer pink ones.

Given the estimated range of value that had popped up during her internet research on the gems, the odds were next to nil that the killer had forced their Jane to don those diamonds before he'd set her on fire—meaning those earrings belonged to Jane.

And just how long would the bastard have let his victim hang on to something she'd have most likely valued?

Not long at all.

No, their Jane had been missing for a day—two to three tops—before she'd been killed. Which meant there was an excellent chance she wasn't in the system yet.

Regardless, Kate copied the file of potential NamUS matches into an email for Seth, so that he could make the calls, then added a brief note to the senior deputy and hit *send*.

Ruger stirred from his napping spot at her feet as she stood. She headed to the kitchen to swap out her coffee cup for a stainless-steel travel mug, topping off the latter with the remainder of the pot for her coming trip. The Shepherd's mood drooped along with his bushy tail as she returned to the table to gather up her remaining notes and turn off her laptop. By the time she'd slid her Glock into her shoulder holster and grabbed her Braxton PD jacket, he'd accepted that she was leaving the house.

But he still wasn't happy about it.

She checked his dog door and made sure it was unlatched, then leaned down to ruffle his ears. "Sorry, buddy. I've got an autopsy. If we're lucky, I'll be back earlier tonight than yesterday." Quite possibly, for good.

But first—she needed to get the hospital in Conway. According to the email Tonga had sent her late last night, he'd be making the first cut at ten on the dot. She wanted to get inside that sterile room well before then. She needed to get re-acclimated to the ghastly sight and the lingering smell that went with their victim's body *before* Owen and Lou joined her, and Tonga came in to open the poor woman up.

Kate grabbed her travel mug. But as she reached for her Braxton PD jacket, she spotted the barely healed band of red at her left wrist.

Lou had already noticed it—and deduced the cause behind the excoriated skin and older, permanent scars encircling her wrist. Her hours with the department might be numbered, but she didn't need anyone else figuring it out.

Like it or not, the shrink had won another round.

Sighing her defeat, she made a detour to the hall bath and dug an old ace bandage out of the linen closet. She wrapped the lengthy bandage around her wrist, deliberately layering the elastic fabric far enough above the reddened skin so it appeared as though she'd suffered a sprain—and, nope, she didn't feel guilty over the subterfuge.

What lay beneath was no one's damned business but her own.

Kate headed back to the kitchen to grab her jacket and her travel mug.

It took sixteen minutes to reach the hospital, leaving her nearly twice as many for her personal mission. She bailed out of her Durango and was heading for the glass doors when she spotted the sheriff's sedan turning into the lot.

So much for snagging quality time alone with their victim.

She pivoted until her boots were pointed deeper into the lot and met up with Lou as he was locking up his sedan.

"Mornin', Kato."

She returned his muted nod as they turned together toward her original destination. "You're early, boss."

And he was not in a good mood. Was it her imagination or had the crevices in Lou's craggy features deepened overnight? His generous thatch of gray was mussed too, as if he'd been raking his fingers through the strands during the drive here.

She knew what was eating at her—but him? "What's wrong?"

Please, Lord, don't let there be another burnt body out there.

"We're havin' shit for luck this week, is all. Owen and the boys were wrappin' up the scene after I left. It was dark and they was headed up that hill in Weaver's yard when that blasted mutt of his got loose and tore down from the deck to see what all the fuss was about. The lab knocked Owen on his ass and sent him tumblin' all the way down to the field. He broke both bones in his lower right leg. He'll be out for today, then hobblin' 'round with a cast and crutches for the next six to eight weeks."

Holy *shit*.

They were out another deputy.

Kate stopped short as the implications for the department—and herself—socked in. She was aware of the hospital entrance's glass doors swishing open as Lou reached them, but she couldn't seem to move, much less accompany him through.

The sheriff stopped. Turned back. "Kato?"

She managed to meet that dark, frazzled stare.

"You okay?"

Hell, no. But that didn't matter, did it? Not anymore. With Owen all but out of commission—and Drake now pulling triple duty while Lou tried to hold the rest of the department together as he searched for both Bob Feathers' and Seth's replacements, there was no one left to track down the monster who'd torched the woman in Nash's field.

No one but her.

Christ.

She straightened her spine and dragged the surrounding chilly air in deep. There was nothing else she could do. Tonga was due to make that first cut in half an hour. She needed to get in there and get acclimated even more now than she had a minute ago.

Like it or not, this case was hers—until it was solved.

She corralled her self-doubts and shoved them down deep, then nodded to Lou as she stepped briskly past him and through the doors. "I'm fine."

As for Lou, he was still looking seriously haggard as they moved deeper into the regional hospital's antiseptic maze, toward the bowels where they kept the morgue. But while Owen's shitty break and the frantic morning Lou had to have spent rearranging the shifts and duties within the department would explain those deepening crevices, she still had no idea why Lou had shown up so early for the autopsy.

What else had gone wrong?

Kate was about to ask when they turned into the corridor that led to the autopsy suite Tonga tended to use when the need arose. Nash Weaver was seated in one of the two chairs along the wall opposite the door. His sandy head slightly bent, the man appeared to be praying over the leather-bound Bible in his hand —and from those reddened eyes and damp cheeks, he'd been crying.

She could feel Lou's stress ratcheting up as he spotted the same evidence.

"I got it, boss. I'll talk to him; see why he's here." Though knowing Nash as she had in school, she had her suspicions. He'd always been a sensitive soul.

The lines bracketing Lou's mouth eased a bit.

Kate pressed her fingers into his forearm. "If Tonga's ready, please tell him to go ahead and get started. I'll be right in."

A swift nod from the sheriff, and she and Nash were as alone as they'd been the night he'd hosted their senior class party out behind his barn while his folks had been visiting the grandparents. Everyone, including Liz and their mutual best friend Dan, had been at the bonfire they'd all created, well on their way to getting toasted. She and Nash had taken a walk down the farm's lengthy drive instead. Nash had been hurting pretty badly over his recent breakup with his girlfriend of three years. She'd been royally pissed with her father and the truth her dad had finally dumped on her regarding the depth of his feelings and doubts about her aspirations to enlist in the Army and follow him into the Military Police.

She'd listened while Nash had vented, and he'd done the same.

Not only had she and Nash never revisited the conversation they'd shared, they hadn't even been alone again in the thirteen years that had followed.

Until now.

Kate slipped into the padded vinyl chair beside Nash's and patiently waited for him to complete his prayers.

It took a few minutes, but his lips finally ceased moving. Nash opened his eyes, but he didn't turn his head. He kept his stare nailed to the autopsy suite door instead.

The why was a no brainer.

Nash was seated on her right. If he shifted that light blue stare, even a bit, he'd be forced to confront what was left of her face. Old classmate and newly ordained pastor or not, it wasn't a sight anyone wanted to focus on first thing in the morning, if ever.

So, she continued to wait.

He finally sighed. "Someone needed to be here for her while Dr. Tonga cut her open. To speak for her. To pray."

"It's not your fault, Nash. None of it."

His lips moved again, this time settling into a darkened twist. "Feels like it."

Yeah, as many homicides as she'd worked, she knew that feeling. It was as familiar to her as that worn leather in Nash's hands was to him.

But she didn't share the personal assessment. There was no point.

He dropped his attention to the Bible, smoothed his fingers over the faded gold letters on the cover. "How do you do this, Kate? And stay sane?"

Yikes. Sensitive soul or not, Nash had also always possessed a way of cutting right to the torturous crux of things.

But while he might've asked, he didn't really want the answer to that either. No one did. Least of all, her.

She offered up her own, silent shrug.

To her surprise, Nash turned his head and looked squarely at her face for a long moment, then found her eyes. "I'm sorry I never called or stopped by after you got back. Dan used to email me, you know. When he was over there."

She tensed. Smothered the urge to snatch that leather book from Nash's hands and anchor it within her own—desperately. "No, I didn't know. Dan and I lost touch after we all graduated." Despite the fact that Dan had joined the Army too. Because of her.

One more thing to feel guilty about.

Nash nodded. "He kept track of you. Your career. Your life. He...cared about you. Right up to the end."

"I know." At least, she'd known about the caring.

And that was the most important part, right?

"Dan believed in you, Kate. I know you told me that night,

years ago, that your dad didn't. That you swore he never really had. But Dan—he did believe in you. I do, too. I've just been lousy at showing it. But I'll do better." Nash fell silent. His gaze drifted down to the book in his hands, then crept back up on another sigh. "You'll find him, won't you? The beast that did this? Before he has a chance to do it to someone else?"

Oh, man. Having an old friend who'd stayed in contact with Dan offer up that dicey confession was one thing. Having the man of the cloth Nash had become look at her as though she was almost a savior herself was quite another.

And disconcerting, to say the least.

There was only one response she could offer in return to both—even though it was the one response a cop shouldn't.

The hell with her endless string of night terrors and tenuous sanity.

"I'll find him." Somehow.

Nash offered her a sad smile. "Thank you."

She stood. She was about to follow Lou across the corridor and into the autopsy suite when something else Nash had said trickled back through her brain. *Someone needed to be here for her while Dr. Tonga cut her open.*

While?

Kate reached into her right trouser pocket to retrieve Max's watch so she could check the time, then tucked it home.

Based on the creases in Nash's gray trousers and the otherwise crisp white shirt he'd donned, the man had been here for a significant amount of time already, bent in prayer. But according to Max's watch—and Tonga's email—the autopsy wasn't scheduled to commence for another ten minutes. The email that had been addressed solely to her and *not* everyone in the department, as was the ME's wont.

"Excuse me, Nash."

"Of course."

She crossed the hall and pushed through the door to the autopsy suite. Tonga and Lou were on the other side. But there was no body. The only items on the stainless-steel table between the two men were photos that smelled faintly as though they were fresh from the printer. What she couldn't smell were traces of grilled meat and sulfur.

At all.

From the visible tint of red staining Lou's face and even tinging Tonga's darker skin, she knew why. Tonga had lied about the time and the autopsy suite location.

And Lou had been in on it.

The autopsy was already finished.

She didn't know if she should be grateful or pissed.

Given the apprehension that was pinched in to both those male blushes, she opted for grateful. Like the men, she ignored the reason behind it all—namely her trauma-riddled brain—and stepped up to the table on Lou's right.

There were a dozen photos in all, splayed out in a line. Next to the close-ups of various areas of the blackened outer body, and shots of the inner lungs and heart, lay a copy of Tonga's preliminary report.

It, too, was already complete.

She glanced past the photos and report to take in Tonga's weary form. Not only was he not wearing his usual scrubs, the man had re-donned the same blue plaid shirt and jeans he'd worn to the crime scene yesterday. Tonga had been here all night, conducting Geraldine Oakley's autopsy, and then the one for their Jane Doe.

For her.

"*Thank you.*"

The ME's answering nod was as soft as her whisper had been. The knot at the front of his throat worked as he cleared it. "We don't have much more than we did yesterday, Deputy, but we do have cause of death. Despite the extensive charring, I was able to count at least thirteen wounds—possibly from a hunting knife—to the woman's neck, torso and inner thighs." The ME tapped an ebony finger over the close-up of the heart. "This wound is the one that killed her. It severed the left anterior descending artery, causing her to bleed out. I also found evidence that she was penetrated vaginally prior to death...and she was beaten. Given the depths of the contusions, severely so."

Well, shit.

"Was the woman dead before she was set on fire?"

Relief flooded though Kate with the ME's second, gentler nod of the briefing.

That was something.

Given the screams that still haunted her dreams of Sergeant Gault and Corporal Babin in that overturned and shattered Humvee, possibly everything.

But those stab wounds. They were telling.

At least thirteen separate wounds to the woman's neck, torso and inner thighs? Deep enough that the charring hadn't been able to obscure them?

That suggested extreme, *personal* hatred.

"What about the stone?"

Tonga's frown caused the lines bracketing his mouth to deepen. "I did find flecks of soil within the woman's vaginal canal, and the flecks are consistent with the soil in Weaver's field. But since we don't know where she was killed—" The ME shrugged.

"The flecks may also be consistent with soil at the primary scene."

Tonga nodded. "That said, there were no other stones found between the crease of the legs or within any of the body's cavities. Nor were there traces of vaginal epithelial cells or secretions on the scorched piece of quartz you recovered."

Thank God. That would've added an element to this case that she just didn't need. Hell, that none of them did. Namely, a seriously twisted sexual component to the crime—and the increased likelihood of a pending repeat.

Kate released the breath she'd been holding.

Lou did the same beside her. The sheriff reached out to scoop the photos together, only to stop and pull his hand back as his phone pinged.

A split second later, her phone pinged as well, followed by Tonga's.

She retrieved her iPhone from its slot on her utility belt. A quick check of her texts revealed who'd contacted them all and why. Seth had tracked down the owner of the diamond in that earring and had already called and spoken with her.

...Mrs. Shah bought them as a wedding gift for her daughter. Aisha Kharoti's been missing for over a day. Mom's headed to the station now to give DNA—

No, she wasn't. Not *right* now, anyway.

Unless Kate was mistaken, Mrs. Shah was at the Conway Regional Medical Center, on the other side of the door to this autopsy suite—and she was shouting at Nash.

4

Kate reached the door to the autopsy suite before Lou and pulled it open.

Nash stood beside the chairs, holding a now sobbing petite woman in floral scrubs. His left hand cradled the dark, thick bun at the nape of her neck as his right patted the woman's upper back while he murmured, "I'm so sorry," over and over.

Lou glanced her way. "I've got Weaver."

Leaving her with the potential witness she needed to speak to anyway. She nodded as she stepped toward the mother. "Mrs. Shah?"

Kate held her breath as the woman turned. There was always the chance that her face would upset the grieving woman more than Mrs. Shah already was, possibly tip her over the edge into hysteria. Nor would it be the first time that had happened.

The woman didn't even blink.

Given those scrubs, it might've been her profession. But more likely, the lack of response was due to the grief clouding those dark brown eyes.

Right now, Kate suspected that Mrs. Shah couldn't see or feel anything beyond the news of her daughter's death.

The woman accepted the linen handkerchief that Nash pressed into her hand just before he turned to follow Lou down the corridor and around the corner to give them privacy.

Kate reached for the door to the suite, closing off the sight of Tonga scooping those graphic photos into a pile as the woman dried her tears and blew her nose.

A soft hiccup filled the corridor. "I'm sorry."

"Don't be. My name is Deputy Holland—Kate. And your reaction is absolutely normal. Though I confess, I don't..." How did she put this delicately?

"Know how I knew Aisha would be here?"

Kate nodded. Based on those scrubs, Mrs. Shah was likely hospital staff, but—

"I work upstairs. I'm a pediatric nurse practitioner. I was on my break when your detective called...about the earrings."

Kate offered up a second nod—but no correction on Seth's detective title.

There was no need. Heck, if her town's voters hadn't stubbornly clung to the old deputy and sheriff titles left over from before Braxton's incorporation when the county had still policed its buildings and roads, that was how she, Seth and the others would've been addressed anyway. Like the rest of the municipal police officers in their state.

The woman lifted the handkerchief Nash had given her and blew her nose again. "Detective Armstrong said he was from Braxton. That one of m-my daughter's earrings had been found near a b-burnt body. I've shared a table with Dr. Tonga in the cafeteria a few times. He conducts your town's autopsies here. So I took a chance and—"

"Came to see her?"

Another lift of that handkerchief and another soft blow. "Yes."

Which meant the woman had known her daughter was missing, or at least suspected it, and had feared the worst.

Kate tipped her head toward the pair of chairs behind the grieving mother. Nash had left his worn Bible atop the seat on the left. "Mrs. Shah, I know this is a difficult time. But I have a few questions about Aisha. Would you mind—"

"Of course." The woman sank into the empty seat.

Kate retrieved Nash's Bible and swapped it for the small memo pad and pen she kept tucked inside her jacket as she claimed the other chair. "I understand that you purchased the diamond earrings as a wedding gift for your daughter?"

"Yes. Three years ago this February."

"And was the marriage still valid?"

"Yes." The deep pinch to the woman's lips revealed more than that single word offered. Mainly that Mrs. Shah would've preferred that the marriage wasn't valid.

"And her husband's full name?" Kate flipped the pad open to take the information down since Seth's text hadn't provided it.

"Haidar Kharoti. He's a soldier."

Kate stilled as the irony bit in. The implications.

Don't. Damn it, she had to stop seeing connections where they did not exist. Her PTSD had been raging all morning. Hell, for the past four weeks.

She was just being paranoid.

After all, Little Rock hosted an Air Force base, not an Army post. Yes, the Robinson Maneuver Training Center was just down the road from Conway, but Camp Robinson hosted the National Guard, not the US Army. Soldier/Sailor/Airman; active duty/reserve/guard—there was enough terminology spinning around the military that civilians often got it mixed up.

Still, she needed to be sure. "Your son-in-law; he's in the Air Force?"

"No, the Army. Haidar is a sergeant. A translator. Like my husband and I, he was born in Lahore, Pakistan. But unlike us, Haidar became a naturalized citizen much younger, while still a boy. He works with the Green Berets now."

Definitely a solider then. And yet another weird similarity to those bodies Burke had hacked up and left around Braxton a month ago. A similarity she and her jagged nerves didn't need. Kate pushed past it. This wasn't about her. "Ma'am, can you tell me where Sergeant Kharoti's currently stationed?"

"At Fort Campbell, in Kentucky. But Aisha, she lives—*lived* —" Another hiccup and a soft blow of the nose punctuated the woman's grief. "—here in Conway. Aisha moved to an apartment this fall to attend college at UCA while Haidar was deployed to Yemen. She said there was another option, but that it was permanent. She wanted to try UCA first. But Aisha didn't tell him she'd come home. He found out when he returned to Fort Campbell last week and discovered her note saying she wanted a divorce. On Wednesday, Aisha phoned to tell me Haidar had called. He'd taken leave and would be here in six hours. She was afraid he would force her to drive back with him."

"Was she reconsidering the divorce at all?"

"No. She was tired of being told she was not a good Muslim wife. She did not want to cover her hair when she went out or stay in the house because she refused to wear the *dupatta*."

"And he'd insisted on that?"

She nodded. "Yes. With Haidar and his family, it was a matter of honor, and he would not relent. Please understand. Though their marriage was arranged, my daughter came to love her husband. But it wasn't enough. She was just eighteen when they wed. She wanted more than to be a wife and bear children. She wanted to get her degree and open a business of her own someday. Haidar refused. And so—" The handkerchief made another pass through the leaking tears. "—they fought. So many times that Aisha decided she must leave."

That made sense. Apart from the timing. Why bolt in the dead of night—or in this case, the middle of the sergeant's deployment?

Except that those bruises Tonga had noted during his autopsy suggested an answer, and it wasn't pretty either. "Mrs. Shah. Do you know if your daughter's fights with her husband got physical? Did Haidar ever strike her?"

Was there a precedent?

The woman nodded slowly. Sadly. "Once. Before he left for Yemen. Haidar apologized, blamed the stress. But Aisha was worried it would happen again."

As much as Kate hated to admit it, soldier or not, odds were that the man would have done it again. Abusers came from all walks of life. All careers and income brackets. Just ask the cops who ended up fielding the plethora of so-called domestic dispute calls.

Somehow, that made it all that much more depressing.

As for this couple, even if the abuse had occurred just the once, it could be enough to cause Aisha Kharoti to flee. If the abuse *had* only occurred once.

The daughter might have been too humiliated to say otherwise.

Either way, had the marital fights and the admitted instance of abuse led to the level of rage indicated by the number and depths of those knife wounds? To that charred body? And if so, "Ma'am, do you know if your son-in-law has a connection to Braxton? Did he grow up nearby or have military friends who hail from around these parts? Or did he serve as a recruiter in or around Little Rock, or possibly attend training at the airbase or at Camp Robinson?" Something to explain why Sergeant

Kharoti might've chosen that particular field to dump his wife's body.

"No, he never lived here. Haidar and his family immigrated to New York when he was a boy. But I don't know about his friends."

Kate nodded. "Then, you don't know where he stayed after he arrived in Conway on Wednesday?"

"That I know. The apartment."

"Your daughter's?" Had Aisha agreed to let him in the door of what had in effect become her sanctuary, after all? Possibly even let him back into her bed?

Or had the sergeant forced his way in—to both?

A fresh wave of those desolate tears coursed down Mrs. Shah's cheeks. "That's why I've been so worried. When we spoke on Wednesday, Aisha said Haidar had agreed to stay in a hotel. She assured me she would call after he arrived to let me know how their dinner went. But I didn't hear from her on Thursday, nor did she answer her phone. I thought perhaps he had taken it away again, so I stopped by her apartment on Friday before work. His duffle bag was in the bedroom, a uniform in the hamper. But he was gone, and so was Aisha. I found his green truck in the lot, but her car was nowhere. I thought—hoped—they had gone for breakfast. It was finals week, but she was supposed to be finished by Thursday afternoon. I sent her another text and went to work. I wish...I wish I had stayed and called the police instead."

There was nothing Kate could offer to that. No platitudes would ease this mother's profound grief. And she sure as hell wasn't about to add to it by pointing out that her daughter had mostly likely been dead by the time she'd arrived at Aisha's apartment—and already on fire. Not now. Not ever.

But Kate did need visual confirmation so that she could use all the tools available to her to investigate that daughter's death.

She retrieved her phone and pulled up the picture Seth had texted late last night of the earring after it had been cleaned and sanitized. She turned her phone so the mother could see the pink diamond and post.

A fresh wave of tears welled up in those dark brown eyes. The woman's tortured whisper followed. "*Yes*. That was hers."

"Do you have a photo of Aisha on you?"

The woman's breath shuddered out, causing her nod to wobble. "Do you have your iPhone's airdrop set to accept files from everyone?"

Kate clicked into her settings and toggled the appropriate one. "I do now."

A fresh wave of tears slid down Mrs. Shah's cheeks as she slipped her right hand into the pocket of her floral scrubs to retrieve her own iPhone. Her fingers shook as she tapped the screen several times.

Moments later, the photo of a gorgeous twenty-something Pakistani woman wearing a scarlet sari with silver flowers airdropped onto Kate's screen. Thick black hair fell to the woman's waist and...she was well-endowed.

They'd need to run a DNA comparison before the department could issue an official confirmation, but the body already tucked back inside its refrigerated drawer down the hall was definitely Aisha's.

The victim's mother had accepted it, too. Mrs. Shah was still scrolling through her app, stopping now and then to airdrop another photo featuring those dark eyes and that caramel skin and captivatingly vibrant smile to Kate's phone.

Six airdrops later, the pictures ceased arriving and the devastated woman who'd probably taken them all finally looked up. "Haidar is a distant cousin to our family. My husband insisted on the marriage, and then he had a heart attack shortly afterward, leaving Aisha to live with his decree and her new husband. And now, my beautiful girl is dead too."

Because of *him*.

Though the mother hadn't added that last aloud, Kate heard it all the same. But for all she'd discovered about the Kharotis and their marriage, was it accurate?

It was time to find out.

They'd yet to locate the primary crime scene. Though if Haidar had killed his wife—at the apartment, no less—chances were the sergeant had already cut and run.

"Mrs. Shah, do you have the address to your daughter's apartment? And would it be possible to borrow your key?" If she'd accessed the apartment on her own two mornings earlier, she had to have one.

Though Kate hated troubling the woman, borrowing it would be quicker than waiting on the department's locksmith.

The mother wiped her eyes again, then traded her phone for a ring of keys as she offered up the address to a student complex just off the University of Central Arkansas' campus. She worked a key free and held it out. "I want to see my baby."

Kate pocketed the key, as she shook her head softly. Firmly. "No, ma'am, you don't."

"I *do*. Detective—"

"Kate."

"*Kate*. Please. I know my child was burned, but I'm a nurse. I *need* to see her."

Kate reached out, gently touching the woman's arm as she shook her head again. "Aisha was your child—and that's exactly why you shouldn't. Mrs. Shah, you don't need that image in your heart." Nor did the woman need the horrific smell that came with it, faint though it would be by now. "You would carry it forever. You don't want that. Aisha wouldn't want that. Let me do it for you. That's what I'm here for."

Hell, she'd be carrying that image and smell around with her for the rest of her life anyway. Especially in her dreams.

Might as well have some sliver of good come out it.

Those silent tears started up again, but the woman nodded. Accepted. "Okay."

The handkerchief returned as well.

Every inch was soaked.

Kate was about to retrieve the travel pack of tissues she kept in her jacket's inner pocket for apparently the same reason that Nash carried his square of linen, when the door to the autopsy suite opened.

Tonga stepped out. As usual, the ME's timing was spot on. "Nida, I am so sorry for your loss."

Mrs. Shah came to her feet to accept the consoling hug he offered. "Thank you, Armand."

Tonga met Kate's stare over the mother's dark head. His silent nod toward the elevators at the opposite end of the corridor spoke volumes. He'd accompany the woman up to the ER and obtain her DNA for comparison to the body's.

Kate returned the ME's nod as she retrieved one of her business cards. She passed it to Aisha's mother along with her repeated condolences and an invitation to call at any time, for any reason.

She waited for Tonga to escort the woman down the hall, then took off in the opposite direction, snagging her phone and punching the sheriff's number as she reached the stairs.

Lou picked up on the first ring. "Please tell me you got a bead on this asshole."

"I might." She gave him the condensed version of the mother's side of the Kharoti marriage as she made her way out of the hospital and across the parking lot—including the fact that the husband was an active-duty Army sergeant.

"Holy crap on a crawdad. *Another* one?"

Kate paused as she reached her Durango. "Yup."

First Joe, Grant and Burke. And now this.

At this rate, she should've stayed CID. Except, they all knew that wasn't possible. Especially her. Despite what her shrink had been arguing.

"Hang on, boss." She climbed into her Durango and slammed the driver's door, sealing out the world as she switched the call to hands-free mode. "Okay, you're on speaker now, but we're still private. I have some pics to text you. They're of Aisha."

She sent the photos winging Lou's way, then fired up the SUV's engine.

Lou's soft whistle warmed the cab as she pulled out of the hospital parking lot and headed for Aisha's off-campus apartment complex. "That was one pretty lady."

"Yeah." Only Aisha Kharoti wasn't so pretty now. Some sick bastard had made sure of it.

Lou must've had the same thought, because his heavy sigh filled the SUV. "Alrighty, then. Seth's still workin' on the electronic dumps for Aisha's phone, but the warrant for her student apartment has come through. Seth'll join you at the complex with a hard copy shortly."

"Sounds good." Kate paused at a red light and waved to a wide-eyed, toffee-haired toddler strapped into the back seat of the sedan beside her. She tried adding a smile, but it fell flat. "I'm a block away from the place now. The mother gave me a key."

"You think the sergeant's camped out there?"

If the mother's story panned out? "I doubt it. You?"

Lou's snort filled the line. "Nope. And I'm willin' to put money down."

So was she.

"Either way, you'd best get in there and secure the scene. I'll give Conway PD a courtesy heads-up for you. You just concentrate on gettin' us another Kato case cracker like you done with that earring."

Yeah, right.

Kate frowned as the sheriff severed the call. With her current track record, she was more likely to miss something huge and right in front of her face—like Joe's, Grant's *and* Burke's guilt.

Her wrist began to itch.

By the time she'd located Aisha's building and parked the Durango, the need to scratch was all but clawing in.

She forced herself to ignore it. She didn't have time to dig Max's watch out from her pocket and slap it on, much less wallow in her mistakes.

She couldn't even spare a few minutes to phone Fort Campbell to give the duty CID agent a heads-up that one of their soldiers was a person of interest in a homicide. No, she hadn't spotted any green pickups on her way through the lot, let alone one with Kentucky plates. But on the off chance the husband was inside—and guilty—she needed to get in and make sure he wasn't destroying evidence.

If there was any left to destroy by now.

Kate swung around to the rear of her SUV to pop the hatch and grab her stainless-steel crime kit. Mrs. Shah had been trying to reach her daughter for three days. A man could do a lot of deep, effective cleaning in that amount of time. Especially if he was savvy enough to have been tapped to deploy with Special Forces.

Screw her father's beliefs. Lou was depending on her. So was Nida Shah.

More importantly, Aisha herself—wherever she was now.

Kate headed for the covered stairs. She set the stainless-steel case down beside the first-floor door on the left and knocked.

No answer.

Fortunately, there was enough overhead to the stairwell to

conceal her presence from the rest of the complex. Retrieving her 9mm with her right hand, she used her left to insert the key Mrs. Shah had provided and eased the door open.

"Hello?"

Once again, silence greeted her.

Her Glock front and center, she nudged her kit inside the door and quietly followed it into the apartment. She cleared the tiny living room, kitchen, bedroom and bath. A final check of the bedroom closet confirmed Lou's assessment.

Haidar Kharoti was gone.

Even more telling, the duffle bag his mother-in-law had spotted in the bedroom Friday morning was missing as well.

The blanket and top sheet on the twin bed were twisted and rumpled. Kate holstered her Glock and donned a set of latex gloves. Peeling the bedclothes from the bottom sheet revealed the dried, telltale traces of bodily fluids from a sexually active couple—along with the distinct smear of oxidized blood.

She opened the camera app on her phone and snapped a photo, then returned to the bathroom. A deep dive through the laundry hamper produced four long-sleeved shirts, a pair of waitressing T-shirts from a local bar and several pairs of jeans, along with an assortment of D-cup lace bras with their matching, barely-there panties.

But no Army uniform, camouflaged or otherwise.

Haidar had definitely abandoned the apartment.

If the sergeant had killed his wife before he'd left, he'd removed that evidence too. Not only were the living room and bedroom carpets devoid of blood, liberal use of the luminol and the black light from the crime kit revealed no evidence of blood on the bathroom sink, tub or floor. The kitchen sink and floor were clean as well.

Had he forgotten about the blood on the sheets, or had he not even known it was there?

She'd have to ask the sergeant—when she found him.

The garbage can beside the bedroom desk produced the only other discoveries of note. The first was an invitation to an "epic" end-of-semester kegger hosted by a local frat for the previous night. The second was a cheap, ink-jet produced business card with a phone number on the front and *L. Basque* penned in ink on the reverse. Intriguingly, the card had been crumpled up inside the party invite. And when she added the waitressing T-shirts, lace bras and barely-there panties that she'd found in the hamper to the sergeant's insistence that his wife could only leave their home if her hair was modestly covered—and most likely the rest of her as well—she just might've found a motive.

The level of anger that had fueled those stab wounds cut in. The smear of blood on the sheets in the bedroom down the hall. The evidence of vaginal penetration that Tonga had noted during the autopsy. The fact that Aisha's body had been dumped in a field of wheat and then set on fire.

How had Mrs. Shah put it outside the autopsy suite? *With Haidar and his family, it was a matter of honor, and he would not relent.*

According to his mother-in-law, Haidar had immigrated to New York as a boy. Kate had assisted with several so-called "honor" killings during her years with Army CID. Although those crimes had been committed by non-US citizens and had taken place in multiple war zones on the opposite side of the globe, she was getting the same chilling vibe now that she'd gotten then.

The perpetrators of those distant homicides might've hidden behind Islam, but it was a sham of an excuse. Islam had had nothing to do with the murders.

So-called honor killings came down to culture and dominance.

Not to mention the men who craved that dominance—especially the men who were willing to slaughter the very women they should be cherishing to maintain it. Haidar had supposedly been set on molding Aisha into his ideal of a good wife before he'd left for Yemen. Had his latest tour strengthened those beliefs?

Kate could only pray that wasn't the case.

Because if it was—and the media got a hold of the rationale—she, Lou and their dwindling department would find themselves squatting on yet another ticking bomb.

And this one came with devastating fallout for the entire US Army.

5

A solid knock on the outside of the apartment door jarred Kate from her funk. Seth's deep voice followed it.

"You in there, Holland?"

"Yeah—just a sec." Kate bagged the flyer invite to the frat party, then the business card. She set both envelopes on the breakfast bar that separated the living area from the kitchen and headed for the door to open it.

Seth's dark, uniformed bubba build dominated the tiny apartment as he stepped inside, brandishing a crisp manila folder. "Got a hard copy of the warrant here and the cellphone data dumps for Aisha Kharoti. Also, Conway PD is officially in the loop and should have someone showing up ASAP to watch and assist."

Had she misheard Lou on the phone?

"You're not sticking around?"

To her surprise, Seth flushed. "You...sure you want me to?"

Okay, so she shouldn't have been—surprised that is. Her fellow deputy was deeply ashamed. Because of her.

That stupid Silver Star.

With one of Seth's boots already out the department's door, her hurting friend of three-plus years actually believed a decorated, former POW like her would have her combat-forged boots ready to kick his inadequate ass out the rest of the way. Since, of course, the demons that plagued her were *so* much worse than his—at least, according to Seth's freshly bruised psyche.

What a crock. Pain was not a contest.

If she'd learned one thing from her sessions with her shrink, it was that everyone's trauma—and their reaction to it—was different. Unique. Just as everyone's path through that trauma was equally unique.

But with the way Seth had closed down on her when she'd tried to broach the subject of PTSD with him last week, he wasn't ready to accept that. Until he had, and until he was willing to put in the work and learn how to push back against the demons of his own that he'd racked up at the crematorium four weeks ago, there was nothing she could do except wait. This, too, from the ever-sage Dr. Manning.

But she could let Seth know she was there for him, whether or not he was still wearing a Braxton deputy's uniform.

Intent on conveying just that, Kate grabbed the sleeve of his jacket and tugged the gentle giant deeper into the apartment. "Conway PD notwithstanding, you're staying. I don't just need help, Deputy. I need you."

The relief that washed Seth's features was so swift and so profound, *she* was embarrassed.

Kate turned away to cover it, pointing toward the narrow hall that led to the apartment's sole bedroom, laundry closet and bath. "There's not much here. Just some fluids with a smear of blood in the victim's bed." She swung back around to tip her head toward the items she'd recovered from the trash. "And those."

Like the smear on the sheets, neither the kegger flyer nor the homemade business card appeared to assist with her overriding question of the moment. Namely, where the hell was Sergeant Kharoti?

Already back at Fort Campbell, fine-tuning his alibi?

Seth laid the manila folder he'd brought on the counter beside the evidence envelopes, then doffed his departmental ball cap. "Do we have a motive yet?"

Her sigh was as dark as the answer to that question. "Possibly. Honor killing."

"What?" The ball cap landed atop the folder with a slap. "*Here*? In Arkansas?"

"Yep."

"Are you sure?"

Until she'd managed to track down Haidar and grill him herself? "No. But it's looking like the best working theory at the moment."

Kate summed up the conversation she'd had with the victim's mother outside the autopsy suite at the hospital, along with the results that Tonga had shared from his external and internal examination of the body, finishing up with a quick recap of the contents of the laundry hamper and a description of the already bagged kegger invite.

One of those oversized hands of Seth's made a raking pass through his hair, causing a crop of short curls to spring forth. "Well, *shit*." A heavy sigh followed. "Though, I gotta confess. I'm a bit torn between apprehension and relief."

She was right there with him on that.

The apprehension came from knowing that if Aisha's decision regarding a divorce and the contents of the hamper and trash had set the sergeant off, the press was going to have a field day with the implications that Islamist behavior had taken root within the US Army. Accurate or not, comparisons with former Army Major Nidal Malik Hasan and his horrific massacre at Fort

Hood, Texas, would undoubtedly follow. Along with yet another flock of microphone-wielding vultures swooping in to pick through the battered bones of Braxton as they attempted to get their stories and make their collective salacious case.

They'd just gotten rid of the last bunch.

As for the relief? Aisha Kharoti was dead. If this was about "honor", no more bodies, charred or otherwise, would be turning up in Braxton's fields. With all those paper sacks filled with body parts that should never had been hacked up in the first place—and wouldn't have been if she'd been the investigator everyone seemed to believe she was—that was something. Right now, everything.

Seth stepped closer. He reached out to gently lift her chin so he could look her in the eye. Something that, given her shredded face, not many were able to do. Not this close. Including her friends.

Not without pity staining their own features.

"Kate, what can I do to make this easier?"

Was her crappy mood that obvious?

Based on the concern knitting those dark brows of Seth's and the darker frown beneath—it was.

She reached out to tap the corner of the manila folder he'd laid on the counter. "You can tell me you found a solid lead in that data dump."

Heck, she'd take a flimsy one at this point.

Unfortunately, he shook his head. "Nothin' solid. There was one thing though."

"What?"

Seth nudged his ball cap off the folder as she approached so he could splay the pages within out along the counter. "Right here. See this Manchin number? It shows up five months back. Three calls over the course of a week. The victim initiated all three. Then nothin' until this month and this past week when

Aisha calls the number again—five times and *all* on Wednesday."

"Wednesday?" The same day the woman's husband had phoned to tell his wife he was driving to see her?

Curious. And something else.

Kate snatched her iPhone from her utility belt and clicked through the most recent crime scene photos she'd taken until she reached the one she'd snapped of the front of the business card before she'd sealed the evidence envelope.

The phone numbers matched.

Seth gathered up the sheets and tucked them back inside the folder. "The number comes back to a Lily—"

"Basque."

"Yeah. How'd you know?"

Kate tapped the corresponding evidence envelope on the counter. "That's the surname handwritten on the back of the business card, with that number printed on the front. Any idea who Lily Basque is?"

"Yeah, a doctor. She's a—" Seth reached into the inner pocket of his jacket and pulled out a memo book identical to the one Kate carried. "—general surgeon outta Little Rock. Has privileges at Baptist Health, though her office appears to be in Manchin. I figured you'd want the info on the office too, since the number had popped so many times this week. Got the address right here."

Kate nodded. But she was still hung up on the hospital where the doc evidently operated. "Baptist Health?" Basque was a civilian? "That doesn't make sense."

He shrugged. "Maybe Aisha needed surgery? Sure, she was young. But there could be any number of reasons why—"

"No, not that. Seth, Aisha Kharoti was a military wife. Pending divorce or not, she still had a dependent's ID. That card entitled Aisha to see any number of doctors at the Air Force hospital on the base just up the road from Baptist. And those T-shirts in the hamper? I haven't verified it yet, but she's got to be a waitress at Stu's bar."

"She is. Seems the woman refused to accept money from her mom. Wanted to prove that she could make it on her own. Aisha took out a student loan for the tuition."

Kate's brow shot up at that last—causing her fellow deputy to flush.

That was some great case info he'd offered. But it was also some seriously *quick* case info.

The man tacked on a slight shrug. "I figured you'd want as much as I could get on the victim, too, so I called the mom back just before I left for here. Mrs. Shah didn't mind. She's even more anxious than we are to nail this sonofabitch."

And Seth thought PTSD made him less of a cop?

Not in her book. He was as on the ball as they came.

She nodded briskly. "Okay. She was definitely a waitress. Now riddle me this, Deputy. Why would a student living off tips, minimum wage and looking at four years of tuition loans that she was eventually going to have to pay back seek out a surgeon she'd have to pay full price to see, when she had access to free medical care, damned proficient Air Force surgeons—and any surgeries they deemed necessary—a mere twenty miles up the road?"

Seth scratched his jaw. "Dunno."

"Me neither." But she would find out. She reached out to tap the bound top of Seth's memo pad. "I don't suppose you have Basque's home address in there." The man appeared to have everything else she'd needed.

Seth shook his head. Which was odd because that beaming grin of his had also taken up residence, automatically lightening her mood and causing a genuine curve to blossom on her own face for the first time since she'd left Ruger's lovable, huggable hide earlier that morning. Why? Because there was something else skating around the corners of that grin, too. Something she liked.

Satisfaction.

"Seth?"

"You don't need her home address. The doc's in her office until four."

"On a Sunday?"

"Yep. I noted her schedule when I googled her. She's off on Fridays and Saturdays. Ten to four the rest of the week. Bit strange if you ask me."

Not really. Just unusual. At least around these parts.

Dr. Basque's offices kept to an Islamic work/weekend schedule.

Curious and curiouser.

Kate hefted her stainless-steel case up onto the counter so she could secure the combination lock. "Can you do me a huge favor?"

"Lemme guess. Stay here and continue processin' the scene until Nester and his boys show while you drive to Manchin and pay the good doc an impromptu visit?"

"Bingo."

"Sure thing. Got my crime kit in my truck. I'll text you the office address."

"Great." She peeled off her gloves and wedged them in her trouser pocket. "Can you call Lou while you're at it? Fill him in on the briefing I gave you?"

She had another, equally critical call to make during her coming drive. One to Fort Campbell's Criminal Investigation Division. The information she was about to relay to the duty CID agent about Sergeant Kharoti and what she hoped to gain in return—namely, the sergeant's current location—just might crack this case open before she even reached Manchin and Dr. Basque's office.

If they were lucky.

"Consider the sheriff briefed."

"Thanks."

She left Nida Shah's key on the counter and signed the evidence envelopes over to Seth, then departed.

Thirty minutes later, Kate and her Durango were less than a mile from the doc's medical office, headed down the tree-lined country highway that led to Manchin.

She hoped to heck her coming interview with Basque would be productive, because the call she'd made to Fort Campbell's CID during the drive had been anything but.

All the duty agent had been able to offer was that Sergeant Haidar Kharoti appeared to be a stellar soldier. According to the information in the records Agent Castile had pulled up, Haidar's translation skills were so savvy, he'd been tapped by Special Forces last spring to accompany a team to Yemen for a six-month rotation.

As the sergeant's mother-in-law had already stated, Haidar had returned to the States early last week.

As far as Castile had been able to determine while Kate had patiently waited on hold, Haidar was still in Conway visiting his wife. Now that Castile knew the sergeant wasn't there—and that the sergeant was wanted for questioning in the brutal murder of that wife—the entire US Army would be looking for the man. With Haidar also not where he'd told the Army he'd be and not scheduled to return to post for two more days, Castile would begin by talking to the sergeant's fellow soldiers.

Unfortunately, since the majority of those same fellow soldiers had also just returned to the States and were on leave too, interviewing them would take time.

Castile would call back as soon as he had something.

Kate had thanked the agent and hung up—and had promptly followed up her Campbell call with another to Seth to make yet another request of the deputy. This one for a warrant for *Haidar* Kharoti's phone.

If they were lucky, the resulting GPS data would lead them straight to the sergeant, wherever the man had escaped to.

Until then, she'd continue to follow the sole clue his wife's calls had provided.

Surprise filtered in as Kate turned the Durango down a barely marked drive. If she hadn't clicked on the GPS pin Seth had texted, she'd have driven right past the entrance. Stranger still, while the single-story, gray brick structure at the end was new and impressive, it was also in the middle of nowhere.

A densely forested nowhere at that. Unless her internal human map was off, Little Rock and the Baptist Health Medical Center were a good twenty-plus miles down the country road she'd abandoned. Every other civilian surgeon's office she knew of was smack in the thick of things—as in inside or within sneezing distance of the hospital where the surgeon in question operated.

Kate parked her Durango beside the only other two cars in front of the building. Hopefully one of them belonged to the doc. But since both muted silver sedans were cheaper and older than her SUV, the odds weren't good.

Perhaps she should've called ahead.

Never give 'em time to prep their story, Holland—much less compare notes.

She'd clearly spent too long on the phone with Agent Castile and immersed in the Army again, because her old CID mentor's advice had begun to filter in. Kate smiled at the memory of Art Valens and his favorite mantra for suspects and witnesses alike as she reached the frosted doors at the front of the medical building.

Automatically removing her ball cap as she entered, she swapped it out for the black leather bifold she kept inside her jacket. The one that contained her badge.

The faint scent of medical grade antiseptic greeted her as she stepped into a light blue carpeted waiting room filled with plush chairs, a matching floral couch and a trio of rich cherry accent tables with an assortment of home and lifestyle magazines on top—but no patient window.

Odd.

An attractive, thirty-something woman of at least partial Middle Eastern descent stood near a closed door at the opposite end of the room. Arab, Persian, Algerian: Kate couldn't be sure. The woman was wearing a long-sleeved white T-shirt beneath a set of pastel pink scrubs. She held a glass horse and a feather duster in her hands.

The receptionist?

"May I help you?"

The smile within those dark, thickly lashed eyes faltered as they reached the right side of her face. A revealing glint assumed its place.

Not the receptionist then. That glint was too familiar.

Kate held up her credentials and went through the motions, anyway. "Deputy Kate Holland, Braxton PD. I need to speak with Dr. Lily Basque."

The woman set the rearing horse and feather duster down on the cherry accent table beside the door. "I'm Dr. Basque."

Kate tucked her credentials home.

She hadn't needed the words. The visual confirmation still lingered in the woman's eyes. Oh, Basque was trying to hide it, but she couldn't. Kate would recognize the gleam of clinical curiosity anywhere. She could almost feel the doc trying to work out exactly what had caused the collection of pockmarks and scars that made up the right side of her face...and how the doc could fix it.

Until, suddenly, something else entered the mix. Something downright intriguing.

Over the past four years, Kate could've sworn she'd collected up every human reaction under the sun to her revised features. But this one?

It was new—at least with adults.

Fear.

What on earth had caused it? Their current location?

According to Seth's preliminary research, not to mention the sign out front, Basque wasn't a plastic surgeon—and Kate had offered up her Braxton credentials. But perhaps the doc was afraid she was here for a medical opinion anyway and didn't want to be the one to tell her that it was impossible. That there was no fix for her face.

As if she hadn't been able to figure that out on her own these past four years.

Kate waited, her curiosity with the woman growing.

It took another few moments for the doc to realize she was staring. Basque jerked her focus down and flushed. "My apologies. I—"

"Not a problem. And I'm not here for a surgical consult."

That must have been the source of the woman's reaction. Because the flush and embarrassment also faded as the doc's professionalism took over. Though, strangely, Basque still wouldn't quite meet her gaze.

"How can I help you, Deputy?"

"Kate. I'm following up on the cellphone data of a woman by the name of Aisha Kharoti. I understand Mrs. Kharoti phoned your office this past Wednesday. Is she a patient of yours?"

Instead of answering, Basque surprised her again. This time

by reaching out to retrieve the duster. She held it in front of her body. Tightly. "I'm sorry. The name doesn't ring a bell."

The grip on that duster? The fact that Basque appeared preoccupied with the feathers sprouting out from the end?

The doc was lying.

And that odd glint of fear was back. Because of the cop's uniform this time, not her shredded face.

That reaction from adults, Kate had dealt with before. She calmly retrieved her phone and brought up the first of the photos that Mrs. Shah had provided of her daughter during happier times. "Mrs. Kharoti may have been afraid of her husband. Hence, she may have used another name when she stopped in. If you could take a look at this photo—" She turned her screen around so the doc could get a clear view.

Kate needn't have bothered. Basque barely glanced at the screen.

She did shake her head, however. Firmly. "I'm so sorry. She's a beautiful woman, but I don't recognize her. Sorry."

That was a lot of sorry for someone the doc had never met.

Instinct had Kate swiping through her photos and bringing up a graphic close-up she'd taken out behind Nash Weaver's house in that field of wheat. "Here's another view of the same woman." She turned the phone again.

The doc blanched. "*Please*. Why would you show me—"

Kate held up her hand, cutting Basque off. She hadn't wanted to play it this way. Hated it, in fact. But she didn't have time for more lies. Aisha's husband was most likely in the wind. And the longer Basque stalled, the farther away Haidar would get. "You're right, Doctor. Aisha Kharoti was a beautiful woman. Emphasis on *was*." She held up the grisly photo once more. "This is what Aisha looks like today. Now, I know Aisha called this office five months ago and again this past week. As a matter of fact, Aisha made five separate calls to your service on Wednesday. I have the data dumps to prove it. As to your question: why am I showing this photo to you? Because I need to find the person who did this to her. So, would you care to study the first photo I showed you a bit more closely, perhaps even check your records for her name?"

The doc nodded. "Of course. I can check now. If you would like to take a seat—"

"I'll stand."

This second nod was even more wary. But the woman turned, taking the duster with her as she opened the door beside them. Basque entered a deserted hallway and closed the door, leaving Kate to stew in the waiting room in silence.

Four minutes later, Basque returned.

Color had returned to the woman's face, and her hand was no longer shaking. But Basque still couldn't quite make eye contact.

The doc focused just beyond the ruined side of Kate's face as she smoothed an errand strand of inky hair into the oversized messy bun at the nape of her neck. "I spoke to my assistant. A woman named Aisha Kharoti did phone my service this past week. We have no record of the earlier calls several months back, but on Wednesday, Mrs. Kharoti wanted an appointment for a surgical consult. She scheduled one, then phoned back several times to reschedule, until she finally called to cancel completely."

"Do you know why she needed surgery?"

"No. If I did, we both know I'd have to wait for a warrant to offer more, but it turns out that Mrs. Kharoti didn't give a reason during any of her calls. And since we offer an array of in- and outpatient services, there's no way to narrow it down." Without that duster in her hands, the woman's fingers had begun to fidget and twitch.

Basque was still lying. The doc knew exactly why Aisha had phoned her office.

And there was the rest.

We offer?

There was only one name on the sign out front. So who did the other car belong to? Basque's nurse? Possibly. Hell, probably.

Either way, why was she getting the distinct vibe that there was more going on in this office than just surgeries? And that it centered around women.

Given Aisha's comments to her mother, Kate had her suspicions, but—

"*...to burn her.*"

She stepped closer to the doc. "Excuse me?"

Basque blinked. "I didn't say—"

"You did. You whispered, 'to burn her'. "

"I didn't mean to."

"Then what did you mean?" Kate stepped that much closer to the doc. Deliberately stared the woman down, making it painfully clear that she wasn't budging from her spot, let alone leaving the office, without an answer.

The real answer.

The doc finally shook her head. Sighed. "It's just—I don't know how much you know about Islam. But cremation? It's *haram* to Muslims. Forbidden. Whoever burned that poor woman hated her a great deal. He or she wanted her punished for eternity."

Kate didn't bother asking how the doc knew about Aisha's religious practices. She'd only get another lie. She went for the unexpected instead. "You're Muslim too, then?"

"*No.*" For the first time since she'd arrived, Basque's stare met hers hard and square on—and remained there.

The doc had a spine after all.

And whole lot of hardened anger and disgust had locked in with it.

Interesting.

A phone pinged. The doctor's. "I'm sorry, Deputy. I must take this. I trust you can find your way out?"

Kate might not be in the Army anymore, but she knew when she'd been dismissed.

She nodded. Why not? She had a feeling she'd be back.

Until then, she had a slew of new questions that needed answers. And they didn't all concern Aisha Kharoti.

Kate retrieved her ball cap, donning it as she crossed the waiting room and departed the building. She retrieved her phone next, surreptitiously snapping photos of the license plates of both those silver, Arkansas-registered sedans on the way to her Durango. But as she climbed into the SUV's driver's seat and slammed the door, she didn't run the plates for the cars.

Instead, she brought up the browser on her phone and typed *Lily Basque, general surgeon* into the search engine.

A slew of local physician reviews and surgical consultation-related links filled the screen. A seemingly unrelated link at the bottom intrigued her more.

Al Jazeera?

Kate clicked the link to the Qatari news site and skimmed the article that loaded. It was a "day in the life" feature detailing the activities of several physicians as they treated and patched up twenty-four hours' worth of unlucky coalition troops and unluckier locals at the Craig Joint Theatre Hospital in Bagram, Afghanistan, during the war. And one of the surgeons of the day, complete with a lovely close-up photo?

Dr. Lily Basque.

Suspicion bit in—along with the memory of that near-constant, evasive stare and the inexplicable glint of fear she'd spotted in the doc.

What were the odds?

Kate scrolled back to the top of the page to check the article's stats. It'd been written just over four years ago. Suspicion turned to certainty as she did the math. The date of the article added to the day that a particular IED had blown her face and her sanity to hell and back. One plus one didn't equal two; it totaled up to a million.

At least.

Lily Basque had been part of Craig's staff the night Kate had killed her captors and escaped to become a *former* POW. The same night she'd been found by an Army patrol and brought to Bagram. The same night she'd been shuttled into that quiet room at the hospital.

Even if the doc hadn't been on duty when she'd been brought in, Basque had to have heard the tale. Hell, according to her childhood friend-turned-shrink Liz, it was still making the rounds of military medicine. The way she'd walked Max's carefully wrapped severed head all the way into the hospital and laid it on the reception counter.

So why hadn't *this* doc mentioned it?

But Kate knew. Most people who were aware of what had happened to her that day also still believed she couldn't remember it. That glimmer of fear she'd noted in the waiting room finally made sense. Basque hadn't *wanted* her to make the connection.

But why?

Kate was torn between biding her time for her coming deep dive into the remaining secrets of the good doc's life and simply bailing out of the Durango to head back inside and nail the woman to the wall when her phone rang.

It was Lou.

On a FaceTime call?

Not the sheriff's preferred method of communicating. Ever.

Please, let him just be checking up on her. Even reaching out to let her know Owen and Drake—hell, even Nester and his boys—had decided to quit too.

Anything but another body.

She braced herself for the worst as she accepted the call.

6

Lou's weary face filled her iPhone's screen. "Hey, Kato. Where're ya at?"

"I'm parked outside a medical office just shy of Manchin. Following up on a slew of numbers from the data dump. A general surgeon by the name of Lily Basque."

"Yeah, Seth said somethin' about that." Hope flickered in. "You got anythin' to show for it?"

"Not yet." But she would. Kate tucked her fingers in her lap, firmly crossing them as she forced the query out. "What's wrong, boss?"

The flicker of hope fled the sheriff's face—with the hounds of hell in hot pursuit.

Shit.

Her mental assessment must've made it to her own features, because her boss sighed into their connection. Nodded. "Yep. We got another body."

Kate pressed the back of her suddenly throbbing skull into the Durango's headrest as she absorbed her own disappointment and fury. There she sat, for several long moments, until she found the strength to straighten. To press for the rest.

"Where?"

"Mazelle. Outskirts of town. Two teenagers stumbled across it this morning. It was layin' in the parkin' lot of that defunct box plant on the north side of town."

"Female, charred?" Of course it was, or why would Lou be calling?

But it needed stating.

"Yep. Looks to be stabbed too. Either our guy's gettin' lazy or there weren't enough fuel around to keep the fire goin', 'cause this one's not as charred as Aisha was. Leastways, that's what I gather from what I been told." Lou scrubbed the silver sprouting along his jaw. "We do have a bit more info off the bat with this one though. They found a purse. From where it was found, they think it fell out of the bastard's vehicle while he was dumpin' the body. But that asshole's mistake is our gain. The purse had a wallet inside it—and in that, a photo ID. A couple of 'em, actually."

Multiple IDs? "What types?"

Another scrub of that silver.

The man was stalling.

Why?

Ah, shit. Multiple *photo* IDs. She was willing to bet both her and Ruger's second vegetarian dinner in a row that one of them was a dependent's card. "This victim was married to a soldier too, wasn't she?"

A half-hearted twist bit into the man's lips. "No doubt about your instincts, Deputy." Lou nodded. "The name on the military dependent card's Tahira Larijani. And, yep, there's a Muslim connection. The husband's stationed out at Camp Robinson. No idea on the state of the marriage. That'll be up to you and your new partner to ferret out. But I'm guessin' it weren't no blissful union, 'cause the detective they got on it is already hoistin' the same tattered flag you've been wavin' at the Kharotis: honor killin'. Chief Barrows and I go way back. He knows we're stretched beyond thin. I'll keep Seth, Owen and Drake close to home. You're to meet up with the detective from Mazelle at the scene. You two'll link the cases together and share the load 'til further notice."

She appreciated the backup—especially now.

But another military spouse *and* another tie to Islam?

Kate caught a blur of motion at the corner of her eye and glanced over to the door of the medical office. It was opening. Basque followed another woman of Middle Eastern descent into the lot, then turned to lock up while the unknown woman kept going until she'd climbed into the farther sedan and started the engine.

The doc waved as the other woman abandoned the lot, then headed for the remaining sedan to do likewise.

Not once did Basque so much as look at the Durango, let alone her. The doc simply left.

What the hell was going on?

"Kato?"

She jerked her attention back to her phone's screen. To Lou.

"Everythin' okay there?"

That remained to be seen, didn't it? "Boss, I—"

"*Don't* have to do this."

She stilled.

That near-nauseous, hellishly reluctant look that had slipped into Lou's tired eyes? The fact that he'd FaceTimed her for the first time—ever? She knew full well what *this* was. The sheriff was giving her an out. On a silver platter, no less. Yeah, that stunning offer was almost as tarnished and banged up as she was, but he was extending it.

The fear that she'd take him up on it locked in and pulsed amid the silence.

But he didn't pull it back.

If anything, the man's stiff nod nudged it closer. "I can send Drake to Mazelle instead. He's new. But the detective that Chief Barrows assigned won't be. It'll work out."

Would it?

But Lou was right about Barrows. Mazelle's chief of police was as solid as they came. Barrows would make sure their collective asses were covered.

So why wasn't she tempted? Hell, her wrist wasn't even itching.

Shouldn't it be?

Or was Dr. Manning's magic bandage simply that good?

"Hon?"

She shook her head. Her decision was already made. "I'm good. Let Barrows know I'm thirty minutes out."

"Kate...I gotta warn you. Their ME is on site, so they mighta moved the body. But they might not have. And if it ain't cooled enough, it could be there for the duration of the search." For the entire time she would need to be there.

Kicking off that godawful odor.

Lou hadn't added that last out loud, but she'd heard it all the same. Had already accepted it too. "Understood."

His voice caught as he leaned closer to the screen, turned gruffer. "You sure?"

Mrs. Shah's face slipped through Kate's mind. The woman's tears sliding down her cheeks as she'd swiped through the last photos she'd ever take of her only daughter. Nash's tented, trembling fingers as he'd sat in vigil for a woman he'd never even met. The twitchy doc as Basque had stood there in her *Architectural Digest* of a waiting room, lying through her glistening, uncharred teeth about knowing the same woman.

"Yeah, I'm sure."

"Alrighty, then. Check in when you can."

"Roger. Out." Kate clicked off her phone and tossed it onto

the passenger seat as she pressed her still throbbing skull into the headrest once more.

What the hell had she just done?

She'd had her out—right there in her hand.

And she'd tossed it back.

She stared down at her wrist, at the ace bandage she'd donned that morning. Maybe it was magic, after all. Because the skin beneath still didn't itch.

But she could feel that old, familiar panic pinching in—and she knew why. It had to do with the blackened body that was waiting for her.

The smell.

The buried memories that were bound to surge to the surface once she got to the crime scene and crash in along with it. Hell, they already *were*.

And there were so damned many to choose from.

The aftermath of her first IED explosion. Bending down to gather up the scorched and bloodied remains of a fellow squad-mate. Countless other horrific memories followed—anchored in by the worst. That flipped and shattered Humvee; being trapped inside with Max...and those hellishly ravenous flames that had blistered, charred and eventually consumed Sergeant Gault and Corporal Babin before her very eyes—and ears. Waking in that mud brick hovel and *knowing* she'd been raped. Killing that kid who'd come back for more. Desperately searching for her fellow soldiers and finding two of them dead. Raising that AK-47 she'd stolen and mowing down her captors, one by one. And finally, her best friend's final moments. Hearing that sword slice down, watching his head hit the dirt and then bending down to wrap him up and cradle him close as she began the walk back to friendly territory.

Back to home.

Kate lifted her hands and scrubbed at her cheeks, but the

tears wouldn't stop. She gave up and lowered her fingers, digging Max's watch out of her trouser pocket so she could slip it on over the bandage, sighing as it settled home.

She turned the watch around and around her wrist, just as she had so many times these past four years. But she turned it slowly now, gently, as she forced herself to follow the shrink's other instructions as well.

She acknowledged what she was feeling. Allowed the pain, the fear and the soul-shredding horror of it all to burn in...and out.

It actually worked.

The panic began to ease, then ebbed damned near completely.

Without her having spun into a total meltdown and vomiting up her non-existent lunch.

Closing her eyes, she offered up her heartfelt thanks to the shrink, then reopened them. She activated the portable cherry atop her Durango, drawing her breath and the lingering echoes of the pain in deep as she fired up the SUV's engine as well.

Determination locked in as she followed the silver sedans out of the deserted parking lot and up the wooded drive toward the county highway that would swing her and her Durango around to the north side of Mazelle.

She didn't need a GPS pin this time. She knew where she was headed.

As for her case?

She was back to square one and without a single signpost in sight. At least, not one that made sense. Two women. Both military spouses, both Muslim. And both seemingly killed by their husbands to assuage some twisted sense of personal honor?

Days apart?

It didn't make sense.

In Pakistan? Sure. Mainly because the country was unfortunate enough to possess the highest number of documented cases of so-called honor killings in the entire world. A solid fifth, in fact. It was why she'd been willing to entertain the motive so quickly with Haidar Kharoti. Especially in light of the Pakistani-born sergeant's preoccupation with the concept—at least according to his mother-in-law.

But now?

She had no idea what to think. Only what she was beginning to fear.

But until she had proof, she refused to voice that fear out loud.

Intent on beginning the search for that proof, Kate pressed her right boot firmly into the Durango's gas. Twenty minutes later, she'd arrived at the outskirts of Mazelle. Five more and she'd reached the vast parking lot to the city's defunct cereal box plant and the dozen-plus police, fire and other emergency vehicles that were haphazardly slotted in around the crime scene's outer perimeter.

Parking her Durango next to a patrol car, she got out to better scan a cluster of uniformed personnel well beyond the yellow tape.

With twilight beginning to set in and this many cops and technicians milling around, she figured it would take a bit to locate the detective in charge.

It took seconds.

Though halfway across the parking lot, she'd recognize that tall, dark-haired, impressively muscled suit anywhere. Detective Arash Moradi. They'd met a month earlier, during the height of the Garbage Man investigation. Arash had worked the three Madrigal Medical staffing company deaths that had spilled over into Mazelle and had been crucial in ferreting out just how involved the Madrigal CEO and his two trusted employees had been in the coordinated slaughter of countless US soldiers as well as homeless veterans—and the harvesting of every single transplantable organ and otherwise abusable body part.

And of course, there'd been that near-missed meet when both she and Arash had been stationed near Bagram, Afghanistan, four years earlier. The day she'd been taken prisoner, and Arash had joined his men in searching for her.

US Army Captain Moradi might've just missed her back then, but Detective Moradi was headed straight for her now, swinging around a cluster of cops who'd stopped to discuss something.

Regret bit in as she noted the phone sealed to the detective's ear.

Embarrassment followed.

To her surprise, Arash had also attended Grant's funeral. Arash had called and left a slew of messages in the weeks before and after as well, intent on checking up on her since she was a fellow cop and military vet to boot.

Messages she'd been too screwed up at the time to scrape together the courtesy and courage to return.

She really should've called the man back, because now they were—

"Evening, partner."

"Hey, Arash."

He slipped his phone inside the jacket of his dark gray suit and ducked beneath the crime scene tape, folding those impressive arms as he came to a halt in front of her.

He didn't say a word. He just looked down at her, waiting.

Damn it, just say it. Get it over with. "I'm sorry I ignored your calls." All eight of them. "I wasn't up to talking."

"With anyone—" A deep smile cut through the man's dusky features, enhancing his appeal tenfold. Because it was genuine. "—or just me?"

"Both."

He laughed. "At least you're honest about it." Arash swung back around, lifting the crime tape and motioning for her to precede him beneath.

They struck out across the rapidly darkening lot, dodging the cluster of now loitering uniformed cops.

The cops nodded to them en masse as they passed. Not a one reacted to the shredded side of her face—and it wasn't because of the fading light. It was just that here, completely cocooned within the blue, it didn't matter. They all *knew*.

Respected.

As much as the latter was unwarranted, it was also a relief.

Because it kept the rest at bay.

Arash waited until they'd cleared the group, then glanced down at her, lowering his voice as they kept walking. "Victim's Tahira Larijani. She's still at the other end of the lot, directly below the first set of loading doors. She'd cooled enough for them to get her in a body bag. They'll be taking her to the morgue soon."

Kate nodded as she spotted the shadowy length of plastic still twenty feet away—and took the blessing. The snug zipper on that bag and utter lack of breeze were working in tandem to keep the odor contained.

For now.

"My boss said she's a dependent?"

Arash nodded. "Husband's name is Bilal. Sergeant Larijani's US Army, currently posted at Camp Robinson, serving as an advisor to the National Guard. He's not there, though, and he's not home either. No one's seen the sergeant since Friday afternoon when he got off work. Wife hasn't been seen since last Wednesday. I sent an officer by their duplex to question the neighbors. That's who I was on the phone with when I saw your Durango pull up. According to my guy, a retiree named Ellen

Reid owns the duplex and lives in the other half. Reid says the Larijanis were having issues."

Oh, boy. "Was Reid getting that through the walls, or did the wife confide in her?"

"Both. Seems Tahira joined a local women's group without her husband's consent. A Bible group. And, yeah, they're practicing Muslims. At least the husband is; Reid felt Tahira was just going through the motions. As for the Bible group, the neighbor says Tahira joined for support. Seems she was raped nine months ago. Scooped up from the parking lot of a grocery store one night and dragged into the back of a van. There's no record of a report, but Reid claims Tahir's husband wouldn't let her file one."

Shit. This was starting to sound doubly familiar. "Let me guess. Sergeant Larijani insisted that it was a matter of honor —his."

"Yup."

"And he didn't have a problem with his wife joining a Bible group?"

"Oh, he did. When he found out about it. Reid heard him shouting at Tahira last week. Bilal was pissed about the group and pissed over his wife's continued refusal to submit to his husbandly 'rights'. Claimed that by cavorting with Christians and leaving the house uncovered, Tahira's loose ways had seduced her rapist."

"Sounds like a piece of work."

"He is."

Kate hiked a brow and waited. Because that "is" had been definitive—and, unless she was mistaken, personal.

Arash's shrug confirmed both. "I know the guy. Well, I knew of him. Haven't seen him for nearly two decades, though. He's first generation Iranian-American. Like me." The detective flashed a twisted smile that was part self-deprecating and the rest grim. "Yep, I freely admit I landed this gig 'cause of my looks. That said, knowing Bilal, even in passing, was a surprise." They were still good ten yards from the sealed body bag when Arash came to a halt, lowering his voice further as he stared down at her. "We attended mosque together as boys—in Dallas."

That would explain the hint of Texas twang that occasionally pricked its way into the detective's otherwise lazier and warmer Arkansan drawl—but not the shadow that had entered his eyes. The tension that was now gripping his shoulders.

Instinct had her focus dipping to settle on those four Arabic letters that were tattooed on in the inside of Arash's right wrist. The ones she'd noticed when they'd first met outside the Madrigal Medical CEO's house.

Their translation? *Infidel.*

She snapped her attention to his face. Flushed. With as many stares as she and her rearranged features received, she should've known better than to gawk. "Sorry."

"No problem." To her surprise, the detective shifted his cuff as he turned his wrist to offer her a clearer view of his ink. "And, no, contrary to common assumption, I didn't get this after I deployed over there. I got it at fourteen, shortly after I arrived in Little Rock. After my father and my uncle murdered my only sister...for *honor*."

She waited for him to offer more. Even thought he was about to—until a uniformed cop approached from their right.

The officer quietly informed Arash that they were about to move the body.

Kate turned toward the loading dock as Arash murmured something in response. She took a step forward, then stopped. There was no "about to" about the movement of the corpse. Two technicians had already lifted the bag and were carefully setting it on the waiting gurney. There was no point in asking the men to draw the zip down so that she could view the woman within. The photos were probably already waiting for her in the electronic case file. Whether or not she wanted to, she'd also be seeing Tahira in the flesh—charred and otherwise—at the autopsy in the morning.

Arash must have been of like mind, because he waited patiently beside her for the techs to finish securing the gurney's burden and begin slowly rolling it toward them. Once the gurney had passed, Arash waved her forward, slowly turning around in the nearly darkened lot, his upturned palm encouraging her to do the same.

Although it was eerie as hell to stand almost on top of where the victim had just lain and execute her own slow, three-hundred-and-sixty-degree circle, Kate did.

Because it was necessary.

Arash reached into his charcoal jacket and withdrew a memo pad similar to the ones she and Seth carried. "I haven't had a chance to visit your scene yet, so you tell me, Deputy. Does there appear to be a connection between the two?"

"Other than the military and Muslim ones?" And the fact that both husbands seemed to be in the wind?

He nodded.

"Well, there's the Bible angle."

Arash's fingers paused as he slipped them into his jacket again, this time presumably for a pen. "You got a church group tied to your murder too?

"No. But the field where Aisha was dumped? It belongs to Nash Weaver—a local pastor. Nash wasn't there when it happened. He's been away on a retreat for the past week. But not only was that retreat well publicized, you can see the spot where the body was dumped from the back of his deck. It felt almost...framed. Whoever killed Aisha—" And she was no longer convinced it was Sergeant Kharoti. Or at the very least, that Haidar was acting alone. "—he wanted her found and quickly."

The pen surfaced. "Now that is interesting."

"The Christian connection?"

"Maybe, maybe not. Definitely on the rest." Instead of opening the memo pad, Arash returned it and the pen to his jacket, then waved her along the cracked and crumbling concrete in front of the loading docks. "I want to show you something."

She followed the detective up to the corner of the building, then around. But instead of more cracked concrete, she came face to face with a full-sized, freshly blacktopped and painted basketball court, complete with working floodlights.

And beyond the court? A shadowier, but equally well-maintained soccer field with pristine white nets anchoring both ends.

"Impressive."

"Yeah. The guy who owns the land this old plant sits on also funds a charity for underprivileged kids. He keeps up this outer area so they have a place to practice. But here's the rub. Kids from the closer neighborhoods walk over here too. You can find them practicing every day, in fact. Especially on the basketball court. And—" Arash turned slowly to study the spot where they and the body had recently been.

Kate finished for him. "—you have to pass through the parking lot, and that loading area we just left, to get to the basketball court."

Another nod.

And another solid case connection.

Whoever killed Tahira Larijani had wanted the woman's burning body found, had planned on it. Just like with Aisha.

That ominous feeling Kate had gotten when she'd driven up Nash's drive prickled in.

"Deputy?"

"Yeah?"

"You thinking what I'm thinking?"

"That we may be dealing with a homegrown Islamist plot within the US military? Yep."

"Agreed." Arash ran a hand down the side of his face as he sighed. "Be a good time to put it into motion, wouldn't it? Damned excellent morale-wise, in fact. What with the dregs of the drawdown playing out in Afghanistan and the current administration determined to lasso up the soldiers we got left in Iraq—and keep 'em that way."

Worse, it made sense jihad-wise.

It wasn't even that farfetched. If a terrorist was willing to blow himself up to take down his enemy, why not sacrifice his wife to accomplish the same?

The murders of Aisha Kharoti and Tahira Larijani should not be related. Not if they were the supposed honor killings they appeared to be.

But they *were* related.

Because they'd been coordinated.

7

Her father tensed.

Kate didn't.

Not even when the man's temper crackled dangerously close to the surface.

He took another step toward her, then another, until he was right there, blocking out the forest of trees on the opposite side of their gravel drive as he loomed over her. Deliberately. Just like he always did. "What did you just say?"

"You heard me."

"Oh, I heard you. I just didn't think you were stupid enough to go behind my back and flat out disobey me."

She held her ground. Stupid or not, "It's done. I signed the papers." And there wasn't a blessed thing this man could do about it.

No matter who—and what—he'd once been.

"*Fuck.*" Her father tugged off his Braxton PD ball cap and slapped it on the hood of his cruiser. Tense, leathery hands dug through the unruly salt-and-pepper waves on his head. "Fine. I'll drive down to Little Rock tomorrow and talk to the recruiter. I doubt he's filed the paperwork yet. I can get you out of this."

That already filthy glower turned filthier. "But you are gonna owe me, young lady."

The hell she would.

And the hell *he* would.

"I'm eighteen now, Dad. I'm legal. And I told you; I signed the papers. I took the oath. They have photos. Several. You couldn't get me out of it if I wanted you to. Which I don't. I leave next week for Fort Leonard Wood for basic training, then MP school."

And then, Iraq.

"Damn it, I've told you. Over and over again. You do not have what it takes to be a soldier." That charming sneer this man seemed to reserve just for her set in as he shook his head. "And you sure as shit don't have what it takes to be an Army cop. Not a good one, anyway. And no amount of training at Leonard Wood —or anywhere else—will fix that. Or you."

She crossed her arms. "I *will* make it. The sheriff says—"

"I don't care what Lou says. That man doesn't know his ass from a hole in the ground. He polices a village of Girl Scouts, for Christ's sake. Hell, *Brownies*. Worse, he's been building you and that ludicrous fantasy of yours up for years now, and that's just plain wrong. *He's* wrong. The man's a—"

"How can you say that?" Any of it? "He's your friend." As near as she could tell, other than Bob Feathers, Lou Simms was her father's only friend.

Probably because her dad was a complete asshole.

Look at how he was willing to crap on the sheriff just to make his case.

Damn it, it didn't matter. She could not do this anymore. She'd busted her butt to make the two of them work ever since her mom had died. For three years now.

It was time to move on.

From her dad, and—yes—this admittedly podunk town he'd dragged her back to.

He stalked around her and leaned into the open window of the cruiser to wrench his keys out of the ignition. "I said I'd get you out of this, and I will. But don't even think it's for your sake. Because it's not. You are just not cop material, Kate, let alone detective. Certainly not for a war-footed military. Not even for this sleepy pissant town, no matter what Lou says. And I ought to know. I've been there, remember? I did it. And I was damned good at it."

Oh, yeah? "Then why'd you up and quit?"

His glower returned. Deepened. "I had to, and you know it."

Here we go again. "Right. For your precious baby girl—me."

"Yes."

"Bullshit." That excuse might make for a great parental sound bite for the town in general and her senior high teachers in particular, but it was a bald-faced lie and she refused to swallow it anymore. This man didn't give a damn about her. He never had.

She'd figured that out years ago.

So, "What's the real reason, *Daddy*? Because we both know you didn't leave Brussels, much less the Army, because of me." She crafted a sneer of her own and offered it up free of charge to the man who'd weaned her on them. "You may as well give me the truth for a change—because you won't get another chance. I'm headed to MP school, whether you want me to or not. And then I'm going to work my ass off for as long as it takes, because I will make CID. And no washed-up, has-been agent is going to stop me. Especially you."

It was the *washed-up* that did it. Egged on by the *has-been*.

An unholy fire sparked within the man's eyes, deepening them to emerald flint as he shoved his keys in his trouser pocket and stepped closer. He abused his bulk, as usual, to loom over her. "You want to know why I really flushed my career down the toilet? All right, then. I did it for your mother. I made that woman a promise—on her goddamned deathbed—and I mean to keep it. I swore I'd get out of the Army and bring you back to Braxton and look out for you, whether you wanted it or not. So that's what I'm doing."

Seriously? "By telling me—"

"The truth, damn it! You just refuse to accept it. You simply *do not have* what it takes for law enforcement—military *or* civilian—and you never will. You're just a pig-headed, barely B-grade kid from the sticks who doesn't have the brain power to solve a tricycle theft, let alone a terror case or a full-blown, multiple homicide. You'll make a shit cop, Kate, and deep down, you know it. Mark my words, you follow through on this, and you're gonna end up dead. Or someone else will, and it'll be *your* fault."

Bastard. "The hell, it—"

Something solid slugged into her torso, knocking her down to the ground—

Except...she was already there. Down that is.

On a bed?

How—

A muted whine filled Kate's ears as she pushed through the thick fog of sleep gumming up her brain. A cold, rubbery nose amid a warm, fuzzy snout followed, frantically nuzzling into her neck as the whimpering strengthened.

Ruger.

The German Shepherd was doing what he did best. What the dog had come to believe was his number one mission in life, especially this past month. Ruger had alerted to her twisting up the sheets, and he'd woken her.

Again.

At least this time she'd been immersed in one of her usual rotten dreams and not a sweat-drenched, heart attack inducing night terror—and, hey, she was still in bed too.

That was something.

Given how and where she tended to wake lately, it was a lot.

She also knew why she'd had that particular dream. Variations on the gem had begun after her father's death. The very night she'd received the American Red Cross message informing her that her dad had been struck by a reckless driver during a midnight traffic stop on one of Braxton's county roads.

She'd had the same dream the next night, and again the next. They'd continued to torment her off and on for months. And each time she'd woken in a cold sweat, *knowing* that whatever case she'd been working, she was bound to screw something up eventually—and badly.

Max had noticed the circles under her eyes and had badgered her until she'd finally come clean. She'd told Max about her father—and her dad's views on her skills.

Max had promptly deemed her father a jackass and a lousy judge of military cops, despite the fact that her old man had been one too. He'd labeled the man a lousy pop, as well. But since her father was dead, Max had been willing to let that character flaw slide. Max had refused, however, to let her father's acidic analysis of her professional skills continue to consume her confidence.

Max had insisted that *he* believed in her. As did countless others. Max had sworn up and down that she was a great cop and an even better CID agent. He'd said it so often in the months that had followed that she'd eventually come to believe it.

And then—that ambush. Max was dead.

And she'd been left with the inescapable truth that her father was right.

Ruger burrowed his face deeper into her neck and chuffed out his morning greeting as her pulse finally steadied.

The irony of her latest dream bit in as she hugged the Shepherd tighter, nuzzling her face into his sturdy warmth as well.

Those fights with her father had been one of many reasons she'd left home when and how she had. The man had been dead for four years now, and she was still fighting with him.

Maybe Dr. Manning was right. He had been about the magic wrist wrap. Maybe it was time to root out the power that her father held over her and let it die too.

But how?

Kate sighed as she pulled back just far enough to lose herself in Ruger's gorgeous, deep brown adoring eyes—and realized she could.

Daylight?

What time was it?

She twisted to her right, knocking her Glock to the hardwood floor as she hooked Max's watch from the nightstand.

7:43?

"Crap!" She wiggled out from underneath Ruger's weight and jackknifed off the bed.

How the heck had she slept for so long?

It didn't matter. "Buddy, we've got company coming." In *seventeen minutes*. "Let's go."

Ruger was at her bare heels as she spun around and jogged down the hall. She hooked a right into the open eating area, passing the brown, granite-topped counter on her way through the kitchen proper until she'd reached the dog door on the opposite side. She unlocked the flap and left Ruger to find his own way through the portal. The second flap at the rear of the garage was set to be unlocked by the chip attached to Ruger's collar twenty-four/seven. Given her job, a necessary failsafe in case Ruger got out and became caught in the heat or the rain.

As the Shepherd set out to take care of his morning business, she whirled around and raced back up the hall and into the bath to take care of hers.

Thank God for every one of her Army tours in the sparsest of locales with even sparser amenities. They allowed her to push through her shower with record speed. She was dried and dressed in a fresh deputy's uniform by the time she heard the flap in the kitchen swinging open again. She finished rewrapping her wrist with Manning's magic bandage as Ruger bounded into the room and up onto her unmade bed.

The twisted sheets would have to wait.

She still had coffee to perk. Securing her utility belt to her waist, Kate scooped her Glock off the floorboards and holstered it, then snatched up Max's watch, glancing at the time as she slipped the loose metal band over the elastic wrap. She had three minutes before Detective Moradi was due to arrive for their breakfast meeting.

Last night, she'd filled the detective in on the curious slew of calls Aisha had made to the lying doc—and the fact that Lily Basque had recognized *her* from her sedated stint at the Craig Joint Theatre Hospital at Bagram and been clearly terrified that Kate might do the same. She'd shown Arash the photo of the doc from the *Al Jazeera* article. Unfortunately, Arash hadn't recognized Basque from when he'd been in country and had stopped by Craig a time or two himself to donate blood.

So they'd decided to split up.

She'd driven north to the Braxton PD to spend some time at her desk, poking further into the doc's life to see what popped and also to catch up on the forensics reports that Seth and Nester had been adding to the Kharoti electronic case file since their search of Aisha's apartment.

Meanwhile, Arash had driven further south into Little Rock. The detective might not be a practicing Muslim, but it seemed he had solid connections in the community. Connections that just might yield results or, at the very least, rumors.

Anything that might suggest a lead for them to investigate.

Arash had also planned on cashing in a few dusty camouflaged markers with several of his fellow Army Intel officers who were still actively employed by Uncle Sam.

They were to link up this morning, at her house, so they could bring each other up to speed on their individual activities before the autopsy.

In two minutes now.

Scratch that. The Mazelle detective was already here.

Why else had Ruger's ears perked up?

A moment later, the brawny Shepherd thumped onto the floor, his giant paws and nails digging into the distressed slats as he tore down the hall. Several more moments, and she could hear the kitchen flap swinging again.

So much for her plan to ease her personal and professional partners through a polite introduction.

Hopefully, Arash wouldn't take Ruger's standard, growling greeting for males to heart.

Kate unlocked the front door, an all-too-familiar apology on her lips as she stepped out onto the wooden porch. "I'm sorry, Ruger's—"

Fine.

Scratch that. He was more than fine. Not only was the Shepherd chuffing out a downright friendly greeting to the kneeling, petting detective in her drive, her traitorous mutt was wagging his tail and shamelessly head butting the man for more.

Jeez. What if Arash had been a serial killer?

The last two men she'd had over had been.

Hell, the only other person Ruger had taken to this quickly was her friend Liz. And, well, Liz was a woman.

Kate couldn't help it; the sight of Ruger burrowing into a man's legs for attention was so unexpected, she laughed.

Arash stood, seemingly unbothered by the dog hair and the dust from the pea gravel that now smudged his dark gray trousers.

"Good morning, Kate." The detective grinned as Ruger finally deigned to notice his supposedly beloved mistress.

Evidently now cognizant of his flagging guard duties as well, the Shepherd spun around and bounded back up onto the porch, executing a swift, second spin just before he plopped his traitorous rump down beside her.

"You've got quite the four-legged welcoming committee there."

"Thanks." She scowled down at Ruger as the detective bent down to dust the vestiges of that same welcome from his trousers. The source of it all gazed lovingly up at her, pink tongue flopping out of the side of his goofy mouth. "*Suck-up.*"

She swore the mutt's grin widened.

Kate smiled back, shaking her head as she waved the detective onto the porch. "I was about to put the coffee on. I don't have anything for breakfast, though."

All she had in the fridge by way of traditional morning sustenance were eggs: chicken and duck. The thought of stinking up her kitchen with yet another source of sulfur a mere two hours before Tahira Larijani's coming autopsy was—

"Not needed." Arash popped the passenger door of his black Explorer. He slung the strap to a computer bag over the left shoulder of his subdued suit, then hefted a cardboard carrier from the seat. "I picked up an assortment of bagels on the way." Slightly scuffed leather dress shoes ate up the flagstone walk. "Hope you don't mind. I made do with a side salad last night, so I'm starving. Unfortunately, in light of our coming agenda, I'm leery of ingesting anything more than bread this morning."

Amen to that. She and Ruger had shared a small cheese pizza the previous night. Well, Ruger had polished off his half. Most of hers was still in the box, long since congealed and—yep, because she'd overslept—littering the kitchen table.

"Not a problem." She opened the door and stepped aside to

let Ruger lead the way for his new friend. "Just follow my mutt. You can set the bagels down on the table. I think I've got butter and jam."

The butter was a certainty. But the jam?

Lou had brought over a giant jar of his wife's amazing homemade blackberry preserves shortly after Grant's funeral, but Kate had already opened it. Meaning there was an excellent chance that Della's efforts were sprouting psychedelic fuzz by now.

Arash set the box of bagels down beside her snoozing laptop and took in the array of forensic reports and crime scene photos that were scattered across the table as he lowered his own computer to the seat of a chair. He scooped up the photos and flipped them over as she reached his side. "There's cream cheese in the container."

"Sold. And apologies for the mess." Not only had she been more tired than wired last night, she'd actually stayed asleep for a change, right though her alarm.

Go figure.

Kate snagged the pizza box off a stack of papers, ignoring the hope that twitched through Ruger's ears as he followed her into the kitchen. The twitching ceased, his ears now drooping with disappointment as she opened the cupboard beneath the sink to set the box atop the waiting garbage can. She'd deal with the recycling later. "Sorry, buddy. You've still got kibble in your bowl, and you definitely don't want to risk a belly ache."

His soft *huff* disagreed, but he shuffled back to Arash and the table while she prepped the coffee pot with grounds and water, and set it to perk.

"Want some help?"

She flinched—and spun around, every single cell in her body on instant, excruciating alert. And her right palm? It was already fused to the butt of her Glock. The muzzle of which was inches from clearing her holster.

Those leather shoes she'd noted must've come with soundless soles, because Arash had made it all the way into the kitchen without her picking up on the man's surprisingly light tread.

He was three feet away now—the dusky skin of his face and neck turning duskier due to the current, underlying tide of red.

Good Lord, she'd almost drawn down on him. A detective. Her new—albeit temporary—*partner*. And he knew it.

The fire in her own face increased along with her humiliation. "Sorry."

"No. I screwed up. This isn't my house. I should've stuck to the table." A wry curve slipped in. "Or made a bit more noise."

She appreciated his attempt to lighten the mood. But she was too keyed up to even try and follow up on it.

Grabbing two plates instead, she added a pair of butter knives and napkins, and shoved the entire stack at him. "Here. Coffee's almost done. I'll wait for it."

Arash opened his mouth, then closed it. He nodded and turned to carry the breakfast ware to the table. Silently.

Thank God.

By the time she'd abandoned the kitchen with two steaming cups of black coffee in hand, Arash had straightened the remaining papers into neat stacks and arranged their plates at the opposite end of the table. His dark gray suit jacket, brown leather shoulder holster and Glock were hooked over the back of the chair at the head of the table. The chair that commanded a view of the kitchen, as well as the living room beyond.

And he was seated inside it.

In her father's chair. The chair that no one had sat in since her father died. Not her, not even Lou. Because she hadn't been able to deal with the thought.

Maybe it was that dream she'd had, but she was okay with it now.

She had no idea why.

Maybe she'd ask Manning, maybe not. She was just glad that the visceral reaction she'd been having to that seat since her return to the States had been stunted.

At least for now.

She set the coffee mugs down. Reaching into the box of bagels, she selected a plain one and sat cater-corner to the detective.

Ruger caught sight of her burdened plate. His hope for people food renewed, he commandeered the empty section of hardwood between them and settled in for the count.

Arash thanked her for the coffee and waved off the need for cream and sugar as he tipped his head toward the elastic bandage beneath Max's watch. "I noticed that at the scene yesterday. You wrench your wrist during an ugly arrest or something?"

Or something.

She offered up a silent shake of her head and waited patiently, stubbornly, for the detective to get off the personal and down to business with his side of the briefing.

Arash took a sip of his coffee, savored it a moment, then set the cup down, shaking his head as he dove in. "There's nothing new on my end, forensics-wise. Probably won't be 'til the autopsy. I also did as we agreed—put out feelers with a few Army Intel buddies last night, along with some folks in the surrounding Muslim communities. Both Sunni and Shi'a. Nothing's come back yet. I've also got an elder from the Little Rock mosque who brings me stuff from time to time. I stopped by his place and hit him up in person. He hasn't heard anything—no whispers about honor killings, much less a coordinated plot to discredit the military from within. He'll keep an ear out."

"You don't think he'd withhold, do you?"

"This guy? No. When he left Iran, he swore he'd never look back. And he hasn't—for good reason. I'm sorry; I wish I could say more."

"It's okay." All cops had their sources. The smart ones protected those that needed and deserved it. With their lives, if necessary.

"What about you? Did you get anything more on the doc?"

"I came up dry too—so far. But like you, I'm still waiting on someone." Someone new. She tore off a piece of her bagel and tossed it to a patiently waiting Ruger.

The dog snatched it from midair, his happy half-gulp, half-groan causing an instinctive smile to slip into place.

Her smile slipped away just as quickly when she glanced toward the end of the table, at the notes she'd scratched out on her legal pad the night before.

"What's wrong, Kate?"

"I'm not sure. It's not about Basque, though." Nor was she even sure why it was bugging her. "It's Agent Castile. He's gone. They sent him to Afghanistan."

"In the middle of the drawdown?"

"Yep." Hell, in the middle of a dozen serious, open cases from what she'd gathered on the phone when she'd called Fort Campbell on her way to Basque's office.

"They say why?"

"No. But I spoke to Castile earlier yesterday at length." She tore off another piece of bagel and tossed it to an even more appreciative Ruger. "He had no idea he was leaving."

Like her old CID instincts, Arash's Army Intel antenna was quivering too. She could practically feel it vibrating between them. Along with the implications of a CID agent's sudden, inexplicable transfer to a war zone that damned near all his fellow agents and regular soldiers were actively abandoning.

"Something just went down in Afghanistan."

And it was huge.

Arash took another sip of his coffee. "You think it's connected to the mess we got going on here?"

"I doubt it. I spoke to the oncoming duty agent. A guy named Paul Frantz." She hadn't worked with Agent Frantz when she was CID, either. "Castile left so quickly, I had to bring Frantz up to speed. He had no clue what I was about to say until I said it."

And if their two supposed stateside honor killings were connected to whatever had caused Agent Castile to be punted to Afghanistan, Frantz would have.

Arash took another sip of his coffee, sighing as he returned the cup to the table. "Shit. I confess, I'm disappointed. A connection to whatever's going on over there might've made this easier. I still have zero leads on Larijani. No one at Camp Robinson has seen the sergeant since Tahira's murder—and they are looking. Bilal was also officially declared AWOL at zero seven hundred this morning."

Kate nodded. "Same with Sergeant Kharoti—though Haidar's not legally AWOL yet. He won't hit that mark until tomorrow." When the sergeant was scheduled to report back to Campbell, also by 0700. Of course, there was always the chance that Haidar would show up on post early.

But she doubted it.

Kate shrugged as she tossed the simmering suspicion as to why out onto the table. "Kharoti might've fled to Pakistan."

And if he had, then where would they be?

Not only had the sergeant been serving as an Urdu and Arabic translator for the US Army, Haidar Kharoti had been working with Special Forces during this last tour of his—in Yemen. Agents with Pakistan's Gestapo-esque Inter-Services Intelligence would be clubbing each other for a change for the mere chance to get a crack at what was in the sergeant's brain.

"If I was Kharoti?" Arash rubbed a hand along the side of his jaw. "I'd have headed there too."

As would she. Why not? If Haidar could evade the ISI's torture-hungry agents long enough to slip into Pakistan's Federally Administered Tribal Areas, he'd be home free, since his chances would be excellent that even the ISI wouldn't find him amidst that country's own zealous, Islamic fundamentalists.

And if Kharoti managed to sneak across his birth country's northwest border into an increasingly Taliban-controlled Afghanistan?

Kate rubbed at the knot of tension that had begun to throb at her temple. Kharoti's possible flight to Pakistan wasn't their only worry. They had Sergeant Larijani's connection to the Middle East to consider too. If Larijani made it back to *his* birth country—Iran—they'd never see him again either. Ever.

And there was the rest.

With no whispers swirling around among Arash's Little Rock Muslim and Army Intel connections, there was a reasonable chance this wasn't a plot to undermine the US military's Islamic soldiers—and their acceptance—from within. While that would be a good thing—great, in fact—they were left with a nearly equally heinous alternative.

Suicide pacts existed. Why not an "honor killing for jihad" pact?

Arash must've been thinking the same thing, because he nodded. Frowned. "If this is some sort of twisted jihadi agreement, and those two sergeants made prearrangements to bolt, we're screwed."

"Agreed." Frustration forced Kate to her feet. Arash had drained his coffee on his last swig. She scooped up her cup and held out her free hand for his. "Refill?"

"Sure. Thanks."

She accepted the second cup and headed around the

counter and into the kitchen proper to recharge both with the remaining caffeine in the pot. The detective broke off a piece of his bagel as she swung around, dabbed it in the cream cheese on his plate and held it out.

"Oh, Ruger won't—"

Ruger *did*.

Worse, he made that same happy half-gulp, half-groan as he accepted the treat from a heretofore unknown hand that he reserved for her alone and *sometimes* Lou.

Who the hell was that hound at her table, and what had he done with Ruger?

Arash must've mistaken her shock for peevishness, because pink tinged the skin at the base of his neck again, highlighting the starched white collar of his dress shirt, not to mention the knot of the ice-blue tie beneath. "Did I overstep?"

She switched her attention to Ruger—who was patiently waiting for another piece...and not from her. She shook her head, bemused. "Not at all. I'm just experiencing a surreal, canine twist on an *Invasion of the Body Snatchers* moment."

She held out the recharged cup. "Here you go."

"Thanks."

She took her coffee with her, leaving Ruger behind with his new treat-doling bestie as she advanced on the cluttered end of the table.

The cuckoo on the far wall of the kitchen squawked out nine.

Yeah, they supposedly had an hour to go, but Arash had informed her last night that he liked to get to his ME's autopsies early. It seemed the Mazelle doc tended to start when he was ready, whether or not a particular victim matched a previously scheduled time.

Then again, maybe Dr. Arquette had decided to pull a Tonga and had worked through the night. There might even be a stack of photos and an official finding already waiting for them.

She should be so lucky.

Kate reached for her sleeping laptop—and froze. She couldn't move, much less pick up the computer. All she could do was stare at the stack of papers beside it.

Manning had sworn to her weeks ago that if she came to their sessions, was open and honest when they spoke, did everything he asked of her, filled out every worksheet to the best of her ability, that things would get better.

That she would get better.

Last night, she'd redoubled her efforts. After all, that snug bandage on her wrist appeared to be holding fast to its weird magic. That in mind, and despite the pain and the renewed flashbacks, she'd dragged out the stack of fresh ABC worksheets the shrink had handed her on Saturday and had worked on several of them, all the while praying that Manning was right.

Because like it or not, she had a homicide to work—two of them now.

Or she *had*.

Because that uppermost sheet that she'd forgotten to tuck back into its folder before she'd let Ruger out one last time and crawled off to bed? It was lying there—right next to the stack of crime scene photos that Arash had scooped together and overturned upon his arrival. And in that centermost block of the ABC worksheet?

Pretty much the worst tidbit that a cop could share with her brand-new partner—and have that budding professional relationship survive the entire day.

My judgment can't be trusted.

Not only had Arash seen that damning statement as he'd straightened up the table while she'd been in the kitchen making their coffee, he hadn't bothered to slip that still unworked sheet beneath a finished one to hide it.

Nor did the detective bother pretending ignorance now as he realized what she was staring at and came to his feet as well.

He stood there, looking down the table at her, as silent as she was.

What the hell was he going to do with the single piece of intelligence that he had managed to glean since they'd left the crime scene yesterday?

Inform his boss?

Hers?

Either option would spell the death knell for her position as co-lead on their recently combined cases. A position that, until this very moment, she hadn't realized that she desperately wanted to keep...now that it was on the verge of being torn from her.

Or was it?

Silence continued to greet her newfound terror...and that was it.

Arash simply stood there, those dark brown, nearly black eyes and impassive features of his giving nothing away. He didn't respond as Ruger's snout came up to bump at the back his hand for attention, either. The detective just kept standing.

Staring.

She never wanted to sit on the wrong side of an interrogation table with Arash Moradi. The man was damned near impossible to read. She could see the barest of tics pulsing in at the left edge of his jaw now...but what did it mean?

Now that he knew *she* knew, what the hell was he going to do?

Evidently, the last thing she expected.

The detective finally lifted the hand that Ruger had been attempting to schmooze and glanced at the watch on his wrist.

And then he frowned. "We'd better get going, Deputy. Like I said last night, our ME's been known to start early."

~

TWENTY-TWO MINUTES LATER, her luck ran out.

Granted, the stench of sulfur and grilled flesh that wafted up from the charred body lying on the autopsy table in front of her wasn't nearly as intense as it had been in Nash's field, but it was still splintering though her.

Kate drew on an old technique that Max had shared with her nearly a decade earlier. She closed her nasal passages from within and took a shallow breath through her mouth as she concentrated on the individual parts, instead of the whole.

Those that she could make out, that is.

A blistered left cheek. The barest hint of an outer ear.

A bit of singed hair, hung up just past that.

A mostly blackened neck. A deeply charred shoulder.

Kate drew another breath, but this breath didn't help any more than the previous one had—or the one before. Worse, she lost her focus for a split second and accidentally inhaled though her nose on the next.

Just like that, individual parts instantly coalesced into the whole. Only that was no longer Tahira Larijani lying on the table; it had become Corporal Babin. And not only could Kate see the corporal's flesh as it charred and blistered up again right in front of her, she could hear it. Just as she could hear Babin screaming. Then sobbing as the corporal had begged God, and everyone else, to end the pain—to end her.

And the *smell*.

Kate stiffened, desperately trying to hold on. But the panic was growing. Swelling. Sweat popped out along her pores. Her entire body had begun to shake with the force of holding it all in. She was going to vomit up the coffee she'd had.

Now.

And then—she wasn't.

Arash's left hand had come up to cup her right shoulder from behind. The shredded one. His touch was light, warm and soothing. Steady. Still, the pads of his fingers and palm had to be feeling the knotted scars and hollowed-out pockmarks beneath; they were too thick to ignore full on. But they didn't seem to bother him. Because the detective kept standing quietly beside her, his concentration seemingly focused on the charred body in front of them as the Mazelle ME systematically examined and commented upon each decimated limb in turn for the voice recorder in the suite.

That light, steady hand worked. The sweltering interior of the Humvee faded. Corporal Babin and Sergeant Gault slipped out the room, and her thoughts.

Tahira Larijani slipped back in.

The panic had faded.

Kate was about to turn to let Arash know that she was okay, that she could handle this, when the ME glanced up.

"Detectives, I think we have something here."

Arash's hand eased off her shoulder as they both moved closer to the vee Dr. Arquette had managed to create between the victim's legs. The skin along both sides of the woman's inner thighs was red and blistered, even blackened in spots, but it wasn't charred. At least, not as extensively as Aisha's had been.

And there was something else.

Something startlingly familiar. "Stab wounds." Piercing the woman's flesh in nearly the exact same manner as Aisha's—if not the exact manner.

The ME nodded. "I reviewed Dr. Tonga's results before I began."

Dr. Arquette glanced up, meeting both their stares. "Yes, the wounds are nearly identical to the ones on Aisha Kharoti. But there's more." The ME drew an invisible line along this woman's left thigh with his gloved index finger. "These wounds are not random. You see the pattern, yes? It's difficult due to the blistering of the epidermis, but the wounds appear to form numbers: thirty-nine here on the left thigh, and possibly a nine carved into the right. I can't be sure of the nine, though, or if it's supposed to be part of another thirty-nine, due to the portion of charring that extends inward."

The ME straightened and skimmed a gloved hand over the array of instruments and medical testing supplies laid out on the stainless-steel tray beside him. The doc selected a sterile swab and returned to the woman's genitals. "Hmm."

"Is something wrong?" *Arash.*

A slight frown marred the ME's brow. "Possibly." He exchanged the swab for a pair of tweezers, his frown deepening as he moved back to the inner thighs to work the tips where the end of the swab had failed to go. Arquette angled his blond head for a better view—causing her and Arash to step back in unison, because they'd lost theirs.

Kate sucked in her breath as the doc finally straightened.

Cradled in the palm of his gloved left hand was a stone. Or, as her boss would say, a common milky quartz.

She heard Arash draw in his astonishment as well. "Is that—"

"Similar to the one recovered from beneath Aisha's thighs? Yes."

Small and nearly round, with its glittering surface perfectly smoothed out and polished, the rock appeared identical to the one found with Aisha, in fact. But there was one difference, however, and it was crucial. This stone was completely unscorched—because it had been found *inside* the victim. That discovery alone made the humble bit of quartz more valuable than a pink diamond in any earring they might find.

At least to their case.

The implications of which were still reverberating in.

Déjà vu followed as Arash stared down at her as he had the day before, out behind that defunct cereal box plant. "Deputy, are you thinking what I'm thinking?"

"Yep."

He'd asked that same question then, too. And she'd given the same response. But they'd already moved past the older working theory that had generated both.

This morning's alternate theory too.

While it was still possible that Sergeants Kharoti and Larijani had murdered their wives in a bizarrely coordinated terror attack from within, it was no longer likely. Nor was it likely that the men had entered some sort of bizarre honor-murder pact. Because that second stone and those numbers carved into Tahira Larijani's inner thighs suggested a new theory, especially if the cuts on Aisha Kharoti's thighs weren't random either. And not only did this new theory incorporate what appeared to be distinct psychological elements to the crimes—if those elements were correct, they weren't looking at the handiwork of a determined Islamist, but a coldly determined serial killer.

And with their current timeline?

They had a day, perhaps two, before the next body turned up.

8

Kate mouthed her thanks as Arash motioned for her to precede him out of the hospital's main elevator bank, then returned her attention to the phone at her right ear—and the request she'd made of the stunned sheriff on the other end.

"A *cadaver* dog?"

"Yeah, I know, boss. Tell the handler and any other state troopers that show up with him to start the search for the bodies at the south end of Nash Weaver's wheat field, moving into Old Man Miller's trees from there. If they come up empty, have them swing around to that patch of woods on the east side of Nash's property." But her gut was leaning toward Miller's trees.

"And if they come up dry there too?"

Kate shrugged as she and Arash continued down the corridor. "Send them down here to Mazelle. They can start with the woods next to the soccer field behind the box plant."

Though Lord only knew what the well-to-do homeowners in the gated community on the far side of the soccer field and woods would say.

Not that seeing a cadaver dog sniffing around his crops and

trees was going to help Nash sleep any easier tonight. Definitely not with the image of what Nash had found lying on the top of that field still excruciatingly fresh in the pastor's mind.

The deepening depression in the sheriff's voice matched her mood. "Alrighty, Kato. I'm hangin' up now and callin' the state police to arrange the handler and death sniffer. It may be a day or so before we can get 'em out here though. I suspect most of 'em are still searchin' for survivors in that apartment buildin' collapse up in Jonesboro. I'll phone Tonga afterwards and let him know he needs to take a second look at the stab marks on Aisha's inner thighs and compare 'em with what Dr. Arquette found."

"Thanks, boss."

Kate ended her catch-up call with Lou and slipped her phone into its slot on her utility belt as Arash held open the door that led to the hospital parking lot. She paused to cleanse her lungs with a deep pull of chilly, but blessedly sulfur, cooked meat and formaldehyde-free noon air, then turned to find Arash staring at her oddly.

"What? You do think they're dead too, don't you?"

A wry smile tipped in, followed by a slow shake of his head. "Well, I do now. Though I have to be honest, my brain hadn't gotten that far since we'd yet to clear the building. But now that it's caught up with yours—" The shake shifted to a firm nod. "Yeah, I'm thinking the sergeants are dead. Both of them."

Kate nodded. Why else were Haidar Kharoti and Bilal Larijani still missing?

Heretofore solid soldiers didn't go AWOL just for the hell of it.

If those two sergeants weren't guilty of murdering their wives for honor or any other reason, the men were already dead. Which meant it was past time to begin the search for their corpses—and any clues or evidence on, in or around them.

Whether or not they found the husbands' bodies together would reveal a lot, too. The last known contact with Aisha had occurred on Wednesday, meaning Sergeant Kharoti had most likely been taken then too. While Tahira had been seen last on Wednesday as well, her husband hadn't fallen off the map until late Friday afternoon when he'd left Camp Robinson. So if the Larijanis had been taken together, that was their timeline.

But the Larijanis' timeline might be tied more firmly to the Kharotis' than she and Arash had thought. Because if that dog did locate the men in Miller's trees, it meant that Sergeant Larijani had been disposed of more than twenty-four hours before his wife's body had been found at that box plant. Why? Miller's trees bordered Nash Weaver's field. A killer smart enough to do what this one was doing wouldn't have risked coming back to bury his dead in a forested area that abutted an active crime scene.

As for their sergeants' vehicles?

She'd had Seth put out an all-points bulletin on Kharoti's green truck following her interview with Aisha's mother. From the note she'd spotted in the Larijani file that morning, Arash had done the same with his sergeant's black Chevy while Tahira's body had still been smoldering at the scene. Neither truck would be turning up. If she was right about Miller's trees, both vehicles had long since been dumped at some chop shop and stripped down to their individual parts, never to be ID'd again.

Arash's phone pinged. He checked his texts as they crossed the hospital lot to where they'd parked their vehicles nearly three hours earlier. "It's from one of my guys. The data dumps on the Larijanis' phones are in. They've been uploaded to the case file. But according to Lance, there are no calls from either Tahira or Bilal to that office number for Dr. Basque, or vice versa."

Kate nodded. "What about that other number?"

"Thirty-nine?"

"Yeah. Does it mean anything in Islam?"

Arash shrugged. "Not that I remember. But I stopped attending mosque when I was fourteen. I'll ask around." He paused between the rear bumpers of their SUVs. "What about the Bible?"

"Dunno. I've been lapsed since my teens too. Though I lasted a year longer." Until her mother's death. "I'll ask Nash."

"Sounds good."

Kate used her remote to unlock her driver's door. She and the detective had agreed to a late dinner at her place to compare notes again. Until then, Arash was headed to back into Little Rock to revisit his Muslim contacts with their new serial murderer theory in mind, and she was returning to Manchin.

Despite what the Larijanis' phone dumps hadn't revealed, her gut was still leaning toward a connection between Mrs. Larijani and the evasive doc—especially since Tahira's postmortem x-rays had revealed evidence of several fractures, most likely caused by abuse. Arash would be asking around about that too. Namely, if any of the detective's contacts had heard of an Underground Railroad of sorts for battered or emotionally abused Muslim women...and if Lily Basque was running it.

And there was that odd fear about the doc's own stint at Bagram, when Kate had been drugged up and placed in that quiet room at Craig. It needed exploring.

But there was something she needed to do first.

Kate glanced pointedly across the lot toward the glass doors of the hospital, then met the detective's dark stare square on. "Thank you."

Arash didn't pretend ignorance or try to pacify her, much less brush off the enormity of the gift he'd offered when he'd reached for her shoulder in the autopsy suite to gently pull her out of that flashback and re-anchor her in the present. He simply shrugged. "Yeah, I saw a few of those hellish sights when I was over there. Smelled the nauseating odors that went with them. More times than I care to remember. But I was never trapped in a Humvee when it all went down."

She held his gaze, that palpable respect, and nodded.

"Kate...you ever want to talk about it—or, hell, get together and *not* talk about it—I'm here." A slow smile slid in. "I'm pretty sure you have my number."

She actually laughed. Eight calls?

She had his number.

The unexpected blip of humor was promptly displaced as the rest of what this man had done settled in as well. More importantly, what he hadn't done.

At least, not yet.

Scrounging up her remaining courage, she tried to find the words to address the rest. What neither of them had mentioned at her place this morning.

"What you read on that worksheet—"

A sharp shake of his head cut her off. "What I read—which, incidentally, was accidental—were the honest, private thoughts of a damned good cop working hard to get her head back on straight after life, and more than one person who professed to care about her, had smashed her to the ground with one hell of a nasty punch. A punch, mind you, that would've landed well beneath *anyone*'s belt. Mine included."

She let that lie. Because, really, how could she respond? Especially to the last part. Argue? Agree?

Worse, she knew precisely to whom Arash was referring with that "more than one person who professed to care". After all, the detective had shown up to support her at Grant's funeral along with the rest of the Braxton PD.

And Joe?

Kate pushed her fists into the pockets of her uniform jacket, turning to brace herself against her SUV as she chickened out altogether and opted for silence.

Arash left her alone with her ghosts for several moments, then appeared to change his mind, pointedly rousing Joe's. "Have you talked to him since?"

She shook her head. Hell, she hadn't even opened the letter Joe's wife had mailed to her, just in case it contained a note from the bastard himself. She'd given the envelope to Lou and asked him to not share the contents with her unless they pertained to the case. They hadn't, because Lou hadn't.

"Yeah, me neither."

She pushed off the SUV. "I didn't know you knew Joe."

"Oh, I don't." Any and all remaining warmth within the detective faded as that frown and that stare of his turned cold. Black. "I met Cordoba for the first time the day I met you. But after all that shit came out about how he and the others were hacking up soldiers and homeless vets, and selling off their organs?" The black grew colder, until it fairly crackled with ice. "Let's just say I wanted to meet Agent Cordoba again, and badly. Alone. But I wouldn't have had much of a career left when all was said and done, so I thought it best to stay away."

She had too. Only her excuse had been significantly less noble.

"Meanwhile, I just stuck my head in the sand." Kate slumped back against her SUV. "According to a friend of mine, I'm good at it."

Though, granted, Liz had cut her more than her fair share of slack over Joe. Especially once her friend had found out she was seeing Manning about it all.

"Yeah, well, I'm the last one to give you crap for that. You'll pull your head out and face reality—in time. And, trust me, it does take time." The ice had thinned. But those eyes were still black. They were hoarding more than anger now.

Pain had swirled into the mix. Regret. Guilt.

His sister.

When it all drifted down to settle on the ink at his inner wrist, Kate was certain. She was also certain she wasn't the only one who'd been forced to endure a monstrous memory in that autopsy suite. Given this man's loaded confession as they'd approached the body bag at yesterday's crime scene, his must've been a doozy.

Now was not the time to ask Arash about it, though, much less offer condolences. A young mother with a shrieking toddler had passed within yards to unlock a third vehicle parked beyond both of theirs and was seating her fractious child within.

The moment had evaporated.

Arash retrieved his keys. "See you tonight, partner. Good luck this afternoon."

"You, too."

They climbed into their respective SUVs and departed the lot.

Kate made two hands-free calls during the half-hour drive to Manchin and ended up leaving detailed voicemails for both. The first call had been to Fort Campbell to loop her replacement CID liaison and the US Army in on the autopsy results from Tahira Larijani, and to share the suspicion she and Arash now held that Aisha's husband—Sergeant Kharoti—might not be mustering with his platoon on the morrow, or ever again, and through no fault of his own.

Her second call had been to her shrink. Fortunately, the impetus for that outreach had been professional as well.

As a senior psychiatrist with the Veterans Administration, Dr. Manning was hardwired into the local and even national VA communities. Not only was she interested in the shrink's take on the new theory regarding the possibility of a serial killer targeting the wives of active-duty Islamic soldiers, she was even more interested in finding out whether or not Manning knew of a specific service member in the area whose unresolved trauma might be nudging him in that direction.

And if their killer wasn't a vet, but a homegrown, civilian Islamist bent on taking revenge on the nation's Muslim soldiers by targeting their wives?

God willing, one of Arash's contacts would be able to ferret out a viable suspect, because right now, they had none.

Determined to change that, Kate turned her SUV into the parking lot in front of Lily Basque's medical office. Like late yesterday afternoon, there were just two other vehicles in sight. The same older silver sedans that had been there the day before.

It was a quarter to one. Was the doc closed for lunch?

Kate parked her Durango in the same spot as before, reaching across to retrieve the medium-sized manila envelope she'd secured in the SUV's glovebox after she'd left Ruger guarding the house that morning. She tucked the envelope into the inner pocket of her Braxton PD jacket and donned her navy-blue ball cap as she bailed out.

Basque had lied to her yesterday. About several things. But it was the withholding of information about the first victim that really burned. With two autopsies in as many days under her belt, it was past time to cut through the bullshit.

Especially when she added on the very real possibility that she and Arash would soon be attending a third.

Kate entered the frosted glass door of the clinic and plowed across the waiting room. A woman of Middle Eastern descent with short, black curls and mauve scrubs stood at the far end. It was the same woman who'd followed Basque into the parking lot the day before. Today, the woman appeared to have just exited that more enticing door.

The one that led deeper within.

Kate kept the shredded side of her face averted to keep

things as smooth and breezy as possible, flashing her credentials as her boots ate up the plush carpet. "Deputy Holland, Braxton PD. I need to speak with Dr. Basque. Immediately."

The woman smiled politely even as she shook her head. "I'm sorry, but Dr. Basque is on her lunch break."

"Excellent. I won't be interrupting a patient exam, then."

"Oh, but she—"

The rest was lost as Kate breached the inner door of the waiting room as easily as she had the glass portal behind her and kept on walking.

There, on the right side of the hall. Near the end.

Another door. And not only was this one partially opened, sunlight glowed invitingly from within.

Kate entered what was indeed an office in time to see the good doctor lowering a set of green lacquered chopsticks from her mouth. Basque balanced them atop a matching bento box centered on the Queen Anne desk in front of her.

Sushi?

Could this impromptu interrogation get any more perfect?

Kate closed in as the woman attempted, and failed, to chew her food and protest at the same time. "Hey, Doc. I brought more pictures. And since you're on your break—" Tugging the manila envelope from her jacket pocket, she dumped the 4x6 inch photos from within directly onto the cherry wood in front of that bento box of raw fish.

The flesh in the photos, however, was decidedly cooked.

And human.

Basque shot up from the cream leather chair, her sudden coughing and choking fit threatening to morph into something more involved and humiliatingly odiferous as she clapped her hands over her mouth. A split second later, the woman bolted around her desk, across the office and out the door.

Kate had zero sympathy. She hadn't consumed an entire

meal in nearly three days, not since the hot roast beef sub she'd shared with Ruger late Friday night.

Leaving the glossy color photos on the desk, she turned, carefully taking stock of the doctor's professional digs as the muted sounds of retching filtered in from somewhere down the hall. Like the waiting room, the plush carpet, floral loveseat and sleek brass accents in the woman's retreat were designed to soothe and relax. Despite all the lovely decor, the room was as sterile and weirdly hollow as the one out front.

Personally, at least.

As far as Kate could tell, there wasn't a single intimate item on the oval coffee table beside her or on the surgeon's gorgeous desk. No pictures of proud parents or a significant other, much less kids. There were no qualifications or awards gracing the walls either. Given the money that appeared to have gone into this place, she'd have expected a prominently displayed piece of sheepskin from an Ivy League university and/or medical school at least.

But again, there was nothing.

Heck, Kate couldn't even find a subdued framing from an obscure state college with a diploma from an even more obscure Caribbean medical school.

But for the sign out front, she'd never know she was in a doctor's office—let alone *this* doctor's office.

The owner of the beautifully generic space finally returned.

The low bun secured at the woman's nape was tidier than it had been yesterday, but the doc's features were decidedly more damp, leery and wan. Her fingers were trembling again, too. But not from fear. From horror.

Blossoming anger muted the latter somewhat as Basque joined her at the patient side of the desk. "Why would you bring more photos of—"

"Aisha?"

The doc clipped a frigid nod.

"Oh, these aren't photos of Mrs. Kharoti." Kate waved a hand over the haphazard pile of crime scene close-ups that she'd printed from the Mazelle case file. "Though I can see how you could make that mistake." Kate lifted a particularly graphic close-up of what was left of the victim's charred face and head, and held it up. "This is a photo of another woman. She, too, was stabbed, set on fire and left to burn. Mind you, not in a field in Braxton, but near the loading dock of an abandoned plant in Mazelle."

"I'm sorry, I don't—

"Recognize her? Try this view." Kate retrieved her phone from her utility belt and clicked into the wedding-day close-up that Arash had provided of the second victim. "Her name is Tahira. Tahira Larijani. Mrs. Larijani was raped roughly nine months ago. Based on the healed fractures evident in her post-mortem x-rays, she may have suffered spousal abuse as well. Physical and emotional. Though Tahira's physical abuse was more extensive than Aisha Kharoti's. But you knew that, didn't you?"

Silence.

"Doc?"

Again, there was no answer. Not because the woman was being deliberately uncooperative—but because her attention had been hijacked by the pile of photos. Not all of them. One photo in particular. It had slid free of the stack and come to rest near the edge of the cherry desk. It was one of the close-ups that Dr. Arquette had taken of the stab wounds on Tahira's thighs, and that Kate had printed in the ME's office less than an hour ago and added to the stack. The numbers on both thighs were clearly visible.

Kate reached out, lightly touching the woman's arm. "Dr. Basque?"

She flinched. Flushed. "I'm sorry, I—"

"Does that number—thirty-nine, or possibly thirty-nine and nine—does it mean something to you?"

"No."

"Are you certain? I haven't heard back from my own medical examiner yet. But that number, or those numbers, may have been carved into Aisha Kharoti's thighs as well."

The doc's arms came up to rub at her upper arms. "Yes, I'm certain."

Basque was lying. Again. The proof was right there in those wide, doe eyes, just as it had been the day before. But there was something else glittering within too.

Absolute terror.

"Ma'am—"

"*No*. I'm sorry; I don't know this woman. And I don't know anything about any numbers, especially those. Please, I don't know *anything*." The doc followed up the over-denial with a stubborn shake of her head as she swung around her desk. But instead of sitting, she drew the creamy leather chair directly in front of her.

Protection.

From the photos? Or the truth?

Basque might not be clued in to the meaning behind that number, but she was withholding something. Though it wasn't necessarily something she needed to conceal, at least from the police. And definitely not from Kate. Not today. Not when that something could very well help catch a killer.

Two women of Middle Eastern descent, both possibly trapped in high-stress marriages that possessed indicators of abuse? "Ma'am...were you helping Aisha and Tahira? Did the women want to leave their marriages, or escape—"

"No!"

"No?" Kate reached down to spread the photos across the

edge of the Queen Anne, turning the more horrific ones around so the doc could get a better view of what had become of Tahira. "But you said you didn't know them. Her."

"I don't. I m-meant, no, I was not helping them—just *her*. Mrs. Kharoti. And with surgery. But I don't know what she needed because she canceled."

Kate ignored the fresh round of denials, as well as the telling quaver that had taken up residence in the doc's husky voice as she softened her own tone. "Ma'am, if you were helping them, either of them, or anyone else, I can help you. Protect you. From whatever you're afraid of. From whom."

"I don't need protection. From anyone."

Reaching down, Kate tapped a finger over the centermost close-up. The one that had mesmerized Basque earlier. "Tahira did. Aisha, too. But I don't think either of them needed protection from their husbands. At least, not these past few days. You see, the autopsies revealed something distinctive. Something I'm not at liberty to share. But I can tell you that our theory of these two murders has shifted. I now think someone else has proven to be more of a danger to these women than either of their husbands were. Now, if I could speak to a person who knew both these women and ask this person questions, I might be able to figure out who did this—" Kate lifted that close-up and held it over the center of the desk to force Basque to look at it again. "—to both Tahira and Aisha in time to stop it from happening to another innocent woman."

"I told you; I don't know *anything*."

Kate returned the photo to the desk and sighed. "Dr. Basque, I meet a lot people in my line of work. Quite frankly, a number of them have something to hide. Naturally, those that do, they often try to keep it from me. But I usually end up seeing hints of it. Sometimes it's a certain look in their eyes. Sometimes it's in the tension in the muscles around their mouths. And, well, sometimes it's in their fingers. For example, in the way a woman —a surgeon even—might dig her nearly nonexistent nails into the back of a cream-colored executive chair so hard that she's leaving marks in the leather."

Basque jerked her hands down from the shoulders of said chair and tucked them behind her back. "I'm not hiding anything. This new woman? Tahira Larijani? She never called the office. Ever. Check my phone records if you need to. There—I've answered all your questions. Now, unless you have a warrant, I would like you to remove those photos from my desk and leave."

Kate nodded. Mainly because she didn't have the warrant that was now on official demand, nor was she likely to any time soon.

All she had were five cryptic calls from Aisha made on the same day to this extremely nervous doctor, along with several other calls to Basque made months ago. Every one of which could be explained away to a judge's satisfaction by a first-year law student.

Kate scooped up the photos and returned the envelope to the inner pocket of her jacket. But instead of turning to leave, she waved her hand at the beautiful furnishings that surround them. "This is a lovely office. So's your waiting room."

A polite, if somewhat stiff smile appeared. "Thank you."

"I have to be honest, though. The rooms are also a bit cold and impersonal. Have you thought about livening them up? Say, with some handcrafted pottery? I mention it because I know another doc who has an extensive collection of cobalt blue pots and bowls from Afghanistan. He might be willing to part with some."

The smile bled off. "That won't be necessary, Deputy. I have everything I need."

As did she.

The fresh thread of tension had stitched in right where Kate had expected it—with her mention of Afghanistan. And with that thread? The same terror she'd spotted in the doc the day before. And, again, a few minutes ago...when she'd mentioned her new theory that someone other than the victims' husbands had killed them.

Kate had already known that Basque was terrified that she'd connect the doc to that year of surgical work at Bagram. But she was now forced to wonder if the fear that was still emanating off the doc wasn't also somehow connected to the two women who'd just been murdered...and whoever had murdered them.

Unfortunately, the doc's rigid posture suggested Basque wasn't going to offer anything more. Not without a warrant.

The warrant she and Arash still had zero probable cause to obtain.

Out of options, she offered the doc a polite goodbye and left.

She made her way up the hall and through the waiting room. The woman in mauve surgical scrubs was no longer inside, nor was there a second sedan parked in the lot.

Had Basque taken the time to warn her co-worker after she'd finished flushing the vestiges of her lunch and told her to leave? Because the other woman knew something?

Kate folded this latest pair of unanswered questions into the rest and headed for her SUV. As she unlocked her Durango and climbed in, she caught the slight sway of blinds in the building's far-right window.

The doc had entered another room just to ensure that she pulled out of the lot.

What the devil had Basque so scared?

Kate forced herself to slide her key into the ignition. She was about to start the engine when her phone rang.

Hope rose as she swapped her keys for her phone. If Lou or

Arash, or even Seth, had hit on something that would get them that warrant...

Unfortunately, her caller was none of the above.

Nor did she recognize the number. But the first three digits? Those formed one of two area codes that Fort Campbell used. Did her new CID liaison have something?

Hope surged anew.

"Deputy Holland speaking."

"Holland? As in, the infamous former Army MP who once ticketed General Harrington's wife for speeding in front of the general and his *entire* staff at HQ?"

That definitely wasn't Agent Frantz.

Hell, her caller wasn't even male.

But it was a friend.

Kate grinned as the years fell away. Memories tumbled into place. Most were darned good ones too, despite the tense and often unpleasant circumstances that had surrounded the creation of each. "Sergeant Regan Chase, how the hell are you? Oh, excuse me, I understand that it's Chief Warrant Officer Two —and *Agent*—Chase now."

Rae's husky, infectious laughter filled the line. "It *is* Agent Chase. Because of you. Thanks again, by the way. For helping me get here."

"None needed." Because, really, Rae had done the hardest part.

All Kate had done was sidle up to one of CID's living legends while they were working that mass grave in Iraq and suggest to Art Valens that his latest referral to CID was right there in front of them, leaning over an obscenely large collection of recently unearthed child-sized skulls, carefully sweeping away the debris so they could catalogue and bag them. Why? Because Rae had been that good at her job—and theirs too. And everyone knew that CID applications with a letter from Art got accepted.

Hell, that was how Kate had snuck in the door.

But they'd all lost touch. Gotten busier in different areas of the globe. Art and Rae had been transferred to the States. Art to teach at the CID agents' course at Fort Leonard Wood and, eventually, Rae to attend it. A couple of years later, Kate had drawn orders that routed her back to Afghanistan. Both Art and a newly minted Agent Chase had eventually followed her—with Rae ending up completing her probationary period with none other than Art Valens right around the time of that ambush.

The proof was still crammed into a folder and shoved in one of those stacks of papers and crime scene reports that Arash had piled up that morning.

And inside the folder?

Another report. This one, four years older than the others that had accumulated on her kitchen table this week. It was also the report that she'd promised Dr. Manning she'd reread—the investigation into the crime scene where Max had lost his head and she'd taken out those terrorists. And the two CID agents who'd overseen that Afghan POW investigation and affixed their names and reputations to the bottom? None other than Art Valens...and the agent on the line with her now.

The irony of it.

"Kate?"

"Yeah?"

"You're thinking about it all, aren't you?"

She managed a half-smile, even as she saw those blinds at the far right of the building shift once more. "The silence was that deafening, eh?"

"Not really. I just recognize it. It's been pummeling in with Art and me these past few weeks too. Ever since the news broke about what those bastards had been doing to vets and soldiers in Arkansas and elsewhere—and how Cordoba was part of it."

Art. *Shit*. How could she have forgotten?

Like her, Rae had known Joe personally as well as professionally. But Art? He'd been Joe's best man at his wedding all those years ago. Hell, Art Valens had introduced her to Joe.

Kate closed her eyes briefly to rub her free hand over her face. "How's Art doing?"

"Oh, you know. Same as the rest of CID, only worse. He keeps flogging himself with endless questions and a massive case of self-doubt. How could he not have known? Had the signs been there, but had he just been so stupid or incompetent that he'd missed them?"

"Yeah." She knew those questions. That monstrous doubt. They were knotted firmly to the ends of her own personal cat o' nine tails. Not to mention crammed into the statement scrawled into the center block of the worksheet Arash had spotted on her table. The one she'd yet to scrape up the courage to finish filling out.

A dark, self-flagellating sigh bled into her SUV.

It wasn't hers. "Point is, Kate, none of us knew. Christ, how could we? Cordoba was good. Damned good. At being an agent and, apparently, an asshole too. And let's face it, being good at the former can make someone that much deadlier at the latter. Because they know what to hide and how to hide it." Another sigh bloodied the cab. And again, it wasn't hers. "Anyway, that's what I keep telling Art. Hell, even legends can get it wrong. Especially if they don't have all the information."

Kate clamped down on her phone.

She knew she was supposed to agree. Part of her even wanted to. A large, growing part. For Art's sake, if nothing else. But she couldn't. Because if she did, what would that mean for her? About her?

Despite the magic wrap on her wrist, her skin began to tingle. Then itch.

Kate reached for the watch looped over the bandage, was a

millimeter from giving into the temptation to touch and turn when yet another sigh drifted through the cab, letting her off the hook—because this one had eased that itch.

This sigh was softer than the others. Resigned. And it was fueled by a shift in topic. "Speaking of information, I have some. Sort of."

Kate jumped on the reprieve—and that curious qualifier. "Sort of?"

"As in, some of it's missing. And the information that is there, may be more telling than what isn't."

"Excuse me?"

Rae laughed. "Sorry. I've had a couple of long days with not a lot of sleep woven in. I'll start at the beginning. I know you dealt with Agent Castile before he was shipped out. Frantz filled me in this morning. Problem is, Castile's current cases got dumped on him. I'm not officially on the roster yet; I just returned to the States from a stint at Hohenfels. Heck, I don't even check into the command until later this week. I've been on leave, securing an apartment and getting it set up. But my household goods got delayed, so I stopped in to get a feel for the place this morning and offered to help Frantz out."

"You're tracking the Kharoti case?"

"Yeah. Hope that's not a problem. I took oversight on the Larijanis too. But that's not why I'm calling. I don't have anything to add to either of those cases, nor have I been able to discern a link between the two men, duty station or schoolwise —yet. I found a note, though, that Castile had scribbled about a Dr. Lily Basque and your concerns about the woman. I ran the name through official Army channels as you requested and got nowhere."

"Nowhere?" How the hell did a CID agent get nowhere on a doc who'd spent a year operating on US and other NATO troops at the Craig Joint Theater Hospital? "That doesn't make sense."

"Oh, it gets even more interesting."

"How so?"

"Well, the *Al Jazeera* article was correct. The woman did do a year as a contracted civilian at Bagram. But her name? It's not Lily Basque. In fact, every legal document I found with that name on it disintegrated upon further digging. And, well, you know me. I'm stubborn. So I dug deeper. I'll forward the documents I already have with that name on them."

"But?" Though Kate knew.

"I got a call right before I phoned you. No number. I'll trace it, but I suspect it'll come back to a burner. The man didn't give his name. Just told me to stop digging."

"Shit."

"Yep. He also told me that if I disobeyed, let alone pulled in another agent or agency into the search, there would be repercussions. Official ones."

"CIA—he's gotta be." Because while a dangling identity smacked of the US Marshals and the Federal Witness Security Program, there were also hints of Afghanistan and the broader Middle East seeded into all of this—and *those* tended to be cultivated and nurtured along by the Central Intelligence Agency.

"Agreed. Given everything else I uncovered—or didn't? There aren't too many other options agency-wise. At least not good ones. Though why the man didn't just say so, I don't get. Then again, spooks really don't like to go on the record about anything, do they?"

True. "Okay—stop digging."

"You sure? I mean...don't take this the wrong way, Kate. But unless you've got contacts who can reach that high up at the Braxton PD that I don't know about—"

Kate actually laughed—but it came out short and harsh. "I don't. Not here, anyway. But I do know someone who isn't connected to my department and does, or did, have contacts that high."

Up until four weeks ago, that is.

Joe.

Evidently Liz, Dr. Manning and even Arash were right. It was time to pull her head out of the sand. Finally face the man whose betrayal had caused her to shove it down in there in the first place.

Silence invaded the line as another old friend and fellow CID agent caught the implications behind what she'd said—and what she was about to do.

The air in the cab thickened, turned hot and stifling, despite the significantly cooler temperature outside.

The blinds moved within the window on the far right of that building once again, and this time, two slats parted noticeably.

Evidently Basque was determined to wait her out.

Kate thought about turning her head so the doc could tell that she was on the phone. The sight might help Basque relax.

But why?

Let the liar sweat.

Lord knew, she herself was all but covered in perspiration now. At the mere *thought* of what she was about to do.

"Kate...have you spoken to him since the arrest?"

"Nope." But she was about to. Just as soon as she called in another marker and then arranged her flight to the military's maximum security correctional facility at Fort Leavenworth.

Sure, she could ask the agent on the other end of the line to keep digging. Regan Chase would undoubtedly get to the bottom of this mystery, too.

But there would be repercussions. Quite possibly a significant and permanent dent to Rae's Army career.

So why risk it?

A month ago Joe Cordoba had been just as dialed in as

Agent Chase, if not more so. And Joe didn't have an Army career to protect anymore—just his own busted-down-to-private and now firmly incarcerated ass. If Joe got hurt in the process, or suffered permanent repercussions for speaking out of turn, so what?

He owed her.

He owed the soldiers and vets he'd murdered even more.

And he *would* be paying up.

9

Kate drummed her fingers on top of the stainless-steel interrogation table. Other than the skeletal chair she'd claimed and the empty one opposite her, there was nothing else within these four claustrophobic walls save the closed door across the room and her increasingly raw, jangled nerves. If anyone had told her as little as two and a half hours ago that she'd be spending the afternoon in an interview room at the US Disciplinary Barracks at Fort Leavenworth, Kansas, she'd have dragged them to the VA hospital in Little Rock to see Dr. Manning...for a psych eval of their own.

And yet, here she was, waiting none-too-patiently for over ten minutes to speak with yet another Army CID agent. Though like her, the man was no longer authorized to carry those credentials. Of course, the removal of Joe's badge had been a bit more violent and definitely more permanent than her own.

But the strangest part of all?

While the entire two-and-a-half hour journey to get inside this room still felt surreal, it also felt good. *She* felt good.

What the heck was up with that?

She knew what Dr. Manning would say. Fortunately, the

shrink hadn't had a chance to return the voicemail she'd left when she was still in Arkansas, driving to whoever's surgical consulting office that really was in Manchin, so she'd yet to suffer Manning's *I told you so* firsthand.

Okay, so the shrink wouldn't actually use those words.

But Kate could hear them...and she was definitely feeling them. She had been since the moment she'd cleaned the figurative bloodstains from her very own silver bullet and given Fort Leavenworth's current commandant a call. Despite the fact that Colonel Stillwater was away from Leavenworth and at the Pentagon for a day of back-to-back meetings, the senior MP had picked up. She'd worked with Stillwater on more cases than she could count during her Army career. That professional history, combined with the hefty medal no one seemed able to get past, would probably have been enough to swing her pending meeting with Joe, but she'd also done a personal favor for Colonel Stillwater years ago when the man had been a major.

Neither of them had spoken of it since. But it seemed picking up the man's wife—then a lieutenant—for solicitation and driving her home to face her husband and her own bout of combat-infused PTSD, instead of taking the woman to the stockade, had earned Kate the right to a private, off-the-books meeting with Joe Cordoba today. It had also earned her the hastily arranged military hop that Colonel Stillwater had set into motion. The one that had flown Kate from the Little Rock airbase to Kansas.

The moment the C-21A had landed at Fort Leavenworth, she'd been greeted by an MP master sergeant she'd also served with, and had been driven straight to US Disciplinary Barracks where it seemed the entire cadre had wanted to shake her hand.

Ironically, not because of that medal.

They'd wanted to meet the former agent who'd sent one of

their newest and most notorious prisoners to them, all wrapped up with a gilded bow stapled to his head.

The only thing off about the entire experience was her weapon.

Because her trusty 9mm was literally off—of her.

It didn't matter that Leavenworth had a zero-weapons policy, guards and staff included. Braxton PD uniform aside, she felt flat-out naked without her Glock.

Jittery.

And the longer she sat at this table, waiting for the MPs to hook up Joe's shiny new bracelets and bring him here, the more jittery her nerves were getting.

She tried smoothing her fingers over the orange face of Max's watch, then slowly twisting it around the elastic bandage on her wrist, but neither helped. She was too keyed up with everything else that was ricocheting around in her head.

Namely, the fact that she was about to see Joe. Talk to him.

Be forced to listen to him in return.

Only this time, she'd be seeing all those stolen organs and the decaying, discarded husks of her dead brothers and sisters in arms piled up around him.

Kate caved in to Manning's relentless advice and tugged her iPhone off her utility belt. She should've been forced to relinquish that upon her arrival at the Disciplinary Barracks too, as any normal visitor would've been. But it seemed there was a silver lining to that battered star after all. While her phone had been noticed by every MP she'd met, not a one had held out their hand and asked for it.

Hence, the phone was now in hers. And stored within were electronic versions of the ABC worksheets Manning had been having her fill out for over a week now.

Would filling one out now while she waited—actively *thinking* about what she was feeling and why—really help temper the tension that was beginning to ratchet in tighter with each passing minute...before it morphed into a full-blown panic attack?

She was just desperate enough to try.

But as Kate tapped into the CPT app on the phone, she discovered that her impact statement was still loaded up. That very private, searingly painful statement that Manning had asked her to write two weeks ago on why she really thought things had gone down the way they had that day—and how the fallout had affected her life.

The statement *Lou* had read.

The statement she couldn't help but reread now.

I hate that goddamned Silver Star. It's a lie. I'm a lie.

The ambush might've happened because of Joe. But Max's death —and the death of Sergeant Cutter and Private LeBeck—they're all on me. Hell, even that Afghan kid's death is my fault. Yeah, he was there to rape me again. But if I hadn't been so shaken and desperate, I would've been able to incapacitate him instead of murdering him.

But most of all, I should have been able to save Max. I was an MP before I became CID. Our motto: Assist. Protect. Defend. I failed at all three—spectacularly—and Max paid the price. I'm the one who should be missing my head, not him.

You want the emotional fallout? Okay, I hate looking into the mirror. Seeing what's left of my face. It's not that I don't deserve what I see, because I do. But it's a constant reminder and inescapable proof that my dad was right. I never should've enlisted. And I sure as hell wasn't cut out to be CID. If I'd stayed in Braxton where I belong, Max would be alive. Another agent would've been in my spot that day—a real one. He or she would've saved Max and the other two soldiers who'd survived the ambush. Hell, if the other agent had known Joe the way I supposedly did, he'd have figured everything out sooner and there wouldn't have even been an ambush.

I hate myself for sleeping with Grant. I hate myself for being so screwed up and desperate to connect with someone that I couldn't see who Grant really was. And I hate myself for not realizing who Joe was either. Every memory I have of Joe, Grant and my entire goddamn Army career is tainted, which is pretty much my entire life. I hate myself for liking Burke—and, hell, not seeing him for who he really was either. I hate myself for killing a kid. I hate myself for not getting to Cutter and LeBeck in time. Most of all, I hate myself for letting Max die.

It should have been me.

It was too late. The panic had set in.

Kate jackknifed to her feet as the sweat began to pop out along her flesh, turning cold and clammy as it pooled beneath her armpits and soaked into her deputy shirt. She spun around, her nervous boots eating up the length of the cramped interview room as she attempted to force the surrounding air to slow its path through her lungs.

She did another about-face and retraced her march.

Then did it again. And again.

Damn it, she shouldn't have sent that vague, *I'll be out of touch* text to Arash. She should've called the man instead. Shared her plans. Arash was co-lead on this case. And smart. Humiliating or not, the detective also knew how tightly wound she was over these murders and everything else in her life right now. He'd have probably talked her out of coming here—or at the very least, insisted on accompanying her.

How the hell had she ever thought she could do this alone?

Talk to Joe. *Know* if he was telling her the truth?

Every day of the last five years of their decade-plus friendship had been filled with the foulest of lies and she'd never even been suspicious. What made her think she'd be able to recognize them now? Trust her instincts? And, yeah, her so-called judgment?

Damn it, she should leave. Before it was—

Too late.

Kate stiffened as the door to the interview room opened. She nearly dropped her phone, her fingers visibly fumbling as she slotted it into her utility belt.

Fortunately, Joe hadn't caught her display of nerves, just the three MPs who escorted her neon-orange, jumpsuit-clad former partner into the room.

The MPs politely ignored her minor freak-out.

As for Joe, her old friend appeared to be actively avoiding her. His dark stare remained fused to the tiles beneath his black low quarters as a buff, Hispanic sergeant and a female corporal walked him all the way up to the table, ensuring the shackles at his ankles didn't get tangled in the legs of the chair as he sat.

An equally buff Asian corporal moved in to secure the steel cuffs at Joe's wrists to the interrogation table.

Kate didn't argue. That was the deal she'd struck upon her arrival.

Her old colleague, Master Sergeant Becker, had agreed to allow her and Joe to speak in the room alone, and with the door closed—so long as she remained on her side of the table and Joe remained cuffed to his.

Kate waited as the sergeant ushered the two corporals out, returning the senior MP's crisp nod as he paused at the door.

"We'll be right outside, Deputy. If you need assistance, just holler."

She wouldn't.

The door closed.

Joe finally looked up. His lips were pressed into that bruised half-smile the man tended to give whenever he was pushing through a particularly shitty stretch of life.

Welcome to the club. Hers had been going on four years now.

And this past month? It had become damned near unbearable.

Because of him.

"Fancy meeting you here, Holland. Bit out of your way, eh?"

"It is. Had to a call in a favor and climb aboard a C-21A just to get here. But you could've refused to see me." She'd half expected he would.

Truth be known, she'd hoped for it as she'd made that call to Stillwater and, again, for pretty much her entire flight.

But Joe hadn't refused.

"I'd never turn my back on you." The man's bruised smile faded into thrumming humiliation—as it should. "Kate, I know you don't believe me. But I—"

"You're right. I don't." Nor did she want to hear whatever excuse he'd been about to give. Though something Master Sergeant Becker had told her was bugging her. "I understand I'm your first visitor."

Joe nodded. "I saw my lawyer a few times when I was housed across the way while he worked out the details of the plea. But, yeah, you're the only one to stop by following my sentencing and my move here to the SHU." The shoulders beneath that neon-orange fabric kicked upward—but she'd knocked down enough doors with those same shoulders in Afghanistan and Iraq to know the nonchalance in that shrug was fake. "Anyway, that's how it's gonna stay for the duration."

Now there was a surprise.

Because the "duration" Joe's lawyer had worked out in that agreement was life without parole in exchange for a guilty plea and full disclosure of every single detail that Joe remembered about Madrigal Medical and the murders of all those soldiers and vets. Joe had been damned lucky the Army had been willing to bargain for those details too. Otherwise, he'd have joined that bastard Nidal Hasan and the six other death-row inmates housed in a remote corridor of this same prison complex.

Those neon orange-clad shoulders tried pushing out

another shrug, only to falter. Indifference hadn't hung this one up, though. Pain had.

And Kate knew why.

Joe's wife. Where was she?

Kate would've expected Elise Cordoba to be settled into a nearby Kansas farmhouse by now, along with the woman's overflowing animal entourage. Elise was the love of Joe's life; she'd been so since junior high. Not to mention the reason Joe had gotten sucked into that nauseating black-market organ harvesting scheme in the first place. Deathly ill from a lifetime of type 1 diabetes, Elise had evidently believed Joe had purchased a kidney for her five years ago on the Pakistani black market. It'd been a lie. Elise hadn't received a single kidney from a seriously desperate soul who'd received a pittance in return, she'd been given Sergeant Tanner Holmes' entire life-sustaining pancreas and kidney block—for free. Monetarily, anyway. In return, Madrigal Medical had received the former CID agent's assistance when needed to conceal any and all future murders of his fellow brothers and sisters in arms.

Had the stress of Joe's arrest and incarceration taken its toll and dealt the woman a serious setback?

Concern simmered to the surface, unbidden.

Kate shoved it down.

Damn it, she wasn't here for this. And she was not here to care. Not for Joe *or* his wife. Not anymore.

Because Elise hadn't come forward when she'd finally figured out just how many organs she'd received and from whom they'd come, had she?

Still, Kate was curious. "Did something happen to your wife?"

Joe blinked. Then frowned. "You didn't read it, did you?"

The letter. The one Elise had sent to plead on her husband's behalf. Or so Kate had assumed. Either way, she'd handed the envelope to Lou, still sealed. Kate shrugged. And this time, the indifference was real. "I gave it to my boss. Sheriff Simms handled whatever exculpatory info Elise thought—"

"That's not what was in there." Joe shook his head slowly, almost sadly. "Kate, I'm guilty. I admitted that to your sheriff even before he booked me while you were getting that gunshot wound stitched up. I asked Elise to pass along a personal apology from me to you for the gunshot—and everything else—that's it. Well, and the news."

She ignored the apology reference and everything it covered, even as she regretted asking, "News?"

"She's pregnant. Sixteen weeks now. I didn't know until after the arrest, because Elise didn't know. At least not then. She told me when I was able to make my first call. That was the last time I spoke to her—and the last time I ever will."

He'd cut Elise from his life? Completely?

That was difficult to swallow.

Joe and Elise had been married for over a decade now—since the day after she and Joe had graduated from MP school. Hell, he and Elise had been trying to have a kid for at least that long. Why would he kick the love of his life to the curb now?

But Kate knew. It was right there in the shadows of those dark brown eyes. In the slight tinge of pink that lay beneath that dusky skin. Once again, there were too many missions, too many cases worked together for her to fail to recognize it.

Shame.

Joe knew she'd seen it too, and it pissed him off. He came up swinging, verbally at least, straining against the steel cuffs that were locked to his wrists as he surged halfway up from his chair. "Christ, Holland. Don't you pity me, because that is not what this is about. Much less who. I don't give a shit about myself. Look at how your bastard of a father contaminated your life, and he wasn't even in prison."

"And *guilty*."

"Yeah—" The cuffs clattered against the rail, settling onto the table as Joe sank back down into his seat. "—and guilty."

She waited for him to meet her stare, then nodded. Because she might know this man well enough to know what was really behind that outburst—but Joe was damned well going to have to spell it out. "That's it, isn't it? You don't want your kid growing up knowing an honorable, decorated soldier was murdered and posthumously labeled a traitor before the entire world to give him or her life."

"Would you?"

Hell, no.

And despite her best efforts, she could feel that insidious pool of pity Joe had rejected oozing back in, smothering out the anger and the disgust.

Damn it, he had no right. No matter what had happened in the past. No matter how many times this man had saved her ass while they'd been over there, *he* had no right to get to her. Not anymore.

It was time to get back on track.

She wasn't here for some IED-riddled stroll down memory lane, much less for herself. She was here for Aisha Kharoti and Tahira Larijani—and the woman who was about to be violated, stabbed and set on fire next. Because if she couldn't figure out what Dr. Basque was hiding—and how it was connected to those first two deaths—there would be another one.

And if she didn't get her head on straight, that coming death would be *her* fault.

Kate reached for her utility belt and removed her phone. She clicked it on and opened up a new page in her notes app. Setting the phone down on the table, she scooted it across until it was within reach of those shackled hands.

"I came here for a name."

Joe glanced at the blank screen, then her. "And you think I have it? Still?"

Oh, he knew this name—and he would be coughing it up. "You remember the case we worked way back at the beginning? That bastard of a warlord we picked up outside Kandahar? The one with an...unnatural fondness for young boys."

Even Joe couldn't keep the disgust from pressing into his lips. "Yeah. I remember that fucker. What about him? 'Cause I also seem to recall him disappearing during a personal pit stop that turned violent while he was being transferred to Bagram."

"He did. But before he left Kandahar, you spoke to him a couple of times. Alone. At least, you thought you were alone. I was outside the interrogation room during your last run at him, waiting to speak to you about another case. I heard you brokering a deal with him. That shit's life—and the ability to live it outside of Afghanistan—for his Taliban contacts. I want to know who was on the other end of our side of that deal." Because that name had been active in Afghanistan and around the greater Middle East right about the time that Lily Basque's identity had been created—at least according to the dates on those documents that Regan Chase had found and forwarded.

There weren't too many people pulling double duty for the CIA and the US Marshals' WITSEC program in those particular neighborhoods back then.

Most likely *one*.

And Joe had worked with him.

"Kate, that name's classified."

"I know."

He shook his head. "The guy's still in the game. And he's not a lightweight. There could be repercussions—for both of us."

She knew that too. The terse phone call Regan had received from their mystery man had also confirmed that the body attached to that name was still active and operating overseas and undercover—and not afraid to abuse his position or anything else to remain so. Why else call?

That was why she'd had to fly here to collect the name in person. Despite Joe's current, already-incarcerated-for-life sentence and surroundings, it was the only way he'd give it up. Because, eventually, Joe's part in spilling it would come out.

It always did.

Like her, Joe knew that too. Just as she'd known, even as she'd made her arrangements with Colonel Stillwater and boarded the C-21A, that it would take seeing her face to face to tip Joe over the edge and into cooperation.

Why?

He still wanted to apologize. Needed to.

Why else had he asked Elise to send that letter?

Joe continued to sit there, silent. No doubt weighing the rest.

Ironically, in this particular prison with these particular inmates—namely, the fact that every single one had taken the oath to defend their country against all enemies, foreign and domestic—there was still a rather notable distinction between homicide...and treason. And depending on the name Joe gave her and the circumstances surrounding how Joe had come by that name, the latter just might apply.

For him.

She didn't care.

Because the former agent sitting across from her in that neon-orange jumpsuit with his legs shackled and his wrists locked to this table? He owed her.

She turned her face far enough to her left to give him a damned good reminder as to the depth of that debt.

Joe took in the full force of the mottled scars and collection of equally ugly pockmarks that his betrayal had permanently carved into her flesh and nodded. He picked up the phone and tapped out a succession of letters, then switched it off before sliding it back across the table as far as those cuffs would allow.

He kept his fingers on the phone, however. As though in doing so, he'd be able to maintain his contact with her.

As if.

"I wish you'd read that letter from Elise."

Why?

She now knew exactly what it contained. Joe was sorry. Not that he'd murdered his fellow soldiers and vets, mind you, but that she—one of his former partners and closest friends—now knew him for the monster he truly was. And that bothered him.

Big fucking deal.

Except—*her* part in all this still bothered her. Tortured her.

What *the hell* had she missed?

Joe sat there while she studied at him at length, searching every inch of those familiar, dusky features until she'd reached those dark, fathomless eyes and delved within, until she was combing the man's very soul.

And then, she gave up.

She had no choice.

There just wasn't anything else to see.

No remorse. Not even a trace. The shame she'd noted earlier was simply because he'd been caught. Exposed for the hypocritical murderer he really was. Period.

And if there was nothing to see now...how on earth could Art Valens have picked up on it back then?

How could she?

"You'd do it all again, wouldn't you?" Cover up the slaughter of all those soldiers and vets. Even knowing how it would all turn out. That he'd end up here.

"To save Elise?" He nodded calmly. Sincerely. "Yeah, I would."

Bastard.

He pulled his breath in deep, purging it on a soft, ragged sigh that somehow managed to tumble across the table...and into her. "Everyone has a price, Kate. Everyone. Most people are just lucky enough that no one ever finds theirs. I know you—"

"Thirty-nine."

His dark brows furrowed. "What?"

"The number: thirty-nine. Or possibly thirty-nine, thirty-nine. Or even thirty-nine, nine. Do any of those combinations mean anything to you? Biblically or Qur'anically?" Or, heck, "Even secularly?"

After all, the ex-CID agent in front of her might be a certifiable demon conceived at Lucifer's feet, but he was still scary smart. A profoundly skilled investigator. How else had Joe been able to do what he'd done for so long? Fool everyone he'd fooled.

All those CID agents.

Regan was right. Hell, so was Dr. Manning.

And her dad?

That particular asshole might even be wrong. At least about her.

Kate could feel the seismic shift within, even as the admission filtered through her brain. Her heart. It was something to consider. And it felt good. Damned good. But it was also something she'd have to think through later. After she'd left this place.

This man.

Joe leaned forward. "Do those numbers concern your current case? The one I assume you need—" He dipped his chin to the phone still tucked beneath his fingers. "—this name to solve."

"Yes. Do they mean anything at all? Especially if carved into a raped and charred Muslim woman's thighs?"

"*Jesus*. That's some case you've landed." But the shoulders beneath that bright orange fabric pushed up once again, even as the head above turned slowly from side to side, regretfully. "I can't think of anything those numbers might apply to in the Bible or in the Qur'an. Sorry. But I'll ask my guard if he'll call—"

"No, thanks." She leaned forward and slipped her phone from beneath Joe's hands before he could stop her, then stood. "I've got a flight to catch."

Asking had a been a long shot, and it'd failed.

It was time to leave. Finish working her case. A case she *would* be solving.

Despite what her own bastard of a father had believed.

The C-21A airframe, pilot and crew Colonel Stillwater had standing by to take her back to Little Rock were at her *whenever* disposal, but Joe didn't need to know that.

"Kate—"

She shook her head, cutting him off as she headed across the room, not even bothering to glance back as she did so. She'd gotten what she'd come for. That name in her phone—and, stunningly, the return of her professional confidence.

She was done.

They were done.

She reached for the handle to the door.

"Damn it, Kate! You have to listen to me. Please. I didn't know you would be on that mission. In that Humvee. I'm—"

"*Sorry*?" She spun around, shattering her agreement with Master Sergeant Becker as she stalked over to the table—right up next to Joe so that she could vent her hate directly down onto him. And then she bent even closer as she tapped the mottled ridges and valleys of her now mutilated flesh. "Take a good look at your fucking *mea culpa—friend*. But don't think this is the only mess you left behind. You should see the scars on the inside. Do you know how many times I was raped, *buddy*?"

He swallowed hard. "No."

She actually managed a smile as she stared into those filthy pools of regret that had the nerve to glisten up right in front of her.

But the twist was grim.

"Me neither. But based on the number of DNA profiles that came back, I entertained at least half a dozen of those bastards before I came to. For how many rounds? Who knows?" After all, DNA could only reveal so much. "But I do remember the teenager whose throat I was forced to slit to prevent my final rape. I remember it so well, I can still see the kid's face every time I close my eyes—when I'm not getting a full-on flashback of that ambush, including sound and smell, or the aftermath of the bullets that took out the back half of Cutter and LeBeck's brains. And let's not forget Max. I see his severed head hitting the ground, rolling across the dirt. And, of course, feel myself wrapping it up and clutching it as I tried to find my way out of that shithole—the location of which you knew about *for every goddamned second that I was stuck there*. Hell, I'm still stuck there. Who knows if I'll ever find my way out? Again, because of *you*."

With that she straightened, whirled around and headed for the door.

"Wait! Please—"

The door slammed, severing Joe's final excuse and leaving it trapped in that room with him as she nodded to the trio of waiting MPs before heading down the corridor to pick up her Glock.

It was time to get the hell out of here. Joe could rot in his brand-new digs for all she cared.

But he might not.

The US Disciplinary Barracks at Fort Leavenworth was a unique place. Unlike the rest of the nation's federal prisons, there was no time off for good behavior. Those incarcerated at the USDB tended to do ninety percent of their allotted time. And those who did that time were unique too. Soldiers, Sailors, Airmen and Marines once trained to fight the nation's wars; to relentlessly track down, rout and kill her enemies. An unfortunate number of whom had then turned around and used that training to ruthlessly brutalize and even murder their fellow citizens closer to—and at times inside—their own homes. Indeed, forty-one of the USDB's inmates fell into the latter category.

Hardened lifers to a man, all with very little left to lose.

As a former Army CID agent, Joe had helped to put at least six of those lifers here...in the same place where he'd be spending the remainder of his pathetic days.

Every morning of which Joe would be forced to wake—and wonder—if one of those six had decided to make *this* morning his last.

10

Charles Praeger.

Kate stared at the name glowing up from her phone as she sat in the darkened parking lot just off the Little Rock airstrip, waiting for her Durango's engine to warm.

Joe had come through. But then, she'd known he would.

She'd been so certain she hadn't even turned on her phone to check that the man hadn't left a pithy "*Screw you*" in place of the classified intel she'd flown all that way to obtain today—not until after she'd departed the outer doors of Leavenworth. It wasn't worth the risk. Having Joe type that name inside a lawyer-safe interview room was one thing; flashing it for the security cameras as she departed the Barracks was another.

So she'd bided her time.

It seemed her judgment could be trusted after all. It was Joe's basic moral code that couldn't. Something else to think about.

Later.

Kate switched off her phone as the air bleeding from the vents on the Durango's dash began to warm. Leaning forward, she cranked the heater up several notches and sat back to consider the name she'd been given—and her options.

While she seriously doubted the man she was after had been baptized Charles Praeger following his birth, that alias would open doors.

But which to try first?

It was just past 5:30 p.m. The early December sun had set half an hour ago.

She might still be just north of Little Rock proper, but the local US Marshals office located southeast of the capitol had closed a half hour before that.

Search engines would be useless too.

She could always call the main switchboard at Langley and leave a message...and most likely be ignored.

Her gut circled back to a Marshals offensive. Unfortunately, her opening salvo would have to wait until the office reopened in the morning.

Kate leaned forward once more, this time to clip her phone to the holder attached to the Durango's dash. Using the phone's voice control feature, she had Siri access her missed calls log and begin relaying the information within as she shifted the SUV into gear and headed out of the airstrip's parking lot to cross the darkened base. By the time she'd cleared security at the main gate, she'd reached her final voicemail.

Dr. Manning had received the message she'd left for him on the way to Dr. Basque's office earlier in the day and had recorded a voicemail of his own.

"*Hello, Kate. I wanted to let you know I reached out to several colleagues about these disturbing murders in Braxton and Mazelle. While my colleagues and I agree that you may be seeking a killer obsessed with Islam, no former or current patients come to mind. I wish I could be more helpful. Sorry.*" Manning had followed up the investigatory dead end with a gentle query as to how she was faring personally before he'd ended the message.

Kate was tempted to return the shrink's call and let him know that not only had she taken his advice to heart during her meeting with Joe, but she'd managed a bit of a breakthrough. That, despite the pending Diamond Award at the capitol, as well as the dog and pony show that was scheduled to follow at the governor's mansion next month, she was all but certain she wouldn't be quitting her job any time soon.

But she needed to do some serious thinking first. Possibly even fill out a few more of those sheets and see what other potentially life and career-altering conclusions she ended up jarring loose.

Plus, Manning's voice had sounded tired and frazzled. Their heart to heart could wait until Saturday. Unless her case blew up, she'd be seeing the shrink then, anyway.

Besides, she needed to call Lou. The man was most likely staying late to push through on the deputy hunt to round out their dwindling department. But if not, he'd be heading home to Della for dinner soon. She needed to fill the sheriff in regarding her recent jaunt—and find out when the cadaver search was scheduled to commence.

Hell, if it was even scheduled yet.

Kate merged her Durango onto I-40 North and settled in for the drive to Braxton. She was about to have Siri initiate her call to the station when her phone rang.

It wasn't Lou.

"Hey, Seth—what's up?"

"Hey, stranger. You still out of state?"

"No. My flight landed at Little Rock Airbase about twenty minutes ago. I'm on my way back to Braxton." Her headlights picked up several deer in the distance off to the right, causing her to ease off the SUV's gas. "I won't be stopping by the station though. I've got a working dinner with Detective Moradi at my place."

"Yeah, the sheriff mentioned we might not see you for a bit, also that you might not be able to access the electronic case files. That's why I'm callin'. A couple more reports came in, including the one on the biological fluids from that bed in Aisha Kharoti's apartment. And I've got a message to pass on from Dr. Tonga."

Kate returned to speed as the Durango cleared the foraging animals. "Hit me. And start with the ME's info first."

"Well, Tonga took another look at Aisha's thighs as requested. While the left is badly burned, he says he *can* extrapolate the traces of the number thirty-nine cut into the deep muscle. But the right thigh's simply too charred to make out anythin' more than a single knife wound. Also, I've been researchin' variations of thirty-nine and thirty-nine, nine on my end."

"And?"

"I made a couple of notes on a few items I came across and uploaded them to the case file, but I wouldn't put money down on a single one of them. Sorry."

She caught the frustration in the deputy's sigh, along with the grip of his growing depression, and understood both. Like her, Seth tended to immerse himself in the evidence when he was working an investigation. In this case, that meant autopsy photos. Which meant the man had spent the afternoon staring at close-ups of charred flesh—Aisha's and Tahira's.

Just what Seth didn't need right now, given his own nightmares.

When this was over, she was going to have to corner the man and get him to open up to her—whether he quit the force or not. Until then, "You okay?"

A rough chuckle filled the line. "You know me, Kato."

Yeah. She did. Which was why she was doubly worried.

Despite their profession, her favorite bubba tended to meander through life overflowing with smiles, rainbows and hope. All of which had been seriously singed around the edges lately.

Just like that chuckle.

She let the sound slide. For now. "Yeah, I do. You mentioned the fluids report?"

"I did—and we do have something positive there. So much so, the sheriff's now champing to set that cadaver dog you ordered loose on Miller's trees."

Kate mentally crossed her fingers as she caught sight of her approaching exit. "We got the dog?"

"Yep. Be here around ten in the morning."

Yes. "That fluids report. The blood that was smeared onto Aisha's sheets—it was menstrual, wasn't it?"

This chuckle was a bit lighter and definitely surprised. "How'd you guess?"

Why else was Lou now anxious to set the dog loose? Because if the blood on those sheets wasn't from rough sex, chances were good that Aisha had voluntarily let her husband back into the marriage bed. If that was the case, where was he?

And where was Tahira Larijani's husband?

Surely one of the sergeants would've turned up by now?

"Kato?"

"I'm here." Just annoyed. At a fellow driver.

Kate frowned as a silver Ram extended cab sped up, clearly intent on cutting her off before her exit. Late for dinner or not, the driver must've caught a glimpse of the dormant police cherry attached to the roof of her SUV, because he quickly and wisely backed off, letting her take the lead onto the interstate off ramp.

Smart man. She was inside her jurisdiction now.

But she was bucking up against the clock herself.

One of the messages she'd listened to as she'd left the airbase had been from Arash, letting her know that he was on time to make their dinner meeting—in just under twenty minutes now. While she appreciated the additional information Arash had offered, namely that he'd made a command decision and picked up food for both of them again in exchange for fresh coffee, she hadn't had a chance to clear off her kitchen table. It was still littered with their current casework and those PTSD worksheets from that morning.

And there was her pending hot and soapy, if quick, shower. The one she desperately needed so she could wash off the dried sweat from that mild panic attack she'd had that afternoon at Leavenworth—hell, so she could wash *Joe* off her—along with the autopsy she and Arash had been forced to start their morning with.

In light of it all, "I need a favor, Seth. Actually, two of them."

"Sure thing."

Kate turned onto the county road that led to her private drive. "Dr. Basque said something to me earlier this afternoon that's bugging me. She claimed Tahira Larijani never called her office. Heck, the doc all but dared me to verify it."

"You want me to?"

"No, there's no need. Detective Moradi got a text after the autopsy. One of his guys already checked. Basque is right; no calls." But there'd been something threaded within the belligerence of that statement the doc had made. Certainty. How could Basque be so sure a potential patient had *never* used her office number...unless she'd spoken to Tahira via another one? "We're looking for a different number, Seth. I've got photos of two license plates. Both from older silver sedans. I'll shoot them to you as soon as I get a chance. One should belong to Basque. Just hang on to that one. But track down the name and any phone numbers that are attached to the second plate. Run those phone numbers against the Larijani dumps. Go back a while. At year, at least."

"Will do. And the second favor?"

"Can you call the sheriff for me and tell him I got what I needed this afternoon? Also tell him I'll be heading back to Little Rock first thing in the morning to follow up on it. I'll let him know how it goes."

She hated to be so vague. But although she'd called Lou before she'd boarded the C-21A in Little Rock to let her boss know where she was headed, as well as who she planned to see and why, she knew Lou wouldn't have passed on the details to Seth.

Not even if her fellow deputy had planned to stick around.

Fortunately, her cryptic comment hadn't bothered Seth. "Will do. I see him headed down the hall now. I'll go catch him. Talk to you soon."

"Thanks."

Seth severed the call as Kate turned into her gravel drive.

She could already hear the faint yet growing strains of Ruger's heartwarming excitement over her return as she took the left side of the Y of the drive to swing around the front of her house. The motion detectors kicked in, lighting up the exterior of the modest, split log ranch just in time for her to see Ruger barrel up the side and come to a pea-gravel-spitting stop as he planted his rump at the very edge of the drive.

The German Shepherd's entire body quivered impatiently as he waited for the garage door to lift so she could nudge the Durango inside and kill the engine.

The moment she stepped out of the SUV, ninety-plus pounds of frantically licking canine launched into her, bathing her face so thoroughly she could probably get away without showering—even as Ruger growled and whined out his annoyance and frustration over being abandoned for so long.

He continued to chuff at her as they awkwardly waltzed their way into the minimally lit kitchen. "I know, buddy; I know. I'm late. And I couldn't stop by for lunch again. I'm so sorry."

A final round of happy slobber forgave her.

As did the extra, guilt-induced slice of cheddar from the oversized tub that she retrieved from the refrigerator. She topped off Ruger's water and measured out his evening kibble, leaving him to enjoy his dinner as she headed down the hall for her shower.

Ten minutes later, the ends of her damp hair clung annoyingly to her neck and shoulders, but she was dressed in her favorite faded jeans and a long-sleeved Braxton PD tee. Her wrist was wrapped in a fresh elastic bandage with Max's dive watch secured around it. She wished she didn't still need the instant and profound quelling of nerves that came with tucking her Glock into her waistband at the small of her back as she headed up the hall, but capable of "sound judgment" or not, she did.

Maybe she always would.

Either way, she could only hope Arash wouldn't be offended.

Ruger had finished his kibble. He bounded deeper into the kitchen as she entered from the opposite side and sat down smack in front of the refrigerator, glancing from the stainless-steel door to her several times in a pointed attempt to guilt her into a third slice of cheese.

"Sorry, buddy. You've had enough."

His sharp snort disagreed. But he gave up, curling up at the corner of the area rug at her feet with a resigned huff as she combined several piles of papers that Arash had made that morning into a larger one to free up more of the table.

She reached the ABC sheet that Arash had accidentally read and stopped, then drew out a chair and sat. Snagging the pencil near the middle of the table, she stared at the stuck point

Manning had filled out in that center block at the end of their session the previous Saturday: *My judgment can't be trusted.*

She shifted the pencil decisively to the left, to the box underneath *Something happens*, and wrote *Joe murdered a soldier and covered up other killings while I knew him.* She shifted the pencil again, this time down to that pointed question waiting beneath the trio of boxes: *Are my thoughts above realistic or helpful?*

She took a deep breath and filled in the blank lines with the truth. *No. I wasn't the only one who couldn't see Joe for who he really was. Or even Grant and Burke.*

One more breath—though, surprisingly, this one was normal—and she'd reached the final question on the sheet: *What can I tell myself on such occasions in the future?*

Even good cops can miss things. Focus on the successes—and work harder on the rest.

She laid the pencil down, knowing Manning would be pleased with this particular sheet. Even better, she was. She'd finally accepted that there was nothing she or anyone else could have done to prevent Max's murder—except Joe.

Manning was right. It was past time to lay the blame where it truly belonged.

Moments later, her cuckoo chirped out the time.

6:30?

Crap. Kate stood and headed into the kitchen. Arash was due to arrive with dinner in hand any moment now, and she hadn't started the coffee.

Scratch that. The detective was already here.

Either that or Ruger had caught the scent of his vixen fox again, because he'd jumped up to his paws and shot across the kitchen behind her. A split second later, the flap on the inner dog door was swinging wildly.

She left the Shepherd to greet their guest and quickly added coffee grounds and water to the machine before setting it to perk. By the time she reached the front door and opened it, Arash was headed up the flagstone path, wearing the same dark gray suit he'd been wearing that morning and carrying a topless brown cardboard box with several smaller, white takeout containers inside. Ruger was dancing around his heels with joy.

Oh, Lord. "What did you bring?"

The man grinned. "A small bribe."

Meat. She'd stake the badge she'd decided to keep on it. Based on the amount of drool dripping from Ruger's tongue, Arash had brought red meat too.

Ruger's favorite food group, and one he hadn't partaken of in days.

Pending case review complete with charred photos or not, she couldn't deny the hopeful hound any more than Arash evidently could.

She held the door open and waved the duo up onto the porch. "Come in."

This grin was just for her. "Thanks."

Kate laughed, though not at Arash. At her dog.

His behavior at breakfast might've been surreal, but apparently, it hadn't been a fluke. Not to Ruger. As far as the Shepherd was concerned, he and Arash were already lifelong friends. She could tell by the way the dog led the detective and that cardboard box of admittedly delicious smells all the way up to the kitchen counter, then plopped down onto his rump beside it. Ruger wasn't gazing at the box, though—but at Arash.

She shook her head at her crazy mutt and turned to retrieve two plates from the upper cupboard to her left. As she turned back, she found Arash staring as well.

At her.

And the man was still smiling.

"What?" Had her hair dried weird?

"You seem...lighter. Happy."

She took a page from her sessions with Manning and took stock of what was actually going on inside her at that precise moment—then nodded. Because she was. "Yeah. I guess I am."

"Productive day?"

In more ways than one. "You could say that."

"And does your productivity and mood have something to do with that cryptic text you sent saying you'd be out of touch this afternoon and to cross my fingers?"

She passed the plates over the counter and into Arash's waiting hand. "Yup."

He arranged the plates where he'd set out their breakfast, then took a moment to remove his suit jacket and shoulder holster while she filled two glasses with ice water and set them on the counter near his side. But instead of hanging his jacket and Glock from the back of her dad's chair, Arash hung them from her old childhood spot before returning to retrieve the glasses, napkins and cutlery she'd added.

"So, you ready to tell me where you took off to today?"

"Fort Leavenworth."

His brow hiked.

She nodded. "It was time to take my head out of the sand."

"You saw Cordoba."

She retrieved two mugs, filled both with coffee and passed them over with surprisingly rock steady hands. "I had to. I got a call from another former fellow CID agent at Campbell, but she had more questions about Dr. Lily Basque than answers. Turns out Basque doesn't exist off paper—and even that fantasy falls apart on closer examination. So I called in a favor with an MP colonel I've worked with who just happens to be the current commandant of the USDB."

That earned her a whistle. "Did Cordoba cough up the name of the guy who gave the doc her new life?"

"Yeah. You want it?"

That dark stare captured hers and held it for several thick moments. The hesitation that elbowed in to linger amid the murky depths was prudent.

Possession of the alias she'd already deleted from her phone could easily create more problems than it solved. Especially for the man standing on the other side of her kitchen counter. She might be buffered to some extent by her current career status and her solid relationship with Lou, but Arash wasn't. Not that the detective's boss over at the Mazelle PD wouldn't back him up if need be, because the man would.

It was the rest.

Unlike her, Arash still had one spit-shined boot planted firmly inside the US Army. She'd abandoned the service completely upon her return to the States; Arash hadn't. He'd transferred into the Reserves. Major Moradi still donned his camouflage one weekend a month, along with an additional two weeks during the year. Major Moradi was also still beholden to his country. Uncle Sam could decide to plug him back into active duty at any time and send him anywhere for even longer.

And there was his branch.

Military Intelligence was rather big on the dissemination of classified information and somewhat particular about how that dissemination occurred.

Security clearances were one thing—even a top secret one—but the *need to know* was quite another. And the two conditions did not always meet.

Arash shook his head. "You hang on to that name. Work it. No need to share it further, unless you decide you need backup."

"Will do. I'm heading into the US Marshals office first thing in the morning. It should get me in the door, at least." From there? She'd find out soon enough, wouldn't she? "I'll let you know how it goes."

Though they both knew they needed this name to pay off.

They had no other leads.

If she could get Praeger to contact her, she just might be able to get the man to contact Lily Basque as well—and force the doc to share, with Praeger at least, what Basque knew about the murders she and Arash were trying to solve...before there was a third.

"So, Detective, how was your day?"

The man shook his head. "Not nearly as productive as yours." He carried the cardboard box to the table and reached inside, dividing up the rice he retrieved between the dinner plates as she swung around the counter to join him. "I revisited several contacts to see if they had anything that meshed with the new theory. I also asked about an Underground Railroad for Muslim women. Two have heard rumors of assistance for the abused, but nothing specific. As for leads on our killer, my last stop did yield a possibility, but it's a long shot. Also, Hashem has to check with a relative on the name."

Next up from the cardboard: a thick vegetable stew that Arash poured over the rice. "Basically, Hashem heard of a Christian who attended mosque a year ago. Late twenties, early thirties. According to gossip, the guy was there because of a Sudanese woman. She'd insisted that he convert before they could even date. So he starts learning Arabic, and then about three months in, he makes his *shahada*—and she immediately announces that she's gotten married...to someone else. But like I said, Hashem can't remember the guy's name." Arash tipped his head toward the plates. "That's where this came from, by the way. Hashem and his wife have a restaurant off Markham."

"It smells delicious." Kate accepted an equally fragrant circle of flatbread from Arash and followed his example, tearing it in two and tucking a piece beside each plate. "So this guy goes to mosque at least twelve times, dives into a very difficult foreign language, then publicly declares that he too believes there's one god—Allah—and that Mohammed's his messenger...and the woman ups and says she's already married another guy? No warning hints, no apologies?"

"Yep."

Yikes. That was harsh. But there would've needed to be a lot more going wrong in their mystery guy's head for him to decide to take out his anger on at least two other women, the way anger had been taken out on Aisha and Tahira.

And there was race to consider. Mostly because Arash had already admitted to his doubts without even meeting the guy, much less hearing his name.

"The convert's black?"

"Yeah. So's the Sudanese woman." The detective shrugged. "Like I said—long shot."

She was forced to agree. Serial killers tended to stick within their race. Not always, of course. And while that didn't mean their suspect was necessarily Persian or Pakistani, especially since they were dealing with other factors here, including a rather distinctive religion and the current geopolitical considerations that unfortunately stemmed from it, both Aisha and Tahira were decidedly light-skinned. Or had been, before the monster who'd taken their lives had set them on fire.

Either way, her gut was leaning toward a Caucasian killer.

From the terse press of his lips, Arash was too.

She stared at the final, oversized waxed bag the man had retrieved from the cardboard. "Please tell me that's dessert."

But she knew it wasn't, because she could smell that it wasn't. Even before Arash shook his head. "This is for the head of the house."

The bribe he'd mentioned.

Only the bone inside that bag wasn't *small* as Arash had promised out on her front walk. Worse, from the ripe scent oozing from that waxed sack, it had been slowly baked, too, in its own juices. And Ruger knew it was his.

The Shepherd was on his very best behavior too, sitting perfectly, handsomely, motionless beside the detective's shoes—utterly mesmerized by that bag.

But then Ruger's attention shifted to her, as if he could sense her suddenly queasy stomach.

Both man and dog were looking at her now.

Both silently pleading.

"Fine. But give it to him in the kitchen." She could smell each and every one of the generous bits of roasted beef that were clinging to that bone. She didn't need to see them, much less the scorched marrow within. Not for another week, at least.

She waited for Arash to deliver Ruger's prize.

Despite the jacket and shoulder-holstered Glock hanging from the back of her childhood chair, she was actually hoping the detective would claim her father's seat.

Otherwise, she would have to.

Happy, slurring groans emanated from the kitchen as Arash returned to the table, only to hook his hand on the back of her childhood chair and pause. He was clearly, politely, waiting for her to seat herself first—at her father's place.

Damn.

"Did I forget to bring something?"

She faked her first smile since Arash's arrival and swore he knew it. "Nope."

She dragged the chair away from the table before she could chicken out and claimed the forbidden seat. She sat there for several moments, as motionless as Ruger had been mere minutes earlier, but for an entirely different reason. She half expected a bolt of lightning to crack straight down through the roof and split her into two for daring to plant her butt where she had so often been told that it did *not* belong.

But there was no lightning...or anything else.

"Kate, are you okay?"

She released her breath and smiled again. This time, the curve felt warm and genuine. "I'm fine." And she was.

Arash was still considering her curiously, so she quickly forked up a bite of her dinner. "What is this?"

"Vegetarian *khoresh bademjan*. It's an eggplant stew. It's one of Hashem's specialties."

"It smells wonderful." She took an experimental bite. "Tastes even better."

Arash let go of whatever he'd been about to say regarding her odd behavior and smiled back. "I'll tell him you said so."

The man proceeded to dig in, as well.

Between forkfuls of the rice and stew, and the backdrop of steady gnawing from deep inside the kitchen, Arash briefed her on the remainder of his day.

He was right; though he'd made quite a few colorful stops, there wasn't much information to share. At least not anything that advanced their case.

She swallowed her last mouthful of that addictive flatbread and sat back. "Did you get a chance to access the Braxton case file?"

"Yeah. I saw the fluids report and the supplemental memo about the numbers on Aisha from Dr. Tonga. What about the cadaver dog?"

"It'll be here at ten a.m.; I might still be in Little Rock though." As much as she wanted to oversee at least the setup of the grid search, she prayed so.

Because that would mean the Praeger alias had gotten her through the door and a Marshal had agreed to run interference regarding the rest.

Arash held out the remainder of his flatbread. "I can head this way and check on the search, if you'd like."

Kate waved off the extra carbs, delicious though they would be. She took the man up on his spoken offer, instead. "Sounds good. I'll text you a GPS pin for Miller's trees. They can be difficult to find." Especially to those who didn't hail from Braxton.

She pushed her half-empty plate aside. As amazing as the stew had tasted, she hadn't eaten much lately. Her stomach must've shrunk, because less than halfway into her plate, she'd become stuffed.

"Thanks for dinner." She could hear her greedy mutt still gnawing deliriously away in the kitchen. "Ruger's, too."

Arash nodded, pushing his slightly more than half-empty plate to the side as well. "Yeah, my appetite's been off this week too." Clearly caffeine didn't apply, though, because he glanced at his empty mug, then hers. "Would you like more coffee?"

"I'll get it." She retrieved both mugs and stood, giving the Shepherd and his ripe, culinary contraband wide berth as she entered the kitchen.

She refilled the mugs and walked to the table to slot both into place. But instead of taking her seat, she headed for the opposite end and retrieved the worksheet she'd filled out shortly before the detective's arrival.

Arash had seen what was written in the center box, and he hadn't ratted her out to Lou or anyone else in her department, or his. He'd also assured her that he trusted her to work Praeger's name and the CIA/WITSEC angle alone.

He deserved to see what she'd finally scrawled onto the rest of the page.

She set the worksheet down beside him and retrieved the remnants of their dinners, leaving the man to skim her innermost thoughts and fears as she retreated to the kitchen to deposit the food in the trash and the plates in the sink.

The worksheet was waiting for her at her spot when she returned.

"Thank you, Kate. And for what it's worth—" That dark stare drifted down toward the final line she'd written: *Even good cops can miss things. Focus on the successes—and work harder on the rest.* "—I agree."

She returned his nod, slid the worksheet down the table and sat.

Arash leaned back to loosen his ice-blue tie as she sipped at her coffee. He unbuttoned his sleeves as well, and rolled them up several inches, leaving her with a clear view of that tattoo on his inner, right wrist as he reached for his own mug.

He took a sip, then set the mug down. But his hand remained where it was, atop the table and turned slightly. They were both staring at the Arabic lettering now.

كافر

Infidel.

She was curious as hell about the story behind that word, especially after the bombshell of a hint that he'd dropped at the Larijani crime scene, but she refused to push it. How could she, given everything she preferred to not share?

Arash finally sighed. He looked straight at her and smiled softly. Sadly. "Her name was Azizah. It means esteemed, cherished...but she was not. I knew that long before they killed her, of course. Because Azizah raised me. Our mother died shortly after she, my father, my sister and I came to the States. I was two. And even though Azizah was only seven, the job of caring for me fell to her. She did it well, and I *adored* her. So much so, I supported her when she wanted to go to college. I even assured my father that in the States, she would make a better—wealthier—marriage with a degree. For that reason alone, my father agreed."

The detective's smile faded, and he fell silent.

Kate waited, even as that dark gaze eased away from hers to drift down again and settle on the small black inking.

Arash kept his focus on that single Arabic word as he pushed out another sigh. "She fell in love with a classmate her freshman year. But Reza was not rich...and my father found out. Why?" A short, stunted laugh escaped, but it held zero humor. "Because Reza was a good guy; responsible. He came to our father and asked to marry Azizah. For that my sister was branded a whore." Another sigh escaped, and this one was dark. Tortured. As were those eyes when Arash finally lifted them. "And she was murdered. They attacked her while I was sleeping. I woke to Azizah screaming. I ran into the garage and found my uncle beating her. I tried to stop him, but my father—"

Arash broke off. He swallowed hard and opened his mouth, but this time, nothing came out.

Those tormented eyes found hers as he stood. He carefully tugged his shirt from his trousers and began to unbutton it. Slowly—almost as though he wasn't quite sure he would be able to share what lay beneath.

By the time he'd parted the fabric, Kate wished to hell he hadn't.

Nearly a dozen white, knotted scars greeted her, cutting in and around the darker skin and generous muscles of the man's entire chest and abdomen. All appeared to be the result of long-healed, if horrific, knife wounds. Several of which surpassed the dimensions of the largest scar that tore across her own face.

The detective's breathing took on a stunted, almost cautious rhythm as he turned to lower the shirt from the muscles of his upper shoulders and back, murmuring, "This was the first." Though gentle and hoarse, his words filled the kitchen...and her.

Kate dragged in her breath much more deeply than Arash had and cursed.

She couldn't help it. There might be just the one, bright-white scar here. But like the others, she knew it had not been forged in combat. Not in the traditional sense.

Hell, not executed by any rule of fair play at all.

No, Arash's own father had come up from behind his back and tried to stab him in the heart.

The shirt slipped up, covering those tense shoulders as he turned around and began to slowly re-button the edges.

Ruger's continued gnawing added a surreal backdrop as Arash finished, then slowly tucked the tails of his shirt back into his trousers.

"I lost my gallbladder that day. A good chunk of my liver. Nearly a foot of intestine." He shrugged. "Fortunately, all ileum. But it was enough that I still had to get a waiver to join the Army."

Kate nodded. Because, really? What else could she do? What could she say?

Because that wasn't all Arash had lost that day.

He'd lost his innocence. Trust in the man who'd given him life.

His sister.

To her surprise, Arash glanced at the sheet of paper she'd left near the center of the table. "There's a reason why I recognize those worksheets. And why whatever's written on them doesn't scare, much less repulse me."

She nodded as she finally connected the dots between this man's pain—and her own. The phone calls he'd made. His offer to talk...or to not talk.

Arash hadn't reached out to her, wasn't continuing to reach out to her because of what she, a fellow vet and cop, had survived as a POW or even during the Garbage Man investigation. Arash had simply recognized another tortured soul twisting alone in the dark and had sought to ease her burden, and his, through friendship.

They were partners for the moment, yes.

But like it or not, they shared a deeper, permanent connection as well. One forged between two broken people who worked to survive each day with the sight of a loved one's murder seared into their minds—unable to escape the soul-piercing reality that someone else they'd once cherished had caused that horror and that death.

Was that why Ruger had taken to this man so quickly and so completely? Did the Shepherd recognize yet another kindred spirit?

Either way, she really should have phoned Arash back. "You saw someone too, didn't you? Filled out your own worksheets?"

He nodded. "My aunt is a therapist. She's married to an older uncle I hadn't known I had—because he'd left Islam. He'd emigrated before his brothers and settled up in Fayetteville. I was pretty messed up by the time I came to live with them, and my aunt knew it was only going to get worse. Of course, she couldn't treat me, so she insisted I see someone. I was furious with her at first."

"And then?"

"Grateful. Very much so. Cognitive processing therapy was still fairly new then, but my aunt had read of Dr. Resick's work. She was encouraged by the results, so she encouraged me." He reached out and cupped his palm to her cheek.

The shredded one.

Weirdly, she didn't flinch. Nor did he.

"Stick with it, Kate. It does work—and you are worth it."

She managed a smile. "That's what my shrink says."

"Your shrink's right. So listen; do the assignments. And don't feel as though you have to explain what's on those sheets to anyone but yourself."

She was about to nod when her phone pinged.

Arash's hand fell away from her cheek. He stepped back to give her space as she pulled her phone from the back pocket of her jeans and checked her incoming text.

It was from Regan Chase.

Got a call from Chaplain Shilmani out of Bragg. Sgt. Kharoti called after he struck his wife. Chaplain's been counseling Kharoti via Skype the whole time the sgt was in Yemen. See email for more.

That sealed it.

Kate didn't know if the cadaver dog was going to find those bodies, but the husbands were definitely not headed back to their respective posts.

She turned her phone around.

Arash frowned as he read the text. "Well, shit. They're dead."

"Yep."

The cuckoo in the kitchen chose that moment to chime out 8:00. Arash half frowned at the obnoxious series of chirps as he turned toward the clock—then outright cursed, and more creatively than he had a moment earlier.

He was staring at the clock. Transfixed.

"What's wrong?"

He swung back to her. "They're closed."

"Closed?"

He nodded as he strode to the table, rifling through the larger stack of casework she'd created before his arrival until he'd located a close-up of the thighs of one of the victims. Based on the lighter amount of charring, and the fact that Kate could make out the numbers formed by those stab wounds, Tahira Larijani's thighs.

Arash tapped a finger over the nines in the wounds, and he was shaking his head, sharply. "Not nines. Fours. The tops of the numbers—the *fours*—are closed."

Kate glanced at the cuckoo.

He was right. The fours on that clock face were closed too. The flourish was common enough in industrial typesetting and design.

And, although not terribly common in handwriting, some

men and women did create their scripted fours with points at the tops. "So we're looking at a killer who's carving thirty-fours into women."

But again, Arash shook his head. "Not quite. Especially if we don't read the pairs of numbers from left to right, as in the Western world, but right to left, as one would read something in Arabic—or in the Qur'an. But we also need to take the sequence as written—because it's complete. In other words, *four, thirty-four*."

Oh, Lord. The detective was onto something. She could see it burning within that intense stare. "So what does 'four, thirty-four' mean in the Qur'an?"

Because it did mean something.

Instead of words, she got another shake of the man's head.

Arash retrieved his smartphone from his pocket and typed the numbers into the Android's waiting search engine, then clicked a link. "I'm not great at reciting the Qur'an. Wasn't as a kid either, much to my father's disgust. But I know the gist. *Surah* IV, verse thirty-four concerns men and how they should supposedly treat women. Here." He turned the screen, so she could read the words he'd highlighted.

...those on whose part you fear desertion, admonish them, and leave them alone in the sleeping places and beat them...

She stepped back to signal that she'd finished.

He clicked off the phone and pocketed it. "Kate, that passage serves as the basis many fundamentalists use to defend the practice of isolating, and even beating and murdering female family members. It's what my father and uncle used to rationalize the murder of my sister. And it's what they would have used to rationalize my murder if I hadn't regained consciousness while they left to bury Azizah's body and crawled to our neighbor's house for help."

Honor killings. "Basque knew."

Arash stiffened. "You're sure?"

The way the doc had stared at the same charred close-up that Arash had just shown her—and had been unable to turn away?

"Oh, yeah." The doc definitely knew.

Sure, Basque could've made a general realization about that Qur'anic verse. But when Kate combined the look in Basque's eyes with the palpable fear that had all but radiated off the woman both times she'd been in the doc's presence?

Basque was connected to this. Somehow.

Arash tidied the stack of casework he'd rifled through. "You think the doctor's protecting the identity of the killer? Possibly even involved in the killings?"

"I don't know." Her instincts might be yelling no, but why else was Basque so unwilling to share information about not one, but two murdered women?

Arash's phone rang.

The detective retrieved the Android from his pocket for the second time in two minutes. Before he could answer it, her iPhone rang as well.

His frown matched hers. "It's my boss."

"Mine, too."

Two calls from two department heads at the same time?

Definitely a bad sign.

Kate headed into the living room to give them both space as she brought her phone to her ear. "Hey, boss. What happened?"

But like Arash, she already knew.

Nor did Lou waste any time with niceties. "We got another body. Female. Possibly violated and stabbed. Definitely burned. And, Kato?" She could feel the sheriff's anger...and his growing fear. "The bastard dumped this woman at the airbase you just left."

11

Forty minutes later, Kate turned her Durango onto East Maddox Road. But for the mix of naked deciduous trees and clothed pines on both sides, this part of the two-lane blacktop that circled around the northern part of Little Rock Airbase was fairly empty. That was normal for this time of night, especially for early December.

The red, white and blue glow of emergency lights in the distance was not.

Lou had been off about one thing. Their latest victim hadn't actually been dumped *at* the airbase...but pretty damned close to it. According to the text that Arash had sent a minute ago, and that her iPhone's hands-free, voice feature had just read out loud, the entire length of their latest blackened corpse was touching Jacksonville's side of the twelve-foot, barbed-wire-topped, chain-link fence that formed the base's outer perimeter.

And since the corpse was physically touching the fence, not to mention lying on a scorched strip of military frontage, the Air Force had assumed jurisdiction.

Fine by her and Arash.

Neither one of them was greedy. Both of them had learned

the hard way that more eyes meant more mental and physical effort directed toward the case.

With three burnt bodies racked up in as many days, they could use all of the above and as much as they could get.

More, if it would prevent a fourth murder.

The glow of red, white and blue grew closer and brighter until the Durango was all but on top of the makeshift light show. Kate slowed down, then came to a halt beside the cruiser parked and facing her in the middle of the oncoming lane. She retrieved her Braxton PD credentials and held them up for the uniformed patrol officer bracing himself against the plummeting temperature in the night air out beside his car.

Another five degrees and they'd hit freezing.

The man's breath billowed between them. "Evenin', Deputy Holland. Special Agent Wynne's expecting you."

She nodded and thanked the cop as he waved her through, coming to yet another halt, this time to park her SUV behind the string of police and emergency vehicles lining the north side of the road. She climbed out, zipping up her own patrol jacket against the icy night before she swapped the Durango's keys for the fresh set of forensic gloves she'd tucked into her trouser pocket while still at her house. Snapping on the latex, she scanned the mishmash of civilian police and military camouflage interspersed with half a dozen firefighter ensembles across the road.

To the far left of that larger, collective cloud of frosted air: the increasingly crushed gray suit that had departed her house as she'd been heading down the hall to her bedroom to swap out her jeans and tee for a fresh deputy uniform and jacket. Swap complete, she'd passed through her kitchen and bent down to tweak Ruger's fuzzy ears on her way to the garage to link up with Arash here.

Ruger hadn't minded her departure. Not with the giant,

pungent bribe Arash had provided still locked between the Shepherd's gnawing jaws and paws.

Unfortunately, it smelled so much worse out here than it had in her kitchen. And as Kate crossed the blacktop, the nauseating odors got stronger.

She steeled herself against the memories that began to rouse themselves and knock up against her psyche. It helped that the body she'd come to see was a good twenty yards further up the road with a sole camouflaged utility uniform kneeling beside it —and decidedly *down*wind from her.

For the moment.

Arash caught sight of her and waved her over.

The detective tipped his head toward the set of towering camouflaged utilities to his right. "Deputy Kate Holland, Braxton PD, meet Special Agent Bill Wynne, US Air Force Office of Special Investigations." Arash turned to the man who would have been her Air Force counterpart back when she was still Army CID. "Bill, Kate's—"

"—the agent who took down that group of bastards four years ago in Afghanistan." The blond giant grinned down at her. "Pleasure to meet you."

Latex met latex as she accepted the agent's equally oversized, but thoroughly inappropriate jackhammer shake. At least here, already gloved up against crime scene contamination as they were. "Likewise, Special Agent W—"

His camouflaged cap shook too, from side to side. "*Bill.*"

"Bill."

The agent's enthusiasm faded as someone yelled "Wynne" from across the road. "Just a sec." The giant turned to Arash. "Feel free to pass on what I just shared with you. Meanwhile, I'll be passing on what you shared with me."

"Will do." Arash waited for the agent to depart, then extended a latex-gloved hand toward the lone living figure at the fence line twenty yards up the road. The one still kneeling beside the source of the hydrogen sulfide and sizzled meat that permeated the night. "The Air Force's medical examiner is already here. A Captain Stan Raub. Ready to take a look at the body?"

Hell, no. But she nodded.

She'd have to do it eventually. Might as well get it over with now. Frankly, with the memories that were still stubbornly banging on the door to her brain, she appreciated having as small an audience as possible while she did so. Nor did it hurt to know that the detective at her side understood. Which was probably why she allowed the fingers of her right hand to slip across her body so she could twist Max's watch around the elastic bandage in an effort to anchor herself against the strengthening sounds, sight and smells of that shattered Humvee.

They were all still there as she and Arash walked, but they weren't able to hijack her present and jerk her all the way into the past.

That was something. A hell of a lot, in fact.

She knew Arash had noticed what she was doing with the watch. But that was okay. Somehow, it was easier to expose herself to him than it was with Liz or even Dr. Manning. Probably because Arash had been there.

And, unfortunately, she was *here*.

Despite the snail's pace Arash had set, they reached the body far too quickly.

Kate released the watch as the ME came to his feet. Another blue-eyed blond in Air Force camouflage, though this one was nearly a foot shorter than the OSI agent she'd just met, putting Captain Raub midway between her five-six and Arash's solid six feet.

Raub stepped forward to greet them. He might've recognized her too, because her scars didn't give him pause. Though there was an added, odd, glint to the ME's eyes. Perhaps the physician in Raub simply didn't feel the need to draw attention to her past as he settled for the usual, forensically conscious introductions nod.

Thank God.

"Good to meet you, Deputy. Wish it was under better circumstances." A hint of humor threaded through that crystal blue as it shifted to Arash. "Decided to wait and finish the briefing with your partner in tow, eh, Detective?"

"Figured it was prudent. The first victim was found in a field half an hour up the road in Braxton. Deputy Holland has the case."

The ME caught her eye and stepped to his right so that Kate could get a good look at the body.

From the singed breasts and genitals, their victim was obviously female. While the body had been laid on top of what appeared to be a foam camping mattress before it had been set on fire, the flames hadn't ignited as evenly or as thoroughly as they had with either Aisha or Tahira.

Because there hadn't been enough fuel in the foam to feed and sustain the flames? Or because the fire department had arrived in time to douse the fire?

Kate's gut pointed to the former, given that she couldn't see the vestiges of aqueous foam or another fire-fighting chemical, or a discarded fire blanket.

Also, while the victim's hair and any clothes appeared to have been completely consumed by the flames, her skin wasn't as deeply charred as the other two victims. Yes, it was severely blistered and thoroughly blackened in spots, but that was it.

Though that was more than enough, because it was also—

"Damned sick work, this." The ME frowned heavily.

Agreed.

Raub motioned for the two of them to hunker down beside

him, then stretched his right index finger out over the scorched torso. "As you can see, she was stabbed at least two dozen times, beginning here—" The gloved finger circled the wounds in and around the victim's breasts then moved down to the blackened abdomen and paused. "—and here—" The ME's finger moved once more, this time to hover over the woman's thighs. "—and ending here. From the lack of blood beneath the body and other considerations, she was most likely killed elsewhere, brought here and set on fire. Of course, I'll need to confirm this with the autopsy."

Raub's gloved hand retracted, leaving a clear view of the woman's scorched and blistered thighs. Hunkered down this close to the body, and from this angle, Kate could make out the distinctive pattern created by those lower stab wounds.

The ME nodded. "Detective Moradi shared your theory about the *Surah* angle, and I concur. Taken together, the wounds clearly form the numbers four, thirty-four."

While she'd expected the corroboration, it wasn't entirely welcome.

Confirmation always cut in multiple, and at times conflicting, ways. Each would play havoc in the minds and hearts of nearly everyone involved in an investigation like this in the days, weeks and even years to come. There was no escaping it.

But there were others who would feel that pain so much more intensely and for so much longer. Aisha's and Tahira's loved ones, and those of this poor woman.

"Do we have an ID yet?"

Arash shook his head. "Agent Wynne's working on it. I gave him the particulars on the Kharoti and Larijani cases. In light of the marital and religious commonalities, he's arranging for base security to begin canvassing the command's Muslim couples—in person. If we're lucky, we might have her name by morning."

But would this woman's husband be missing too?

From the glance Arash shot her, he was wondering the same. He was also visibly feeling the weight of this new death.

No surprise there. Given what the detective had shared of his past at her kitchen table, it was clear he hadn't accidentally fallen into police work. He'd deliberately pursued it. Arash was here for all the right reasons, too. Most especially: the need to protect.

How many pieces of his sister had he seen in those whom he'd already helped?

From what Kate already knew of the man, far too many.

And not nearly enough.

"Detective?"

Arash turned to the ME. "Yes?"

"I found something after you left earlier. I've bagged it." The ME leaned over to retrieve a paper envelope from his crime kit. It was unsealed. "I don't yet know if she was raped, but this was at the entrance to her vaginal canal. It looks to be—"

"A rock. Milky quartz."

That clear blue gaze swung to hers. "Yes. You found one in your victim?"

Kate shook her head. "Not quite. It was underneath. It was partially scorched, so we weren't certain it was important...until it turned up at the second autopsy."

The ME's sigh was as dark as the surrounding night. The resignation within could have just as easily come from her or Arash. No one who did this for a living welcomed a sexual component to a crime. No one.

"Deputy Holland?"

She stood and turned to find Agent Wynne headed toward her.

Kate met the man halfway and filled him in on what she knew, and still didn't know, about the first murder. She wrapped up her case brief with a summary of her visits to the mysterious general surgeon's office in Manchin—and included what she and Regan Chase had yet to uncover about that only lead. Specifically, Lily Basque's real name.

Like Arash, the OSI agent was happy to let Kate follow up on the matter.

As for Agent Wynne's reciprocal briefing, his was even shorter than hers. "Guys, I've got nothing else to share that you haven't just seen." The shake of his head encompassed them both. "My recommendation? Head home for some shut-eye. Arash, unless you've got something else to work on, you and I can reconvene at the hospital on base first thing in the morning for the autopsy—zero eight hundred."

The agent turned to her. "Meanwhile, you keep to your Marshals' plan. Use that name you've got to beat the damned door down. Let us know if anyone's inside."

Kate nodded, as did Arash.

As much as she hated leaving a scene, Kate was forced to agree with Wynne's logic. The OSI agent's investigatory instincts were still well-rested and sharp.

Theirs were not.

She and Arash waved to Wynne and headed across the road, then turned to walk up the deserted side of the outer scene toward the string of dormant emergency vehicles.

Five paces in, she was forced to smile.

Her temporary partner's brow kicked up. "What?"

"Nothing." But it was something. Her judgment had come through again. This time about the detective who'd managed to pause in mid-step just long enough to smoothly alter his previous position on her right side and back around to her left, so that his body was now serving as a physical buffer between her and the raw edge of the road. A road that, while desolate and dark, was anchored by cop cars at both ends.

But those cop cars didn't matter. And from that quizzical

brow, Arash had no clue as to what he'd done. The detective's protective instincts simply ran that strong and that deep.

In a weird way, Arash reminded her of Ruger. Not that she'd tell him. He might not view the comparison as a compliment.

Though from the way that dark brow had hiked up further, he still wanted to know what amused her. "Did I say something back there with Raub or Wynne? Do something?"

She shook her head again and outright laughed. "You're fine. It's me. I'm just having a strange day." She stopped beside the driver's door of her Durango.

Arash stopped with her.

Her smile bled off. But the instinctive reaction wasn't due to him.

"What's wrong?"

She shook her head as the chill settled in. The one that had absolutely nothing to do with the surrounding temperature. "I don't know."

And she didn't.

But something *was* wrong.

She was getting the same feeling she'd gotten while heading up the drive to Nash Weaver's house. The same feeling she'd gotten while standing in Nash's field of winter wheat next to Aisha's body and looking up at his deck. The same feeling she'd gotten as a military policeman on too damned many foot patrols in Afghanistan and Iraq.

Only, now, it was worse.

The tiny hairs at the back of her neck had shot to attention.

She could feel the night breeze plucking at each and every one.

She shifted slightly, subtly. Just enough so she could stare into the woods on her right. Study them. The spaces in between were lonely and black.

Was that all it was? The desolation inherent in all those bald, winter trees? Or was the day finally getting to her? That charred and blistered body behind her? Her meeting with Joe?

No. It was more than that.

The fingers of her right hand crept up on their own. But they didn't settle on her watch. They eased in around the butt of her Glock. And they did not want to let go.

"Kate?"

"He's still here...somewhere." Watching.

"You see him?"

"No." But she could feel him.

Unfortunately, there wasn't a damned thing she could do about it. There was too much forest around them. Miles of it. And every acre was currently pitch black.

Arash's left hand came up and around her chest to open the Durango's driver's door. "Get in. Go home. Text me when you get there. Keep Ruger and that Glock loaded and handy tonight—and double check the locks on your windows and doors."

"Arash—"

"I mean it, Kate. Go. Now. I'll alert Wynne. Let him know. He can have a patrol car make a pass up and down the road, but there's nothing any of us can do unless the bastard decides to reveal himself. Not out here, with all of us exposed like this."

Arash was right. The suspect they were after had managed to kill three women in nearly as many days, leaving absolutely nothing behind forensics-wise but what he'd wanted them to find. Hell, the bastard hadn't even left at least two of his victims' husbands.

Both of whom were combat vets.

Someone that smart was not about to screw up and reveal himself now.

She also knew Arash wasn't going to give in regarding that charming set of *me, Tarzan; you, Jane* orders he'd just issued. To a fellow cop, no less.

Part of her was pissed. The rest of her understood.

Those damned protective instincts of his had locked in, and they had nothing to do with a nighttime stroll down the raw edge of a busy, or not so busy, road—and everything to do with the man's own traumatic issues.

Fortunately for Arash, it wasn't worth the argument.

Because the feeling was gone. Which meant *he* was gone. At least for now.

The only way the bastard could've accomplished that was to have moved deeper into the trees. They'd lost their prey before she'd even realized he was here.

"*Kate.*"

"Fine." She slid into the Durango's driver's seat. "I'll leave. I'll even follow the rest of your orders—*partner*." She'd absolutely secure the perimeter of her home. Heck, her PTSD-riddled paranoia wouldn't let her do anything else. "But I am not texting."

She wasn't some teenaged kid headed home after dark. And with that body lying out behind them, still kicking off heat, this sure as hell wasn't some date.

She started the Durango and shifted into gear.

Arash had no choice but to offer a stiff nod and an even stiffer "Goodnight" as he closed the door.

Her pique lasted just long enough for her to clear the outer patrol car and the gradually freezing uniformed cop blocking the road at the opposite end of the scene.

She and Arash had just had their first spat. In an odd way, it had solidified their friendship. She would've smiled at the thought, but she didn't.

It seemed she truly could trust her judgment.

But right now, she almost wished she couldn't. Because the reason behind that feeling she'd gotten out on that road with Arash followed her all the way home.

SHE WOKE SLOWLY, gently—and in her own bed for a change.

Kate stared at the lingering shadows on the ceiling of her room, her relief fading as last night's crime scene and that pricklingly exposed sensation she'd experienced while walking along the road with Arash filtered back in.

She'd texted the man after all. Roughly an hour after she'd arrived home, and only after Arash had reached out with an inane *Did you see...?* about a report that'd been uploaded to the Larijani file the previous afternoon. A report Arash had known she'd seen, because he'd mentioned it while they'd been eating dinner.

At the time, she'd thought about feigning sleep. After all, his initial text had come through after eleven last night. But she just wasn't petty. And, hell, why risk a budding friendship?

What would Ruger think?

Who was she kidding? She knew why she'd responded to that text. She'd seen those scars on the outside of the man's body before they'd left for the airbase. Given her own scars, she knew the wounds on the inside were bound to be a thousand times worse—with far too many still raw and seeping.

She just could not add to them.

So she'd sent back a pithy *yep, saw it* and then caved into the guilt and had followed those typed words up with the ones Arash had really needed to see. *I'm home. Windows & doors locked. Glock next to bed. Ruger inside it. Nite.*

His response: *Thank you. Sleep tight.*

She'd promptly put the phone down, lest she was tempted to add more.

But, seriously? If the man tried that Tarzan routine with her again, they'd have to have a talk. And Arash *would* be listening.

As for her?

Right now—this morning—she was listening to something she hadn't heard in weeks. Months even. Ruger. The German Shepherd's deep, contented snores were drifting up from the foot of her bed. For the first time since that first line of bags had appeared out on Ol' Man Miller's road, she hadn't woken Ruger in the throes of terror.

Nor had Ruger been forced to wake her.

No nightmares.

Sure, with her history there was always the chance she'd trembled through one or two and dreamt she was back there in that hellhole with Max and just couldn't remember it. But she didn't think so. Not only was Ruger soundly asleep, she felt good.

Kate eased her right hand out over her Glock to snag the dive watch from the nightstand beside her bed.

06:55.

That explained the beginnings of daylight that were bleeding into the room. But she still couldn't quite believe that she'd slept for over six hours at a stretch, much less that her body and brain were so well rested, she felt as though it had been sixty.

But she'd take it. More importantly, she needed it.

Especially now.

Last night their case had changed. The actual killings aside, those first two crime scenes had several psychological elements in common—including the fact that whoever had stabbed and burned Aisha and Tahira had wanted the women's bodies to be seen. But last night? That placement of the third body out on that particular deserted road with all that natural cover and concealment on the other side said something new.

Yes, shoving the victim up against the northern perimeter of the airbase and setting it on fire had guaranteed it would be seen, and quickly. By the next car to pass, in fact. But something had changed within the killer.

He had wanted to see *them*.

Yes, he could've been hiding in Miller's trees, watching her, Tonga and Lou at the first scene. And he could've been hiding somewhere in or around the second scene too, possibly even holed up in a concealed space inside the old box plant—again, watching. But he hadn't been. She would've felt him. Like she had last night.

Like he'd *wanted* them to feel him.

But why? And what, if anything, did this new need to see and be felt have to do with those numbers he'd carved? With the Qur'anic verse that appeared to be behind them?

Despite the discovery of the third body, there was still only one way to find out.

Lily Basque.

Unfortunately, the only current path to Basque ran through Charles Praeger and the US Marshal who could connect Praeger and Basque long enough to get the doc to open up about what she was hiding...in just over an hour when the Marshals' office was scheduled to open in Little Rock. Kate glanced down just as the second hand completed a sweep around the orange face of her watch. The alarm beneath began to bleat.

Make that one hour, exactly.

Ruger's head popped up as she killed the alarm. The moment he spotted her looking at him, his dragon's tail began thumping atop the bedcovers.

"Morning, buddy. Ready to go outside?"

His lazy yawn and stretch said...eventually. But the Shepherd's bladder must've chimed in with a radically shorter timetable because he hopped off the bed, glancing back expectantly as his paws clipped along the hardwood toward the door.

"All right. I'm coming."

She attended to Ruger's needs first, heading to the kitchen to unlatch the dog flap so he could pass through the door. While he was out doing his job, she refreshed his water and measured out his morning kibble. That done, she set her own liquid breakfast of caffeine to perk and stopped at the table to rouse her laptop from sleep and check the electronic case files. She skimmed a memo and forensic report that Nester had added to the Kharoti folder, but there was nothing pertinent inside. Likewise, with the Mazelle Larijani folder. She hadn't been looped in on the Air Force OSI agent's casework yet, so that would have to wait.

Her review complete, Kate headed back up the hall.

Twenty minutes later she was showered and dressed in a fresh Braxton PD uniform with her Glock already holstered. Not only had she had enough time to leisurely wrap her wrist, she'd made her bed for a change.

Life was looking up.

Heck, Ruger had even dragged that giant piece of contraband Arash had given him into his plush, memory foam dog bed in the den while she was dressing and had settled in for a serious morning chew. She could smell the residual marrow drifting across the dining area and into the kitchen as she set her phone on the counter, and it wasn't even bothering her.

Surely that boded well for her coming showdown with the Marshals?

Or not.

The moment she finished filling her travel mug with coffee, her phone rang. And the number glowing up from the screen? It did not belong to Arash or Lou or Seth, or even Agent Wynne. Hell, it didn't even belong to Regan Chase.

But it was the number that had shown up on Regan's phone at Fort Campbell's CID office the day before. The same unlisted number that Regan had forwarded to her. The same number that Kate was absolutely certain was still unlisted.

Not that it mattered. She knew who was on the other end. "Morning, Chuck. How's life with the Company?"

As for her case? That was about to slam into a solid, incommunicative wall.

Why else was Charles Praeger calling her now? Less than a minute from her stepping out the door?

Praeger knew exactly where she'd flown to yesterday and who she'd visited after the C-21A had landed. Praeger also knew she'd flown back to Little Rock too late to abuse the information she'd obtained from Joe. Just as Praeger knew precisely when the closest US Marshals office was scheduled to reopen and exactly how long it would take her to drive there from the home address that the spook had also taken the time to locate.

Together, that all meant one thing. She was on the right track regarding the doc. She'd be damned if she'd let this asshole knock her off it.

"Leave Lily Basque alone." A nice generic, Midwestern newscaster accent.

Of course, that accent was probably as fake as its owner's name.

Kate switched off the coffeepot's warming feature. "Sorry, Chuck. I can't do that. I'm working a murder investigation, as you well know. Three now, in fact. We just had another body turn up late last night. And Dr. Basque—well, whoever she really is—has information that I need."

"Find another lead, because that one's a dead end. Basque doesn't know anything about your deaths. *Leave her alone.*"

A decisive click filled Kate's right ear.

Praeger had hung up on her.

Shit.

She hit redial, but the man didn't pick up. Not that she'd expected him to.

Now what?

Her visit to the US Marshals' office was moot. No one would be speaking with her on the record or off, if they even let her in the door.

While this would be a prime moment to head to Manchin and confront Basque, the doc wouldn't be in her office for another two and a half hours. And Kate still had zilch evidence-wise to support the warrant the doc had demanded. Without that flimsy piece of paper supporting a third visit, she wouldn't get through that door either.

Not legally.

Which was frustrating as hell, because Lily Basque was on the verge of cracking.

The proof? The SOS the doc had sent out to Praeger.

Kate could spend the next few hours reviewing the entire case file and looking for alternate leads they might have missed, but she'd done nearly that after she'd returned home from the crime scene last night, and she suspected that Arash had done the same.

Why else had the detective texted her as late as he had?

If anything promising had been added since she'd last checked upon waking, Arash would've sent her a text by now.

No, she still wasn't looped in on Wynne's folder. But given that jackhammer handshake at the scene last night, if the OSI agent had anything new, she suspected he'd have called up the supposed war hero himself and passed on the info to her directly.

Hell, she couldn't even run an internet search for connections between the doc and their current victim, because they still had no idea who the woman really was.

That left the one place and activity Kate would prefer to avoid given the charred state of their current victim.

The autopsy.

What the hell. She'd been on her way into Little Rock anyway.

If she abused the electronic cherry attached to the top of her Durango and applied a bit of extra pressure to the gas, she might even arrive early enough to acclimate herself to the inevitable smell before Arash, Bill Wynne and the ME arrived.

Kate attached her phone to her utility belt and donned her deputy jacket on the way to the den to tweak Ruger's ears. The Shepherd was so caught up with his new favorite toy, he offered up a few thwacks of that dragon's tail, but that was it.

He was good to go for the day.

So she left.

Traffic on the interstate was thicker than usual. Worse, a fender bender involving two SUVs chewed through her buffer. By the time she reached the airbase and cleared security at the front gate, she was racing the clock for first cut.

Kate finally arrived at the hospital clinic's information desk and followed the instructions she was given to the corridor that led to the autopsy suite. To her surprise, Arash and the OSI agent had yet to enter. The two hadn't even breached the door.

Arash took one look at the lingering frustration she could still feel pinching her features and met her halfway up the corridor. "What happened?"

She nodded to Arash, then Wynne as he too closed in. "I got shot down—by the main name himself."

Arash nudged aside the left sleeve to a fresh charcoal suit and checked the time on the smartwatch beneath. "That was quick."

"More so than you think. I didn't get to the office. Got a call from the guy while I was still in my kitchen. His message: 'Leave

Lily Basque alone.' He hung up and refused to pick up when I redialed." Naturally, she'd find another way to get through to the doc, but that was going to take time. And with the cadaver search not commencing until ten, "I figured I'd show up here and lend another set of eyes." She tipped her head toward the closed door to the suite further up on her right. "Is the ME running late?"

"No, I was. Just arrived myself." The OSI agent tucked his right hand into the hip pocket to his camouflaged utilities and surfaced with a smartphone. "Your information regarding religion and marital status paid off."

"You've got an ID on your body?"

"Yep. I was about to brief your partner, then call you. Guess I can run through it all once now." Wynne tapped into the notes app on his phone. "The victim's name is Samara Frasheri. She was married to an aviation maintenance sergeant by the name of Xhafer Frasheri. Sergeant Frasheri had duty yesterday and wasn't scheduled to head home 'til zero seven hundred this morning. After our info was disseminated, he was told to go home and check. He did—and she was missing. He contacted my office."

A solid alibi then. "Have you had a chance to meet with him?"

Wynne nodded. "That's why I was late. I showed him a photo of the left ankle and foot." The agent frowned. "It was the cleanest view I could get, and it had three small moles just below the outer bone. I figured it was a long shot, but—"

"He was able to ID her from the moles?"

"He was. And right off." The OSI agent scrubbed a palm over the exhaustion and hint of blond stubble cropping in along his jaw. "It was a rough meeting. Frasheri claims that he and Samara had a happy marriage, and that they were currently trying for their first kid. And, yeah, he was profoundly broken up."

At least the sergeant was alive. She was still all but certain the other two husbands weren't.

While she suspected Sergeant Frasheri wouldn't feel the same way if anyone voiced that pending reality to him, it was something to the three of them.

And one less stress point for the cadaver team.

Wynne dragged his free palm along his jaw once more, then lowered it to tap into his text app. "Anyway, here's the spelling on the names."

Her phone pinged along with Arash's. "What about a Christian angle? Have you found one?"

Wynne shook his head. "Not yet."

Kate nodded. Heck, there might not even be one to find.

Yes, Aisha had been dumped in a pastor's field, and Tahira had been attending a Bible-based support group for rape victims without her husband's knowledge. But the discoveries could just be one of those true coincidences that investigators stumbled across more often than they liked to admit. Mostly because they could bump an investigator off the real path and, worse, slow the case down.

Or were they simply missing something else? Another, uniting, link?

"What about the sergeants?" Yes, her gut was still telling her the first two wives were connected to Basque—and, hence, quite possibly this woman as well—but Kharoti and Larijani were both Army combat vets. Sergeant Frasheri might be an Airman, but he could easily be in that club. "Do you know if the men were stationed near each other? Or if they served together in Afghanistan or Iraq?"

"I did get a chance to run down that angle. And, no, I don't see an obvious nexus between all three sergeants' careers, or even a solid one between your two Army soldiers." The agent tapped out a second text.

A follow-on set of pings echoed through the corridor.

"That's the electronic link for the Frasheri case file and the password to get in. You can check out the notes I just uploaded on their careers when you get a chance. I'll let Captain Raub know we're all here for the postmortem and that he can get started. Join me when you can." With that the OSI agent headed for the door up on the right and entered the autopsy suite.

Kate retrieved her phone to make sure the case link had made it intact.

As Arash reached into his suit pocket for his phone, presumably to do the same, it rang. He glanced down at his caller ID, then her. "It's Hashem."

The man who'd cooked their dinner last night—and was working on that Sudanese Muslim-convert tip.

"Excuse me." Arash turned slightly and answered his phone in Farsi. He listened for a moment and appeared to answer in the affirmative, then hung up. "Hashem says he has something. But he doesn't want to talk over the phone or at his house. He has a brother visiting, so he asked if I'd meet him at his restaurant."

Kate nodded. "Go. I'll view the postmortem with Agent Wynne and let you know what the ME finds."

Fortunately, Arash didn't comment on her unilateral decision to kick him out of the hospital and across town, leaving her without the flashback buffer she'd somehow become accustomed to. There was no point. This was the job. Despite all the inescapable personal shit she brought to it, it still had to get done.

That said, her smile was admittedly a bit stiff.

But it was real.

"Good luck with Hashem." Whatever Arash's contact had discovered about the Sudanese convert, she prayed it produced a solid, viable lead.

Because they desperately needed one.

Yes, she was willing to apologize to Basque to try and soften her up. She'd even outright beg the doc for help. But deep down, Kate doubted it would work.

The woman was just too scared.

Arash nodded.

She was about to turn when he reached out and touched her sleeve, stopping her. "Something's changed with this bastard, Kate, and I don't know why. We've been looking at him. But last night? He's starting to look at us."

"I know."

"Be extra careful out and about today. Okay, partner?"

"Will do. You too, Arash."

He nodded, and they turned simultaneously. Arash headed down the corridor toward the elevator to leave. She followed the OSI agent to that dreaded door. She didn't bother removing her jacket. Autopsies were on the cold side.

Pausing in front of the suite, Kate drew in her nerves along with the last deep breath she'd be taking for a while, and pushed into the room.

She noticed two things right off. First, the ME had been at it a while.

Unless Captain Raub and the slender black female sergeant assisting him had decided to hold off 'til the end on taking samples from the array of organs that had already been removed from the body and were currently lined up in stainless-steel bowls along the counter on the right side of the suite, she had roughly thirty minutes left in purgatory, if that. Raub had not only completed the external exam and Y incision as best he could, given the charred condition and retracted musculature of the corpse, the ME had already made his way through the entire chest cavity. He was currently examining the victim's intestines as he offered up a stream of medical jargon for the microphone suspended inches above the clear shield covering his face.

Kate would've allowed her inescapable relief at the stunted session to filter in a bit longer had that second observation not taken hold as well. Agent Wynne's towering form was not posted near the body on the table, but was looming beside the door.

Wynne was clearly waiting for her...and he was royally pissed.

Because the ME had started so early and without him?

No. That wasn't the vibe she was getting from the blond brows clashing together above the agent's disposable face mask. Something else had angered Wynne, and she was fairly certain it had to do with their victim—and their case.

She accepted the mask and pair of latex gloves Wynne held out for her and donned them. "What's wrong?"

"The victim's husband lied to me."

Well, that did tend to happen in their line of work, didn't it? A lot. But to earn that scowl, this lie must have been a doozy. "What happened?"

"As you see, Raub got an early start. We had two airmen in the queue ahead of Mrs. Frasheri. But since those two airmen died as a result of a motorcycle accident, Raub wanted to take the serial homicide first, so he wouldn't miss anything due to exhaustion. He had Sergeant Lanier over there arrange for a set of X-rays before Mrs. Frasheri was brought in here."

Oh, crap. Kate knew where this was headed.

Given Aisha's issues with her husband and the X-ray results she'd already seen on Tahira Larijani, "They found multiple healed fractures, didn't they?"

The precise nature of which suggested abuse.

"Yep."

Yet another possible connection to Lily Basque and that

Underground Railroad for abuse that Kate was now all but certain Basque was participating in.

Were they looking for the husband of someone Basque had helped? A husband bent on defiling, stabbing and burning other women because his own wife was now out of his reach—due to Basque? Or was his wife still trapped in the marital net, and was their killer simply raging against his wife's nerve at wanting to be free—and taking it out on other women seeking their own escape through Basque?

Either way, why murder the husbands?

Was there a message there, too? Or, as Kate's gut was insisting, had Sergeants Kharoti and Larijani simply gotten in the way? After all, Sergeant Frasheri had been on duty. Leaving his wife unprotected. In this instance, as well as others.

Unfortunately, while Samara Frasheri's X-ray results connected her to Lily Basque in Kate's mind, it wasn't nearly enough for a judge.

That warrant.

Something that, as much as Kate hated to admit, she would need to physically have in hand when she headed back to Manchin to confront Basque now that Praeger had called and officially shut her down. If she didn't, at this point Basque would be within her rights to call another cop...on Kate.

"You want a closer view?"

She shook her head. "I'm good." The cold made the smell almost manageable from back here, along with all those insidious memories that, unfortunately, were still knocking against her jangled nerves.

Why push it?

Nor did the OSI agent argue.

If anything, Kate felt the man's stance settle in, though it was still tense. She glanced up and swore from the fresh pinch to those brows that Wynne, too, was fighting the stench of scorched flesh. His own private hell littered with battered Humvees, exploded IEDs and the bodies of far too many dead friends.

Welcome to the real War on Terror. Drawdown or not, it was still being fought on a damned near daily, sometimes hourly, basis. And would be for decades to come.

By those who'd been there.

Unwilling to draw attention to another soldier's pain, Kate shifted her stare to where she'd rather it not be. To that charred body on the table. She focused on Mrs. Frasheri's better foot. The left one her husband had been forced to ID. Kate was dimly aware of Captain Raub removing the woman's intestines and placing them in the sterile bowl his sergeant held out, before the ME turned back to what now had to be an all but empty abdominal cavity.

"Agent Wynne? Deputy Holland?"

Oh, shit. She knew that tension too, though this one had been sheering into the ME's voice. Raub had found something else. Something that didn't mesh.

But what?

The ME glanced up as she and Wynne approached the autopsy table. "Though it is not in her military dependent's medical record, Mrs. Frasheri has been hospitalized recently. *Very* recently. Take a look in here and tell me what you see."

Sergeant Lanier stepped back to allow both her and Wynne to move in close enough to peer into the victim's abdominal cavity. The muscle within wasn't charred, though it was cooked. But that wasn't the incongruous part.

Kate looked at the ME. "Stitches."

Raub nodded, even as he pointed back to the cavity. "Do you see anything else? Or rather, do you *not* see something?"

She glanced at the stitches that ran along the top of the

woman's cervix. The ovaries were present as well. But, "The uterus. It's missing." Surgically.

Wynne stiffened beside her. "Son of a bitch. Frasheri lied again."

That, the sergeant had. Because why would a couple try to get pregnant when there was no place for the fetus to grow?

But Raub wasn't paying attention to the peeved OSI agent. He was staring at her. He had more to offer. It was right there in those clear blue, *suspicious* eyes.

"What's wrong, Captain?"

The ME retrieved a pair of tweezers and used them to point to the cervix. "You see this knot in the suture thread on the far right? That daisy-petal flourish to it?"

"Yes?"

"I know who performed this LAVH and tied off that flourish. I should. I worked alongside her for six months at Bagram."

Craig.

Apprehension rippled down Kate's spine. For a split second, she thought about severing her stare. If only to protect herself from everything else she could now see inside the blue. *Recognition. Acknowledgment.*

"You were there, weren't you, Captain? At the Craig Joint Theatre Hospital. When I was there." Drugged up and strapped down in that quiet room.

When Basque was there.

Raub nodded. And then he flushed. "I didn't want to say anything last night. Figured you got put on the spot often enough. But, yes, I was there. I started out as a general surgeon —until a brush with an IED forced me to give up live patients."

"I'm sorry." And she was.

The ME shrugged. "I adjusted. I wasn't sure she ever would. Not to surgery, mind you. To the patients, to our surroundings. To life. She was always so...nervous."

"She?" *Wynne.*

But Kate knew. "Dr. Lily Basque. She removed this woman's uterus."

Again, Raub nodded.

Kate was about to question the ME further—and not about the woman lying on the table—when her phone pinged.

Kate retrieved her phone and glanced at the incoming text.

It was from Arash.

call me

Had Arash discovered something too? Something they could add to that flourish to gain a warrant?

At that moment, Kate wanted nothing more than to find out.

12

Both the medical examiner and Agent Wynne nodded as Kate excused herself and turned to depart the autopsy suite.

The second the door closed behind her, she peeled off her gloves and hit the tiny phone icon above Arash's intriguing *call me* text to do just that.

The detective picked up on the first ring. "Sorry. Hope I didn't interrupt. Did you get anything from the autopsy?"

"Yeah. It might even be enough for a warrant for Dr. Basque." She filled him in on Mrs. Frasheri's missing uterus and the rest.

Arash cursed. "That's definitely warrant material. But we may not need it."

"The warrant?"

"Yep. Just a sec."

Kate heard a car door snap shut. Probably the driver's door to his Explorer. A moment later, the engine turned over.

"Okay, I'm back. Hashem came through. We got a name. But it's not for the Sudanese guy. One of Hashem's customers recognized the photo you sent me from that *Al Jazeera* article. Lily Basque was born Layla Baqr. According to Hashem, Layla was born in Illinois. But nineteen years ago, Layla was married...and living in Iran."

"Wow." That Underground Railroad the doc had yet to confirm was making more and more sense. "How the heck did he stumble onto that?"

"Easy. He didn't stumble—the man jumped and willingly. Hashem's got a female first generation, Iranian-American customer whose sister left her husband. Rumor had it, it was because of abuse. Normally, he would never have broached the subject, even for me. But while he isn't military, Hashem is Muslim and married. He's terrified for his wife right now. So much so, he called the customer and asked if he could forward the *Al Jazeera* photo to her. Turns out there was no abuse, but the customer and her sister both recognized Layla. They all attended mosque together as teenagers near Chicago. They were in the same study group in fact, until Layla left for Iran a few days after she turned fourteen."

"They're sure that's where she was headed?"

"Oh, yeah. Her leaving made a huge impression. At the time —a good ten months before 9/11 went down, mind you—they all thought it was *exotic*."

Back then, and at fourteen, she might've too.

Not now. Nothing could persuade her to head back that way again.

Ever.

As for where she was currently headed, and just as soon as she informed Agent Wynne of her intentions? "You want to join me in confronting the doc?" Because she definitely had enough to get her inside the door. And with what she now had to offer, there was no way Basque would be threatening to call on any other cop but her.

"Wish I could. But I've got another stop to make. There may be more to learn."

Now that was tantalizing.

"How much more?" And where did he plan on stopping to get it?

From whom?

"The town that Basque was headed to all those years ago? The teenagers looked it up on the map before she left. Karaj is northwest of Tehran. It's basically a satellite city of the capital."

"Is that significant?"

"Not really. But I have another contact whose in-laws live up near Searcy. They moved to the States ten years ago. But they're from a smaller village just outside of—"

"Karaj."

"Yep. Unfortunately, they're Luddites, so I'll have to drive out to see them. Their son-in-law's meeting me to perform the introduction—also necessary. But even with an intro, I'll need to do more. They're older and more than a bit suspicious of authority figures. It'll help if I spend some time chatting and do the tea thing before I ask. If they have any real dirt to share, that'll be the way to get it."

"Go."

She could hear him grin. "Figured you'd say that. I'm pulling out of Hashem's parking lot now. I'll let you know what I find. Either way, I should be back sometime this afternoon, hopefully early."

"Good luck."

"You too, partner."

She hung up. Before she could return to the autopsy suite, the door opened. Agent Wynne's camouflaged form stepped out to dominate the corridor.

"The ME's done?"

Wynne nodded. "Yeah. They're putting it all back and stitching her up now. No more revelations to share."

"Well, I've got a huge one." She passed on the information

Arash had given her. But like Arash, the OSI agent turned down the invite to head to Manchin with her to corner Basque.

Wynne's reason?

"I need to have another chat with Sergeant Frasheri. See if he'd like to repeat that passel of lies he fed me this morning about his perfect marriage—in an interrogation room and under oath."

As with Arash, she wished the agent luck as he turned to stride further away from the autopsy suite while she headed back inside.

Captain Raub was about to stitch up the body. When he realized she was there to discuss Bagram and Basque, he passed both the thread and his task to his assistant.

Unfortunately, their conversation didn't last long.

Less than a minute after the OSI agent's departure, Kate was following Wynne's path out of the autopsy suite and all the way to the parking lot of the hospital clinic.

It seemed Lily Basque had kept to herself during her stint at Craig.

No shock there.

As many times as she'd worked undercover when she was CID, Kate knew exactly how much effort went into creating and maintaining a faux identity. It was amazing the amount of chitchat that filled the average person's day. Innocent comments about parents, lovers and friends. Memories of childhood. Schools. First jobs. Kids.

And when someone offered up their own tidbits about their life? Convention dictated you do the same. If not? Well, that was just odd. Suspicious even.

Since even minor comments could add up and eventually trip a person in a major way, it became easier to avoid people.

Lonelier. But easier.

Kate would've felt sorry for the doc, but for the fact that

she'd shown up at Basque's office twice now to ask for help in identifying Aisha and Tahira's killer, only to receive lies. She now had three murders to solve. A third visit to make.

Agent Wynne was right about one thing.

There would be no more lies.

Kate reached her Durango and climbed in. Slotting her phone into the hands-free attachment on the dash, she started the engine and drove across base toward the Arnold gate. She was about to phone Lou to bring him up to date when her ringer kicked in.

The call was from Seth.

"Hey, Kato. Is this a good time?"

"Absolutely." Talking to her favorite easy-going bubba just might help her walk back from the edge of her rapidly spiraling fury. Or not.

"Got a couple things to share. First off, I just wanted to let you know the cadaver dog and his handler arrived a few minutes early. No worries; I told Lou I'd deal with it. We're on site now and the dog's already begun sniffin' his way through Miller's trees."

Seriously? Not that they'd started earlier, but that Seth had volunteered?

While that was great news, "You sure?"

She or Lou could always call Drake and get him to stop by; take over if need be. Granted, Drake was still learning the ropes.

But the dog was doing all the work.

"Yeah, I'm sure. I've been feelin' like crap for dumpin' this all on you."

While that was a good sign, and actually boded well for the deputy's recovery, there was more here to consider. Like the fact that it might be too soon—for Seth.

If that dog was successful, the next step would be digging. Photographing. Identifying.

After several days in the ground, none of that was going to be pretty. With as many victims as she'd helped pull out of those mass graves in Iraq, she ought to know.

She cleared the base gate. "Seth—"

"I know. Like I said, no worries. Time to buck up, is all."

"Okay." This was his decision to make, not hers. "If you need me—for any reason—I'm just a phone call or text away."

"Thanks, Kato. I do appreciate that—and you." That last had come out a bit hoarse. Embarrassed. There was no need; they'd been friends for too long. But that raw note was probably why the man cleared his throat. "Anyway, about that other reason for my call?"

Kate mentally crossed her fingers as she stopped for a red light. *Please, please, let it be more ammo to use against Basque.* "Yeah?"

"Your gut was right about that second license plate. The sedan comes back to a nurse at Basque's medical office, though I'm guessin' you knew that. Name's Daria Farid. Single with no kids and no adults registered at her address either. But she's got two cellphone numbers registered to her name, and damned if one of 'em doesn't pop up on Mrs. Larijani's data dump. The calls started up six months ago. They were hot and heavy for a few weeks, then steadied out. Last one occurred a week ago Monday."

Kate caught Seth's yawn as he finished. He must've worked through the night to get the information. Heck, she knew he had, because she hadn't had a chance to forward the plate photos to Seth until after she'd returned from the Frasheri crime scene outside the airbase last night.

His efforts had paid off in droves.

No surprise there. Seth was a damned good deputy. He might hold to his initial decision and honor that resignation, but he wouldn't be happy about it. And their department would be the lesser for it.

The light changed to green and she nudged the Durango's gas. "Outstanding work, Seth. And exactly what I needed. Tell the sheriff I'm headed to Manchin to grill the doc, will you? I've got a new angle to work. With this added info of yours tossed into the mix, we just might get somewhere."

There was no need to offer more. Much less to get Lou's or Seth's hopes up. Not until she had something solid.

"Will do." Seth severed the call.

A mere ten minutes later, she'd reached the parking lot to Basque's medical office. A quick check of Max's watch revealed that it was barely 9:40. The office wasn't due to open for another twenty minutes.

The doc was here, though. At least, her sedan was.

It was also the only other vehicle in the lot.

Kate parked her SUV beside those aging silver wheels and bailed out. If her luck held, the frosted front door to the clinic would be unlocked.

Surprisingly, it was.

But where was the doc? Across this empty showcase of a waiting room and past the closed door that led to the hall beyond, calmly sitting at her desk and catching up on paperwork...with the front door unlocked and a killer Kate was damned sure Basque knew something about still on the loose, targeting Muslim women?

Or was the killer here—*with* the doc?

There might not have been tool marks on the lock to the front door, but three autopsies in three days for women whose profiles not only matched the doc but whose lives had also converged right here had Kate drawing her Glock as she crossed the waiting room. She reached the door at the far side and eased it open.

Silence.

No, not quite.

There. At the end of the hall. Coming from the room across from Basque's office. The muted sound of a drawer being pulled open, its contents rifled through.

Kate crept down the hall, 9mm front and center as she turned swiftly into the tiny room to find Basque wearing light blue scrubs with a long-sleeved white tee beneath and standing at the foot of an examination table with her back to her.

Basque turned, spotted the Glock and shrieked. The stainless-steel tray of instruments in her hands clattered to the floor.

Kate stepped all the way into the room and checked behind the door.

Clear.

She and the doc were the only ones there. "Sorry, Ma'am. I—"

"Why would you *do* that? Draw your gun in my surgical suite?"

"Surgical suite?" This was a surgeon's office, yes. But a consulting one, correct?

Or did Basque do more here in this weirdly sleepy, almost hollow practice than simply consult? Something beyond minor, outpatient procedures for her fellow local residents. Beyond helping Muslim women in need.

Something for which Charles Praeger would feel compelled to intercede on her behalf—officially?

From the fresh bout of fear in the woman's dark eyes, Kate was certain all of those conditions had been met at one time or another, including the final one.

The CIA didn't merely protect the doc; Basque worked for them.

Furthermore, from the lingering terror at getting caught, not to mention the array of formerly sterile surgical instruments scattered about the floor, the doc had been in the process of preparing to perform the latter.

Well, this could get interesting, couldn't it?

Fortunately, with Seth handling that cadaver search, she had plenty of time to wait around this place and see—from the inside.

Kate holstered her Glock then bent down to retrieve a stray scalpel, extending it handle first. "Got a patient coming in for minor surgery this morning, Doc? Or something a bit more involved? Say, an under-the-radar hysterectomy for a supposedly happily married Air Force wife?" Or something even more interesting?

And classified.

"What are you talking about?"

Oh, Basque knew. Unfortunately, the woman snatched the scalpel from her hand and spun away before Kate could get a clear shot at the second wave of emotion supplanting that guilt and fear.

Panic?

Based on the tremor that had taken hold of the woman's slender fingers as she laid the blade on the counter, definitely panic. And there was the way Basque continued to face the counter as those quivering fingers fine-tuned the position of that scalpel. "Never mind. I don't have time to speak with you, Deputy. I do have a patient arriving, however. Soon. And I need to be ready. Now leave."

"I will. After you tell me about your Underground Railroad for Muslim women in need." She'd get to what Basque did for Praeger and Company soon enough. "Specifically, I want to know what you did for Aisha Kharoti, Tahira Larijani and Sa—"

The woman spun around. "*Stop*. I wasn't exaggerating. I can't deal with your questions today. You need to leave. He'll arrive any moment now. He's—"

"Already here, Lily."

Kate spun around, her hand instinctively drawing her Glock. She took one look at the seemingly unarmed man wearing a black henley, matching cargo pants and boots leaning against the door jamb and shoved the 9mm home for the second time since she'd entered the building.

Basque was safe and so was she. At least from this man.

Asshole or not.

Like Arash, the newcomer holding up the jamb was dark haired and roughly six feet tall. He was similarly built, though not as impressively as the detective. His facial features appeared more Brazilian or Argentinian than Middle Eastern. This man was also two decades older than Arash, and his hair was salted generously throughout. His eyes were a muted, muddy green too, instead of rich, dark brown. He shared her partner's easy, unflappable demeanor though. And there was the generic Midwest accent the man had just used. The same accent she'd heard this morning.

On the phone.

Standing in her kitchen.

"Hello, Chuck."

Charles Praeger smiled. The generous twist was almost friendly. "Hello, Kate. For a soldier, you don't follow orders very well, do you?"

She shrugged. "*Former* soldier."

"Ah. That explains it."

They both knew it didn't. Just as they both knew exactly why she wasn't on Uncle Sam's payroll anymore.

Hell, so did the woman beside them. The one still quietly quivering in her baby blue scrubs and sensible, white tennis shoes.

How Basque operated with those nerves, Kate had no idea.

Praeger reached out to pat the woman's shoulder. "It's okay.

I'll handle this, Lily. You go tend to the other item on the agenda. I put him in the first room on the right. Daria just arrived. She's with him now."

The doc escaped, leaving the scalpel on the counter and the rest of the decidedly unsterile instruments scattered across the floor.

Kate ignored the spook's "handle" comment and focused on that more intriguing word. "Him?"

Praeger's smile strengthened. "No one you need concern yourself with, Deputy."

"I've got three dead women, Chuck. Each one stabbed and burned." She fixed her own faux smile into place. "Trust me; I'm concerned."

The man stepped into the room to scoop the remaining blades, a pair of tweezers and several other surgical looking instruments from the floor. He set them all on the counter beside the scalpel. Then turned around to lean up against it. "She doesn't know that I know about her—how did you phrase it? *Underground Railroad for Muslims.*" This smile was real. "I like that." The smile faded as he shrugged. "Anyway, the side job doesn't matter. It makes her happy, and it—"

"Doesn't interfere with the work she does for the Company?"

Another shrug. And another genuine twist. "Precisely."

Why not?

If the CIA could run a dusty, cargo plane airline/agency front out of the middle of Florida, Arizona, or even the northern hills of Montana and the like—why not a sleepy surgical practice hidden in the woods less than a sneeze's distance from Little Rock, Arkansas? She should probably take a look at their surrounding cargo plane companies.

"And how exactly did the doc land this gig of hers?"

That twist faded somewhat. "Well, we'd have to back up a few years for that explanation. Something I'm willing to do, mind you, given the seriousness of the circumstances. In light of what you used to do, I know you can keep your mouth shut. But I will need an assurance that you'll keep the details out of your casework, too."

"I can try." And she'd probably succeed. "But I have to be honest, Chuck, I'm working three murders. And my gut's telling me that Layla Baqr's tied firmly to them."

The twist returned at the use of the doc's birth name. "My guy was right. You are good. Guess I shouldn't be surprised. You took down that other bastard."

Joe.

Even if the spook hadn't known who she'd flown to see yesterday to get Praeger's own cover name, the reference would've been obvious. It was threading through those muted green eyes. In the spook's own issues with failing to see Joe for who he really was.

Welcome to the club. It was a pretty damned big one.

As for that thread of respect, she offered up a stunted nod, finally ready to own up to her part in the win on that one. She had taken Joe down. Eventually.

It was the eventually that would haunt her to the end of her days. She didn't need any more regret piled in.

There would be *no* fourth victim on this one.

Her determination must've made it into her own eyes, because the spook offered up a stunted nod in return. "I've been working for the Company for a couple of decades now, all over the globe. I started with them the year before 9/11. I was working in Iran when the Twin Towers fell. The country was desperate and so was I. I took my job seriously. A week later, I was on my way back from an early morning meeting with a contact, when I heard a commotion within a walled courtyard. Then screaming. A man stormed out, but the woman was still screaming. So I entered. I found Lily—as you surmised, then Layla Baqr—stabbed multiple times...and she was on fire."

Shit. The connections went deeper than she feared.

It also explained those long-sleeved T-shirts the doc wore under her scrubs, and the burn scars they were no doubt covering.

That realization must've shown too, because the spook offered another nod. Though this one appeared to be turned inward and more than a bit pained. "Yeah, quite the thing for a twenty-five-year-old kid to have to deal with. I put out the flames and staunched the bleeding as best I could. When I realized she was the eighteen-year-old American wife that I'd heard an Iranian bureaucrat had married, I did suffer a mild panic attack. But I calmed down and got her to a nearby safe house. While a friend and I treated her burns, she told me the rest."

The man broke off long enough to offer up a filthy scowl. "She wasn't eighteen; she hadn't even hit *fifteen* yet. She'd been raised just outside Chicago by her mom. Her Iranian father had abandoned them when she was three, then had the balls to circle back around when she hit her teens. Assured by her mom that she was still a virgin, the lying bastard brought the two of them to Iran for a second honeymoon and to 'get reacquainted'. She was married off within hours of the plane's landing. Never saw her mom again. I looked for the woman until I got reassigned. Even retraced her old haunts when I got back here to the States, but—" That shrug said it all. The spook believed the woman to be dead.

She probably was.

"Anyway, Lily's husband was two decades older than her and also her father's cousin. She was his second wife. The fucker married her to have the sons that eluded him. She was raped almost nightly for ten months. That last morning, she woke to news of a family wedding. But because she wasn't pregnant, she was forbidden to attend. But that lady down the hall? She may look fragile, Deputy, but she's tough. Damned near as tough as you are. She was determined to make a break for it, even if it meant her life. Unfortunately, the bastard had forgotten something. He caught her packing food when he came back. He was more than twice her size and royally pissed to find her on the verge of 'dishonoring' him, but Lily had made up her mind. She made it to the courtyard before he caught up with her. She told me that when she felt the flames, she knew it was over. Hell, if I hadn't been out in the street, it probably would've been." The spook shook head at that and fell silent.

The quiet settled for several long moments, thickening until the air in the room fairly pulsed around them.

From the darkness clouding into that muted green, the spook was still caught up in his retelling. In the memory. The horror of his own introduction to the inescapable reality of what one man or woman was capable of doing to another.

As tragic as the tale was, Kate wasn't shocked. Not much succeeded in doing that anymore. Not after what she'd lived through as a POW and in the years before. The things she'd seen done in the name of hate, and even love.

By soldiers and civilians.

The spook finally scrubbed a palm along the side of his weary jaw and sighed. "Okay, Deputy. I gave you our side. Now you share what you've got. Let's figure out who this fucker is and take him down, so I can get back to my day job."

Who could refuse an offer like that?

She couldn't. Not with three charred bodies in the state's morgues. "Given your...connections, I assume you've managed to access and read the case files?"

He nodded. "The first two. I haven't had a chance to skim the reports for the woman you found out at the airbase. It's the second file that made me realize I had to get my ass here and have a face to face. But I couldn't afford to have you coming at Lily without me by her side. That's why I called you this morning. I'd hoped it would buy me a bit more time. You gotta understand. Lily's strong and smart, but she's been through enough shit. And I had to make a stop to pick up a package on my way here."

Package? "The 'him' down the hall, I presume?"

Muted green met her query.

And that was it.

Right.

Well, that part really wasn't her business anyway, was it? Much less her job.

She had a killer to catch. Like it or not, it would take going through the evidence with the man silently staring at her...and waiting.

What the hell. "Well, Chuck, with three victims comes a new theory. At first, Detective Moradi and I were worried about an infection of radical Islamist behavior in the Army. Individually or as some sort of coordinated attack designed to appear that way. But our physical evidence now points to a serial killer. One who's religiously and sexually motivated."

The spook's brow spiked up at that last. "Sexual? Because of that weird rock you found beneath the first woman and inside the second?"

Kate nodded. "The ME found another stone inside last night's victim. And when you add that stone to four, thirty-four—"

"Thirty-four? The reports I read said it was a thirty-nine. Most likely, two of them."

Hence the need to snoop at *all* the files. "We now think the nines are angular fours. Also, the charring on the first two bodies was too heavy for us to be sure, but with last night's corpse came confirmation: we're looking at just a four on the left thighs of the women with a thirty-four carved into their right thighs. So, if you stand at their feet, and read them right to left you get—"

"*Surah* IV, thirty-four."

"You know of it." Given where on the globe Praeger had operated all these years, and that he'd have been expected to blend in culturally, of course he would.

The spook was already nodding. And frowning. "So you think it's someone who's connected to a woman Lily and Daria have helped?"

She had. Until today. These past thirty minutes. "You said Lily was stabbed by her husband and then burned—"

"No. It's not him. I wish it was that easy, Deputy. But it can't be. For one thing, while the bastard's still alive and kicking, he's doing it in Iran."

"And the other reason?" Because there was another. Something Praeger believed was impossible to get past. It, too, was churning through the muted green.

"Her ex thinks she's dead. Hell, her father must too. I...put another body in her place."

"*What*?"

He shrugged. "It was all I could think of on the spot—and I was damned lucky to get that inspiration. The man was a diplomat. Low-level, but still. He had serious connections. He had to believe he'd finished the job, or he'd have hunted her to the ends of the earth. I'd heard rumors about his dealings with folks who'd crossed him, and after seeing what he did to Lily, I believed them. So I pulled a switch. Like I said, he'd left for a wedding. In Iran, they can be a multi-day affair. Which meant I had time. I'd heard about an honor killing on the outskirts of Tehran the night before I stumbled across Lily. It too had ended in flames. Sick, I know. But it's not that unusual in that neck of the woods. So I did some checking. No one had claimed the corpse. The body was roughly the same size as Lily and so fucking charred her own mother wouldn't have been able to tell the difference. And, hell, it wasn't as though anyone was gonna run a DNA test. So I called up another operative and we paid off the guy in the morgue and put that woman's body in the courtyard in Lily's place."

A sharp gasp from the doorway cut her off. She and Praeger turned in unison to find the doc gaping at them.

"Ah, shit. I'm sorry, Lily. I should've told you. But you were so young. You'd been through enough. I didn't want to toss anything else on your back."

Basque nodded calmly. Too calmly. She was in shock and Kate was fairly certain it didn't have a blessed thing to do with whatever the doc had been doing for that *package* down the hall, but with what Basque had just heard her savior confess.

The woman scraped out a whisper. "Deputy Holland, you mentioned a hysterectomy when you arrived. Samara Frasheri. She's dead too, isn't she?"

"Yes."

Basque swayed with the verbal confirmation.

Kate lunged forward, but the spook beat her to it. Or rather, to Basque. He looped his right arm around the doc and guided her all the way into the examination room, settling her into a molded plastic patient chair at the wall.

Tears filled the woman's eyes, spilling over those thick lashes and soaking into the light blue scrubs that were still pristine, despite whatever medical procedure had been performed in the other room.

Given how many tears were falling and the depth of the shudders that were wracking those shoulders, Kate suspected this was the first time Basque had opened the floodgates this week and allowed herself to grieve for any of those murdered women.

By tacit agreement, both she and Praeger left the doc to her sorrow until it played out. The doc suppressed a hiccup as she finally wiped her tears with the cuffs of the long-sleeved T-shirt beneath her scrubs. "I'm sorry. I just saw Samara last week." She met Kate's stare square on. "Yes, I did her hysterectomy. It was that or let her bleed out. She was six weeks along, but she hadn't told her husband yet."

"Did Sergeant Frasheri beat her?"

Those dark orbs filled with more tears. "No. It was her father. She said she'd angered him over something she said, but Samara couldn't even remember what. A friend of hers knew about Daria—my nurse—and what we do." Basque turned to the spook, but before she could open her mouth, he shook his head reassuringly.

"I know. The Company knows."

"Of course." Her shoulders sagged that much more. "How did I think I could hide it from you?"

"It's not a big deal, Lily. I won't lie and tell you it hasn't proved awkward at times, but for the most part, the higher ups are fine with it. So am I." The spook tipped his head, directing the doc's attention back to Kate. "Now tell the deputy what she needs to know."

As those still streaming eyes found hers again, Kate took a moment to root through the stainless-steel cupboard beside her until she found an opened box of tissues.

She passed the box to Basque.

"Thank you." The woman blew her reddened nose. "Sergeant Frasheri was away last week for training. Samara refused to go to the hospital. By the time my nurse got her here, she was hemorrhaging. I had to do what I did to save her life. She was grateful, but she and her husband wanted that child. Samara begged us not to tell him what happened. She was terrified that if her husband found out and confronted her father, and that if her father lashed out as he always did, she'd lose her husband too."

The spook reached down to retrieve a fistful of damp tissues.

Kate waited as he tossed them in the trash in the corner of the room, then prompted, "And Aisha and Tahira?"

"I didn't lie about Tahira—exactly. My nurse still attends mosque. Daria's found many of those we assist through friends she's met there. They often come from many states away. But they don't need to be Muslim or married, just in need. With Little Rock's large, transient military community so close by, it's not that difficult to conceal them. And who would look for them here? We do what we can and help them to move on in Arkansas, or elsewhere if they need or want to go further. But Tahira? I never met or even spoke to her. Tahira was raped several months ago. Her husband blamed her for the crime. Daria found a support group for her to attend, and she was trying to empower Tahira to leave her husband. We would have assisted if need be."

"And Aisha?"

The doc's eyes filled with tears once more. "Aisha, I knew. She wanted to try a divorce first, so she wouldn't have to leave her mother. Daria and I were assisting her, but then she called a few days ago. She was terrified because Sergeant Kharoti was on his way to Conway. She called twice more to go over the procedures to file a restraining order, but then she called again. She said he was in town, at her apartment and that he was truly sorry he'd struck her. He swore he was in counseling with a Muslim chaplain and was working through his issues. She told me she loved him enough to give him another chance and then she hung up." A fresh tissue came out of the box. A fresh mopping of tears and a fresh blow of that excoriated nose. "That was the last time I spoke with her. Then you arrived and terrified me with all those photos."

"I'm sorry." And she was. But that didn't mean that given the same circumstances, the same stonewalling, she wouldn't do it again.

"I know. And I'm sorry I lied to you, Deputy. Especially about the numbers. You're wrong about them. This monster, he's not carving thirty-nines, but—"

"*Surah* IV, thirty-four." Kate nodded. "My partner figured it out, and it's supported by the cuts on Mrs. Frasheri's body. But you knew that the moment you saw the close-ups of Mrs. Larijani, didn't you? The ones I dumped on your desk."

"How could I not?" The question was rife with the terror and agony that had created it. "It was his favorite *surah*."

"Your husband's?"

"My jailor, my rapist." She shook head slowly. Defiantly. "That bastard was many things. But he was *never* my husband."

There was no way she could argue with that. Didn't want to.

Basque was right. You couldn't trap a woman in your home, abuse her for months on end and call it a marriage.

But from the furrows that had taken root between those finely plucked brows, the doc was also confused. "I don't understand. Why Aisha, Tahira and Samara? It's me, isn't it? I'm the only connection that makes sense. Except, it doesn't."

That remained to be seen. Kate hoped. Otherwise, she'd just investigated herself into a corner with no foreseeable way out. "Have you ever had a run-in with the husband of someone you helped? You or your nurse?"

"No. We're careful. *Very* careful." Her stare flicked to the spook for emphasis. "He taught us how to be for the other work we do. No husband has ever come to the clinic."

But that didn't mean one or two didn't know where it was.

That the killer hadn't been watching from somewhere amid all those surrounding trees. Recording the clinic's comings and goings, even taking photos of the license plates in the lot as she'd done, and using those numbers to gain more information.

Like names and addresses.

But since the doc appeared to be unaware of all of that or at least unwilling to consider it, she'd have to jar the woman's memory from another angle. "Dr. Basque—"

"Lily, please."

"Lily. According to my partner, *surah* IV, thirty-four is a favorite among many fundamentalists. Did any of the women you've assisted mention a husband who was obsessed with that verse? Or possibly a verse that involves stones or stoning?"

"Stone?" The doc's fingers gripped the box of tissues, crushing in the sides. "What kind of a stone? Was it white?"

Oh, boy.

Now they were getting somewhere. "As a matter of fact, yes. We found a small piece of white, milky quartz beneath Aisha. Another inside Tahira and another in—"

The box of tissues dropped to the floor as Lily jackknifed to her feet, only to sway so sharply both Kate and Praeger reached out to guide the woman back down. She fell into the seat, more tears dripping free as she bent over to blindly reach for the tissues.

Kate snagged the box and pulled half a dozen free, tucking them into the woman's hands so she could staunch this wave.

It didn't work. The tears kept falling.

"It's my fault."

"You do know him then? The man I'm looking for?"

"*Yes.*" Horror filled the woman's eyes, every taut muscle of her face. Hell, her entire body. "Vahid Baqr, my so-called husband. It has to be him. Who else would do that? With *that* stone? I never told anyone." She shook her head as she looked to Praeger, guilt and embarrassment tinging the pain. "Even you. I was too ashamed."

And with that telling comment, Kate knew exactly what else had happened in that courtyard. Unfortunately, the words needed to be on the record, not simmering in her gut or in her brain. But something told her that, after nearly two decades of having the memory behind them fester inside, the doc finally needed to say them too.

"Lily...what else did Vahid do to you that morning?"

Those swollen, tear-ravaged lips moved, but the doc couldn't quite seem to push out the words crowded up behind them.

The spook slipped the wad of tissues from Lily's hand and replaced them with his, then gently squeezed. "Can you tell the deputy what happened? Can you tell me?"

The woman took a deep breath and started again. But she wasn't looking at either of them now. She was looking into the past. At the pain. "After Vahid stabbed me, he grabbed one of the white, decorative stones that surrounded the base of the tree. He pulled my legs apart and shoved it inside me. Then he spat in my face. He said...he said that was all my opening was good for. Stones. Ten months and I'd yet to conceive a child, and now I never would. Then he dropped that match onto my chador."

The woman's gaze found Kate's, but those dark eyes had turned glassy. Sightless. "Late at night, I can still hear the scrape of the match lighting. Feel the flames licking up the fabric, consuming it. Consuming me. I remember screaming for him to make it stop, to help. But Vahid was gone." Those sightless eyes turned to the spook, finally managing to focus as one of Praeger's weathered hands came up to cup her shoulder. "And then you were there, putting out the flames and telling me it was going to be okay."

"It will be. I swear it."

The doc was back in the present now, but still clearly caught up in the terror of it all as she offered a soft, disbelieving shrug. "How can it be okay, ever again? Vahid is back. He found out I'm not dead, and he's determined to settle the score. But first, he's murdering those around me. Women I care about. That's why I stayed so long. He threatened to hurt my mom if I didn't submit. Aisha, Tahira and now Samara; it's my fault they're dead."

Kate shook her head firmly. "No. Lily, you can't—"

But the return shake she received was just as firm. And even more ashamed. "You don't understand. I know you, Deputy. I was there, at Craig, when they put you in the quiet room. I wanted so badly to go to you and support you as Charles had done with me; assure you that, in time, the horror would ease. But I was *terrified.* I wasn't supposed to be there. My WITSEC handler had warned me. He said if I went to Afghanistan, I might be identified. I disagreed. Vahid insisted I cover my entire face and body in Iran, and I obeyed. Those who did see me—other than my father and Vahid—they were all women. But then you showed up at Craig. And reporters began crawling over the hospital like flesh-eating bacteria consuming a deer. One of them saw me and decided to write an article about an Iranian-American doctor working in Bagram. I couldn't even say no, because that would've made him suspicious. Dig deeper into me. So I made it all about the patients, which was why I was there anyway. To give back. I told him my father had issues with my being there. He swore he wouldn't include a photo—"

"But he did."

Like the shake, that nod was filled with shame. Full disclosure had taken another knock between Lily and the spook, because that was something else the doc had left out of her conversations with him. "I'm so sorry, Charles. I don't even remember it being taken. I hoped it wouldn't matter. I was in profile and wearing a headscarf in the picture. And it was online, but at *Al Jazeera* not *The Chicago Tribune* or the *Sun-Times*. And the women who had seen my face in Iran would never have been allowed to watch or read the news, so I kept my head down and I waited. When a week went by, and then a month, then six, and no one noticed, I started to breathe again. I assumed I'd gotten lucky. Instead, I got those women killed."

Praeger shook his head, squeezed the woman's shoulder. "It's okay. Now that we know it's Vahid, we can find him. Stop him." He turned to her. "Right, Deputy?"

That was definitely easier said than done. The article had come out four years ago. Lord only knew when Vahid Baqr had seen it. How long he'd been plotting his revenge. The research he'd accomplished. The resources he'd been able to put into place.

And he was supposedly a diplomat?

Low-level, yes. But what kind of connections did he have?

Where were they?

What had the spook said? The man would hunt his wife to the ends of the earth if he discovered she was still alive. He'd just about gotten there. And he had every intention of going further. If Vahid had figured out how to make his way out of Iran and into the United States—to Manchin, Arkansas, no less, he had no plans to stop.

Not until Lily Basque was dead.

13

"I've ruined everything, haven't I? For everyone."

Kate waited for Praeger to reassure the doc, as he had several times during their discussion. When he didn't, those tears started up again.

Kate wasn't surprised. It had been a hell of an interview.

Even she was feeling raw. And desperate.

How on earth was she going to find a man savvy enough to have murdered three women the way Vahid had—in a country foreign to him, no less—and remain at large? Where was Vahid even staying? In a remote cabin somewhere? In Little Rock or in some other relatively nearby southern city with a fellow, like-minded Iranian expat?

If so, would Arash, with even his array of connections, be able to get a bead on the man in time for them to prevent a fourth murder?

To prevent Lily Basque's?

The quickest and surest path to protecting this woman would be to get Lily out of Arkansas. But while that would undoubtedly be safest for the doc, would removing Lily from her ex-bastard's reach enrage Vahid so much that he would continue to murder others in her stead? If he was even done with murdering others.

How many women had Vahid ID'd from the clinic?

Kate swore she could see the same questions and considerations whirling through the spook's brain as he stared intently across the exam room. While she too needed a decision from the man, at this precise moment, his charge needed reassurance more. And not from her. "Chuck?"

Muted green focused. The weathered cheeks beneath flushed. "Sorry." He reached up to give the doc's shoulder a squeeze. "I need to do some thinking. Arranging. I can't lie, Lily. Vahid's involvement does change things for everyone, but especially for you."

The doc nodded, albeit numbly.

He glanced from Lily to the hall. "I need you to do me a favor. Go check on our patient. I know, I know. Daria's good. But I'd like your call on whether or not the man's ready to move." Calm, steady. Praeger's voice and his words. Kate knew they were designed to get the doc focused on medicine again. An area of her life that Lily understood and where she'd feel a measure of control.

The spook was good.

And it worked. The tears dried up as the doc nodded. "And then?"

His hand came up to gently squeeze the shoulders of those scrubs once more, to soothe the still clearly terrified woman beneath as the inevitable followed. "And then I want you to gather up anything you need from your office. You might not be back for a while."

From the look he shot Kate as Lily stood to follow through on his orders, Kate was fairly certain the doc wouldn't be back at all—let alone remaining in the world as her current self.

Praeger reached out as the scrubs cleared the room and carefully closed the door behind their owner. "She's going to need a new identity. But I need time. I have..."

"A patient to secure."

This nod was not numb. It was decidedly crisp. "I've got a flight to get him on, and it's critical that I do so. I've also got a vital event that I need to attend this afternoon."

The spook wasn't going to share the who, what, where, why or how for that pending event any more than he'd be sharing his patient's identity.

Nor would Praeger be sharing his own real birth name. She wouldn't bother pressing for that identity either. Despite their newfound detente, the spook wouldn't give it—not unless information was mission essential. That was just the way the CIA worked.

It was also clear that the spook's pending event was not one that he could attend with Lily in tow.

No matter. Kate had her own agenda.

Fortunately for Praeger, one of the leading items on her To Do list involved his charge. Specifically, keeping the woman still known as Lily Basque safe. Her motivation had increased a hundredfold too, now that she knew the doc was an innocent target in all this.

"I'll take her. I'm sure you know where I live, Chuck, so you'll know where to pick her up when you're ready."

Not to mention that her place was easy to secure. There were enough trees cut down around the split log home that no one would be able to sneak up on her. And she had Ruger. Those ears and that nose of his would hear and sniff out anyone she couldn't see. The Shepherd did it on an hourly basis.

There were her own skills as well. Taking down eleven jihad addicts after as many hours of captivity in Afghanistan tended to provide one hell of an *I can keep the woman safe* bullet point to her own professional résumé.

Despite that résumé, the spook stared at her for a solid eleven seconds. One for each one of those bastards. Then nodded. "Okay. You need anything? Backup? Specialized equipment to extend your perimeter? I can call it in."

"Nope." That all came with Ruger. And she trusted the dog more than a van full of electronics.

Especially over some stranger she'd never met, and that would be who'd show with those electronics if Praeger made his call.

"I'll let Lily know. Back in a few."

The unspoken *wait here* reverberated off the walls as the spook closed the door behind him. Firmly.

Evidently, he didn't trust her not to try to finagle a peek at the only other man in the clinic. The one down the hall in what she suspected was closer to a surgical suite in a hospital than the bare bones exam room she was currently incarcerated within.

Admittedly, she was curious. But no matter. Kate retrieved her phone from her utility belt, determined to use the time and the privacy wisely.

First up: a lengthy text to Arash—albeit, sans names—to fill the detective in on the basics in case he needed the information to round out his tea date with Lily's former neighbors. She'd have preferred the give and take of a phone call to this much typing, but she was loath to disturb Arash.

Who knew if he was at a critical juncture?

From his *I'll be there ASAP* she knew he wasn't thrilled with the plan to babysit their killer's prime target at her house. But her suspicion that Arash was currently immersed in his own impromptu mission was sound, because he didn't take the time to offer more, much less insult her by arguing the decision.

She took the win and pasted the bulk of the text she'd sent Arash into one to Lou, highlighting her need to serve as babysitter for a few hours, then hit send.

Her third text was truncated and sent to Agent Wynne to let the OSI agent know the case was shaping up on her end and to provide the ID on their suspect. Her fourth and final text went to Regan Chase at Fort Campbell to inform the Army.

That done, she was about to call Seth to check on the cadaver search when her phone rang. "Hey, boss."

"Hey yourself, Kato. That's some mornin' you're havin'."

She spotted a stray pair of surgical tweezers on the floor, jammed up against the base of the exam table from when Lily had dropped the tray, and bent to scoop them up. "Yeah, it's been an eye-opener. I'll provide more details in person."

"Sounds good. Gotta be honest, though. Wish you had the time to swing past here. We got our hands full."

Miller's trees. The search. "Seth said you started early. How's the dog holding up?"

"He's done."

What? She pushed back the cuff of her jacket and checked the time on Max's watch. 11:10. They'd been at it for barely an hour and a half. "That's quick."

"Yep. That asshole you texted me about may be smart, but he got lazy. Leastways with the husbands. Cain't be sure, of course, but I don't think he expected or wanted to deal with them, 'cause he didn't dig all that deep. Hell, not that a hound wouldn't a found 'em anyways. But it mighta made it more of a challenge."

"You found both sergeants?"

"In the same damned shallow grave. No obvious cause of death, but we haven't moved them yet. They're lyin' face up and side by side. The bastard buried 'em about three feet down with a layer of dirt and leaves scattered over the top. Seth, Drake, Tonga and I are on site, already processin' the scene. Nester and his boys are on the way. That's why I called. I knew you'd want to see it all for yourself. You want me to send Seth or Drake to your place to swap out the guard duty for a spell?"

You bet she did. But she wouldn't.

Couldn't.

"This woman's too skittish, boss." Too damned terrified. "But I should be turning the task over to someone she trusts within a few hours." Which was the only reason the "Uncle Lou" inside her boss wasn't throwing his own overbearingly protective fit. The timelines they'd been able to piece together for all three women had shown that they'd been abducted after dark. "There should be enough daylight left after the doc's handoff for me to head out to Miller's place and get a sense of the scene."

Hopefully, Tonga would have an idea on cause of death by then too.

"Alrighty. I'll inform the Mazelle chief of police about the find. Keep in touch. And keep that Glock and that mutt at the ready. "

Both went without saying.

Kate severed the call and shot off a follow-up text regarding the discovery of the husbands to Arash, Agent Wynne and Regan Chase. Tea time was definitely underway and steaming along, because that update to Arash went unanswered.

Less than a minute later, the skittish woman at the center of it all opened the door to the room. Still wearing the white, long-sleeved tee beneath those baby blue scrubs, the doc had added an oversized leather bag slung over her right shoulder and a subdued gray herring bone coat tucked between her crossed forearms.

"I'm ready, Deputy."

Yeah, those eyes didn't look ready. They looked terrified.

She nodded anyway and added a reassuring smile. "It's Kate."

She motioned for Lily to don her coat, then led the way out of the building, instinctively scanning the parking lot and the thick stand of trees that surrounded it as the doc locked up behind them.

The Durango was the only vehicle in sight. Even the doc's sedan had been removed.

Lily's face fell as she noted its absence. Evidently, she wasn't looking forward to having her entire life erased along with her car before the day was out—again.

Kate left her charge to her thoughts as she pointed the Durango toward Braxton.

Although she could fake idle conversation with the best of them, she figured Lily would prefer that she concentrate on figuring out how the hell a non-native American had managed to pull off all three of those crime scenes.

And then there was the military connection.

Suspicion had begun to niggle in long before she turned off the highway to take the backroad around Braxton proper. "Lily, did Vahid ever visit the States?"

If so, how and why? The woman's ex might be a diplomat, but the formal exchange of consular personnel between the United States and Iran had been abruptly severed in 1979—and for a significant reason.

Silence greeted her curiosity.

Kate glanced across the front of the SUV. Her passenger was staring blindly out of the window at the passing trees, bottom lip quivering in her reflection. At least the tears had stopped. Or maybe there just weren't any left.

She reached out to tap the doc's arm.

Lily jumped. "I'm sorry. Did you say something, Deputy? I'm afraid I was thinking...about everything."

"It's Kate. If you're Lily, I'm Kate. Okay?"

"Okay."

The woman's whisper didn't sound all that confident, but Kate accepted it as she shifted her full attention back to the road. "I've been trying to think through a few things myself. Namely, how Vahid's been able to move around the States so easily."

Getting here would've been easy enough. But not by air. Given the security checks and the man's ethnic features, he'd have been flagged even with exquisitely forged papers. Coming by sea had its own issues.

That left land as the most likely route. Specifically, the southern border. At the moment, it was little more than a sieve, and honest folks born due south of the country weren't the only ones streaming across. Vahid would've fit right in.

But once he'd arrived?

"How good is the man's English?"

"It's perfect." Kate caught the soft shake of the doc's head in her periphery. "I'm sorry; I assumed Charles had told you. Vahid was raised here. In Chicago. He liked to tell me we had so much in common. We didn't. Not only was I fourteen at the time, he was thirty-four. He was also born in Iran and immigrated with his parents in the seventies when he was five. Vahid became naturalized though. He didn't move back to Iran until after he graduated from college."

Now that didn't seem to mesh. "Why not stay?" Especially if he already had his citizenship and a degree under his belt?

"Because the Army kicked him out."

Whoa. Kate slowed the Durango as they approached a yellow yield sign. So much made sense with that comment. "What happened?"

"Vahid joined the Reserve Officer Training Corps in college. His major was mechanical engineering. He wanted to work with rivers and dams, and a captain in the ROTC unit had assured him that the best way to do that was through the—"

"Army Corps of Engineers."

"Yes."

Kate waited for a Silverado towing a doublewide horse trailer to pass, then turned in behind it. Her private drive was roughly half a mile down the road.

"So did Vahid flunk out?" And had the disappointment been enough to twist him down that path of hate toward women?

"No, he graduated. I don't think his grades were all that great, because he would have lorded that over me, too. I do know that the week before, he was called into his commander's office at the ROTC unit and told that there was an issue with his security clearance. Vahid and my father, they had another cousin. But Bijan was a few years older and still lived in Iran. Bijan was involved in the Iranian Hostage Crisis. It came out during Vahid's background check, and he was rejected. Vahid was furious. At the Army and the country, and it didn't help that his ROTC commander was a woman."

Yeah, if he'd already had issues, that would have definitely jumpstarted a deep dive into fundamentalism.

It also explained why the bastard had begun with military wives.

Getting his revenge against the child bride he'd discovered had bested him all these years was one thing. Why not humiliate Uncle Sam in the process?

Perhaps those grades weren't that poor after all.

"I don't suppose you kept any photos of the man?"

The doc shook her head—firmly. "God, no."

Great. Not that she would've held on to one herself. But still—the absence made their search that much harder.

She'd put in a rush request with the Military Personnel Records division at the National Archives, but she doubted Saint Louis would be able to cough up an image either. Vahid would've attended ROTC in the eighties. Back then, the Army wouldn't have hung on to the man's photo, since he'd never received a commission.

That left attempting to track down an old high school yearbook or microfiched driver's license photo, and hoping like hell that the resulting computerized age progression was even close to what the bastard looked like now—if Vahid was even in the former and/or had bothered to obtain the latter.

Damn it. They needed something current, and they needed it *now*.

Kate turned the Durango into her private drive. Despite tree frontage roughly five acres deep, she could hear Ruger's greeting well before they reached the house.

As usual, the Shepherd was overjoyed to see her. So much so, he was waiting on the far-right side of the drive, near the front of the garage. But Ruger wasn't jumping up and down. He was in guard mode, maintaining a vigilant position at the entrance to the flagstone walkway...because they had company.

Lily tensed as Kate pulled in beside the waiting Braxton PD SUV parked on the left side of the drive and turned off her own engine.

"It's okay, Lily. That's Seth. He's a fellow deputy. I trust him with my life." Though that explanation didn't answer the question burning through *her* brain.

What was Seth doing here? Lou had said the deputy was with him at the Miller scene, and that they'd yet to remove the bodies from the makeshift grave.

Crap.

Lou. She should've expected him to pull something like this.

She pushed down her irritation as she bailed out of the Durango to give Ruger his *I missed you too* hug with her left arm while she waved her right between her guests. "Dr. Lily Basque, meet Deputy Seth Armstrong, Braxton PD." She gave Ruger a final hug and told him to sit beside her. "And this is Ruger."

The Shepherd's tail thumped into the pea gravel as he crooked up his right paw, instantly charming the doc. Even better, his spontaneity had put the woman at ease.

A genuine smile warmed Lily's features as she slung her leather bag over her shoulder and bent to accept Ruger's shake. "Oh, my. He's gorgeous."

That he was. "Thank you."

And *thank you, Ruger*.

If Arash didn't bring another one of those meaty bones by soon, she'd have to risk swinging past the butcher's to grab a few herself.

Kate motioned for Seth to follow as she headed up the flagstone walk to let them all inside the house. She waved Seth into her kitchen and gave the doc a quick tour of the rest of the place before depositing the woman in the den with Ruger and a promise that she'd return after she spoke with her fellow deputy.

Both doc and dog were curled up on the forest green cushions of the overstuffed couch before Kate left the room.

Time to deal with Seth. Find out what he was doing here.

And what was in the manila folder that he'd brought into the house.

The senior deputy was staring down at the stacks of casework on her table when she reached his side. Specifically, at a close-up of Tahira Larijani's desecrated thighs. One look at the fresh lines bracketing her favorite bubba's mouth and carving away his innate humor, and she knew exactly why Seth was here.

Her father was so wrong about his old high school buddy. Lou Simms was a lot of things, but dumb was not one of them. Lou's manner was just...different.

Got a deputy in danger of popping his cork at a crime scene because he was having trouble dealing with all the shit he'd endured at several previous crime scenes? Got another deputy who'd agreed to babysit the target of a serial killer? Why not lie to the first and send him on to guilt the second into accepting makeshift backup?

The proof was in the pristine manila folder still tucked beneath Seth's arm.

He held it out. "Here you go. The initial Miller crime scene photos as requested, fresh off the department's printer. Sorry yours is on the fritz."

Yeah, it wasn't. But she wouldn't embarrass a good friend, let alone their mutual boss by revealing differently.

"Thanks." Kate glanced at the burdened table as she accepted the folder. "The darn thing crapped out after all that printing."

Despite the fib, she did prefer working with hard copies. Which was probably why Seth had swallowed Lou's lie so easily. And since those hard copies were not only here, but in her hand, she opened the folder and flipped through it.

Even with the dirt still clinging to their faces, both men were easy to identify. Their missing sergeants were definitely dead. But like Lou had stated on the phone, the cause was not obvious.

Hopefully, Tonga was already working his medical examiner's magic.

She closed the folder and laid it on the table.

Seth was still staring at that close-up of those charred and mutilated thighs, still looking as though he was about to lose what she suspected was a nonexistent lunch. "How do you do it, Kate?" He waved his hands at the photos. "Deal with all...*this*?"

"And not let it get to me?"

He nodded silently.

"I don't." Because it did get to her. Always. And it should—with every single case. Because if it didn't? Well, she just didn't want to be that person.

Ever.

But *this* was the moment she'd been waiting for with him. The man had finally reached out to her. She had no choice but to extend a helping hand. "Seth, that horror you've got inside you? It's already entrenched. You can stop being a deputy, and I'm not saying you shouldn't, but quitting the force? It won't make that horror go away."

In the end, she hadn't even needed her chats with Dr. Manning to press that point home. She'd bailed on the Army after what she'd endured. It was four years on now.

Look how well that tail-tuck and retreat had turned out.

She extended her fingers and gently squeezed Seth's forearm. "If you want your life back, you're going have to learn how to drive the horror out on your own. But I can give you the number of a guy who can teach you how to do it."

"Is he helping you?"

She shifted her attention to the far stack. To the worksheet she'd shared with Arash. The sheet was turned upside down now. But because of what was written on the other side, she no longer felt as though she was in the same state.

No, things weren't perfect. Heck, they weren't even all that great yet. Manning was right; it was going to take time. Baby steps, even. But, "Yeah, he is helping. I am going to get there. And, Seth, I'd really like for you to get there, too."

The man nodded slowly, thoughtfully. "I'll let you know."

"Okay."

"Meanwhile, Lou wants me to stick around. Provide backup."

"Fine. But you're making the pizza. I've got a cheese one in the freezer. You can dress it up with a few veggies from the fridge. But first, would you grab the basket from the top of the dryer?" She reached out to tap the stack of autopsy close-ups. "I need to put all this out of sight." At least while Lily was there.

As Seth headed across her kitchen to loop around the pantry and grab the basket, Kate combined the smaller stacks she'd created while reviewing the files after she'd returned from the Frasheri crime scene and the airbase the night before.

By the time Seth returned, she'd made two larger ones.

She'd just placed the second stack in the basket when Ruger shot off the couch and across the den and kitchen. A split second later, the inner dog door was flapping in the wind.

Lily came sprinting up to the table next, panic and terror stamped along every inch of her face and body. "Is that—"

"Everything's fine." Kate allowed the amusement that had taken seed with Ruger's near-Olympic dash to blossom visibly. "It seems my partner has arrived."

And the four-legged creature in her life was hoping—praying—the detective was armed with another juicy bag of contraband.

Kate hefted the basket from the table and deposited it into her fellow deputy's arms. "Lily, Seth is going to set my files on the bed in my dad's old room for me." And, hey, she wouldn't have to face any crappy memories with his doing so in her stead. "Then he's going to get a pizza started for our lunch while I brief my partner and take a walk around the perimeter. Perhaps you'd like to help add the veggies?"

The woman relaxed as Seth tipped his head and smiled down at her. Kate wasn't surprised. That sedate bubba mystique of his could soothe a meth head off the ledge of a building in the middle of an active threat to jump.

She'd seen it happen.

As for her own lie of the afternoon, it was a white one. She was due for a briefing, but she'd be on the receiving end.

She hoped.

She could only pray Arash had learned something during this morning's impromptu tea that was worth sharing. While they now knew who they were looking for, they still didn't have a single clue as to how or where to find him.

Arash had parked his black Explorer behind Seth's department SUV. The detective was still hunkered down beside his front passenger door, scratching the base of Ruger's ears as she stepped out onto the porch. From the glance Arash shot her as she headed down the walk, she knew he had learned something during that tea.

From the way that glance shifted tellingly toward the trees, she also knew he'd prefer to share it in private.

She reached the pea gravel.

It took her disloyal mutt a solid five additional seconds of ear scratching before Ruger spun around to join her.

"I think I'm jealous."

The detective laughed as he stood and dusted off the lower legs of the trousers to his suit. "I'm just the shiny new toy. And I confess; I have another bribe in the car."

He turned to retrieve an oversized, brown paper lunch sack from within as she shook her head.

"It's more than that. Ruger likes you."

Arash grinned down as the dog bumped his nose into the back of the man's occupied hand in an attempt to regain his attention—and a closer whiff of whatever was in that sack. "I like him too. I suspect he knows it." He shrugged. "I wanted a German Shepherd growing up. Badly. The kid across the street had one, and I confess, I was jealous as hell. My aunt would've gotten one in a heartbeat, too, but she's allergic."

"And now?"

In anticipation of their coming professional conversation, the two of them headed down the garage side of the house by tacit agreement and kept on moving as they cleared the back of the split-log home to gain distance from the ears within.

Ruger was at their heels. Make that the detective's heels...and that paper bag.

"And now I live in a studio apartment. It doesn't seem fair, trapping a dog inside so small a space, let alone a guy as big as yours."

"You could always move."

"I've thought about it. My lease is almost up, too. But it would have to be a special place." The man's approving glance took in the modest, cedar horse barn near the treeline on their left, before sweeping across the brittle, overgrown grass of the four-acre dormant pasture until it reached the smattering of currently naked oaks, maples and hickory trees mixed in with the shortleaf and loblolly pines off their right. "Someplace like this, in fact."

His gaze had settled on the visible break in the trees.

There was no way she was copping to the vacant log cabin at the other end of that distant, shadowy path. The one perfectly sized for a bachelor ready to give up on life in the city. Ruger would have Arash and that seemingly bottomless supply of contraband moving in before nightfall.

As it was, her salivating mutt was staring intently at the sack in Arash's hands. The man laughed as he raised a questioning brow to her.

"Go ahead."

He pulled out a paper towel and began to unwrap it. "Don't look."

But she did. Not that she'd needed to. The large chunks of beef skewered onto that bamboo stick might be stone cold, but they were kicking off enough of a residual odor that, this close to the source, she'd have known what they were anyway.

Arash pulled off the first chunk and tossed it to Ruger, who neatly snatched it from midair. Her mannerless mutt didn't even bother to chew; he swallowed the chunk whole with a happy slurping groan, before snatching up and gobbling down the three additional chunks just as easily and noisily. There appeared to be something else inside the sack. It must not have been intended for Ruger, because it remained firmly inside as Arash curled down the bag's edges, sealing it.

The dog accepted that his feast was over. He gave the detective's fingers a quick, slobbering, thank-you lick and promptly bounded off past the barn to do his business as Arash watched him go.

Yep, man and beast were officially fast friends.

The detective took in the trio of human silhouettes spray-painted onto the sheet of plywood leaning against the barn's cedar siding. It made for a handy spot to practice her knife work. And she had been practicing. Though she'd replaced the plywood and paint at the start of those sessions with Manning, two distinctive spots within each silhouette had already been gouged down to bare wood—between the eyes and over the heart.

"Impressive." Arash's brow quirked as he glanced back at her. "I'll remember not to reach rudely past your plate the next time we share dinner."

She shrugged. Ironically, one of her dad's fellow deputies—and his only other friend on the planet—had taught her. Bob Feathers had even given her a set of throwing knives to practice with on her own for her sixteenth birthday.

Her dad had been livid.

Feathers had laughed outright and promptly told her father to his face that he was just jealous that his daughter possessed the natural aim he didn't.

As for her, Feathers had drawn her aside later in all seriousness and had admitted the real reason behind the gift—and the fact that he would continue to work with her, no matter what her dad said. Everyone knew she intended on enlisting at eighteen. That meant that, eventually, she'd end up in Afghanistan or Iraq—or both. Feathers had confessed that he didn't want her in danger any more than her dad did, but he also knew she was serious about becoming an MP. So he was going to make damned sure she was as prepared as she could be by the time she became one.

And Feathers was right. She had been forced to tap into the skillset a time or two over the years. For that reason alone, she kept up her practice.

As for Arash, the detective's humor had faded as he turned back to face her.

Well, crap. Whatever Arash had learned today was a game changer. Why else had the mere thought of it eradicated any remaining trace of levity in the man?

She glanced back at her kitchen window. At this distance, and with it lighter outside the house than in, all she could see was Seth's shadowy sequoia shape standing protectively near the doc's significantly shorter and more petite one. It was enough.

She turned back to Arash. "What'd you get?"

"Her mother's still alive."

"*What*?"

Arash had managed to discover in one morning what a CIA operative had tried years ago to get—and failed?

Then again, Arash was Army Intel. Arash was also a dual Afghan and Iraq combat vet, with all that entailed. And the detective had managed to track down and speak with another woman from the doc's former hometown in Iran.

Even with any and all lingering cultural issues, that was a conversation easier had between a man and a woman outside of a Persian stronghold than within.

Especially since it seemed that the male relatives in the doc's previous life enforced strict purdah, right down to the separation of the sexes and the all-obscuring shuttlecock burqa in lieu of the open veil that most Iranian Shias wore.

"Yeah, I was pretty stunned too. I'd hoped for something we could use, of course. But this? It complicates things."

That it did. "How badly?"

"Enough that I wanted to check with you first, before I shared my news with the doc. Dineh—the woman I spoke with —has known Vahid's family for years, including all three of Vahid's current wives and his cousin, the doc's father Masud Baqr. Though that's not really a surprise; the town was simply that small. Dineh left Iran about six years ago. She, her husband and their daughter were smuggled out via Afghanistan with the help of their son-in-law who runs a Persian carpet store in Little Rock. According to Dineh, she and Maya became friends a year after the doc escaped. It took another two years before Maya shared her tale with Dineh. It was the anniversary of her daughter's supposed death and Maya was grieving so deeply, she finally opened up. The reason Maya wasn't kicked to the curb following her daughter's 'honor killing' was because Maya had announced a new pregnancy mere hours before she and Masud learned of Basque's death. So Masud decided to wait. Prudent, I suppose, since his second wife, though younger and Iranian, had supposedly failed with that task."

She could see where this was headed. Hell, just about anyone could. "I'll take a guess here: Maya gave birth to a boy, and Masud decided she was worth keeping."

Arash clipped a nod. "And now the woman's trapped in Iran like her daughter was, along with Naveed, Hassan and Yasmin—the doc's two younger brothers and sister. According to Dineh, Maya had no interest in leaving, because she believed her elder daughter dead and that she was responsible since she brought the girl to Iran."

"And Dineh? Who else has she told about all this?"

"She swears no one. Given her husband's surprise during the telling, I believe her. But there's more. Something Dineh's been holding onto all these years—a picture. It was taken six years ago, just before Dineh left Iran. She's kept it as a reminder of her friend. Dineh wants the doc to have it." Arash shifted whatever was still in that paper bag to his left hand so that he could slip his right into his suit jacket.

He pulled out a worn, three-by-five-inch photo and passed it over.

It was of a seated woman in her mid-to-late forties. A boy about twelve years old and two younger children—another boy around ten or so, and a girl around five—stood beside her. Mother and daughter looked a lot like Lily Basque. And everyone in that photo was still in Iran.

Damned if Arash hadn't called it. This did complicate things.

A lot.

He sighed. "Yeah, I have to be honest. I'm not looking forward to the telling."

Oh, she got that. Because while Lily would be overjoyed to learn of her mother and siblings, the doc was bound to be terrified about her family's current circumstances, doubly so in light of the bloody rampage her ex was on.

Kate flipped the photo over. Someone, possibly Dineh, had written a date on the reverse, most likely when it had been taken. "Does Dineh—"

"Have a photo of Vahid Baqr?"

Kate nodded.

"No. I asked. I figured the doc wouldn't have saved one. Since it's been eighteen years since Lily has seen the bastard and only six for Dineh, I asked Dineh if she'd work with a sketch artist. She agreed, so I called the Searcy PD. They sent someone out. The artist arrived before I left. If we're lucky, we'll have something viable soon."

Kate's phone pinged as Ruger barreled out of the trees near the rear of the barn, the slight hitch to his gait noticeable as he swiftly changed course to chase down a gray squirrel. Fortunately for the squirrel, it beat Ruger back to the trees and skittered up the closest one.

She retrieved her phone from her utility belt and clicked into her most recent text.

It was from Lou.

She shared the latest with Arash. "We've got cause of death on the sergeants. Hypoxia due to exsanguination. Both men suffered a single, deep stab wound to their right lung, followed by a complete severing of their right popliteal artery." The wounds would've occurred in that order too, since the physiological fallout would've been covered during Neutralizing Sentry Duty 101. Stab someone in the lungs and they cannot scream, much less yell to warn others. In the sergeants' cases, their wives.

And that second slice across the back of the leg behind the knee? With the popliteal artery extending down from the femoral, the men would've bled out in roughly a minute, if not less.

And during that minute?

Both Sergeant Kharoti and Sergeant Larijani would also have been immobilized and unable to prevent what was happening to their wives.

What a way to go, even with the Larijani marital issues.

"*Shit.*" Arash scrubbed hand along the side of his jaw. "That would do it. But how the hell would some low-level diplomat know—"

"Vahid was US Army."

The detective's shock rivaled hers upon learning the news. And with each new tantalizing tidbit that she tossed on top—specifically the revelations concerning Vahid's Corps of Engineers aspirations, along with the revocation of his clearance and subsequent loss of his ROTC commission due to his cousin's involvement in overrunning Embassy Tehran in 1979—Arash, too, agreed: the motives, means and opportunities surrounding their cases and Agent Wynne's had coalesced. Become that much clearer.

She wrapped up her side of the briefing with the remaining information that the spook had passed along to her at the clinic, including the man's 'Charles Praeger' alias. Praeger was due to show soon. Arash would be meeting him at that point anyway.

As she finished, Kate held out the photo Dineh had given Arash.

He waved it off. "You give it to Basque, along with the explanation. You've established a rapport with her. Plus, with everything she's been through, I suspect it'll come easier from a woman than a man...and one who looks like her ex."

As much as she hated to admit it, Arash was probably right. "Okay. Let's get this over with then." She used her thumb and index finger to shrill out a whistle.

Ruger spun around in mid-lope and bounded up the middle of the field, tearing past them until he was leading the way to the twin doors at the back of her deck.

The dog might've sensed what was going on, or at least his mistress' mood, because he continued on into the den and hopped on the couch beside the doc, where he was duly welcomed and fêted.

Her fellow deputy was standing inside the kitchen, near the oven, waiting for the pizza to finish baking.

Kate signaled for Seth to remain where he was. Arash paused at the counter to deposit the paper bag he'd brought inside, then entered the den at her side.

Lily must've learned more from Charles Praeger than how to sanitize her Underground Railroad trail, because she took one look at their expressions and jumped to her feet. "What's wrong?"

There really was no easy way to say this. Kate opted for showing.

She held out Dineh's gift.

The doc accepted the modest, three-by-five-inch print. Her lashes flew wide as she realized what it was—*who* they were—but she didn't look up. She couldn't. Vahid himself could've entered the room and the woman would've failed to notice.

She was that absorbed.

A picture might be worth a thousand words, but that single photo was worth so many more...especially in tears. At least from Lily. But these tears were different than the ones Kate had cataloged earlier. Not only were these quiet and slow, they were infused with a thick, palpable joy and an utterly profound relief.

They trickled down for nearly a minute.

But then they changed. And these new tears, Kate knew all too well. Because they were infused with apprehension and absolute terror.

The woman swallowed hard as she looked up. "My mom, my siblings, they're trapped there, aren't they? In Iran."

"Yes."

Lily nodded carefully. A moment later, she sank back down to the couch. A moment after that, before their very eyes, the doc pulled all the way inward as she curled up with that worn photo and a willing and sympathetic Ruger.

Kate retrieved the oversized, sunflower-yellow afghan she'd received from a local knitter the previous Christmas and settled it over the doc, then ran her palm down Ruger's warmer, softer head and neck to let him know she appreciated the comfort he was offering a stranger. She turned around and headed to the kitchen.

Arash followed.

There was nothing else either of them could do, much less say to the doc, until she surfaced from her grief. The realization that three women and two of their husbands had been killed by her own monster of an ex; the reality that she was going to lose everything familiar to her since her life was about to be uprooted again; and now this—to discover that her mother was alive and that she had three younger siblings, but that they were all at the mercy of the man who'd given her to Vahid in the first place?

It was simply too much.

There'd be no connecting, no further information about Vahid. Not from the doc. Not until that shock wore off.

Arash's phone pinged as they reached the table. He slipped the Android from his suit jacket and glanced at his incoming text, then into the kitchen.

Seth, bless him, took the hint and announced that he was going to walk the perimeter of the clearing.

Arash waited to speak until the front door closed behind her fellow deputy. "You think Praeger will be able to pull her out of it?"

"I think so." From what she'd seen at the clinic this morning, the spook had a way with his charge, an almost father-daughter touch. Not surprising, given how old Lily had been when the man had found her, and what Praeger had risked for her back then in Iran and in nearly two decades since in the States.

"Good. Because Dineh came through. We've got a sketch. And it's pretty detailed." Arash tapped his screen several times.

A moment later, her phone pinged.

"I just sent it to you. I'd like to run it past the doc before I leave, see if she can add anything, but—" Arash glanced over at the afghan-covered figure huddled up with Ruger on the couch. Lily was still clutching the photo, but she wasn't looking at it anymore. She was staring at the wall. "—I'm not sure that woman can focus right now."

Kate nodded. "If Praeger's delayed much longer, I'll see if I can talk her out of it."

And if she couldn't?

Well, Ruger could work miracles when he set his canine heart and brain to it, along with his burrowing muzzle and those full-on fuzzy body hugs. Look how he'd managed to pull her back from the brink. More times than she could count.

"I'll show her the photo and let you know what she says. But I wouldn't delay getting it out there." They needed that sketch in front of every cop and especially every married, military Muslim couple in the state, hopefully within the hour.

Accomplishing that would have to be the detective's job, since she was stuck here for the time being. Not to mention that she and Seth had a list of Underground Railroad ticket holders to compile, phone and warn as well.

"Agreed. Good luck. If something comes up and Praeger does get held up, let me know ASAP. I plan on stopping back when I'm done with the sketch to assist with any calls that are left to make, but I can also come prepared to relieve Deputy Armstrong for the night. Until then, watch your back, partner."

"Sounds good. You be careful, too."

Arash nodded as he turned toward the living room. "I'll let Armstrong know he can come in."

"Wait."

Arash stopped. Swung back.

She pointed toward the bag he'd set on the counter. "You forgot that."

"Nope." A slight smile tipped in. "That's yours. By the way, Hashem's glad you liked his *khoresh bademjan*. He expects to see you dining in at his place soon."

Hashem? Surely Arash hadn't—

She reached for the bag as the front door closed. A swift

peek inside had her shaking her head and smiling, because Arash *had*.

The man bribed Ruger with thick bones and chunks of meat. Her treats were vegetarian and far tastier. And this one smelled amazing.

Fresh flatbread.

Ignoring the audible growl in her stomach, she left the bag on the counter for later and pulled up the photo Arash had texted.

He was right. Dineh had done well. There was enough detail here to get their all-points bulletin underway. And with that distinctive mole riding the ridge of Vahid's left cheek? Unless that mark had been surgically removed at some point during the past six years, it might just get the bastard identified—and caught.

She was about to forward the sketch to Lou when her phone rang.

Praeger.

There was only one reason the spook would be calling her again, instead of showing up in person. Arash's feared scenario had come to pass.

There was a delay.

Shit. She opened the connection. "How much longer?"

Praeger didn't miss a beat. "Not sure yet. There's been an issue with finding and securing an adequate location. Given all that's happened to the woman, not to mention the determination of the bastard who's after her, I refuse to just leave her anywhere."

Not only did Kate understand, she agreed. But, "Got an estimate?"

"I may not be able to swing by 'til the morning."

Christ. Kate whirled around to face the den, the couch and the afghan-covered woman still huddled upon it. The hell with Arash's fears, she had her own to deal with.

Her body language must've radiated what her voice had not, because Ruger's head popped up over the padded arm. She could make out that canine concern even with the dining area and the width of the den between them.

"That gonna be a problem?"

"No." Yes.

Because an impromptu sleepover would undoubtedly involve sleep.

Hers.

She and Arash would have to work in shifts, one up while the other slept. It was the only way to keep the guard currently on duty fresh and alert.

Yes, she'd managed to make it through the previous night without enduring a dream so horrific and intense that Ruger was forced to wake her.

But that was one night out of the last four weeks' worth of nights.

What were the odds she'd be able to repeat it?

And while Arash would be okay with her waking up in a cold sweat and screaming at the top of her lungs, would Lily?

Granted, the woman was a doctor. And, yes, Lily knew about those hours she'd spent as a POW in Afghanistan four years earlier. But discovering that half of her protective detail *still* suffered from full-blown PTSD, including night terrors and quite possibly sleepwalking? Yeah, that would make the woman feel safe.

"Kate?"

She could hear the propellers of a twin engine on the smaller side as they cut in. Was that plane—and the spook—even in Arkansas?

"It's fine. Do what you need to do. We'll be here."

The spook shot off a terse "Thanks" and severed the connection.

Kate slid her now dormant phone into its slot on her utility belt as she turned to stare out through the window at the open field and trees beyond.

How she'd be spending her night was the least of her worries. The critical question was—how did Vahid Baqr plan on spending his?

And where?

14

She woke to screaming.

It wasn't hers.

It took Kate a full two seconds to shake the sleep from her brain and locate the source of that terror. It was coming from off her left, deep inside the den.

Kate shoved her chair away from the kitchen table and the laptop she'd dozed off over and bolted. By the time she'd vaulted into the den and reached the couch, a more heavily armed and woodland-camouflaged Arash had entered the house through the front door and was coming up behind her—fast.

Ruger, bless him, already had everything in hand.

Or, rather, muzzle and paw.

Their now significantly quieter charge was sitting up on the couch, her rattled brain and quivering nerves still locked inside a terror that, although completely different from Kate's, appeared all too familiar in the middle of the night.

Lily took one look at Arash's face as the detective rounded the knobby pine coffee table and clutched Ruger closer.

He slung the AR-15 rifle over his shoulder and bent down. "Dr. Basque, are you all right?"

Instead of answering his query, Lily shrank further away from Arash, pulling the Shepherd with her, until doc and dog were cornered by the back and far arm of the couch. Not only did Ruger not complain, he snuggled in deeper.

Arash turned to Kate. "I'll...go back outside. Resume my rounds."

"Okay."

She waited until his bootfalls had left the room, then stepped forward to gather up the yellow afghan, which had fallen to the area rug between the coffee table and couch, holding it out with her left hand as she heard the front door close. A quick glance at the Doxa's exposed face on her wrist revealed the time.

06:09.

Not quite late enough to rise and start the day. Especially since Praeger had yet to follow up on yesterday's call and propose a handoff plan, let alone a time for its kickoff. But how to soothe the doc and lull her back to sleep, even for another hour?

Ruger and Lily were already curled up around each other. But even that warm, burrowing muzzle hadn't succeeded in vanquishing the memories. The ones Kate could see clouding those thickly lashed eyes, keeping them wide open and overly alert.

"Lily? Would you like some warm milk or tea?"

The woman's chin wobbled as she shook her head.

"Would you like me to go back to the table?"

Another side-to-side wobble. But this one was firmer.

"Okay." Kate walked over to the oversized rocking chair that Lou had crafted for her and her dad as a housewarming present years earlier. Dragging the rocker out of its corner at the far side of the den, she parked it between the dormant, wood-burning fireplace and the occupied corner of the couch. "I'll just sit here for a while." Silently.

Why not? It wasn't as though she hadn't been there herself. In precisely that spot on the couch, with damned near that precise time on the clock. And, of course, with Ruger wrapped up around her, and her wrapped up around him.

Mere days earlier.

Perhaps she should've had Seth stick around for the night instead of heading home for sleep after Arash had shown up shortly after dinner to relieve the deputy of his impromptu backup duties. Seeing Lily this torn up, nearly two decades after her bout in hell, might've added more weight to the offer Kate had made to Seth regarding Dr. Manning's assistance and phone number.

The sight was definitely motivating her to stick with her therapy.

"You're wondering why I went there, aren't you?"

Kate focused on the still trembling doc. "Excuse me?"

"Afghanistan. Craig. You're wondering why I risked it."

Well, yes.

She offered a soft smile instead. "Lily, I'm—"

"Not judging me. I know. And I do appreciate it." The woman paused to press her face into Ruger's warmth for a steadying moment, then lifted it. "Not as much as I appreciate you loaning me this incredible guy, mind you, but..." She shrugged. "Yeah. You of all people do deserve an explanation."

Kate shook her head. "You're wrong. I don't. No one does. You don't owe anyone anything you don't want to give."

"What if I do...want to?"

"That's different." If Lily needed to talk, she'd listen. Kate suspected Ruger's hugs would help more, but she'd try. She had a whole handful of sessions with Manning that she could attempt to mimic. "I'm here if you need to vent."

The doc pressed her lips together, then sighed. "It was you.

Your fellow soldiers. All of you. I had to give back. It's the reason I do what I do for Charles and the others at my clinic in Manchin. You have to understand, WITSEC gave me more than a new identity; they gave me a life. And when the time came, they made sure there was money in the form of a scholarship for medical school, too. But back then, when Vahid tried to kill me? The twin towers had fallen the week before. By the time I was able to travel, there was a team of Special Forces soldiers already inside Afghanistan, preparing for the invasion. Charles got me to the border of Iran. Soldiers from that team brought me all the way across Afghanistan and handed me off to another team in Pakistan. Before my burns had completely healed, I was safely home in the States. For so many years, I've needed to pay down that first debt. But all I had to give was my knowledge of medicine and my time. So that's what I offered."

It was a hell of a lot. What her fellow soldiers had done for the doc, and what Lily had turned around and given them in return.

Medical care was everything to a grunt on the front lines. And Kate didn't need that glowing article to know that this woman had given the best.

"I'm sorry I avoided you at Craig."

Kate smiled at that. Then laughed.

The doc stiffened.

"I don't mean to be rude. Truly. But, Lily, I was so drugged up in that quiet room, I didn't remember getting a visit from a soldier who turned into a serial killer. I doubt anything you could've said would've stuck with me long enough to help."

Her admittedly dark humor flagged as the rest of those significantly darker, more current memories of Staff Sergeant Burke simmered in. The ones from the month before.

From the anger and distaste pinching Lily's lips, the doc

knew who and what was behind them too. Anyone who lived in the state probably would have.

Ruger must've picked up on the deepening of his mistress' mood as well, because he shifted his head to look at her.

Kate reached out and smoothed her fingers along his muzzle so he'd know she appreciated that ever-present, steady support. Even now, with a woman he didn't know clutching him close. "Trust me; you don't owe me anything. I went over there, even suffered the consequences, because of my own need to serve my country."

"I'm so sorry you were raped."

That set her back a bit—and made her think. About a lot of things.

The irony of it. That this particular woman would feel so badly for her. Kate might've been raped by nearly as many bastards as she had fingers, but she'd been unconscious at the time. How did that compare to getting violated night after night by the same bastard for ten months—and remembering every single one?

"Yeah, I'm sorry, too. But more so for you. I don't remember what happened to me. Not that part. I was still knocked out while those assholes were having their fun. What I do remember, what has me screwed up to this day, are the things that happened to my friends. So, I guess you could say that I have no right to—"

The doc's hand shot over Ruger's head to latch onto hers and hold on tightly. "Oh, you do, Kate. You *do* have the right. If I've learned one thing helping all those women that I've been fortunate enough to know, it's that horror comes in so many disguises. And there is no way to compare them, nor should there be. What happened to those women, and to me, does not negate what happened to you or anyone else."

Kate couldn't help it; she smiled. She was beginning to see

why Lily Basque—even with her serious case of temperamental nerves and tears—was so successful with that Women's Railroad. Hell, maybe those jitters gave Lily an edge.

They did make the doc approachable. And they definitely made a person want to listen to her. To believe.

Yeah, Seth should've definitely stuck around.

"What is it?"

Kate shrugged. "I've got another friend who should be sitting here, listening to this, is all." She reached out as the afghan started to slip, tucking the scalloped edge beneath Ruger's monster paws so it would stay put. "And I do agree with you. Though I admit it's taken me a while, and I had a lot of help getting there. But what I don't understand is why you're sitting here beating yourself up. You went to Afghanistan to give back—and you succeeded. You should be proud of that. Despite what Vahid's done to taint it."

Given how she'd phrased that last, Kate wasn't sure what she'd expected in return. Agreement? Another argument?

What she got was...nothing.

The doc had done more than fall silent, though. Her fingers were working into the fur at Ruger's neck so deeply that he was beginning to shift and squirm. Another couple of those squeezes and the Shepherd just might abandon the couch—and his charge—altogether.

That said, Kate didn't think the doc was even aware of what she was doing.

She closed her fingers over Lily's and shifted them from Ruger's fur to the tight yellow loops of the afghan. "I'm sorry if I said something to upset you."

That glistening stare finally met hers. It was stained with guilt...and shame. "You didn't do anything. It's me. Giving back? That's not the only reason I went. I did go for the troops, but I needed to prove something to myself too. I'd spent a decade and a half hating my father for giving me to that monster. But I hated Vahid more. For the things he did to me and the things he made me do to him. Helping those women? It wasn't enough. No matter what I did, who I helped, it never quite banished the ugliness inside. I think I really went there because I wanted to prove to myself that I'd won, not him."

"But that's not—"

"A bad thing? But it is. Because that's not all. Deep down, I think I *wanted* him to know I was there. That I was still alive. That I'd *beaten* him. And that means that Aisha, Tahira and Samara, their murders are on my head. Their husbands' too."

"Lily—"

"*No*. You *can't* absolve me. Even if you could, there's more. You and your friends have been protecting me all night. Heck, even your dog spent the night trying to keep me safe and sane. And Charles? He's working through the night to find a new place to send me. If you and your friends and Charles succeed, then Vahid won't. What happens then? Because it's not just about me anymore. What if he gets so angry that he couldn't find me, that he decides to go home? My mom, my brothers and my sister? They're all trapped in Iran with the same monster who gave me to Vahid. And Vahid? He knows where they are. What if he decides that, if he can't kill me, he'll kill *them*?"

Those temperamental tears began to spill again, and this time, there was no staunching them.

Worse, the doc had tuned out of the world—completely. Lily simply tugged Ruger closer and burrowed back down into the cushions of the couch, into herself.

Lily was so upset now that all Kate could do was pray that Ruger would stay long enough for the woman to sob herself to sleep.

Again.

Kate leaned forward and tucked the afghan in around the

doc. She gave Ruger's muzzle one last lingering stroke and stood to depart the den.

Stopping at the table, she closed the lid to her laptop, then headed into the kitchen to start yet another pot of coffee.

As the coffee finished brewing, she looped back through the den to check on its occupants.

Ruger was still on the couch, awake. But the guilt of the Craig confession punching into the stress that had already been steadily beating against the doc's heart and soul these past few days must've done her in, because she was out cold.

Thank God.

Kate caught the motion of Arash's camouflaged form just beyond the shadowy planks of her cedar deck. Since he'd thoughtfully brought along a pair of night vision goggles with that ArmaLite rifle when he'd arrived to take over from Seth last night, she'd agreed that he could take the midnight shift.

The cuckoo clock was chiming out 06:30.

She should've relieved Arash two and a half hours ago. But instead of calling to wake her for the turnover, he'd stayed on watch. He had to be exhausted.

Even before she'd nodded off over those electronic case files on her laptop, she'd begun to suspect that Arash preferred to remain outside while Lily was here, patrolling the perimeter of the property, rather than coming in to crash on the recliner in the den. The hurt and resignation that had threaded into the man's face as the doc had spotted those distinctive Persian features of his—and shied away—had confirmed it.

Kate knew that hurt and resignation well. She should. She'd been best friends with both for four years now. The irony of the turnabout hadn't escaped her, either. Tonight, Arash's face had terrified. And hers?

For once, it had actually soothed.

But at what cost to him?

It didn't matter that she understood Lily's instinctive fear. Kate was still pissed—for Arash.

She donned her Braxton PD jacket, then filled two mugs with coffee and brought them out onto the chilly deck. Ruger seemed to sense that she needed him inside with the doc, because he didn't follow.

Arash had sensed her as well, and he did turn and head back to her. She handed off one of the mugs as he joined her up on the deck, at the rail.

"Thanks."

She shrugged. "I owe you for the bread."

Okay, so it might've been the fourth or fifth cup of coffee she'd handed him throughout the night, but it was fantastic flatbread.

The man's half-smile quirked in, only to fade as he balanced the night-vision goggles atop the cedar rail. Sunrise was half an hour away now. With twilight already beginning to bleed into the four acres of dormant pasture, the NVGs wouldn't be of much use during his next pass.

Or needed.

Her gut was even more certain of the latter.

Arash took a sip of his coffee as he turned to scan the clearing. "Where the hell is he?"

"I have no idea." Nor did Vahid's absence make sense.

Following Praeger's call yesterday afternoon, she'd followed through on her plan to phone the clinic's nurse and had asked Daria to create a list of all the women that she and Lily had assisted. Daria had then phoned each one to warn them and tell them to head somewhere safe—immediately. Seth had taken that same list of Daria's and informed the respective police departments, so that they could conduct drive-bys at the very least, even if they were strapped for personnel.

With everyone covered, Vahid should've felt pressured at the loss of secondary targets and risked going after the one woman he wanted to kill most of all.

But he hadn't.

Surely a man smart enough to do what he'd been doing would've realized that, with his primary prey missing too, she was likely holed up with one of the detectives working the cases? And with Arash in a cramped studio apartment and Agent Wynne living in a suburban home with his wife and kids, surely Vahid would've realized Lily was here? Hell, shouldn't he have stopped by for reconnaissance at least?

"Kate, if he was going to show, he'd have done it under the cover of dark."

"I know." Vahid had for the first three murders. The timelines they'd been able to establish between Aisha, Tahira and Samara's deaths proved that.

So why hadn't he shown up here for that all important attempt last night? And why did the man's absence give her pause?

Either way, her cleared acreage had lightened up even more, the nuances within growing more discernible by the minute. She could make out the faint shapes of the silhouettes on her practice board beside the barn. Vahid would be a fool if he showed now. And that was the one thing the bastard had proven himself not to be.

They'd remain on alert until Praeger arrived for the handoff, but Lily was in the clear. At least for now. After five losses over the past week, three of them seriously sadistic, she'd take the win. They all would.

Arash took another sip from his mug and turned around to brace his camouflaged backside against the rail of the deck as he stared through the double glass doors that led to the den. Their charge was still out cold on the couch.

Ruger, however, was wide awake and watching them in return.

Arash tipped his head toward the doors. "Where'd you get him?"

"Ruger?"

He nodded.

It must've been those bionic ears of his, because the dog knew they were talking about him. She was doubly certain when that dragon tail began thumping against the afghan.

She smiled. "I guess you could say Ruger got me. I found him out behind the guest cabin my dad built." Not that her dad had ever invited a guest to stay in it.

But that was another story.

The detective turned to shift his mug toward the right side of the clearing. "The one through the trees over there? Made of logs?" He settled back in against the rail. "Nice place. I saw it on my passes during the night."

As vigilant as Arash had been?

Of course, he would have.

"Yeah, that's it. It happened three years ago now. The short version? Hunting season had started. I heard a shot, went to investigate and I came across a six-month-old pup bleeding out from some blind asshole's bullet. I caught a glimpse of the hunter's rifle—a Ruger—but declined to give chase. I rushed the pup to the vet instead. Doc Wilson fished a round from his pelvis; that's how Ruger got his name and his limp. We've been inseparable since."

"You're lucky."

That she was. She appreciated that Arash recognized her incredible fortune in it all. Most folks who heard the tale assumed Ruger had been the luckier one that day.

They were wrong. "He hates men, you know."

That garnered a raised brow and a soft chuckle. "I never would've guessed that."

"It's true. He loves Lou and he likes the vet who saved his life, and he tolerates Seth on occasion—though he still refuses to let the guy up the front walk if I'm not home—and he pretty much growls at every other male he's ever met. Except you."

"What about Ruger's mistress?"

"Excuse me?"

"You heard me."

She'd heard him. She just couldn't quite believe what he was asking. Implying.

Look at the man. Look at her.

Sure, Grant had been willing to screw her. He'd claimed that he cared for her, too. Loved her even. But Grant had been tangled up with his own demons.

And Arash? The detective was out of her league. Even before her face had taken that IED-fueled trip through the meat grinder. Men who looked like Arash Moradi simply were not interested in a woman like her. Ever.

Fellow trusted cops? Sure. Battle Buddies even.

But that was it. And she knew it.

Right?

"Arash...I—"

"You have the most incredible eyes, and I'm not just referring to that mossy gold-green. They light up and pull me in when you're happy. They pull me in even deeper when you're not. Either way, I can't look away. I don't want to."

She had no idea how to respond.

Surely, he couldn't be serious about this. About her.

Could he?

That wry smile he'd given her earlier quirked in. "Kate, this can't be a shock. You counted my calls. There had to be a clue in all those rambling voicemails I left. Say around message six, seven or eight?"

Wow.

Okay, then. But she still—

Ruger growled, deep and low, and shot off the couch.

A split second later, the Shepherd was barreling through the kitchen toward his inner dog door. A second after that, she and Arash were locked and loaded.

One more second, and Arash and the AR-15 he'd brought to the party were headed across the back of the house and around toward the front—because that's where Ruger was headed.

She was racing in the opposite direction.

15

As Ruger and Arash sprinted around the house to greet their uninvited visitor, Kate and her Glock breached the double doors that led off the deck and into the den.

She vaulted around her coffee table and grabbed a waking, groggy Lily with her free hand. Pulling the woman to her feet, Kate half carried, half hustled the doc, sunflower afghan and all, out of the den and down the hall into the windowless bathroom. There, she ordered Lily to lock the door behind her.

The moment Kate heard the bolt slide into place, she took off for the front door.

By the time she'd raced out onto the flagstone path that led to the drive of her home, a midnight-blue Bronco had pulled up into the double-wide pea gravel several feet behind the detective's black Explorer.

Charles Praeger turned off the Bronco's engine and sat calmly at the wheel, waiting for her to call off a silent Arash and his not-so-silent assistant.

"*Ruger*."

The dog obeyed her soft order instantly, backing away from

the driver's door and sitting down at the edge of the dried, winter grass. But those low, steady growls of his were still reverberating deep in his chest.

She nodded to the detective as she holstered her Glock. "Meet Chuck."

Arash lowered his weapon.

Praeger smiled at him as he opened the door of his SUV and climbed out, still wearing the black henley, cargo pants and boots she'd seen him in yesterday. "Remind me to call ahead the next time I decide to visit."

Arash's nod was substantially cooler than the surrounding sunrise-lit air. "Consider yourself reminded."

Jesus. She wasn't sure who was more annoying, her dog or her partner.

The spook shrugged. "He's right. I should've given a heads-up. Meant to. Then got sucked into an overseas call on the way here. One that shunted my thoughts in a different direction. Sorry." He glanced up at the house. "Where's Lily?"

"Locked in the bathroom."

"Good. Keep her there for a few more minutes."

Arash's brow rose at that.

Praeger offered another shrug. This one was heavier and significantly more pointed than his first. "That call I took concerns her—in a roundabout way. According to a contact of mine at Homeland Security who's currently in the hot zone, her father was scooped up in a raid on a terrorists' safe house about ten hours ago...in Herat."

Afghanistan?

Kate glared at Ruger to get those intermittent rumbling growls of his to cease completely as she stepped closer to the spook.

First Vahid, and now his cousin? "What's Masud doing out of Iran?"

"Damned if I know. But given everything that's been going on with Lily's ex this past week, it can't be good. I also can't help but wonder if it's connected somehow."

Agreed.

"All the more reason for Lily and me to get moving. The place I've arranged to put her is almost ready, and the new identity is in the works with WITSEC. They should have that finalized soon, too."

Arash slung the AR-15 over his shoulder. "Why the rush?"

Kate's brain echoed the query. For the moment, Lily was safe. Why risk moving her before everything was one hundred percent good to go?

Because while the cousins' behavior *could* be connected, one of the men was still firmly over there, roughly seven thousand miles away, and currently detained by the Afghan government. The other had two armed cops and a zealous Ruger in his path.

"Paranoia. The kind that's kept me alive. That raid? It wasn't us. A local militia executed it—without bothering to tell our guys they were headed out to play. And then they waited damned near ten hours to loop in the central government."

"Shit." US troop drawdown in the country currently in force or not, that didn't bode well. Especially since the local militias in Afghanistan tended to be riddled with informants loyal to anyone and everyone *but* the sitting government in Kabul, including the Taliban, Al Qaeda, ISIS...and the Iranian Quds Force.

Praeger nodded. "Yeah, something stinks in Herat. Unfortunately, I don't have a spare minute to figure out which end of the cesspool this new odor's coming from. Not with that bastard cousin of Masud's running around this continent, carving up military wives. Once I get Lily set up in her new spot, I'll fly overseas and figure out what the fuck's going on. I'll get word back to one of you to pass to the other—*if* I can. That's all I can promise."

It would have to be enough. Especially since both she and Arash knew Praeger's bosses at Langley wouldn't be thrilled with even that potential bit of sharing.

Then again, given Arash's intricate, civilian stateside network, she wouldn't be surprised if someone in *Major* Moradi's overseas military network didn't end up backfilling the information to the detective anyway.

Either way, "Okay. Let's get the doc moving. Do you have clothes for her? She wouldn't accept anything from me, so she's still dressed in yesterday's scrubs."

The spook shook his head. "No time. I landed less than an hour ago. Daria's moving on too. I tried to keep the two of them together for the move, but—" Another shrug, this one weighed down with regret. "—with such short notice, it wasn't possible. They might be able to fix that later. But for now, someone with WITSEC will pack up a few things for the both of them and forward them on separately."

The spook followed her and Arash up the flagstone walk. Ruger was at their boot heels, still smoldering over this new human male's presence on his turf.

But at least he was being quiet about it.

Praeger paused at the steps to the porch. "Almost forgot. Kate, I got your text about Maya and Lily's younger siblings." He glanced at Arash. "If it's at all possible, Detective, I'd like to speak to your contact. See if she's got anything more that can help me get those four out of Iran. Though that, too, will have to wait."

Arash's phone rang. "Let me know when you're coming back through the area. I'll set something up."

"Appreciate it."

Kate opened the front door and motioned for Praeger to precede them into the house as the detective accepted his call.

She was about to follow when Arash touched the sleeve of her jacket.

The detective continued to listen to whoever was on the other end of the phone as he motioned for her to stay out on the porch with him. "Just a moment, Remy." Arash glanced to where the spook had paused too, just inside the doorway. "The doctor's down the hall on the right. We'll be right behind you."

Remy? As in Detective Langlois with the Manchin PD?

Oh, Lord. This was going to be bad.

The dread intensified as Arash kept his hand on her sleeve, silently guiding her to the opposite end of her porch as he informed Remy that he was back on the line, then proceeded to listen to whatever else the man had to say for over a minute.

Arash thanked his caller and hung up.

Crap. First Remy's name and now that grim glint within the shadows that were overtaking the exhaustion in Arash's stare.

"It's Vahid, isn't it?"

"Yup. I know why the bastard didn't show up here last night. He was busy."

Oh, *no, no, no*. "The nurse."

"Yeah. That's was Remy Langlois out of Manchin. I'm guessing you know him, since Remy seemed to know you. Daria won't be needing that new WITSEC identity. Seems she stopped by their clinic in the middle of the night to get something. Water delivery guy showed up about half an hour ago. He saw blood inside, so he tried the door. When it opened, he could smell gasoline. He followed the odor into a back office. Daria was lying in the middle of the floor, stabbed repeatedly. She's dead."

The doc gasped from the doorway—and that was it. No scream followed, no tears. No fainting. The woman just stood there, pale and swaying slightly.

"I want to see her."

"Lily, no. You don't have to do this." The spook reached up

from behind her, settling his hands on her shoulders. The support steadied the doc's entire body.

When her nod came, it too was firm. "I do. I need to see her." She pulled the herringbone coat she'd brought with her more tightly around herself. "I know you all think I'm not strong enough, but I am. I loved Daria like a sister. I want her avenged. The others too, but Daria most of all. You both have been trying to find Vahid for days now. If I go, I may see something that will help. Something that no one else will see. Especially since that office she's lying in is mine." The woman stepped all the way out onto the porch and reached for Kate's hand. "*Please*."

Kate looked to Arash. They both knew Remy would need to speak with the doc anyway, so that he could work his case effectively.

Arash nodded.

She looked to Praeger.

He shook his head.

"Fine. Let's go. Charles can drive you to your next locale from there."

The outvoted and out-jurisdictioned spook scowled as he led his charge down the flagstone walk and assisted her into the front passenger seat of the Bronco.

Kate knew the spook assumed that she and Arash were simply desperate to solve their cases; that that was why they'd agreed. And, yes, they were desperate.

But it was that *please* that had sealed it. At least for Kate. She'd have needed to do the same thing in Lily's place, and for the same reason.

She glanced at Arash. "I'll meet you there."

"I'll wait for you."

"Don't bother. I need to toss Ruger his kibble before I leave."

Arash tipped a nod her way and headed down the walk as well.

Kate entered the house and locked the front door behind her. She took a minute to feed Ruger and secure the doors leading from the den onto the deck, but that was it. Yesterday's deputy uniform and wrist wrap were worn and wrinkled, but they'd have to suffice. Nor would her partner be detouring through Mazelle just to change those camouflaged utilities and boots he'd worn while slipping between the trees of her woods all night.

She gave Ruger's ears one last tweak and headed for the garage to back her Durango into the drive.

Arash's Explorer was still parked on the left side, with the detective standing beside his driver's door, arms hooked along the edge of the roof, patiently waiting. They both knew he didn't need the clinic's address, much less help typing it into his GPS unit.

The man had simply, neatly, avoided the argument —with her.

She rolled her driver's window down. "You're irritating; you know that?"

"So my aunt says."

"Smart woman. Listen to her." She rolled the window up and backed all the way out to the edge of the pea gravel to execute a ninety-degree reverse turn before settling in for the twenty-five-minute drive to Lily Basque's soon-to-be former clinic in Manchin.

Arash and his Explorer were right behind her the entire way.

Her irritation had long since ebbed. It wasn't as though Daria Farid was going to get any more dead because Arash had been determined to wait for her. Or Lily any more upset by it all.

Though the doc was plenty upset by the time they arrived.

And those endless tears had returned.

At least, that's what she and Arash were told by the uniformed patrolman when they stopped inside the frosted glass door to the clinic to don their latex gloves and paper crime scene booties.

Though the doc's absence would've become apparent as they reached Lily's chilly office.

There was only one person inside, the Manchin detective that both she and—from the tenor of that phone call on her porch—apparently Arash knew well.

Remy's nod covered them both. "Hey, guys. Dr. Basque's with a male friend in an exam room at the end of the hall, waitin' to speak to you. She was able to ID the victim, but that was it. Poor thing was too broken up over the sight here to do more."

Kate nodded. "We heard." But Lily had tried. She'd give the doc that.

Remy waved them deeper inside, even as he walked to the door. "Make yourselves at home. Word came down while you were on your way here. My boss has already spoken to both your bosses. Looks like we're all on the same team until we catch this bastard. That said, I need to find out what's holdin' up the ME. Back in a few."

Arash waited until Remy departed, then joined her at the body. "Is this the woman you saw in the waiting room during your second visit?"

"Yeah." It seemed she had met Daria when she'd stormed into the clinic following Samara Frasheri's autopsy, though briefly. "I don't know what's worse, the sulfur byproducts or this stench." Someone had opened the windows to vent the office. But while the surrounding air in the room was decidedly crisp, it still reeked of gasoline.

The pungent fumes jarred with the sleek, Queen Anne cherry desk three feet to their right and the *Architectural Digest*-ready couch and coffee table to their left.

And there was the naked body lying on the carpet in front of them.

Unlike the other victims, the nurse still had her crown of short, raven curls, and except for the smeared blood and dozen stab wounds marring her torso, abdomen and thighs, her skin was smooth and blemish free. But those wide, glassy pupils that had already clouded over?

Daria Farid was definitely dead.

Arash hunkered down near the pads of the woman's feet. "Remy thinks Vahid was interrupted. Could've been the noise. On the phone, he told me they had a housefire up the road about three in the morning. The engine company screamed right past the clinic's drive. Three or four bellowing cop cars followed. Might've spooked the bastard and made him bolt instead of lighting that damned match."

That *damned match* Arash had referred to was lying roughly fourteen, fifteen inches from the victim's right hand, just beneath the coffee table. Beside it was the light blue matchbox that had most likely contained it. And on the top of that box?

The flourish of Arabic script.

Kate retrieved her phone from her utility belt and snapped several close-ups of the box and the unexpended, wooden match. Yes, Manchin's forensic team would be through here any moment now to do the same thing, but it was an old CID habit she just couldn't seem to kick. "You want me to forward these?"

Arash nodded. "Thanks."

She shifted her attention to the woman's naked thighs. Without the charring, the numbers were raw and bloody, but excruciatingly legible.

"*Surah* IV, thirty-four."

"Yeah." She snapped another succession of close-ups of those obscene carvings, then stood to forward the photos to Arash.

As for the potential presence of a small stone of milky quartz shoved inside this woman, they too would be waiting on the arrival of Remy's ME.

"*Fuck.*"

"This is not your fault, Arash."

"It sure as hell feels like it."

"I know." Lord, did she. She'd been so smug in their impromptu plan to keep Lily safe while laying a simultaneous trap for the doc's bastard of an ex.

But Vahid had gotten the drop on them anyway.

And this woman had paid the price.

Kate lifted her phone and took a series of overall photos of the desecrated body, along with the deep splotches of scarlet staining the surrounding carpet.

That chore finished, she carefully walked the perimeter of the room, snapping more overall photos and close-ups of anything and everything she or Arash might need while they were reviewing the case later, together or separately.

Not much fit, but she took the photos anyway. Aside from leaving the immediate scene, it was the only thing she could do to give the detective space.

This uncharred body might be easier for her to view than the others had been, but it was anything but for Arash.

The detective was still standing there at the feet of the corpse, staring at it.

Transfixed.

Despite their plush surroundings and that pungent stench of gas, this woman had to resemble his sister following her murder. Especially with those wounds.

The stench of gas might even be making it worse. He and Azizah had been stabbed in their garage, after all.

From the slight glistening of Arash's gaze, she suspected so.

Kate finished her painfully slow photographic loop and returned to the center of the room, to that defiled body and a still frozen partner.

The glistening had grown worse.

Screw procedure. She'd grab a spare glove off someone later.

Kate reached out, latex and all, and pressed her fingers into the man's camouflaged arm, gently pressing into the taut, quivering biceps beneath.

He flinched.

"Arash?"

That tortured stare finally refocused on her. "Sorry."

"It's okay."

"I was...thinking."

That she knew, just as she knew who he'd been thinking about. But it was equally clear that he didn't want to talk about who had hijacked his thoughts, let alone why.

She let it slide.

Given all he'd done for her, how could she not?

She watched as the man visibly pulled himself from the mired muck of his own past, returning to the present with a sharp, cleansing shake of his head.

He drew in his breath and frowned. "Kate, Seth said that when he spoke to Daria on the phone, she told him that she was holed up at a friend's apartment, that she'd be staying there until her new identity came through. The apartment had a doorman and security. So what was she even doing here? What could be worth the risk?"

That same question had been tumbling through her brain as she'd snapped those overall photos of the body. "Could be a new client for the Railroad called. If the woman was desperate or currently in danger, Daria might not have been able to resist one last assist."

Arash's frown deepened. "Or maybe Vahid put a woman up to making that call and ambushed Daria when she arrived to unlock the door."

Both were equally likely. Remy would forward the data

dumps for the clinic and the nurse's phone once he had them. But even then, would they ever know which?

"Kate, I want this bastard. Badly."

She nodded. "Let's go see what Lily can tell us."

As they headed down the hall, she and Arash realized Lily wasn't in the mood to tell anything. At least not quietly. The doc was shouting, and at the top of her lungs.

"You can't *stop* me!"

Kate used her gloved left hand to knock firmly on the exterior of the door to the exam room, even as she used her right to turn the knob and push it all the way in.

"Hey, Chuck, you got a problem in here? I hope not, 'cause the entire Manchin police department's getting a charmingly audible blow-by-blow."

To her surprise, the doc whirled around and vaulted toward Kate, grabbing her upper arm in nearly the same spot Kate had recently grasped Arash. But these fingers weren't gentle and soothing, they were frantic. As was the woman's tear-stained face.

"Tell him it's *my* life, Kate. *My* decision."

Praeger stepped toward them. "Damn it, Lily—"

"No!" The woman glared up at the same man Kate had seen her clinging to in this very room less than twenty-four hours earlier. "I am *done* sitting around and waiting for that bastard to come after me or someone else I know. Daria is *dead*. If I can do something to help catch him, I will. And I don't care where I have to go to do it."

She and Arash glanced at the spook, but Kate spoke first, parroting the most intriguing word that had come out of the doc's mouth. "*Where*?"

Praeger raked his hands through his hair, hair that appeared more salt than pepper than it had in her drive back in Braxton a mere hour ago. "Lily overheard a phone call and suddenly she's Wonder Woman wielding some asinine Lasso of Truth."

Those fingers dug deeper in Kate's biceps, despite the fact that the Wonder Woman in question was staring at the spook. "Please, Charles, I can get him to talk. I know I can."

Where...and now *him*?

Her *father*?

The man an Afghan militia had scooped up ten hours ago in Herat?

"Okay, wait." Kate eased the tense claws from her arm and faced the spook head on. "We need some context here—*now*. Is she referring to Masud Baqr?"

Praeger nodded. "Yes. I left something out of our conversation in your drive—but only because I was sure it wouldn't fly. And it *didn't*."

"Fine. What did you leave out?"

The spook's hands made another raking pass through the salt and pepper. "I told you, this whole damned mess stinks. I want answers as much as you both do—shit, more, since Lily's involved. I asked my Homeland contact in Kabul to go back to President Ghani to try to broker a deal. Basically, to agree to whatever Ghani wanted in exchange for letting us fly Masud to the States, or at least someplace stable, so we could question him. Find out what the hell Masud and his cousin are really up to. Because I'm not convinced that bastard Vahid's not holed up with a stateside terror cell and that these murders aren't just Act I. Hell, from what my Homeland contact says, Masud even alluded to an Act II in the works."

As much as Kate hated to admit it, the spook might be right. There might just be an Act II, and Masud could very well know about it. But, "President Ghani said no."

A clipped nod confirmed the non-deal.

Hell, given the current political and military deterioration in

Afghanistan brought on by the pulling out of US and NATO assets and forces, not to mention the looming, uglier promise of yet another Taliban rule, she'd have refused the deal too. And there was the rest. The most tantalizing fact of all: Lily's father was Iranian. "Chuck, if Ghani was going to trade Masud to anyone, it would be to President Rouhani and Iran."

"You think I don't know that? But it was worth a shot—not to mention a solid entry position to start the bargaining. My contact? What you also don't know is that he saved Ghani's ass from an IED before he became president. Ghani owes him. And —" The spook sighed, even as he scowled at his charge. "We did get something."

The critical part of the doc's initial bellow filtered back: *I don't care where I have to go*. Oh, shit.

She turned to Lily. "You want to go to Afghanistan?"

Now? With the drawdown almost complete and the remaining central-government-controlled Afghan districts falling to the Taliban as easily as a row of dominoes to a two-year-old's tantrum?

The spook's scowl deepened. "Oh, it's worse than that. Ghani has agreed that if Lily flies to Herat, she'll be granted visitation with Masud. And Masud supposedly wants to see her. Why? Who the fuck knows? It's not like Masud gave a shit about her growing up, much less when he handed her off to his cousin when she was barely fourteen. Hell, Masud might even want her punished more than Vahid does. As for Ghani, he agreed that Lily can bring someone with her for the trip. But I'm a man, and I don't particularly look Persian. Even if I forge papers to prove I'm an uncle on her mother's side, I won't be able to be with her twenty-four/seven. But that's okay with Wonder Woman here. Because she thinks she can get *you* to drop everything, including your murder investigations, and go tagging merrily along."

"*No*!"

Kate flinched. While that particular bellow had been ripping up her throat, it hadn't breached her mouth. It had exploded from Arash's.

But even as the suggestion behind it pummeled through every single cell of her body until it reached deep inside her heart where it began to pound furiously within the walls, forcing the adrenaline to surge in and out along with her blood, even as the sweat popped out to drench her neck, chest and armpits—she was forced to wonder...perhaps this wasn't such a profoundly horrific idea, after all.

It just might be their only viable option too.

"Lily, Chuck. May the detective and I have the room for a minute?"

The spook looked as though he was about to argue with her request, until he glanced at Arash. Whatever Praeger saw in those tense features must've reassured him, because the spook nodded and latched onto Lily's elbow to steer her to the door.

Lily jerked her arm from Praeger's grasp and came to a halt beside Kate. Those slender fingers returned to her upper arm.

They were still trembling, but they were gentle now, beseeching. "I know I have no right to ask you to come. But, please, Kate. I know in my soul that if I don't do this, I'll never see my mother again or meet my siblings. And you need answers. To solve your case, and to find Vahid and punish him for what he's done. But also to make sure Vahid isn't harboring a more monstrous plan. If he is, and he's shared it with anyone, it will be with my father. I lied to Charles just now. I honestly don't know if I can get that man to talk. But I *must* try. And if you accompany me, they will have to let you see him too. I'll tell them I was pregnant when I escaped Iran; that you're his granddaughter. If we're both veiled, even my father won't be able to tell how old you are, much less that we're not related. Not until the guards have left us alone with him, and it's too late."

The woman left.

Kate closed the door on the spook and his charge, then turned around to face Arash. Those crossed and locked forearms? That squared-off stance and that blistering stare?

The detective was beyond pissed. At her.

"A minute? Oh, it's going to take a hell of a lot longer than that to convince—"

She stepped closer, using Lily's gentler gesture against the man as she laid her hand on his forearms. Though she'd like to think her fingers weren't trembling quite as much. "You want him; I want him. Arash, this may be the only way we can get him. It's been eighteen hours now since you released that sketch. No one's come forward who even *thinks* they saw him. Vahid's not one step ahead of us; he's a hundred. We need help finding his damned trail. Especially since he's proven himself patient enough to forgo the bait we all but dangled last night, only to get Daria to nibble instead."

And there was the legal side.

They both knew that someone from one of their departments needed to be there in Herat to conduct, or at least sit in on, the interrogation. With the Afghan government barely in control of its own jails and prisons, it was the only way any evidence obtained there could be used back here in a stateside courtroom to put the man's cousin away for the murders Vahid had committed on American soil.

The muscles within those crossed arms hardened beneath her fingertips, as did that stare. "And if Vahid *is* holed up with a terror cell and plotting Act II? What's to say that getting that woman back over there—*that close to Iran*—isn't the plan? And a trap. One that *you* will be caught up in if you're standing next to her. Praeger's right. Why else would Masud even be willing to talk to the woman? Daughter or not, he wrote her off years ago—twice. When she was a toddler and again at fourteen."

He had a point. About all of it. Especially regarding the geography. Herat was seventy miles from the Iranian border. The Taliban currently surrounded the city of Herat, too; already had its tainted tentacles deep inside.

As for this being a trap? Fortunately, she had a stronger point to counter that reality with. She offered hers up with a shrug. "Been there; survived that. Got the scars and raging PTSD to prove it. Besides, we'll have Praeger as backup."

And there were still a few thousand US forces in the neighborhood. Though, admittedly, only a few. And they were stretched around the country pretty damned thin.

That stare grew darker, turned completely black. "Fine. I'll go."

She shook her head. Because the spook was right about something else too. The whole male-female dichotomy over there. Even with Arash's distinctive features, he'd have the same problem as Praeger. "You wouldn't be able to remain at Lily's side twenty-four/seven either. And that may be what it's going to take to get her safely home."

Not to mention, there could be insurmountable issues in getting Arash or even Praeger into Masud's detention cell once they arrived. To a fundamental Islamist, another man could be a threat.

But two women?

It turned out Lily Basque had learned a heck of a lot from running that Railroad. Kate could only hope the experience would be enough to see them through this.

She stiffened as she felt Arash's hand close over hers. Until that moment, she hadn't realized that she'd let his forearm go. She was holding hers.

Or rather, her left wrist.

Max's watch. She'd been twisting it again.

Great. Talk about subliminal doubts and stressors. And this man had already pegged pretty much all of hers.

Worse, given that Arash's aunt was a therapist and that he himself had been through CPT and had filled out all those worksheets, he knew exactly why she'd been twisting that metal watchband...and why the skin beneath needed protection.

"Kate—"

She shook her head as she turned her hand in his, borrowing the man's strength as she searched for the words to convince him.

Somehow, having heard the confession he'd offered up out on her deck that morning about the real reason behind those eight calls made this harder. But it also gave her the courage to see it through. "I can't tell you that part of me isn't terrified at the mere thought of being back there, but I can tell you that four years ago, I was terrified during that ambush too. Just like I was terrified when I woke up alone in that hovel, and when I was forced to kill the kid who came back to rape me. And I was *damned* terrified when I took his rifle and headed across that compound to kill the rest of those bastards. But I can tell you something else, too. I can deal with the terror, Arash. What I can't deal with—what I can't *live* with—is standing by and doing nothing."

It was the one argument that had a shot with him, and she knew it.

So she stood there for a solid minute, gripping his hand as she watched Arash's own terror churn through that blackened stare of his, along with the ghost he held so very dear as he fought the inevitable. Until, finally, Arash caved in and nodded.

Because he couldn't stand by and do nothing either.

She reached up with her free hand and smoothed her fingertips through the prickly morning shadow that darkened the skin along his jaw, until she was soothing the harder muscles that were still locked down beneath. "Do me a favor?"

"Name it."

"Visit Ruger while I'm gone?" Though Lou would feed him, something told her Arash would need the dog as much as Ruger would need him.

"Okay."

She nodded her thanks and turned to open the door before Arash could change his mind—about any of it.

Praeger stood on the other side, alone. He must've tucked his charge into another exam room so that he could argue without Lily there.

Fortunately for Kate, the spook took one look at her expression and was forced to accepted reality. "Fine. If we're going to do this, let's go. I want this stupidity over with before Ghani changes his mind. Go home; get what you need. Meet Lily and me in Little Rock at the airbase. I'll have a pass waiting for you at the main gate."

"How long do I have?"

"Just get to the airstrip. The plane will be ready."

Probably the same one he'd flown back in on earlier this morning.

The doc came out of the next room over then, evidently having listened in at the door. Relief washed the woman's features as Kate offered a departing nod to her, as well as Praeger and a still silent Arash. But it was the detective's lingering stiff, palpable dread as she turned to head up the hall and out of clinic that gave her pause.

What the hell had she just gotten herself into?

16

Herat International Airport
Herat, Afghanistan.

SHE'D BROKEN the most painful promise she'd ever made—to herself.

Kate executed a slow, three-hundred-and-sixty-degree turn, her frosted breath billowing out against the desolation of the night as she took in her surroundings. Granted, she was standing just off a bare-bones tarmac, roughly four hundred miles due west from where her Humvee had been ambushed and Max had been beheaded, but she was definitely back in the one country she'd sworn she'd never set foot in again.

Afghanistan.

But that wasn't the worst part.

She was naked.

Oh, she had clothes, and they were currently covering her body from her neck down. They even belonged to her. But she'd trade every square inch of her Braxton PD deputy's uniform for the Glock that *should* be tucked inside her holster.

But was not.

Her 9mm was gone. Confiscated back at Little Rock. Moments before she'd boarded the US Air Force C-130 still powering down its engines behind her.

Why? She wasn't military anymore. Given the blindingly broad authority the federal government had once entrusted her with, first as a still pimpled eighteen-year-old MP and then as a combat-seasoned CID agent, losing the right to carry a single 9mm back into this near lawless hellhole would've been downright laughable...were it not for the severe case of jitters that had been dogging her for the last twenty hours.

The result? She'd put serious wear and tear on the ace bandage Manning had talked her into sporting. A recommendation she'd have to thank the shrink for during their next session. Without the wrap, her wrist would've been a raw, bloody mess well before they'd landed in Herat five minutes ago.

The only thing that'd saved her from having a full-blown, sweat-soaked meltdown in the C-130's onboard latrine had been Lily. The woman had finally changed out of those scrubs during their first refueling stop and into the spare black leggings and oversized green sweater Kate had brought to the airport for her.

But that was all the energy Lily had possessed, emotional and otherwise. The doc had spent remainder of the flight huddled into the webbed seat next to Kate, clutching the worn photo that Dineh had given Arash, staring at her mother and siblings. Silently.

And, yes, tears had been present for most of those hours.

She and Lily Basque were quite the pair.

Given her not-so-loving relationship with her own father, Kate understood more than most what it was costing the woman to fly to an Afghan jail a stone's throw from the eastern border of

Iran just to confront Masud. And while she seriously doubted that the pending chat between Lily and her father would yield anything actionable in Afghanistan, Iran or the States, unlike Praeger, she did believe it was worth a shot.

The shock of seeing his daughter alive after all these years just might rattle Masud enough to get him to open up about his cousin. If not, at least she and the spook had succeeded in getting Lily as far away from Vahid as possible.

For the moment.

Even Praeger had been forced to agree that the latter made this entire journey a net positive. Though he was still pissed about it all.

The spook was on edge too. Even now, standing ten feet away, Kate could feel the tension in the man as Praeger loomed beside his charge on the darkened, icy tarmac. Not only was that vigilance understandable, it was prudent. The moment their Army taxi arrived, they'd be leaving for the militia's makeshift Afghan jail.

As for the armed guards who ran that jail?

Even the spook's Homeland Security contact had been unable to verify who those guards really worked for. It was the main reason why Praeger had decided that they'd conduct their meeting with Masud immediately upon landing.

Kate had agreed in the hope that an evening interrogation, after what was bound to have been a ruthless nonstop day of them, would dent her suspect's cousin's zealous resolve...and inadvertently loosen an already exhausted tongue.

According to the time-zone reset she'd long since given to Max's dive watch, it was nearing 8:00 p.m. local. Even the main men's prison in Herat would've stopped accepting visitors by now. Fortunately, Praeger's Homeland contact had arranged for a follow-on call from President Ghani's office in Kabul to the makeshift militia jail.

They were expected.

They'd be there soon, too. From the familiar rumbling that became audible as the C-130's giant turbofan engines cut out, it sounded as though their ride had arrived.

Kate tensed as two and a half tons of Army steel ate up the access road and came to a halt near the tail of the plane. A second vehicle chewed its way into a supporting position behind the first and shifted into idle mode as well. A third sand-colored beast brought up the rear.

Humvees.

From the moment she'd made the decision to come to Herat, she'd known she was going to have to crawl back inside one of those bone-jarring monsters. During the flight, she'd convinced herself that it wouldn't be an issue. She'd just walk right up to one of those growling flashback inducers, take a deep breath and slide inside its deceptively protective belly as she'd done countless times in the preceding years.

But as Praeger drew the doc closer to his side and turned to wave Kate toward them, she wasn't sure anymore.

This really was happening.

She managed to delay the inevitable for an additional two seconds, possibly three, as she turned around to retrieve her small, dark-blue duffle from the tarmac.

"Chief Holland?"

She abandoned the duffle and spun back.

An ascetic, sinewy black man of roughly five-ten and dressed in Army camouflage stood in her path. His utilities were devoid of name, rank and every indicator that would've given her a clue as to his branch and military qualifications. A warm, earthy smile commandeered the man's face, however, softening every single feature, especially those dark, piercing eyes. "First Sergeant Trent Bowen, Special Forces." That inviting smile of his crinkled in deeper as he brandished the distinctive blue fabric of a folded-up, Taliban-approved shuttlecock burqa. "Major Moradi says hi."

Arash?

The detective hadn't so much as hinted that anything out of the ordinary would be waiting for her in the texts she'd received before her phone had gone dark.

But that glint in the first sergeant's stare?

What had Arash done now?

Bowen pushed the folds of cheap blue polyester toward her. The moment the burqa settled between her palms, she knew. There was no mistaking the lovely, solid shape and weight within. The burqa was concealing a holstered handgun.

Bowen's voice scraped down to the barest of murmurs. "Glock19. Locked and loaded. If you need to ditch it at some point, no worries. It's been sanitized. And I can provide another." The man's voice returned to standard, conversational volume as he relinquished his hold on the burqa and stepped back. "The major also says to tell you Ruger's getting fat and lazy on bribes as we speak, so hurry home."

Relief seared in, soothing her nerves.

The doubts.

She might've felt as though she was on her own these past twenty hours, even seated inches from the doc and across an aisle of webbed seats from one of the CIA's finest, but she hadn't been. Her partner had been on her other side, supporting her. Seven thousand miles away now or not, the detective still was.

The Glock was one thing. But that comment about Ruger?

Arash had sent one hell of a message.

I trust this man. You can, too.

So she did. She turned and used the first sergeant's camouflaged body as cover as she slipped her fingers between those cheap polyester folds to accept the priceless gift within, tucking the streamlined leather holster she encountered in at the small of her back. She pulled the elastic ribbed waist of her deputy jacket firmly down over the 9mm and her utility belt to conceal it. Her sigh eased out into the chilly night.

"Better?"

Lord, yes. The hell with beef bones and fragrant flatbread. She'd take the 9mm.

The first sergeant winked as she turned around. "Moradi thought you might appreciate the present. So, you ready to do this?"

She drew her breath in deep. Along with the cold, crisp air came a refilling of the reservoir of inner strength she always seemed to be able to tap into when she needed it most. Though, yeah, the Glock absolutely helped to fill it.

Sure, she liked knives, especially ones she could throw. Thanks to Bob Feathers' tips and relentless training, she could even clip a bonsai tree into shape from thirty feet away on a cloudy day. But knives weren't boomerangs. They didn't come back.

She'd prefer a rifle or a handgun any day of the week.

Because she could reload.

Kate glanced over at the trio of idling Humvees. Praeger was assisting an already burqa-clad doc into the rear seat of the middle vehicle. If Lily could face her father, she herself could damned sure face climbing into another Humvee.

As for the claustrophobic woman-eraser still in her hands, she wasn't donning that until she absolutely needed to. Wadding up the fabric, Kate shoved her burqa beneath her left arm, then reached down with her right to grab her duffle.

"Let's roll out, First Sergeant."

Bowen nodded toward the rear vehicle. "You're with me."

She'd have preferred to ride with Lily, especially now that she was armed and could better protect the woman, but the Humvees that Bowen and the other soldiers had driven to the tarmac only had room for two additional passengers each. She took a final deep, courage-inviting breath and opened the rear door of the waiting beast. Tossing her duffle to the floorboard, she climbed inside. By the time Bowen rounded the vehicle and joined her in the back seat on her right, she'd pulled the wad of cheap polyester into her lap and buried her hands beneath it. She gripped the stainless-steel band of Max's watch and twisted it as she pulled in her next breath.

This inhalation was deliberately slow and even more shallow.

Unfortunately, the air that filled her lungs was still laden with that distinctive blend of military metal, paint, plastics, rubber and even electronics. It was an odor her mind and body knew too well, because that final, horrific memory she held of herself in one of these crowded in with it.

The pungent punch of diesel as the driver shifted the Humvee into gear and moved out behind the lead vehicle didn't help.

But the lack of sulfur byproducts and melting rubber did.

It also helped that she couldn't really make out the Afghan countryside as they headed north up the Kandahar-Herat highway. The moonless, maturing night lay like a suffocating cloak over the buildings they passed, not unlike the waiting burqa in her lap. The thick layer of clouds that blotted out every star of the gorgeous, luminous view of the Milky Way that normally came with this country added to the crush.

Though even if she'd wanted to distinguish between the varying shades of brown as they approached the outer districts of Herat, she wouldn't have been able to.

The reason? She was forced to concentrate on the non-stop chatter from the Special Forces soldier beside her. Only Bowen wasn't providing a commentary on the road, the other vehicles or even the occasional buildings they passed, he was plying her with endless questions regarding her life in Arkansas and Ruger.

She knew exactly what Bowen was doing. What Arash had asked the first sergeant to do from the moment she entered the Humvee, until she exited it.

Keep her distracted.

Strangely, it was working.

Before she realized it, they were there. Only *there* was not quite where or what she'd expected.

She'd known Masud Baqr wasn't being held in the men's prison, or even at a police station inside Herat proper. According to Praeger's Homeland contact, Lily's father was supposedly holed up with the militia members who'd scooped him up and taken him to a walled compound at the southern, agricultural outskirts of the city, mere miles north of the outlying airport.

But even here, in Afghanistan, she'd expected that makeshift jail to be more...jail-like.

While they had parked just outside a compound, and it was agricultural in nature, the entire structure was almost a dead ringer for a fortified rural farmhouse she and Joe Cordoba had cleared several hundred miles east of Herat and over a decade earlier when they were still both junior military police. The thick, hand-formed walls of baked mud in front of the Humvees loomed roughly eighteen feet high. Like the farmhouse she and Joe had secured, the various two-story, flat-roofed buildings that formed the compound were also sealed together along the corners, creating a stark, massive square with an inner, protected courtyard where the owner's animals could roam.

According to the ripe stench that registered within her nose as the soldier in the front passenger seat of their vehicle bailed out, this particular courtyard contained a cow or two, at least. Or had until very recently.

She couldn't see the cows, of course, and wouldn't be able to unless she breached the outer walls.

That didn't bother her. It was what else that she couldn't see that did. Namely, people. In this case, an armed militia guard or two, patrolling the premises.

There were none.

Her old Army instincts tightened.

Evidently, the first sergeant's had too. "Wait in here."

Yeah, not gonna happen.

If she was going to get ambushed in this godforsaken country—*again*—she'd do it outside another US government-provided iron coffin, thank you.

She did, however, pull the shuttlecock burqa over her head and shoulders, letting the cheap, blue polyester billow down to camouflage her deputy uniform jacket, trousers and boots as she abandoned the Humvee. The fingers of her left hand held the human tent in place against the icy breeze that swirled in. The fingers of her right instinctively moved around her waist to tuck in at the small of her back until they were curling about the solid, comforting butt of the Glock Arash had provided.

The meshed threads of the burqa's stingy viewing cutout poked at her eyes as she watched the first sergeant link up with the US soldier who'd ridden shotgun in their vehicle, as well as Praeger and the two Afghan army soldiers from the lead Humvee. Bowen and the other US soldier brandished M4 carbines, and the two Afghan army soldiers carried M16s, as all five men headed for the wooden door slotted into the courtyard wall and disappeared within.

The rest of them were left behind to endure the blind, painful wait.

During which the driver of her own Humvee was evidently not content to remain inside while she stood behind her armored rear door.

"Evening, Chief."

With the soldier's uniform as sanitized as the first sergeant's, she settled for a responding nod.

Half a dozen excruciatingly tense minutes dragged in before Bowen, Praeger and the three others who'd breached the outer wall filed out. Fortunately, the stances of all five men were significantly more relaxed than when they'd entered.

Kate breathed easier, along with the Humvee driver shielded by the armored door in front of hers.

Praeger stopped beside the middle vehicle to assist Lily.

Bowen continued on to her side. "You're good to go. There's an old shitty worktable set up in a room inside the compound, about fifteen feet down on the right from where we entered. Not sure where they scrounged up that pair of rickety stools, but Masud's bound and already perched on one of 'em at the table. Need anything?"

"Yes. Unzip my duffle, please. There's a manila folder on top."

The first sergeant shouldered his M4 and leaned into the rear of the Humvee to retrieve the folder she'd prepared from the basket of paperwork and photos she'd had Seth store in her father's bedroom back in Braxton.

She would've liked to have added in hard copies of photos from the clinic's crime scene with the others, but there hadn't been time. Heck, she hadn't even seen Daria's autopsy results. The initial report would most likely be in by now and uploaded to the electronic case file she and Arash had created. But with the Taliban intimidating cellular companies across the country into shutting down their networks at night for fear that the antennas would be used to track their movements, she couldn't even receive a pithy text, let alone a phone call from Remy or Arash to update her on the latest.

She and her non-satellite, so-called smartphone would have

to wait for daylight, when the civilian networks would be allowed to restart.

"Here you go, Chief."

"Thanks. And it's deputy—or Kate."

"Nah, my team and I stopped by where they held you that day to do a bit of recon and help clean up the ripening, post-party favors you left scattered about." The first sergeant flashed that deep grin of his. "You'll always be Chief Holland to me."

That would be why Arash had called on this man then.

Despite the burqa, she offered a nod of respect for the first sergeant's efforts that day as well. "I appreciate it—and sorry about the mess." Then again, straightening up after herself had been the last thing on her mind at the time. Even if she hadn't tipped into a fugue at the sight of Max losing his head, she'd have left every one of those bodies where they'd dropped in her quest to get the hell out of Dodge. "Got any polite instructions for the chief?"

"Just watch your back. I'm leaving the two Afghan army soldiers we brought along out here to guard the Humvees and our gear. All four of my men will accompany us inside. We'll keep an eye on the dozen militia that I made out and be on the lookout for others that may be lurking within while you do your thing. Most of the militia are huddled up in the northeast corner of the compound, trying to keep warm around a fire they've got going. They bought the story that Praeger's an uncle to you and Basque on her mom's side, so he'll be able to be in the room with you. I'll be just outside in the courtyard with my men—keeping an eye on the rest of them. You need me, you holler. I'll be in there. Hell, we all will be."

"Got it."

They headed toward the opening in the courtyard wall to link up with a patiently waiting Praeger and a completely obscured Lily. Bowen's men had already entered to tactfully secure the premises and had left the wooden door ajar.

The smell of manure intensified.

Given the substantial quiver around the hem of the other burqa, Kate suspected the woman beneath was terrified. Ignoring the smell, she reached out to grasp the doc's arm through two layers of slippery polyester.

"Lily? Are you okay?"

"No. But I want this *done*."

She appreciated the blunt honesty. Not to mention the woman's continued courage, despite the tears that were bound to be threatening beneath that veil, if not already sliding down. Kate could only pray the courage would hold.

Lily's and hers.

Nerves more taut than they'd been in years ratcheted in that much tighter as Kate entered the compound's twenty-by-forty-foot inner courtyard. She caught sight of the source of the smell in the shadows off to her left.

A moment later, a loud *moo* confirmed her suspicion. Those copious piles her boots and the hem of her burqa had managed to dodge upon entering?

Definitely cow shit.

As Bowen had stated, a dozen haphazardly uniformed Afghan militia men were clustered around a fire in the opposite corner, attempting to stay warm.

Bowen slipped around to her exposed left side, as neatly as Arash had done out on the road at the Frasheri body dump near the Little Rock Airbase.

God help her. This time, she welcomed the added layer of human protection.

Worse, her wrist had begun to itch.

She ignored it, concentrating on another familiar odor

riding the telling yellow glow that was spilling out from the open doorway ahead on her right.

Stale sweat and burning kerosene.

Yet another round of unwelcomed mental souvenirs from this godforsaken country clamored in. At the center—a bunch of hyped-up jihadis, a kneeling best friend and that cold, vicious sword.

She forced her mind to let go of the bastards who'd forged the nightmare of her past and focused on four innocent women instead. How they'd looked in life. Those beautiful dark eyes and beaming smiles preserved by their loved ones' cameras before Vahid and his fundamentalist contempt for women had gotten hold of them.

She focused on Daria, the woman whose slaughter she might've actually been able to prevent if she'd figured this all out in time, using it to propel herself forward.

There would be no more senseless deaths.

All she needed was a location for Vahid.

Arash, Lou, Seth, Remy and Agent Wynne would take care of the rest before her plane could even touch down back in Little Rock.

The determination carried her into the room behind Praeger and his charge of nearly two decades now.

Kate hung back at the doorway, just ahead of the first sergeant's protective vigilance as Bowen took up a position just outside the frame, facing the courtyard, so he and his soldiers could watch the cluster of Afghan militia men who—despite that warm fire on an increasingly chilly night—had to be watching them.

As Bowen had stated, a scarred wooden worktable and two rickety stools outfitted an otherwise bare, mud-walled room. A concession to the coming Americans, no doubt. Not that this dusty barnyard of a palace would be sporting a line of pillows for seating along the floor, plush or otherwise.

A dented kerosene lantern hung from a hook to the left of the doorway behind them, providing the room's only source of light. At the opposite side of the table, on one of the stools, sat an oddly bruise-free Persian male in his late fifties, his wrists flex-cuffed together and resting atop the slab of rutted wood in front of him.

Masud Baqr. Lily's father.

The man was dressed in the coarse white tunic and trousers combination common to the region, minus head covering. His hair was as dark and thick as Praeger's, though bone straight and more heavily salted. With that still reasonably fit body and those distinctive—and admittedly attractive—facial features however, Masud more closely resembled an older version of Arash. But only on the surface.

That simmering scowl? The familiar, cold pinch of distaste that bit into the man's lips as Lily complied with the silent flick of her father's flex-cuff-impeded fingers to pull off her burqa and stand trembling before him?

He was Kate's own bastard of a dad brought back to life.

As if on cue, Masud ignored Praeger completely as he shifted his icy sneer toward the doorway. To her. "Well, let me see this new relative of mine."

What the hell. Kate tugged off her burqa.

Masud ignored the uniform that had been hidden beneath as his scowl settled on the plethora of pockmarks, scars and crevices that covered most of the right side of her face. Distaste twisted into outright revulsion. "You are no seed of mine."

"Trust me. I celebrate that fact."

His scowl darkened and shifted to his daughter. A torrent of filthy, demeaning Farsi poured out of the man's mouth. Kate didn't understand a word of it. She didn't need to. The subtle stiffening of Praeger's stance along with the overt shrinking of Lily's offered up the gist of what was being said, and none of it was good.

Let alone helpful.

The doc's composure was already hanging by a thread. One more wave of tears and it would be washed away for good.

"That's *enough*."

The source of that foul stream jerked his astonishment back to her.

Lily's followed.

Even the spook turned to stare at her.

"As supportive and loving as this reunion is, Mr. Baqr, catching up isn't why we're here, is it?" Wadding up her burqa, Kate turned and stepped just outside the room briefly to swap out the resulting blue cloud with the manila folder that had been tucked beneath the first sergeant's left arm. She swung back around and approached the wooden table between Praeger and his charge, laying the folder down between herself and the prisoner. She tapped the cover. "This is."

Masud glanced at the folder. "And what is that?"

"Photos of your cousin's handiwork."

Genuine interest flared within that cold stare.

Kate ignored it as she turned to direct her murmur to the spook. "Take Lily and the other stool to the corner." The doc could use the physical support even the crappy stool and mud walls would provide. Those already shredded nerves of Lily's had deteriorated so much during the vitriol her father had spewed that her teeth were beginning to chatter.

Any moment now, the reaction would become audible.

That, they didn't need.

Kate would prefer to send the doc out to wait in the Humvee. But as prudent as it was to leave a pair of male soldiers to guard their vehicles outside the walls, it was potentially vital for her to remain as part of a female duo inside here.

Lest a righteous member of the militia get curious—and pissed.

And then where would they be?

Kate bent down to open the folder as the spook complied. She could hear Praeger settling Lily against the wall as she removed the 8x10 inch photos that she'd brought of Aisha Kharoti. Laying the grisly crime scene close-ups out along the edge of the table in front of her, she followed them up with a second row containing the close-ups of Tahira Larijani's charred body, anchoring both of those rows with a third, equally grim line of pictures taken of Samara Frasheri's desecrated corpse.

That nauseating glint of interest strengthened as Masud slowly studied each of the photographs in turn. He even lifted his flex-cuffed wrists so he could draw the centermost 8x10 of Samara's mutilated thighs directly in front of him.

Satisfaction slipped into that ever-present distain. "*Admonish them and leave them alone in the sleeping places, and—*"

"Yes, yes; I know. *Surah* IV, thirty-four."

He looked up. "I see you have been studying the wisdom of Allah. This is good."

What she'd give to have the freedom to remove that smirk.

Permanently.

"Not really, Masud. I'm fairly certain the vast majority of Muslims in the world would agree that the murder of any woman and the subsequent desecration of her body does not fall under the umbrella of *admonishment*."

The bastard shrugged. "This is for Allah to decide."

And if Allah existed, he undoubtedly would. But that heavenly determination would have to wait for Vahid's next life.

For better or worse, the authority to affect the bastard's

current, earthly existence had landed into her lap. At least until she could kick it off to a stateside prosecutor and judge.

"Now, see, here's where even you may be forced to agree with me." She tapped the leading photos in each row. "Aisha Kharoti, Tahira Larijani and Samara Frasheri weren't married to Vahid. Nor was Daria Farid, the woman your cousin stabbed in your daughter's clinic yesterday morning." Kate withdrew the remaining pair of photos from the folder and laid them next to the others at the side of the table. "And neither were these two soldiers. In fact, this victim was married to Aisha, and this one was married to Tahira. And, of course, both of them were *men*."

All that earned her was a shrug. "Perhaps they were unable to control their women. After all, they were American men, yes?"

She matched the careless lift of those tunic-clad shoulders with one of her own. "It's possible. But surely that's not a deficiency worth killing over: a man being unable to control his woman. Especially since that appears to be par for the course for your family. After all—" Kate tipped her head toward the corner of the room. "—Vahid didn't do all that great with Layla, did he? Because, well, *she* beat *him*...and you."

To her disappointment Masud simply nodded and offered up another shrug. Not only did this one contain the nonchalance of the first, there was an added chilling quality to it that had the hair at the back of her neck prickling to attention.

As did that smirk. "This is true. Vahid was not successful. But he was younger then. He is older now. Wiser. Vahid will do better with her replacement."

Replacement?

That family photo Arash had obtained filtered in.

Shit. The hell with a snooping, indignant member of the militia. She should've sent Lily from the room earlier.

It was too late now. Masud's smirk had shifted to the corner of the room. Deepened. "Her sister."

The stool clattered to the floor as the doc barreled up to the table to glare at the piece of living excrement piled across from them. "She's a *child*."

Another one of those damned careless shrugs pushed up. "Eleven, just this year. And, yet, already a woman. Your mother has assured me of this."

"You *bastard*. If you give my sister to him, I'll cut off your—"

The rest of that threat was lopped off, and now, as Praeger slipped his right arm around the top of the doc's chest to turn her into his. "Lily, calm down. This won't help Yasmin, much less you."

But it had brought on the tears again.

This time, Kate couldn't fault her for them. The girl was in Iran. If plans were already in place to force her into marriage before she was even twelve, whereafter she'd be raped nightly by the same monster who'd violated the doc for nearly a year, there wasn't a damned thing any of them could do to prevent it, Praeger included.

And Lily knew it.

The spook glanced over the top of the doc's openly sobbing head, then jerked his toward the door.

Kate nodded.

If a member of the militia spotted Lily departing the compound and was affronted enough to interfere with her remaining presence in this room—and realized she wasn't related to Masud after all—she'd deal with it then. Because there was no way she'd get anything out of Masud with his daughter melting down in front of him.

The asshole was too busy getting off on her distress.

As for Praeger, from the snarl of pure hate the bastard shot his way as the spook turned to escort his charge from the room, Masud would've launched himself from that stool and killed Praeger with his bare hands had his wrists not been bound.

Simply because the spook had dared to comfort Lily? Or was it because Masud had realized his daughter was leaving?

And he was not.

The anger faded until it was tucked neatly inside that smarmy smirk of his. "And now, it is down to just you and me. A much cozier pair, yes? Much more...intimate."

"Don't piss me off, Masud. You wouldn't like me when I get pissed off."

He nodded sagely. "Yes, I have heard the tales of the vengeful Agent Holland. But you are currently unarmed—" That gloating grin strengthened as his focus dipped to the name tag above her right pocket and the decidedly feminine curve beneath. "...*Deputy* Holland."

That suggestive, lingering look at her breasts? The filthy implication behind it? It was the worst thing he could've done—for himself.

She smiled.

The confidence Masud spotted within her face must've given the man pause, because that smarmy twist finally faded, and completely. As well it should.

Because the confidence that had spread out until it was thrumming through her entire body hadn't come from the holstered Glock tucked in at the small of her back. Or even her sessions with Manning. It had come from deep within her soul.

This man's religiously fucked-up ilk had gotten the drop on her once before.

Never again.

"You've got one shot, Masud. One. You tell me where to find Vahid and maybe I'll see what I can do about convincing those men out in that courtyard to look the other way after I leave. Long enough for you to head out too."

It was a flat-out lie.

There would be no deal. She'd known that going in. President Ghani had made the dictate crystal clear through Praeger's Homeland contact.

But Masud didn't know that. And after the comment about offering up Yasmin to his monster of a cousin, she really didn't—

Yasmin.

"Deputy?"

She tensed—and pushed the vague tickling to the back of her brain. Or tried to.

It refused to budge.

Why?

The distinctive sound of a US Army Humvee's diesel engine growling to life succeeded in gnawing through the tickling.

Kate stiffened.

The vehicle was departing.

She spun around. The first sergeant was still just outside the doorway, but he'd turned his back on the inner courtyard and his other men.

Bowen was staring straight at her. And those tense lips were angled down.

She closed the packed dust between them. "What's wrong?"

"Your partner just commandeered the two Afghan army soldiers I posted outside the compound, along with one of my vehicles."

Praeger? "He's not my—"

Holy *shit.*

A chill colder than the snow-packed peaks of the nearby Hindu Kush blew up her spine.

Her expression must've given the reason behind it away, because the first sergeant stepped closer as he nudged her to finish her denial. "He's not your what?"

"Partner."

Arash. He'd given her that worn photo that Dineh had given to him. He'd even relayed the names of Lily's mother, Maya, and her siblings in Iran: Naveed, Hassan and Yasmin. But Lily had been too upset for conversation when she'd received the photo and too freaked out by Arash's features after she'd woken from her nightmare just before dawn the previous morning, so Arash hadn't passed the names on to Lily.

Nor had she.

Not even during that twenty-hour flight.

She'd been too consumed with her own inner turmoil over where she was headed again to realize she'd forgotten to share the siblings' names, while the doc had been so upset, Lily hadn't even thought to ask. And although Kate had texted Praeger to let him know that Lily's mother was alive and that Lily had siblings, she hadn't provided the names in the text she'd sent to the spook either.

So how the *hell* had Praeger known Yasmin's name?

And had the spook really believed Lily's mother to be dead all these years as he'd supposedly searched for the woman?

Her gut had to be wrong. Because the answer it offered up didn't make sense.

Except her gut wouldn't stop bellowing.

About Praeger.

She'd never seen the spook scrawl out so much as a lowly zero, but she now knew exactly how he created his fours.

"Where'd they go?" Even as Kate asked the question, she prayed the first sergeant would have an answer.

But Bowen just shook his head. "I have no fucking idea. He pulled the National Security card. Took the doc, one of the Humvees and the two Afghan army soldiers before I was even honored with a text to let me know they were all leaving. And now, no one will answer *my* text, let alone pick up the phone. What the hell's going on?"

Even if she'd had an explanation to give, it would have to wait. The first sergeant's satellite phone was ringing.

She tensed as Bowen answered.

Two seconds later, he held out the handset. "It's not them. It's the major. He wants to speak with you."

Apprehension smelted into a pool of churning, molten dread as she accepted the phone. Kate ducked around the first sergeant, leaving Masud in Bowen's very capable Special Forces hands as she stepped into the darkened clearing. "What's wrong?"

Because something was. That name, and now the fact that Arash had just tracked her down in Herat—on someone else's phone—proved it.

"Remy called. One of his guys found a set of fingerprints at the clinic scene. They came back restricted. Remy was bemused, so he called me."

"They've got to be Praeger's."

"That's what I told Remy. After all, the man's with the Company. But, Kate, the prints weren't on a tabletop or a door. They were recovered from the inside of a right-handed latex glove that the tech found underneath the edge of the couch in the waiting room—and Daria Farid's blood is on the outside."

"*Fuck.*"

The geopolitical needle of their case had just jerked a hundred and eighty degrees about. It was no longer pointed at the Middle East and Iran, but smack in the middle of United States—and the CIA.

"Yeah. Where is the bastard?"

She had no bloody idea. But there was no way she was telling Arash that.

True partner or not, there wasn't a damned thing he could do from seven thousand miles away but worry. And Arash would worry. "I'll call you back. I—"

"*Kate—*"

"I'm fine, Arash. I've got the gifts you arranged. Both of them.

Don't tell Lou about this just yet, okay? And hang tight. I'll phone as soon as I can. Out."

She prayed that Arash would forgive her, because she hung up before he could argue. She spun around, bypassing the terse questions burning in Bowen's stare as well, as she shoved the phone at him. She didn't have answers for the first sergeant either.

But someone did.

Someone who was still seated on the stool at that worktable across the room, those perfect, even teeth all but gleaming in the light from the kerosene lamp hanging from the wall.

A moment later, she was looming over him. "Where is he?"

"Vahid?"

"Screw your cousin. We'll get to him in a minute. Where's Charles Praeger?"

Those teeth gleamed brighter for a split second, then faded along with that smile. The frown that took its place was infested with resignation. "Who knows? But he is not the man you and your friends believe him to be, yes? Nor is my cousin."

She didn't know about Vahid, but Praeger definitely wasn't who she'd thought him to be.

But the resignation that the mere mention of Praeger's name had induced in Masud? That, she knew all too well. Better yet, it was something she could work with.

Along with the anger Masud had directed toward the spook earlier. That fury made sense now. "Praeger and your cousin, they betrayed you."

"Yes. This, I discovered for myself not too many hours ago."

"The terror sweep that netted you. It wasn't supposed to happen, was it?"

"No. We were to be protected when we came to Herat."

"Who arranged that protection?" Praeger? "And why?"

Silence filled the room.

It locked in so completely, she could hear the flames licking at the wick inside the kerosene lamp back at the door.

"Masud, I can still make that deal I offered earlier." And she would.

Somehow.

She'd enter a pact with the Devil himself if it would keep Lily from the monster that *this* bastard had given her to all those years ago at fourteen.

The man's smile returned, but there was no humor in it now. It didn't matter. Because the silence had broken. "There is no need to lie to me, Deputy. We both know you no longer possess the authority to make such deals."

Perhaps...and perhaps not.

She offered up a smile of her own. It was just as grim. "Four years ago, eleven men counted me out a few hundred miles from here. It was a mistake—on their parts." Masud had alluded to the fact that he knew her military history.

Why not abuse it?

His brow kicked up. "Indeed."

The brow eased down into place. But something had come with it. Something she needed. Not only was Masud in agreement over the outcome of what'd happened to her that day she'd been taken prisoner, he was wavering with his decision to hold his tongue now.

She could see it in the self-serving glint that returned to that dark stare.

It drifted downward, settling on the rows of grisly crime scene photos that were still lined up across the table in front of him. He reached out and tapped the one he'd drawn close earlier. "Vahid did not kill this woman." His finger swept out to encompass the remaining photos. "Or the others."

Yeah, she'd begun to suspect that all by herself. Still, "How can you be so certain?"

"These women, they were all killed in the United States, yes? This past week?"

She inclined her head.

"Until two days ago—hours before I was arrested, mind you—Vahid was with me in Tehran and then in Mashhad, before we traveled here to make our deal."

Shit. This was as bad as she'd feared.

And the deepening American national and geopolitical implications?

This time, *she* fell silent.

Creaking filled the tiny room as Masud drew his bound wrists to his lap and shifted atop the stool. "You do not believe me."

Oh, she did.

That was the problem. Because among other things, it meant that Lily was not only trapped in that stolen Humvee heading to God knew where to have God knew what vented upon her, the doc was doing it in the company of a CIA operative willing to slaughter at least four American women and two US Army sergeants just to complete his side of Vahid's *deal.*

Kate scooped the rows of photos together and tucked them into the manila folder as she worked through the remaining implications. "What does Vahid have for Praeger? I know he's only a low-level diplomat. Did he stumble across a critical piece of information on another country?"

Whatever the information and whichever nation it concerned, it would have to be huge for the spook to believe it was worth the lives of six innocent victims—at least.

Masud lifted his fingers, knitting them together as he settled them on the table in front of him. "I do not know. Vahid did not trust me with the information this time."

"This time?"

"My cousin...he is...not a diplomat. That is something Vahid tells people because he cannot say where he truly works. Vahid travels here to Herat on occasion to meet with a scientist from Pakistan on behalf of our government. He even took a local Afghan woman for his third wife, as directed from above, to help conceal the nature of his continued visits. Vahid also meets with Charles Praeger during those visits. Though not at the same time, you understand, and on his own. As his cousin, I accompany him to Herat to deflect attention, but also for his security. I do not know what information Vahid receives or passes with either the Pakistani scientist or Praeger, because while I also work where Vahid works, I do not work with him. He is...higher up than me."

Vahid was a mechanical engineer who'd once wanted to work with water and the infrastructure that contained and tamed it, but believed he'd been denied his dream by the US Army. Where could a man with that background, and harboring that level of simmering anger, work in Iran that would necessitate separate meetings with a Pakistani scientist and a CIA—

Oh, Jesus.

She even heard Bowen stiffen just outside the door behind her.

Masud nodded. "Your suspicions are correct. Vahid is an engineer in our rather impressive nuclear weapons program. So, you see, whatever my cousin has offered in exchange for the opportunity to finally and *completely* cleanse our family's honor, I suspect Charles Praeger will be equally determined to obtain it, yes?"

As much as she wanted desperately to argue otherwise, she couldn't.

Bastards. All of them.

This one, his cousin—*and* the spook.

"Where is Praeger making the exchange?"

But Masud just stared.

"You have to have a suspicion, at least."

And he did. But once again, Masud failed to voice it. That dark stare of his shifted across the room instead, to the doorway and the inner courtyard beyond. "I believe one of those men with the militia intends to kill me."

She didn't doubt it.

She also finally knew who those men were loyal to. At the very least, the one in charge. *Praeger*. That loyalty also explained why there were no bruises, cuts or broken bones marring the Iranian's features. What was the point of torturing Masud if the Iranian was simply sitting on this stool to provide support for Praeger's coming cover story?

And of course, that lack of battered flesh also confirmed that once she, Bowen and the first sergeant's remaining men left this compound, Masud Baqr's hours, possibly his minutes, were numbered.

As much as this man deserved that outcome, the former Army CID agent in her couldn't let his death come to pass. Not here, like this. Because while Masud might be clinging to the lower rungs of Iran's nuclear program, he was definitely on those rungs and willing to speak. With time, those at Homeland or within the CIA could whittle away at Masud for names of others who might also be willing to have a two-way conversation, and they could then climb each of those names in turn, until the CIA reached the very top.

But for that to happen, she'd have to keep this bastard safe.

Which brought them to the real reason Masud was being so chatty. He was attempting to save his own rotten hide.

Though Bowen would undoubtedly argue with her decision, she nodded crisply. "I'll leave the US soldiers here for your protection until I return."

Four of them, anyway.

She'd need a driver. Not to mention that—former, eleven-to-one odds notwithstanding—armed backup while breaching a mud-walled Afghan hovel would be nice for a change. Given the trail of bodies the spook that she was after had left behind this past week, that backup might be desperately needed too.

"Now, where is Praeger making the swap?"

"I suspect where they always meet. The place is somewhat similar to this and even more—" Masud's disdain flicked toward the doorway and the courtyard beyond. "—private. Vahid will need that, for he wishes to take his time. He has spoken of little else these past six months but revenge. Ever since Praeger showed him the photo from *Al Jazeera* and assured my cousin that he could find Layla and bring her back to us. This time, Vahid has vowed to stay beside her long enough to make certain she is dead."

"*Where*?"

The bastard adjusted his knitted fingers and sighed. "You know of the Hadiqat Greenhouse? In the Guzarah District."

No. But she wasn't alone, was she? Because of Arash, she had that backup she desperately needed.

"First Sergeant?"

A split second later, Bowen was at her side. "Yeah, I know the place." His terse stare captured hers. "It's a stone's throw southeast of here."

Masud nodded. "Continue down the road for another kilometer. The compound is on the right. You cannot mistake it; there are no other buildings nearby, only fields."

And one seriously sore thumb of a sand-colored Humvee sticking out and frantically waving at them from just outside the walls—she *hoped*.

If not? Charles Praeger would be in the wind. And Lily Basque, née Layla Baqr, would be dead before they even found her.

This time, for real.

17

She was back inside a Humvee—and had been for the past nine minutes and sixteen seconds. And yet, in all those minutes and seconds, the grisly flashback that had been tormenting her like some next-level horror flick complete with sight, sound, taste, touch and smell for nearly a week hadn't seared in.

Not a single frame.

It might've been because, this time, she was driving the beast.

Task and focus-wise, it made a difference. Even on this dark, desolate and seriously spine- and tailbone-jarring road.

And the panic?

Oh, it was still there. And it was definitely coursing through her veins. But none of the accompanying, adrenaline-laden terror was for her. Every single drop was for Lily.

Evidently that made a difference too. And a definite tactical plus. Bowen didn't have the time to waste holding her hand. Not during this trip.

The first sergeant was busy. While she'd been following the curt directions that he'd occasionally paused to pepper the night air with, Bowen had been on that secure comm link of his nearly nonstop, attempting to scramble a drone and additional ground forces. The latter of which, they desperately needed. Not only to converge on the eighteen-foot-high, mud-walled compound they'd just left behind, but if at all possible, to beat them to the next one.

Hell, Bowen was *still* on that link, pursuing backup.

She and the first sergeant were in sync. Neither of them cared who got to Lily in time to save her from Praeger and her bastard of an ex, so long as *someone* got to her.

Unfortunately, there was no one.

Just them.

The drawdown had left the remaining US and NATO combat forces spread ghostly thin across the entire country, especially this far from Bagram Airbase and Kabul. It was everything Bowen had been able to do to beg, borrow and steal the four US Special Forces and two supplemental Afghan army soldiers he'd brought with him to support Praeger's last minute sham of a family reunion.

The spook had played his hand well.

As a result, she had someone more dangerous than a serial killer to confront. Namely, a rogue and utterly ruthless CIA operative with an agenda.

Never in a million tours on this wretched patch of earth would she have ever thought she'd be praying for the Taliban to show up.

But she was.

The brutal, misogynist assholes were currently making inroads in Herat's outer districts. What were the odds that the Taliban had decided to make a push into Guzarah tonight and had netted the Humvee that Charles Praeger had stolen...with the spook still inside it?

Yeah, not likely. Which meant she was left with the hope that

Praeger had had a change of heart about condemning a woman to the same fate he'd once saved her from. After at least six months of meticulous planning, since that was how long ago Praeger had shown that photo of Lily from the *Al Jazeera* article to her ex.

Even less likely.

Kate winced as the Humvee slammed thorough a pothole so cavernous the first sergeant lost the thread of his conversation as the top of his helmet came perilously close to meeting the steel roof of their vehicle.

"*Shit*. Sorry."

"It's fine. Keep driving, Chief. We're almost there." Bowen switched back to his comm link and whoever was on the other end.

She slowed down to take a right turn onto the final dark, gloomy road, then sped up again. According to Bowen's initial briefing, the compound should be five, six minutes ahead, also on the right. But would Lily even be there?

What if Praeger had chosen somewhere new for the handoff?

The CIA bastard was beyond clever.

Vahid, too.

The hell with the porous US southern border. Since Vahid wouldn't have been able to get inside the States without his *own* country knowing he was gone long enough to get his revenge on Lily, he and Praeger had needed a plan. Given Vahid's visibility in Iran due to his position with their nuclear weapons program, once the man cleared the border at Dogharoon-Islam Qala, they'd have had a span of days to work with, at best.

So the spook had hatched a plan to make those days count—with a series of grisly murders disguised as honor killings. Honor killings that were identical to the final fate Vahid's wife was supposed to have been subjected to all those years ago.

Why? To rattle Lily and herd her back over here.

But that wasn't all. Once Praeger had chosen his victims and tweaked his "serial killer's" MO, he'd set out to find the perfect detective just pigheaded and desperate enough to help it along.

As the Garbage Man case had become public, Praeger must've thought he'd hit the lottery when he realized he had two detectives that fit: her and Arash.

Reporters had clawed through her life, and Arash's too, during the weeks that followed Sergeant Burke's death and Joe's arrest, salivating over all those military connections. Once Praeger's curiosity had been piqued, the CIA operative's security clearance would've paved the way for the rest. A bit of judicious digging into her old Army record would've revealed her multiple rapes by those bastards who'd ambushed the convoy that day—along with the timing of her stay in that quiet room at Craig. Hell, the spook had probably ordered Lily not to mention her time at Bagram, knowing that the doc's silence would pique her own interest and suspicions that much more.

And Arash? One peek at the detective's current Army record—and the detailed background investigation that'd been conducted prior to the granting of his top-secret clearance—would've revealed Arash's horrific part in his sister's so-called honor killing.

Why else had Praeger dumped his first body within her jurisdiction and the second in Arash's? Alone, she or Arash would've easily picked up Praeger's gauntlet.

But together?

They'd actually fed on each other, their combined experiences and, yes, traumas helping to propel their investigations down the enticing trench Praeger had carved out for them, leading them—and Lily—straight back to where Vahid was really holed up.

Hell, Praeger had been so sure he'd had them hooked, he'd

dropped his third victim at the perimeter of the Little Rock Air Base to obfuscate his involvement that much more while cementing the US military's interest and support for the hunt as well. And then he'd killed Daria—but left the nurse's features uncharred and, thus, visible—to tip Lily completely over the edge and motivate her into insisting that she question her father.

And it had worked.

Somehow, Praeger had known about the stone that Vahid had shoved into Lily years ago. If the spook hadn't been there when it had been removed by whoever'd nursed a fourteen-year-old Lily through her burns while she was at that Iranian safe house, Lily had to have relived the experience in her nightmares afterward.

And who was there to comfort Lily during those nightmares while he waited for the Special Forces team to arrive and exfiltrate the girl?

Praeger.

Kate could only imagine the now grown woman's horror at discovering that her cherished savior had become her ultimate betrayer. Worse, all those comforting, paternalist touches the spook had been extending for the past two days, and most likely the past two decades? Lily would see the spook as more of a father. Making the betrayal that much worse. Especially in light of Masud's loving non-protection.

Kate winced as the Humvee blew through another pothole-turned-crater. If nothing else, this week had put her issues with her own dad in perspective.

As for Praeger? Despite all those connect-the-dot hot buttons he'd laid out for her and Arash to trip over, how the hell could they have been taken in so completely? *Especially* her. After all, she was the one who'd spent time with the spook.

"You done beating yourself up about this?"

Kate glanced across the Humvee, spotting what appeared to be a shadowy greenhouse complex in the distance behind the first sergeant's helmet. But was it the Hadiqat Greenhouse? Even without the dense, obscuring cloud cover and with a full, gleaming moon on tap to highlight the sign out front, she'd have been clueless.

The writing was in Arabic.

"Chief?"

The Humvee's rumbling diesel covered her sigh as she refocused on the road. "No."

"Well, you should be." Bowen's attention returned to his comm link for a moment as he gave an affirmative response to something. From what she'd overheard from the first sergeant's side of the conversations, backup was twenty minutes out.

This thing would probably be over by then.

Bowen's sigh was louder than hers, deliberate too, because it briefly overtook the diesel. "If it helps, I didn't see that CIA fucker for who he was either."

Actually, that did help.

What helped even more was that, even with that C-130's flight added in, she'd been in the spook's presence for roughly twenty-four hours total. It wasn't as though she'd worked alongside the man for years as an MP, and then as CID.

That whole "trusting her judgment" thing.

She suspected she and Manning would be working on this incident with a few of those worksheets of his too. If she survived.

Right about now, she was more worried about Lily's survival at the hands of—

"There!"

"I see it, First Sergeant."

Masud had held up his end. Not only was the compound off their right similar to the one they'd just departed, she could make out the distant, murky shape of another sand-colored Humvee—at least, she prayed that's what she was seeing.

She pulled off the road and switched off their lights. They couldn't risk getting any closer to verifying that shape's identity in *this* Humvee. Just as she and Bowen had heard Praeger leaving the previous compound via the vehicle he'd stolen, Praeger and Vahid would be able to hear their arrival in this one.

Killing the engine, she bailed out of the Humvee along with the first sergeant, grabbing the Glock he'd provided upon her arrival at the airport to help soothe her paranoia in country.

Little had she known then that she'd actually need it.

Bowen brandished his M4 as they double-timed across the hardened expanse of dirt and rocks leading up to the compound. Thank God Ruger continued to succeed in guilting her into maintaining her runs whenever possible.

The first sergeant reached the stolen Humvee just ahead of her, his swift glance taking in the camouflaged-uniformed bodies lying face down on either side of the rear of the vehicle in the dirt. Both Afghan army soldiers he'd brought along tonight were dead.

Bowen's soft "*Fuck*" slipped into the dark.

Kate maintained her silence and nodded her regrets.

From the flow of the blood staining the soil, Praeger had taken out the Afghan men the same way he'd dealt with the sergeants married to his first two female victims back in Arkansas. A swift, deep stab to the right lung followed by a severed popliteal artery at the back of the right leg, before he'd left the men to bleed out into the ground.

"Here, Chief."

Kate holstered the Glock and accepted the M16 rifle Bowen had taken off the first fallen Afghan. Reaching down, she retrieved the spare magazine she could see attached to the second soldier's war belt, shoving the extra ammo into her right trouser pocket as she straightened.

"Got a knife on you?"

Her breath frosted out. "No." The Air Force sergeant who'd cleared her for boarding the C-130 in Little Rock had confiscated that too.

Well, she had a replacement now. A gorgeous, if somewhat banged-up Kunai thrower. Bowen had tucked the hilt of the blackened blade into her hand before she could finish shaking her head.

Using the metal ring welded to the butt, she tucked the twelve-inch, double-edged dagger into the pocket of her deputy jacket, creating a makeshift sheath within as it pierced the quilted inner lining of the coat.

"Ready?"

She nodded.

And they were double-timing again, this time around the massive, eighteen-foot mud walls, scanning for an opening. They found it on the southern side.

A decrepit wooden door hung wide open.

Because Praeger hadn't had a free hand or foot to shut it with after Lily had seen her so-called savior slaughter two Afghan soldiers and had begun to fight him?

Or because it was a trap?

Hell, was Lily still even here, much less Vahid and the spook?

They hadn't had time to recon the entire perimeter, let alone look for tire treads. If Praeger had managed to pre-stage a second set of getaway wheels nearby, they were screwed.

Kate came up on the left side of the opening in the towering wall, Bowen on the right, just as they'd discussed between his calls during the drive.

A moment later, the first sergeant breached the compound. He paused inside to cover her entrance.

Once she'd followed him in, they split up.

She skirted the right side of the darkened courtyard, while Bowen took the left, both of them intent on clearing the compound room by room as they went. God willing, one of them would come across a living Lily before they met up in the middle and had to ascend to the second level via the half-rotted wooden ladder Kate had just passed beneath.

At least her eyes were better adjusted to the icy gloom. She couldn't risk using her flashlight—and pinning a bullseye on herself.

Kate cleared her first three rooms in rapid succession.

All were empty save dirt, a mix of old animal feces—large and small—and even more Afghan dust.

The entire place had probably been stripped bare by desperate locals through the years as they and their children had sunk further into war-torn poverty than they'd been at the onset of 9/11 and the initial reign of the Taliban.

She hoped.

Because now that she and Bowen were here, she'd reversed her desire to have the Taliban converging on the place. At least until she and Bowen left—with Lily.

Unfortunately, the doc wasn't in the fourth, dusty room either.

But neither was Praeger.

The fifth was empty too.

The sixth was occupied, however, by the rogue CIA bastard she was seeking...and First Sergeant Bowen.

Oh, Jesus. No!

Bowen was in the middle of the room, lying on his right with his camouflaged back to her, amid a scattering of that ancient feces and dust. Praeger stood in front of the far wall, half hidden within the thicker shadows, looming over the first sergeant's torso and her—holding Bowen's M4. The deadlier end was not pointed at her, but the first sergeant's strangely helmet-less forehead. Blood had begun to pool beneath the lower edge of Bowen's upper-body armor and ribs...but it didn't appear to be spreading out.

She refused to panic. The first sergeant might be paralyzed for the moment, but the expansion of his lungs was still normal. The man just had to hold on for a bit. Long enough for her to figure out how to work this.

"Hello, Kate."

"Fuck you, Chuck."

"Now, now. Watch your mouth. There's no reason to get nasty. As for your companion here, all I had time for was the strike to his lung. Lower that M16 to the ground and gently kick it to the far corner of the room opposite me, and I might delay the slice to the back of the man's knee...or the bullet to his brain."

The opening steps to her recent, deadly dance with Staff Sergeant Burke following the Garbage Man murders reverberated in. She'd lost her primary weapon then too. Along with her backup piece *and* her knife. Worse, this bastard wasn't concussed like Burke had been. Nor did she have a savvy, protective canine lurking nearby.

Right about now, she missed the edge Ruger had given her more.

Hell, she just missed Ruger. If she couldn't find a way to turn this situation around and quickly, Arash would be getting his coveted Shepherd after all. Hers.

"Kate? I know you've developed a latent issue with orders, but—"

"*Fine.*" She lowered the outdated US Army rifle in her hands and laid it in the rat shit at her boots as she kept her stare welded to the current US Army version pointed at Bowen's naked forehead. She had no choice. Not if she wanted to delay that slice—or the threatened bullet—long enough to take down Praeger and save Bowen.

Except...her gut was telling her the spook *wanted* to make that cut.

Needed it, even.

It made sense. You couldn't coldly stab four women as many times as he had, torch the first three corpses and be completely good to go in the brain department. It made her wonder how many other men Praeger had murdered through the years, immobilizing them first and then bleeding them dry with that lung/leg, stab-and-slash combination he seemed to prefer...and in which countries he'd left the bodies.

It seemed she'd been hunting a serial killer all along. Just not the one she'd thought.

"I believed I also said to kick that M16 over here to me."

She complied. Reluctantly. She could make out the rest of the first sergeant's impressive cache of firearms and blades piled near the spook's boots.

"Now the 9mm."

Yeah, these steps and this dance were definitely feeling familiar.

"I don't—"

"You do." The spook's teeth gleamed in the dark. "No, I didn't see Bowen pass it to you. But it was in that burqa, and you slotted it into place a second later. Probably at your back. Either way, you're carrying. Lady, you went from the worst case of jonesing I have *ever* seen to utterly placid by the time you'd turned around out beside that C-130 and headed for your vehicle. I've seen opium addicts take longer to get right."

Shit. Manning was going to have a field day with this worksheet.

If she was lucky.

"Now, give me the handgun, and I'll let you check on the first sergeant. Maybe even offer up a tragic, heartfelt goodbye."

Huh? She should be the one dragging this out, not him.

Or perhaps not.

The man shifted his stance, and she realized what she'd been missing. There was a coating of dust mixed in with the dried rat shit clinging to the knees of those cargo pants. She knew exactly what'd been happening in this room in the moments before she'd entered it. The spook had been kneeling, staring into the first sergeant's eyes.

Watching.

What Praeger had done to the men that the cadaver dog had located in Miller's trees? What the spook had just done to Bowen—and had definitely done to others too? It wasn't about that threatened arterial slice at all. Or the initial strike to the lungs.

It was about what happened in the moments in between.

She wasn't the only one with a deep, insidious need that gnawed at her.

Hell, the spook couldn't *stop* looking at the first sergeant's face. Even now, with her in the room—and still armed.

She knew why. Just as she knew what that shadowy, spherical shape behind Praeger was—and who'd placed it there. Praeger had made that first stab into Bowen's lungs, as he always did. But then the spook had taken the time to remove Bowen's helmet and had hunkered all the way down into the excrement and dirt to meet the first sergeant's stare to get what he *needed*. What Praeger always needed.

Except Praeger hadn't gotten it from Bowen. Not yet.

She'd interrupted him.

Praeger had an obsession too. Otherwise, why not shoot her

now, then finish off the first sergeant lying at those blackened boots, all but frozen in the minutes before his death?

She was certain as she watched the spook's stare flick away from hers to zero in on Bowen's for a split second, before coming right back.

Yeah, the bastard needed it.

But how could she use that need to save Bowen and possibly Lily too?

"Kate? I'm waiting for that handgun."

She removed the 9mm and laid it on the ground at her feet, then kicked it toward the M16 before he could order that too, ignoring the itch that automatically set in with her second weapon's loss. The Glock was still scraping through the dust as she closed in on the first sergeant and hunkered down behind him. The size of the pool of blood was static. From the visible rising and falling of Bowen's chest, his lungs were not.

Thank God.

She couldn't risk turning the man onto his back. Not with the bulk of his body still keeping a decent amount of pressure on that knife wound.

At least, she hoped that was what was happening.

There was an equal chance that the first sergeant's lungs were gradually filling with blood instead, slowly but surely drowning him as those still steady respirations became shallower and shallower until they ceased.

All she could do was pray for the former as she worked to create an opportunity. She'd have to take Praeger down first, and *then* tear into the pouch centered at the rear of Bowen's war belt. That was where she'd kept her own first aid kit when suited up, since from there, she could reach it with either hand.

God willing, Bowen carried chest seals within his.

She risked losing her view of Praeger as she bent over the first sergeant's torso.

Relief seared in as she spotted the first sergeant's open eyes and the gorgeous, if dim, glint of life within. The micro pinch to the left side of Bowen's lips told her the rest. He was still with it enough to understand what they were saying.

He also knew she still had the Kunai he'd taken off the Afghan soldier. But, like her, he knew the timing would be critical.

She'd get one chance. The dagger was jammed into her jacket pocket. How the hell could she outdraw an M4 already aimed at her?

She needed a distraction. Based on the amount of blood soaking into the knees of her trousers, she needed it *soon*.

The spook's glance flicked down to Bowen's again. He was checking to make sure his latest victim-fix was still alive. A split second later, Praeger's focus returned to her.

Not nearly long enough. "Where's Lily?"

The spook tipped his chin upward. "Second level. She's in the middle of her marital reunion. Vahid wanted one last memory to cherish before he did the deed."

As if on cue, a single, piercing scream rent the air.

The terror within cut straight through Kate's gut.

The spook wasn't even fazed.

"How can you just stand here while he rapes and murders her?"

"Come on, Kate. Don't play stupid. If you're here, you know why. You got the gist out of that idiot, Masud."

"I did. And you're a *bastard*."

"Maybe." The man's shrug might've stirred the shadows, but it didn't even ding that reprehensible resolve. "Or maybe I'm just willing to do whatever it takes to get the job done. Like you. Hell, look at how things went down with your friend four years ago in this same shithole of a country."

Max.

"You're wrong." Manning was right; she would've died for Max *if* her death could've saved him. But it wouldn't have. And she'd only had a split second to make that realization before she'd been forced to act on the reality behind it.

The realization just hadn't been conscious.

What this spook was doing was completely conscious and deliberate. The ruthless way he'd gone about accomplishing it was going to trap him in hell for eternity too. And she planned on being the one to send him there.

Somehow.

She checked the first sergeant's torso again. It was still moving. He was still breathing. "We're nothing alike, Chuck. You've sold your soul for a name. One that—"

"You think I did all this for a *name*?" He shook his head sharply, but that carbine didn't move. His glance did. It flicked to Bowen again, then zeroed right back in on her. "We're getting a body for a body, Kate. I give up Lily and we get the identity of a very high-level Iranian physicist who's willing to *defect* to the States. Screw the next limp-dick nuclear agreement. What this physicist has to say will let us undermine Tehran's nuclear weapons ambitions for decades to come, possibly longer. I've been working that bastard upstairs for twenty-one goddamned years, but it's finally paid off."

Oh, Lord. "That's why you were there that day. You weren't in that alley by accident. And Vahid didn't forget something so crucial that he had to leave a wedding to come back and get it. You two had arranged a meeting."

"Yeah. But I confess, I learned my lesson. Like I said, I was new at the game. I made the following get-togethers on more neutral ground."

"Like this place."

The man nodded. "This long damned, drawn-out war did make it easy."

She didn't care about that. Not right now.

"How can you be sure Vahid's even telling the truth?"

"Oh, he is. This job? It's not what folks back home think it is. It's not all spies, lies and James Bond on steroids. It's making connections, person by person—and getting *them* to give up their secrets. To do that, you gotta understand what motivates people. And Vahid? Deep down, he's still that pathetic little prickless cadet, desperate to prove to good ol' Uncle Sam that he never should've been kicked to the curb all those years ago."

"And Lily?" Because he'd played the doc too, right along with her asshole of an ex. Until *this* asshole had realized he could use Lily too. "Damn it, she trusted you."

All that produced was a clipped nod. "And I *earned* that trust. She's the one who blew it. She brought it on herself. I risked everything to help her—and it worked. Vahid still doesn't know that I'm the one who pulled her from the courtyard and put a body in her place. Vahid thinks neighborhood women did it. And Lily? She's the one who risked screwing it up. Time and again. I warned her not to go to Afghanistan. Hell, WITSEC warned her. But she wouldn't listen. So she'll suffer the consequences. Just as I've suffered them because of that asinine Nightingale routine of hers. She and Daria nearly cost me a dozen missions through the years. Fortunately, I'm good at clean-up."

Yeah, not so much.

Even better, it seemed he couldn't control that clawing addiction of his any more than she could. Because yet another glance had flicked down to the first sergeant's, before coming back up to hers.

She followed the spook's driving need to know with her own.

Bowen's ribs were still expanding, contracting.

For now.

"If you're so damned good, why does my co-worker in

Arkansas have a latex glove from the clinic with Daria Farid's blood on the outside and your fingerprints on the inside? And, no, I'm not bluffing. I got a call on Bowen's sat phone."

"So that's how you put it together." Another shrug stirred the shadows, but something about this one told her Praeger wasn't quite as unconcerned as he wanted her to believe. In fact, from the way the man's lips had pressed together, he was actually rattled. "It doesn't matter. The evidence will disappear as soon as I get my human cargo to the States. You've served, Kate. You know how it is. Duty. Honor. Country. In the end, two out of three ain't bad—for Langley and for me."

Yeah, he could talk a good game. But his use of pronouns earlier was telling. *I give up Lily—and we get the identity.*

Not only was tonight not sanctioned; deep down, even Praeger knew it never would be. "What about the murders? You expect me to believe Langley's okay with those too? Or are we just supposed to be overjoyed with your Big Get and consider five women, two US and two more Afghan army soldiers collateral damage?"

"Why not? That's what they were—and what Lily will be." Another glance dipped to Bowen. This one lasted a full, frantic second before it snapped up to her.

It was time.

She shook her head. "Bullshit."

Surprise flickered into the spook's eyes as she stood. Prepared herself. Praeger was six feet away. Distance wasn't the problem. Nor were the shadows.

She needed the bastard facing her when that Kunai flew.

If she didn't hit the T-box between those eyes dead center *and* with enough force to drive that blade deep enough to pierce the brain stem at the back of his skull and cause instant paralysis, he'd still be able to fire the M4. And if he killed her, Bowen and Lily were dead too. "You're right, Chuck. I do need that

Glock." Right about now, she was on fire for it. Not just in her wrist, but her entire body. "But you're craving something, too."

Even now, knowing she was watching him, he couldn't help himself. He flicked his focus to Bowen just long enough to take another look.

Who was jonesing now?

"The hell I—"

"Oh, you are." By his own admission, Praeger had worked undercover for twenty-one years, clinging to that adrenaline-honed edge, never knowing if *this moment* would be his last. That's when the murders would've started. When the spook had begun to wonder what it would be like to *know* he was about to die...and had become driven to find out. "You need to get down in the rat shit and look in that man's eyes. See what First Sergeant Bowen's seeing."

Feel it.

Praeger had murdered those two Afghans out by their Humvee. But because Lily had been in tow, he hadn't been able to get the fix he usually got with killing. That loss made him need it with Bowen all the more right now.

And then he'd need to get it with her.

It was the only reason she was still alive.

She forced herself to wait. The next flick of that glance would be coming any second now. It wouldn't be lasting long enough though. She had no choice. She had to make her move. She'd managed a glance of her own. Bowen's chest was barely rising now. His lungs were definitely filling with blood. If she didn't get to him soon, there'd be no point.

Bowen would be dead.

The moment Praeger caved into his need, she shoved her right hand into her pocket. Out came the Kunai. But as she drew back to launch the blade, a miracle occurred. A loud crash echoed in the courtyard.

Praeger's face turned all the way to the doorway—and her.

The blade cleaved through the air. A split second later, the tip pierced skin and bone, the hilt coming to a solid, thunking rest directly between the spook's eyes.

Kate lunged forward, grabbing his shoulders and slamming the man's entire body toward the wall before it could collapse on top of Bowen. She heard the secondary thump as the spook's back hit the baked mud, followed by a slow scrape as his ass slid down to the floor, coming to rest in yet another pile of rat shit.

It didn't matter; Praeger was already dead.

But Bowen was not.

Yet.

She could only pray Vahid hadn't caused that crash out in the courtyard, because she didn't have time to scramble for her Glock. She was too busy tearing into the center pouch on Bowen's war belt, breathing out her relief as she spotted the sterile chest seals within.

She pulled everything out of the pouch, then flipped the man onto his back. Yanking up his uniform top, she found the wound where she'd suspected.

The blade had penetrated Bowen's chest on the right side, in the space between his protective plating, and just beneath his third rib.

She dug into his stash of gauze and used it to dry the blood from his skin. She ripped into the sterile envelope next, pulled out a seal, and peeled off the backing.

Another swipe of gauze and the seal was in place.

But, damn it, the right side of his chest still wasn't inflating. And while she could see movement on the left, it was shallow.

Dangerously so.

She snatched up the cylinder for the decompression needle she'd dumped in the dirt before flipping the man over, only have a hand close over hers—a woman's.

"Move aside, Kate. I've got this."

She glanced up. Lily's battered and bloodied face greeted her. The doc's left eye was swollen shut. The right was already turning blue with the skin split almost the entire way around. And in the center? An ice-cold determination Kate had never seen or felt in this woman before.

There wasn't a tear in sight.

And the fingers that turned to receive the cylinder?

They might be bloodied and bruised too, but they were surgeon steady.

Kate dropped the cylinder into the woman's hand. Just like that, she was relegated to assistant. She couldn't have been happier.

Praeger was wrong. She had no issue with following orders. Definitely not from *this* doc and about this patient. Because Bowen had a chance now.

Kate spun around, shifting her position into the space above the first sergeant's head to give the doc room to work.

"Lift his right arm and pull up his shirt as high as you can."

Kate complied.

The doc slid the decompression needle from the sterile cylinder. A moment later, Lily was counting the ribs beneath Bowen's raised arm and inserting it.

The soft, beautiful sound of air whispering out of that needle followed.

Another few seconds and the needle itself was out of the first sergeant too, leaving the catheter behind to continue venting the pressure in the man's chest so that his other lung and his heart could resume their normal function.

At least until they got Bowen medevacked out of here.

The doc appeared pleased with her impromptu patient's progress as she thoroughly checked him over, verifying the first sergeant's increased lung capacity and improved mental status. Bowen was doing great, and Lily told him so.

But as the woman turned back, Kate caught a more thorough view of that battered face—and what she'd missed beneath. Holy *shit*. The entire front of the sweater she'd given Lily before their C-130 had taken off from Little Rock was drenched in blood, along with the front of those leggings, right down to and including the soles of the doc's shoes. With her focus zeroed in on the first sergeant, she hadn't even noticed.

"Lily, are you—"

"It's not mine."

"Vahid?"

"Dead."

"Are you certain?"

The woman's nod was as firm and steady as her voice. "I managed to grab his knife. I severed his brachial artery before he could stop me. I stayed until he bled out." She looked at Bowen, at the chest seal that covered the two-inch slash in his skin. "I shouldn't have. If I hadn't, I might not have slipped on that ladder and broken it. And I definitely would've gotten here sooner."

"Trust me—" That distracting crash from the ladder had saved all their lives. "—your timing was absolutely *perfect*."

The doc snapped out another one of those incredibly steady nods, then checked her patient again.

Bowen was visibly breathing easier now. A soft, though admittedly slight version of the smile she'd noted when he'd introduced himself back at the airport in Herat had even slipped onto his lips. A hint of warmth accompanied it.

They'd won, and he knew it.

She was about to retrieve the man's comm link so she could call for a chopper—but there was no need. She could hear it rumbling in.

Backup had finally arrived.

Within minutes, a squad of US Army soldiers had moved in to secure the premises even as a pair of medics were taking over, shifting Bowen onto a spine board and double-timing out of the room and the entire compound—Lily with them—leaving Kate to wait for CID to arrive along with the current in-country forensics team.

It was time to process the compound for evidence and mop up the remaining mess.

Some things never changed.

No matter which uniform she wore.

18

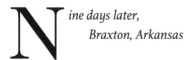

N*ine days later,*
Braxton, Arkansas

SHE'D BEEN GUILTED into bribing her mutt, and they both knew it.

Kate watched as Ruger snatched a French fry from midair and swallowed it whole before patiently waiting for the next. From her carton.

His was already empty and had been for several minutes.

Along with the cardboard container that had held his burger. Granted, the patty had been formed from ground chicken, not beef. But it had been grilled.

That was something, right?

As Dr. Manning had reminded her at the end of their session a mere hour ago—baby steps.

Kate tossed another one of her fries to Ruger, then studied the rapidly cooling chicken burger in the box on the dining table in front of her, aware that Ruger was looking at it too. Hoping. It had taken her six days to return home from her unexpected trip to Afghanistan, and the Shepherd had been abusing her lingering pangs of conscience for every one of them during these last three.

Fortunately, Arash had not.

After First Sergeant Bowen and Lily had left via the medevac chopper, she'd borrowed another soldier's satellite phone to call the detective, as promised. While still securing Praeger's body and any potential evidence on it, she'd assured Arash that she was okay, and had then briefed him on what had happened with the spook.

Arash had agreed to contact Lou, Remy and Agent Wynne to let them know that they'd caught the murderous bastard they were all after—albeit not precisely the one they thought they'd been seeking—and that he'd been taken down in Afghanistan, not Arkansas.

With Praeger's admission of guilt while the spook had been standing over Bowen, combined with the fact that Praeger was now dead, they were cleared to release the various crime scenes and bodies within their respective jurisdictions just as soon as the remaining forensic and administrative processing allowed.

It wasn't much of a gift to the victims' families, but it was all they'd had to offer. That, and the reassurance that the killings had finally stopped.

As for the scene in Herat, once her call to Arash had ended, the official processing of the compound had begun. She'd been photographing Praeger's body and the hovel surrounding it when the lead, in-country CID agent had arrived.

That agent? A sight for seriously exhausted eyes: her old friend, Art Valens.

Not surprisingly, Art hadn't been alone. He'd arrived with

Agent Castile and a forensics team—and yet another CIA spook in tow...as well as stunning news.

From what their new CIA buddy had been able to share, Charles Praeger really had gone rogue. Not only were her suspicions correct regarding the Afghan militiamen at the previous compound, namely that they were working for Praeger, it turned out the Homeland Security contact in Kabul that Praeger had been touting and quoting to her and Arash hadn't even been aware of Masud's arrest. Nor had President Ghani.

So she, Art and their new CIA contact had gotten to work, laying the groundwork for a brokered, US-Iranian body swap of their own.

Because while Ghani and the remainder of the Afghan government were not aware of who Masud and Vahid Baqr were, much less where the men worked, Iran was. And once Iran had been informed that the US had both, they wanted their men back.

Badly.

The US government had agreed. For a price.

Kate glanced down as Ruger snorted softly—his version of a polite attempt to regain her attention and return it to his woefully under-stuffed belly.

Yes, she was out of fries now too. But that chicken burger was still sitting on the table in front of her. Whole. Lonely.

And still giving off that oh-so-enticing aroma...at least to him.

The determined thumping of Ruger's dragon tail, combined with the not-so-subtle slurp of his lolling tongue, let her know that if she still couldn't quite stomach meat yet, he'd be happy to help her out. He was just that giving of a dog.

Kate grinned at her goofy, drooling mutt.

Two seconds after she'd caved in and tossed the top of the bun toward Ruger's talented chops, her phone rang.

It was another old friend.

Kate's smile lingered as she picked up. "As I live and breathe, two calls in two weeks from the vaunted Special Agent Regan Chase. Don't tell me Braxton's finally made it onto the Army's radar?"

Rae's husky laugh filled the line. "Nah, just you. But I know for a fact that you never escaped it. You just thought you had. And fair warning: from what I hear regarding the fallout of your latest visit to Herat, the brass wants you back in *our* uniform—and on active duty."

Yeah, not a good idea.

True, the presence of her newly gifted Glock had been duly noted and ignored by everyone in that same Army uniform for the remainder of the time she'd spent in Herat. And then at Bagram where she and Art had taken Masud and Vahid's body while they'd been finessing the Iranian deal. But Praeger had been right about one thing. She'd definitely needed the 9mm.

That need might've even reared its ugly head when she'd boarded a C-141 for the return flight to Little Rock, because even the pilot had left the Glock, and her, alone.

Yet another Army souvenir to shove inside her dusty footlocker.

Why not? It wasn't as though she could ship the Glock back to Bowen. Mostly because the Army had shipped Bowen to Germany and the Landstuhl Regional Medical Center to recuperate before she'd had a chance to see him again.

But she'd already been officially informed that Bowen was doing well, so that wasn't why Regan was calling.

Crap. Kate tossed the chicken patty and the bottom of the bun to an ever-appreciative Ruger as she stood to pace into her kitchen. "Please tell me the deal didn't fall through."

"Nope. In fact, it's now complete. Art phoned me from Kabul an hour ago. I told him I'd call you. The exchange went down at the Dogharoon-Islam Qala border crossing as planned and right on schedule. We got Lily's mom, her sister and her two brothers—and, of course, Iran got Masud and...Vahid's corpse."

"And how did the guys who Iran sent for the swap take the discovery of the rather ripe condition of the latter?"

Rae's laughter warmed the line once more. "Oh, I understand they were jihad-level pissed. But your new CIA buddy reminded them that you all never actually *said* Vahid was alive. Besides, once Iran's interrogators finish 'interviewing' Masud about those extracurricular meetings his cousin had been conducting with Praeger in Herat, he'll be dead too. Valued engineer or not, they'd have done the same thing to Vahid once they'd 'debriefed' him. This way, they'll always wonder what *we* managed to get."

"True." Were it not for those stabbed and charred bodies, last week's trip back to that hellhole would've been worth it for that alone.

Although, the US government had gotten something out of this entire mess. Though admittedly not nearly as much as Praeger would've given to them. Nor did Washington have the name of the Pakistani scientist who Vahid had been meeting on behalf of Iran—because even a desperate-to-deal Masud hadn't known it. But Washington did have the certain knowledge that there *was* a high-level scientist in Iran's nuclear weapons program who wanted out so badly that he was willing to act on it.

It was up to her new CIA buddy and his co-workers to find that scientist.

As for Masud?

Rae was right. Lily's loving pops would most likely be as dead as his cousin before the week was out. But since Washington would probably never be certain of that fate, Maya Baqr and Lily's younger siblings would be joining the doc in the entire family's new, WITSEC-created life.

Hell, even if the Company did somehow receive proof that Masud was dead, those new identities would remain prudent, since someone in the Iranian government or Quds Force might be pissed enough over being snookered regarding Vahid's decided lack of life upon his repatriation to seek revenge. With as many *fatwas* as the country's grand ayatollah had issued over the past week alone, it might even be likely.

"I appreciate the call, Rae. Thanks for letting me know." Especially on a Saturday afternoon, the week before Christmas.

Kate returned to the table to retrieve the cardboard wrappings from Ruger's very bountiful meal and carted them into the kitchen to dump them in the trash.

"Yeah, I'm not done. I've got two more messages. The first is from Lily. Again, via Art. She says to tell you thanks for the pep talk you gave her at Bagram; that she took one look at Yasmin and realized you were right. I'm assuming that's good news."

"It is." Great in fact.

The confident doc in Lily might've been a force to be reckoned with while she'd been saving Bowen's life, but once the adrenaline had worn off, that confidence had bottomed out. When Kate had stopped by to check on her at Bagram, she'd found Lily depressed and doubting her career, because she'd used her medical knowledge to kill Vahid. How could she continue to practice medicine—as Dr. Basque, or anyone else—when she was guilty of murder? Lily had refused to accept that Vahid's death had been straight-up self-defense. Kate had finally left Lily with a question of her own.

If Yasmin had been forced to marry Vahid and the girl had done the same thing to him on their wedding night, would Lily have called that murder too?

Even then, Lily hadn't been sure. But she was now.

And that was definitely a good thing.

As for that Railroad of Lily's? She'd have to find another way to support it. Praeger had been right about something else. Helping those women in need did risk her cover. But now that the doc had four other covers to worry about, she had a feeling Lily—or whatever her name was now—would find a way to help...and stay safe.

Kate returned to the table to push her chair in. "And the final message?"

Rae had mentioned two. What could be left?

"Oh, that one's from me, and it concerns Art and me. Art said you told him about your visit with Joe at Leavenworth, and that you asked him to pass on your thoughts to the rest of CID where needed. I wanted to let you know the added insight helped me. And Art? He's still frazzled by work, but he's also back to his old, craggy self."

"I'm glad. And I appreciate the messages and body swap info. Thanks for calling. I hate to cut you off, but company just turned into my drive."

No, not invited. But based on Ruger's whirling happy dance, their visitor was welcome—by them both.

"Not a problem. Stay in touch, Kate. And stay safe out there, okay? From what I've seen, you've got some serious assholes populating your neck of the woods."

"That goes double on your end. Bye."

Kate smiled as she hung up and tucked her phone back inside its slot in her utility belt. It was nice to know her epiphany about Joe had helped others. Especially Art, given that whatever Art and Agent Castile were currently trying to keep a lid on in Afghanistan was eating at the man. She hadn't asked about the cause, and Art hadn't told. It was the way of CID. Hell, most cop shops—federal, military or civilian.

All she could do was hope that he and Agent Castile wrapped it up quickly, and that it stayed off the evening news.

What she'd shared with Art had been the truth. She'd looked straight into Joe's eyes—knowing what she now knew about the bastard—and had still seen absolutely *nothing*. Because there was nothing to see. Not only did Joe not regret his actions, he still believed his wife deserved those stolen organs over their rightful, murdered owner.

That just wasn't something a normal person would have sensed.

And so they all hadn't.

Damned if Manning hadn't been spot on again—she'd told him so, too. This morning and last Saturday, as well. Since she hadn't returned from Bagram yet, they'd had their session via a video call over Skype. She and the shrink had spent most of the session discussing her visit with Joe and how it had allowed her to see things—and herself—more clearly now. She'd even filled out another one of those post-traumatic symptom assessments she'd been taking before her in-person sessions at the VA hospital in Little Rock. Manning had been thrilled with the marked decrease in last week's scores—and this morning's too. The shrink was even more pleased with the corresponding improvement to her psyche.

So was she.

She was doubly glad that her personal takeaway had helped Rae as well. She knew from a shared, past Christmas that the merry season that was bearing down on a huge portion of the world was the opposite of merry for Rae, and for good cause. Worse, given the number on the tragic anniversary that would be accompanying it, this year's holiday would be an especially difficult one for the CID agent.

Kate made a mental note to check in on Rae in the coming week, then nudged her attention back to Braxton and the needs of her current department as she passed through the living room to reach the front door of her home.

According to the hops that had entered Ruger's happy dance, not to mention his full body swirls, their not-quite-unexpected guest was headed up the walk. She didn't bother with a perfunctory glance through the slats. With Ruger's bionic hearing and fervent greeting tailored to the man on the other side, she simply opened the door.

"Hey, boss."

"Afternoon, Kato. Figured you'd be back by now. But I wanted to give you a chance to feed that hungry hound of yours before I came over."

"Oh, he ate." Both chicken burgers and two small orders of unsalted fries.

Despite the reluctance of her nose and brain earlier, her now very empty stomach rumbled with what might've been.

Ruger, however, had a non-judgmental bottomless pit inside him. One that, based on the paper lunch sack that Lou had brought, was about to be treated to yet another juicy bone with bits of beef attached. Though this one appeared to be a Della Simms home-kitchen special. Like Ruger, Lou had figured that her taste buds would still be on a meat strike.

And like Ruger, he was right.

That lone can of vegetarian chili in her pantry was in her very near future.

The Shepherd accepted the treat from Lou's hand with a giddy wag and a departing burp that had her boss chuckling as he crumpled up the bag before shoving it in the pocket of his sheriff's jacket.

"So, what's up?" Because something was. Yeah, Lou was checking up on her, and a bit more openly now that she knew that he knew she was seeing a shrink. But there was a glint in his soft brown stare. Lou had brought something beside the bone.

The man had news. And it was good.

"Seth's stayin' on. He stopped by the station this mornin' while I was catchin' up on paperwork and told me that my search to replace deputies was down to just fillin' Feathers' spot. Which is damned doubly good, 'cause I may have found someone to replace Bob. I'll know more come Monday."

"That's fantastic." Both revelations.

But especially the one regarding Seth.

That glint turned shrewd. "You knew, didn't you?"

"Pretty much." She'd gotten a text from Seth while she was still in Herat, asking for her shrink's number. Seth had also pulled her aside yesterday as she'd headed out on patrol to let her know that he'd not only joined Manning's after-hours PTSD support group for vets and first responders, but that his first meeting had gone...well.

"I appreciate what you done for the boy. And I know Seth does too."

"Yeah, he said as much."

Lou nodded. "And you? You doin' okay? You didn't say much at work, but I know goin' back over there cain't have been fun."

Now there was an understatement.

She let the subtle, questioning poke into the current state of her psyche slide. For one, she'd just spent an hour in Manning's office letting him do the same—and the shrink had been a hell of a lot more open and ruthlessly skilled about it.

And two, here she and Lou were on yet another Saturday, the both of them in uniform...when only one of them had actually been to the station that day.

Like the shrink and Charles Praeger, Lou knew full well she'd worn hers into Little Rock once again just so she could openly carry her service Glock.

Baby steps, right?

"I'm good, Lou." She nodded crisply. Firmly. But it was the

use of his first name that eased the man's doubts once and for all.

His returning nod was equally firm. "Well, alrighty then. I'd best get home. I'm supposed to take Della to a matinee movie up in Conway today—and it looks like you and Ruger still have a baby evergreen to chop down and drag inside." His girth turned toward the door, then stopped. "Dang it; near plum forgot. That cold case file I gave you a bit ago? You didn't happen to bring it home with you, did you?"

"I did. I haven't had a chance to study it though." He'd handed the folder to her two weeks ago Friday, when she'd been certain she was going to quit. So what had been the point in even cracking the cover?

But then Aisha's body had turned up in Nash Weaver's field and, somehow, everything had changed.

"Yeah, I know. It's been a busy couple a weeks. I had an idea 'bout it last night though, and I wanted to double-check my memory on somethin'."

"It's down the hall." The folder had been on the table with everything else she'd shoved into the basket that she'd then shoved at Seth. "The doc was freaked when she got here. I didn't want to make it worse by leaving casework lying around." She'd been so busy since her return that she'd just grabbed the work-sheets she'd needed for this morning's session with Manning and had left the rest. "I'll get it."

She winced as Lou followed her down the hall...and got a good look at the thick layer of dust on every single item in her dad's old room, except the laundry basket.

She pulled out the missing person's file Lou had handed her when he'd first asked her to review it. This time, she actually opened the manila folder.

Two things jumped out at her. The date the presumed victim had gone missing—and the original responding deputy's name.

"This is one of my dad's old cases." And it was unsolved?

Wow.

"Yeah, your old man was good. But, frankly, you're better. So I figured, since it was sittin' in that file cabinet, the pages inside yellowin' and the witnesses who mighta seen or spoken to the man last in danger of dyin' off or movin' away—"

"What did you say?"

"About witnesses dyin'?"

Oh, hell's bells, no. "The other part."

"About you bein' the sharper detective?" The sheriff shook his head, clearly bemused. "Well, Christ's toes, missy. It weren't even a contest. You solved your first case at fifteen—and it was a first-degree murder. The bastard got life."

She'd *what*?

"Lou—what are you talking about?"

"The Belton murder. When Ken Belton killed Penelope, his wife of—what? five, six years—for tryin' to leave town with their kid."

Kate shook her head, more confused than ever. "I remember the case." Not only had it been her dad's case, the Belton murder had been one of the only two murders in town before Staff Sergeant Burke had begun leaving those oversized, brown paper bags around Braxton's backroads with body parts in them. "But I certainly don't remember solving that case. Heck, the only thing I do remember about it is—"

"Comin' into the kitchen in the middle of the night, 'cause you was thirsty? Yeah." Lou tipped his crop of silver toward the yawning door of her dad's room and the hall beyond. "Your dad and I were sittin' out there at the kitchen table, hashin' through the facts for the thousandth time. We were desperate. We had Ken in custody and we knew from the bastard's lack of remorse, and flat-out glee that Penn was dead, that he'd done it. But we'd already searched his house, barn and entire property. We couldn't find any rifles, let alone the one he'd used to kill her. We were outta time. We had to let him go the next mornin' or the judge woulda had us all for brunch. You musta been listenin' in the hall, 'cause you just breezed in to get a glass and asked if we'd checked the root cellar."

"Yeah, and Dad laughed in my face."

"He did. And I admit, I mighta chuckled too. 'Cause this is Arkansas. With the water table as high as it is, basements and cellars are about as rare as a barrel racer clingin' to an English saddle. But then you mentioned how Dan Parish had told you that he'd gotten locked in Billy Tennet's grandma's cellar and how her house sat on a hill—and, well, wasn't the Belton place perched on one too? So we made another search at dawn."

Okay, that all she remembered. Mostly because she'd been pissed that her dad had laughed at her in front of Lou, who she'd known for all of six months by then. And, anyway, "You found the rifle in the barn, wedged between last year's bales of hay."

"Nope. We found it in the root cellar that was hidden beneath a rug in a hall off the kitchen. Damned hidey-hole was five feet high with a dirt floor. Three out of four walls had wooden shelves that looked like they been there since the Civil War—along with jars of peaches on one of 'em. But in the back of them peaches?" He nodded. "That old Remington 700 that Ken's granddaddy bought, and that Ken used to hunt and shoot Penelope, and that we used to put him away for life."

Son of a *bitch*. "Dad lied to me."

Hell, Lou had too.

But at least her boss had the grace to be embarrassed enough to turn a deep ruddy red about it now. Lord knew her dad never would have.

"I'm sorry, Kato. He didn't want you to know. And, well, he was your dad. Jack told me that you were determined to join the

Army and be an MP. And I knew he was right. He said if you knew how good you really were, that you'd go for sure...and end up in one of all them flag-draped coffins that were comin' home in droves at the time—" The man shuddered as his eyes glistened with the terror of it. Even now.

Kate reached out and hugged him.

What else could she do?

"It's okay, Lou." And it was. Because at least now she knew. And, Lord, did it make that whole "trusting her judgment" issue settle in easier.

Plus, the man in front of her, still trying to get that glistening under control as he squeezed her back, had truly withheld the truth out of love.

But her dad?

The hug ended. Lou gave the shredded side of her face a final, soothing pat and stepped back, swiping at his own cheeks as he sighed.

Kate stared at the dust covering the dark, heavy headboard butted up against the wall beside them and the equally dark, clunky dresser that went with it. She'd been home for four years now, and she could still count on one hand the number of times she'd been in here. Because of the man who'd once slept in this room...and because of the insidious, inescapable fact that she'd never been able to screw up the nerve to admit to anyone except Max. She hadn't even been brave enough to admit it to Manning.

"My dad hated me. I don't know why, but he did."

That dried up the remaining glistening in Lou's eyes. But his cheeks had turned ruddier. From anger. "Oh, missy, that man hated himself. And, hell, he deserved it."

She blinked at Lou. Several times. Trying to wrap her mind around the words that had just come out of his mouth.

Because they were the last words she'd have ever expected to hear from him.

But that crop of silver bobbed as its owner nodded. "Yep, I know. Jack was my friend. But he could be a donkey's ass. Ya gotta understand. Jack was there for me, offerin' a shoulder when I needed one most. When my ma and pa died in that crash when I was just a kid. Then later, when Della and I got married, and we found out we couldn't have kids 'cause of me—and the State wouldn't let us adopt bein' how she was bipolar. Then your mom died, and Jack came home." Those muddy eyes glistened again as Lou pushed up a shrug. "And he gave us you. Well, loaned you out to us now and then. But it was enough. *You* were enough. 'Cause Della and me? We love you like you was our own. So, I gotta keep all that in mind when I think about the man. But there's the rest too. There's what he done to you. How he'd talk to you and run you down. And that? Well, Jesus forgive me, 'cause I cain't ever forgive that, no matter how hard I try."

Oh, Lord.

She could feel her own eyes glistening now.

Burning.

Kate shook her head, trying to clear the tears before they could leak out and stain her face...and failed. The sniff she managed helped. "I love you and Della too."

"I know that. And so does she. I also always knew that your dad didn't have anywhere else to go. But you do. You were meant for bigger things, Kato. Bigger places. You always were. And you got a taste of it all again this past week, too."

She had.

Nor could she lie to him or herself. It had felt damned good to be back on that razor's edge in Herat. "You might be right, boss. But maybe I've got reasons to stay. A lot of them."

The man standing in front of her, for one. The mutt out in

her den, gnawing on that new bone of his, for another. Not that Ruger had needed it. She'd seen the lion's hoard of older bribes that Arash had been contributing to while she'd been gone.

And there were the guys in the department. Seth, Owen and—

"That detective who stopped by—knowin' where your spare key's kept—to hang out with Ruger while I was here...he included in all them reasons you got to stay?"

Maybe.

She'd phoned Arash four more times since the call she'd made after Praeger's death. Texted him too. It was necessary; they were both wrapping up their casework. She'd even seen Arash twice in the three days since she'd been back. Again, because of their cases. She hadn't brought up what he'd said out on her deck before Lily's nightmare had interrupted them though. And he hadn't pushed for the answer she'd yet to give.

But Arash Moradi wasn't the only one who'd been hooked by a pair of eyes.

She was taken with his too.

Along with the rest of the man.

Manning had been pressing her for five sessions now to allow herself to feel—her memories and the fallout they'd created inside her. He'd encouraged her to feel other things as well, especially what was happening within her right now. The truth was, when it came to Arash, she not only wanted to feel, she already did. She'd admitted as much to Manning during their Skype session last Saturday. They'd discussed it all again in person at the VA hospital in Little Rock today. Her judgment, her meeting with Joe, everything that had happened since, including Arash.

She was finally ready to give the detective his answer.

But it seemed she'd failed to provide a timely one for Lou.

The sheriff just grinned, then laughed and shook his head—and let it go.

Lou looked around at the thick layer of dust coating all that dark, clunky wood. "Well, if you are gonna stay, you need to make a few changes. For one—" He ran his hand through the film on the dresser beside him and brandished the resulting clumps of gray. "—this ugly-ass furniture has to go. Now Della won't believe it, but even I can see that. The Torres family lost it all in the fire you missed while you were takin' your Afghan vacation earlier this week. I heard things were 'specially tight, so they weren't insured, neither. They'd be grateful for a few things while they get back on their feet."

Kate nodded. Smiled.

That was a fantastic idea.

It led to others. Ones she couldn't believe she hadn't thought of until right now. "I think I'll strip off this hideous plaid wallpaper and paint in here, too."

Something bright and cheery, and with wildflowers stenciled here and there.

Just what her dad would've hated.

Lou nodded as well, getting deep into the spirit of it all as he pointed into the connecting bath. "Hell, rip out every single one of them bath fixtures and put in brand spankin' new ones. I'll help. So will the rest of the boys. Della can make her famous, slow-cooked ribs while we all work. Either way, ya gotta make this place yours."

He was right.

"You're on. I'll let you know when it's time for the plumbing. But right now, you've got a movie date to make, boss."

Lou had been right about that still absent evergreen, too. She planned on taking Ruger for a walk in the woods this afternoon, so they could search for the perfect one. Once they dragged the tree into the den, she'd decorate it with the twinkling lights and paper bones she'd hung on last year's, while her mutt gnawed on his gift from Lou.

And afterward?

Well, she had a phone call to return to a certain detective out in Mazelle. A call that had nothing to do with casework, and everything to do with them. Then again, she might just reverse those tasks and make that phone call first.

See how Arash felt about decorating trees.

~

Thanks so much for reading my work. I hope you enjoyed it! As you know, an author's career is built on reviews. Please take a moment to leave a quick comment or an in-depth review for your fellow readers

HERE.

~

Are you ready for
Kate's next gripping adventure?

***Beneath the Bones*:**

Some secrets should stay buried...

CLICK HERE for details on BENEATH THE BONES, Book 3 in the Hidden Valor Military/Veterans Suspense Series.

~

Join Candace's list to keep abreast of book release info & Reader Crew Extras:

CandaceIrving.com/newsletter

For more on PTSD, turn the page to read the Afterward by CPT's creator, Dr. Patricia Resick, Ph.D.

You'll also find website links for real-world PTSD & CPT resources at the end of my Author's Note.

AFTERWORD

BY PATRICIA A. RESICK, PH.D.

In this series, Kate had very severe PTSD which not only resulted in panic attacks but dissociative states in which she had no memory and found herself waking up in strange places. In the first book, *The Garbage Man*, she engaged in self-harm, the twisting of Max's watch until she injured her wrist, in order to try to control her anxiety. Most PTSD is not so severe, but Kate had clearly been through emotional and physical abuse as a child followed by witnessing or finding dismembered bodies in her military service. Her "index" event, the one that causes the most PTSD symptoms, was the death of her good friend Max and the death and burning of others who were riding with her when ambushed. It was followed by her abduction and group rape (although she was unconscious at the time, she knows about them). And although a blocked memory for most of the first book, she killed a number of people and saw Max beheaded. It would have been surprising if she didn't have severe PTSD. On top of that, her police cases include betrayal by others (that she blamed herself for not figuring out sooner), more trauma triggers such as dismembered bodies and burned bodies that were reminders of earlier traumatic events as part of her work.

PTSD is a normal reaction to serious life-threatening traumas to self or others or sexual assault. Most people recover from a traumatic event in a few months unless something blocks the recovery. More about that in a minute. There are four categories of symptoms that must be met in order to diagnose PTSD. The person must have some kind of intrusive reminders when they don't want to think about the traumatic event(s) such as images or smells, flashbacks, or nightmares. The next two categories are natural responses to being reminded of the trauma, physiological arousal such as fear or anger, sleep, concentration problems, or startle responses and being hypervigilant (e.g., Kate always having her loaded gun within reach, even in sessions with her therapist).

Also falling under the physical reactions are physical aggression and reckless or self-destructive behavior (twisting Max's watch). Emotional reactions can be any kind of negative emotions from fear or terror, anger, sadness, or disgust (for Kate, the smell of the burned bodies or gasoline) and detachment from others. Thoughts (cognitions) often include guilt, shame, faulty beliefs about others with regard to the traumatic events and negative beliefs about self or others that have generalized into the present and future (Kate is wracked with unreasonable self-blame and thoughts that she has poor judgment).

In order to cope with all of these types of symptoms, people avoid internal and external reminders in any way they can from intentionally pushing the memories away, to all sorts of harmful behaviors such as drinking, avoiding therapy, refusing to talk about their experiences with anyone, etc. Dissociative amnesia and pain can also serve as avoidance of the memory. The biggest problem with avoidance is that it blocks recovery. We think that people who have a diagnosis of PTSD have stopped the natural recovery process by not allowing themselves, or being prevented from, feeling their emotions and not getting any corrective information about their faulty thinking about the causes and consequences of the traumatic events. Their brains keep trying to find an acceptable place to put the memory but because of avoidance, it just keeps coming up again and again, for some people for the rest of their lives, until something or someone intervenes.

Cognitive Processing Therapy (CPT) helps the patient by teaching them skills to figure out how they got stuck in their PTSD, either by not feeling their natural emotions or by saying things to themselves that increases the desire to avoid other helpful people and keeps the PTSD symptoms alive and active. CPT starts with some education and then an impact statement, about a page long, about why they think the index event occurred (their thoughts) and what the consequences are for their relationship with themselves and others. This exercise is then turned into a stuck point log from which all of the other worksheets are drawn from. We use a series of progressive worksheets to teach the patient to become their own therapist and to learn more fact-based and balanced thinking.

CPT is often 12 sessions, hopefully more than once a week, and can be conducted individually or in groups. However, CPT has also been tested as flexible length and more recently intensively conducted across a week or two. It can be conducted over the computer as well and many people have received CPT during the pandemic. There have been more than 30 controlled studies of CPT with different populations and traumas across the world and dozens of program evaluation studies in clinical settings with civilians, veterans, and active duty military. For more information see the links that are provided at the end of the following Author's Note.

Patricia A. Resick, Ph.D.

A NOTE FROM THE AUTHOR

INCLUDES LINKS FOR MORE ON PSTD & CPT

Dear Reader—

When I first conceived of the character of Deputy Kate Holland, I knew she would suffer from severe post-traumatic stress disorder due to her experiences as a prisoner of war in Afghanistan. As a veteran, I was determined to make Kate's recovery journey as realistic as possible. And since there are no quick fixes for PTSD, Kate wasn't going to get one. Hence, it took Kate the entirety of *The Garbage Man*, book 1 in her Hidden Valor suspense series, to go from denial to the realization that she needed help.

In this second book of the series, *In the Name Of*, I wanted Kate to actually enter therapy, even as she was tasked to work yet another series of grisly murders in and around her hometown of Braxton, Arkansas. I also wanted Kate's PTSD arc to incorporate normal setbacks along the way, as well as her eventual successes —because that's how life works.

I began where I always do: with research. Since Kate's trauma occurred as a result of combat, I initially plowed through a number of profoundly moving PTSD memoirs. From there, I surveyed the various types of treatments that are currently available for PTSD. Upon discovering that Cognitive Processing Therapy (CPT) is the preferred treatment for the military, VA and thousands of psychiatrists and psychologists around the world, I dug deeper.

CPT is a time-tested, effective PTSD treatment created and developed by Dr. Patricia Resick, Ph.D. Created in 1988, it's been in use for decades and is becoming more refined all the time. The therapy involves 12 trauma-focused sessions that center around "stuck points" or problem areas in thinking that interfere with the normal recovery process.

The more I read about CPT, the more I knew this was the right approach for Kate. I quickly purchased Dr. Resick's CPT therapists' manual and began to plow through the chapters. As I did, I deliberately took Kate through the prescribed 12 sessions of therapy laid out within. Not only did I have her character in mind as I read, I filled out the manual's enclosed worksheets as "Kate". The more worksheets I filled out and the more stuck points I uncovered, the more I realized I wanted readers to make that journey with Kate.

And what better way to share Kate's CPT journey than to weave the revelations within those worksheets into the Hidden Valor books?

I also wanted to incorporate the results from Kate's PTSD symptoms checklist. But since the wording on the official checklist is not mine—along with the pointed, probing questions on those CPT worksheets—I did what any writer would do. I emailed CPT's creator, the brilliant and amazingly generous Dr. Resick to ask for permission to use them.

Not only did Dr. Resick respond to my email, she loaned me her incredible expertise as I crafted Kate's therapy. Dr. Resick answered my endless questions. She also helped me dig so much deeper into Kate and her psyche than I'd have thought possible. The result? While Kate's PTSD is pure fiction, her recovery and its timeline are quite real. Even better—because it's based in reality—Kate's PTSD arc actually drives the suspense plot at times, affecting her current murder investigations in surprising ways. How cool is that?

Since PTSD can be such a crippling and pervasive syndrome—not only among our nation's veterans, but also amid folks from every country and every walk of life—I wanted to offer up a few official, real-world links for CPT. If you're suffering from PTSD or know someone who is, please check out the information and assistance at the ends of the links.

For more on PTSD—including symptoms & treatment—visit the National Center for PTSD: https://www.ptsd.va.gov/understand/what/ptsd_basics.asp

For more information on CPT: https://cptforptsd.com

To find a CPT-trained therapist near you or someone you care about: https://cptforptsd.com/cpt-provider-roster/

To listen to the Open Stance podcast with PTSD expert Dr. Patricia Resick, Ph.D., ABPP: https://pod.casts.io/podcasts/open-stance/episodes/open-stance-with-ptsd-expert-dr-patricia-resick-ph-d-abpp

To listen to The Therapy Show podcast on CPT with Dr. Patricia Resick, Ph.D.: https://www.therapyshow.com/podcasts/episode/44795d33/53-dr-patricia-resick-on-cognitive-processing-therapy-a-gold-standard-treatment-for-ptsd

To listen to a real patient undergo CPT: https://www.thisamericanlife.org/682/ten-sessions

Fair Winds & Following Seas,
Candace

DID YOU KNOW?

I'm also writing an active-duty
Army CID Detective series.
Here's a sneak peak for

BLIND EDGE
Book 2 in the Deception Point
Military Detective Series,
Featuring Special Agent Regan Chase

Prologue

THE BIBLE WAS WRONG. Vengeance didn't belong to the Lord. It belonged to him.

To them.

To the twelve soldiers who'd stumbled out of that dank, icy cave, each as consumed as he was by the malevolence that had been carved into their souls. A second later, the night breeze shifted—and he caught a whiff of *him*. He couldn't be sure if that rotting piece of camel dung had been left behind as a lookout or if the bastard was part of a squad waiting to ambush his team. When the combined experiences of countless covert missions locked in, allowing him to place the stench wafting down along with stale sweat and pure evil, he no longer cared. Because once again, he smelled blood.

Fresh blood.

It permeated the air outside the cave, as did the need for retribution. As his fellow soldiers faded into the wind-sheared boulders, he knew they felt it too.

By God, they would all taste it.

Soon.

He shot out on point. There was no need to glance behind as he reached the base of the cliff and shouldered his rifle. His team had followed, protecting his back as they'd done every op these past months. The trust freed him to focus on their unspoken mission. On the blood pooling around seven bodies laid out on the floor of that cavern, and then some. He tucked the blade of his knife between his teeth and began to climb. Rock tore at his fingers as he jammed them into crevice after crevice, causing his own blood to mingle with the death still staining his hands. Moments later, he stopped, locking the toes of his boots to a narrow ledge as he scanned the dark.

Nothing.

He resumed his climb. The same moonless night that cloaked his prey protected him and his team. As long as they were mute, they were safe. Unless—

Shit!

He froze as the wind shifted, shooting his own stench heavenward. He caught the answering scuffle of panicked boots.

Too late, bastard.

He was almost there.

His position compromised, he grabbed a scrub pine, using it to whiplash up the remaining three feet of cliff.

Loose rock bit into his soles, causing him to skid to a halt two yards from his prey. The wind shifted once more, whipping a filthy turban from the bastard's face. A second later, he was staring into pure, bearded hatred as an AK47 rifle swung up. He grabbed his knife and lunged forward. Blood gushed over his knuckles as he buried the blade to its hilt. He hauled the bastard in closer, staring deep into that blackened gaze, for the first time in his life embracing the carnal satisfaction that seared in on a close-quarters kill—until suddenly, inexplicably, the gaze wavered...then slowly disintegrated altogether.

To his horror, it coalesced once more, this time into a soft blue hue he knew all too well.

Sweet Jesus—*no!*

It was a lie. A trick. An illusion. This latest flood of adrenaline had simply been too much to absorb. That was all.

Goddamn it, that was *all.*

He'd never know how he managed to hold his heart together as he released the knife and brought his fingers to his eyes. He rubbed them over and over, praying harder than he'd ever prayed as he sank to his knees. But as he blinked through his tears and forced himself to focus on the river of scarlet gushing into the snow, he knew it was true. The body in his arms wasn't that of his enemy. Nor was he in some freezing mountain pass half a world away. He was in his own backyard.

And he'd just murdered the woman he loved.

Now I lay me down to sleep,
I pray the Lord my soul to keep.

If I should kill before I wake,
I pray the Lord it's my enemy I take.

Chapter 1

Military Police Station
Fort Campbell, Kentucky

US Army Special Agent Regan Chase stared at the five-foot fir anchoring the corner of the deserted lounge. A rainbow of ornaments dangled from the tree's artificial limbs along with hundreds of twinkling lights, each doing its damnedest to infect her with an equally artificial promise of home, hearth and simpering happiness. Fifteen months ago, she might've succumbed. Tonight, that phony fir simply underscored the three tenets of truth Regan had crashed into at the tender age of six. One, no one sat around the North Pole stuffing sacks with free toys. Two, reindeer couldn't fly. And three, if there ever had been some jolly old geezer looking out for the boys and girls of the world, he'd been fired for incompetence a long time ago.

The current proof was handcuffed to a stall in the military police station's latrine, attempting to purge what appeared to be an entire fifth of nauseatingly ripe booze. Unfortunately, the majority of the alcohol had long since made it into the man's bloodstream. Even more unfortunate, Regan had no idea whose bloodstream said booze was currently coursing through.

Not only had their drunken John Doe been arrested sans driver's license and military ID, he'd stolen the pickup he'd used in tonight's carnage.

Regan turned her back on the tree and headed for the coffee table at the rear of the lounge, sighing as she sank into one of the vinyl chairs. She reached past a bowl of cellophane-wrapped candy canes to snag the stack of photos she'd queued into the duty sergeant's printer upon her arrival. The close-up of the stolen pickup's silver grill splattered with blood flaunted its own obscene contribution to the night's festivities. The scarlet slush adhering to the tires beneath provided even more proof of yet another Christmas shot to hell.

Make that crushed.

Regan studied the remaining dozen photos. From the angle and depth of the furrows running the length of the snowy street, John Doe hadn't tried to slow down, much less swerve. Instead, he'd plowed into a trio of teenagers making the rounds of Fort Campbell's senior officer housing and belting out carols to the commanding general himself. One of the boys had suffered a broken leg. Another had dislocated his shoulder as he'd tried to wrench his younger brother out of the way of the truck's relentless headlights. Unfortunately, he'd failed.

As far as Regan knew, the kid was still in surgery.

She should phone the hospital. Find out if he'd made it to recovery. She was about to retrieve her cellphone when the door opened. A lanky, red-haired specialist strode in, a ring-sized, gift-wrapped box in his left hand, the naked fingers of a curvaceous blond in his right.

The specialist paused as he spotted Regan. Flushed. "Sorry, Chief. Thought the lounge was vacant."

He held his breath as he waited. Regan knew why. She'd transferred to Fort Campbell's Criminal Investigation Division two weeks earlier. Not quite long enough for the resident military policemen to know if CID's newest investigator had a poker up her ass regarding midnight rendezvous while on duty, even on holidays.

Regan scooped the photos off the table, tucking them into the oversized cargo pocket on the thigh of her camouflaged Army Combat Uniform as she stood. She scanned the name tag on the soldier's matching ACUs as she grabbed her parka and patrol cap. "It's all yours, Specialist Jasik. I was about to leave for the hospital."

Why not?

She wouldn't be getting a decent statement until their drunken Doe sobered up. Given the stunning 0.32 the man had blown on their breathalyzer, that would be a good eight hours, at least. If the man didn't plunge into a coma first.

Jasik relaxed. He led the blond to the couch as Regan passed. "Thanks, Chief. And Merry Christmas."

Regan peeled back the velcroed grosgrain covering of her combat watch and glanced at the digital readout: 0003. So it was —all three minutes of it. Though what was so merry about it, she had no idea. But that was her problem. Or so she'd been told.

Regan returned the salutation anyway, donning her camouflaged parka and cap as she departed the lounge. Nodding to the duty sergeant, she pushed the glass doors open. Icy wind whipped across a freshly salted walk, kicking up snowflakes from the two-foot banks scraped to the sides. The flakes stung her eyes and chapped her cheeks as she passed a pair of recently de-iced police cruisers at the head of the dimly lit lot.

By the time Regan reached her Explorer, she was looking forward to the impromptu hospital visit. It would give her a chance to stop by the ER and commiserate with Gil. Like her, he had a habit of volunteering for Christmas duty.

For an entirely different reason, though.

Regan unlocked her SUV. Exhaust plumed as she started the engine. Grabbing her ice scraper from the door, she cleared the latest layer of snow from her front windshield. She was finishing the rear when an ear-splitting wail rent the air.

Ambulance. On post.

Judging from its Doppler, it was headed away from the hospital.

The police station's door whipped open, confirming her hunch. A trio of ACU-clad military policemen vaulted into the night, their combat boots thundering down the salted walk. The first two MPs peeled off and piled into the closest de-iced cruiser. The third headed straight for her.

Regan recognized the soldier's tall, ebony frame: Staff Sergeant Otis T. Wickham.

They'd met in front of their drunken Doe's blood-splattered pickup, where they'd also reached the conclusion that Doe's intended target did indeed appear to be the trio of caroling kids and not the commanding general. One look at the tension locking the MP's jaw as he reached her side told her that whatever had gone down was bad.

He popped a salute. "Evenin', Chief. There's been a stabbing in Stryker Housing. Victim's a woman. The captain wants you there. No specifics, but it's gotta be bad. The husband called it in. Man's Special Forces—and he was downright frantic."

Regan tossed the ice scraper inside the Explorer. "Get in."

Wickham wedged his bulk into her passenger seat as she hit the emergency lights and peeled out after the shrieking cruiser. They fishtailed onto Forest Road, neither of them speaking. It was for the best. Four-wheel drive or not, it took all her concentration to keep up with the cruiser as they reached the entrance to Fort Campbell's snowbound Stryker Family Housing. The strobes of the now-silent ambulance bathed the neighborhood in an eerily festive red, ushering them to a cookie-cutter brick-and-vinyl duplex at the end of the street.

Regan brought the SUV to a halt within kissing distance of the cruiser and killed her siren.

Doors slammed as she and the MPs bailed out.

She recognized the closest as the gift-bearing soldier from

the lounge. Specialist Jasik had traded the curvaceous blond for a black, thirty-something private. Staff Sergeant Wickham motioned Jasik to his side. The private headed for the end of the drive to round up the pajama-clad rubberneckers. Life-saving gear in hand, a trio of paramedics waited impatiently for the official all-clear from the MPs.

Regan withdrew her 9mm Sig Sauer from its holster at her outer right thigh as Wickham and Jasik retrieved their M9s before killing the volume on their police radios. Save for the crush of snow, silence reigned as they approached the duplex. A life-sized Santa cutout decorated the front door. A cursory glance at the knob revealed no obvious sign of forced entry. The brass plate above the mail slot provided a name and a rank: Sergeant Patrick Blessing.

Regan moved to the right of Santa's corpulent belly as Wickham assumed the left. Jasik was moving into position when the door opened.

Three 9mms whipped up, zeroed in.

A woman froze in the entryway. Roughly five feet tall, Hispanic, mid-twenties. She was dressed in a long-sleeved pink flannel nightgown and fleece-lined moccasins. Given her wide eyes and rigid spine, she was more startled than they. But she wasn't Mrs. Blessing. Though her cuffs were splattered with blood, the woman appeared uninjured. Definitely not stabbed.

She swallowed firmly. "She—uh—Danielle's out back. I live next door. My husband's a medic." Her voice dropped to a whisper. "He's with them now."

Regan lowered her Sig. The MPs followed suit as the woman waved them in.

Regan tipped her head toward Wickham. She might be senior in rank, but right now, she was junior to the staff sergeant's on-post experience. That included knowledge of Stryker's floor plans. Protocol dictated they assume the suspect was on the premises, possibly controlling the actions of the medic's wife—and search accordingly.

Wickham clipped a nod as he and Jasik headed down the hall.

Regan caught the neighbor's gaze. "Stay here."

The relief swirling into her tear-stained face assured Regan she would. The woman had already seen more than she wanted, and it had shaken her to her core. As Regan passed through the kitchen to join Wickham and Jasik at the sliding glass door in the dining room, she realized why the neighbor was so rattled.

They all did.

They'd found Mrs. Blessing. She was twenty feet away, lying in the snow on her back, clad in a sleeveless, floral nightgown bunched beneath her breasts. Like her neighbor, Danielle was delicate, dark-haired and—despite the gray cast to her flesh—almost painfully pretty. But there was nothing pretty about the knife embedded in her belly. Two men knelt along the woman's left. Judging from his sobs, Regan assumed the bare-chested man just past the woman's head, smoothing curls, was her husband. That pegged the man at her torso, leaning over to blow air through her lips, as the medic. Like the husband, the medic had removed his T-shirt. The shirts were packed around the hilt of the knife, immobilizing the blade in a desperate attempt to keep the flow of blood corked. Given the amount of red saturating the cotton, it wasn't working. Danielle Blessing was bleeding out. But that wasn't the worst of it.

She was pregnant.

"*Jesus H. Chri—*" Jasik swallowed the rest.

The MP regained his composure and grabbed his radio to yell for the paramedics as Regan and Wickham shot through the open slider and across the snow. She'd have to trust that Jasik knew enough to secure the interior of the duplex after his call.

Regan dropped to her knees opposite the medic as the man

thumped out a series of chest compressions. Staff Sergeant Wickham was two seconds behind and two inches beside her.

Odds were, they were already too late.

Danielle Blessing's abdomen was extremely distended—even for a third trimester—and rock hard. An oddly sweet odor wafted up from the makeshift packing, mixing with the cloying stench of blood. It was a scent Regan would recognize anywhere: amniotic fluid. Worse, scarlet seeped from between the woman's thighs, pooling amid the snow.

Regan holstered her Sig and ripped off her camouflaged parka. "What have you got?"

The medic looked up. "No breathing, no pulse. Been that way since I got here—six damned minutes ago." The rest was in his eyes. *Hopeless.*

The medic continued thumping regardless. Working around the knife, she and Wickham covered the woman's lower abdomen, thighs and calves with their coats. Danielle's feet were still exposed to the snow and midnight air. Like her face, they were beyond gray.

Regan shook her head as the medic completed his latest round of chest compressions. "I've got it." She sealed her mouth to the woman's lips. They were ice-cold and unresponsive.

Wickham took over the compressions as Regan finished her breaths. But for the husband's raw sobs and Wickham's thumping, silence filled the night.

Two more rounds of breath, and Regan lost her job. So did Wickham. The paramedics had arrived.

Blessing's neighbor dragged the sergeant to his feet as she and Wickham scrambled out of the way. Two of the paramedics dropped their gear and knelt to double-check Danielle's airway and non-existent vitals as a third probed the saturated T-shirts. Ceding to the inevitable, Regan turned toward the duplex. Jasik stood at the kitchen window, his initial search evidently complete.

The MP shook his head. If someone had broken into the Blessings' home, he or she was gone now.

The slider was still open. The medic had reached the snow-covered steps and stood to the left. Sergeant Blessing had turned and slumped down at the top, halfway inside the slider's frame, his naked feet buried in a drift, his dark head bowing over bloodstained hands, and he was shaking.

From grief? Or guilt?

Unfortunately, she knew. As with the icy furrows left by a drunken Doe's stolen pickup, the snow provided the proof.

Footprints.

They covered the yard. But upon their arrival, there'd been but four telling sets. Once Regan eliminated those left by the his-and-her moccasins of the medic and his wife, she was left with a single, composite trail of overlapping, bare footprints. The leading prints were woefully petite; the following, unusually large. Both sets were dug into the snow as if their owners had torn down the slider's steps and across the yard...all the way to where Danielle lay. Finally, there was the blood. Save for the scarlet slush surrounding the body, there was no sign of splatter —at the slider or along the trail.

For some reason, Sergeant Blessing had deliberately chased and *then* stabbed his wife.

Regan turned to Wickham. "I'll take the husband, question him inside. You take the neighbor. Stay out here." She glanced at the paramedics. "They might need to talk to him." Though she doubted it. There was nothing the sergeant could say that would help his wife now.

Danielle Blessing had been placed on a spine board, stripped down to gray, oozing flesh and redressed with several trauma pads. Half a dozen rolls of Kling gauze anchored the pads and the hilt of the knife. As the brawnier of the paramedics finished intubating the woman's throat and began manually pumping oxygen into her lungs via a big valve mask, his female partner attached the leads of a portable electrocardiogram to Danielle's shoulders and left hip.

Silence had long since given way to a calm, steady stream of medical jargon.

"Patient on cardiac monitor."

"IV spiked on blood set. One thousand milliliters NS. Starting second line—LR on a Macro drip, sixteen gauge."

"I still can't get a pulse."

Judging from that last—not to mention the wad of fresh dressing one of the paramedics used to dry off Danielle's chest—the next step involved shocks. In a perfect world, the woman's heart would restart. But the world was far from perfect. Regan had learned that the hard way. Given that this woman's heart had already been subjected to eight-plus minutes of unsuccessful CPR, the odds that she'd recover were all but nonexistent.

Regan shifted her attention to Wickham. "Ready, Staff Sergeant?"

His nod was stoic. But his sigh was resigned. Bitter. "Merry Christmas."

The past crowded in despite Regan's attempts to keep it at bay. She shook it off. "Yeah."

Wickham doffed his camouflaged cap as they headed for the slider. Though his bald scalp was exposed to the winter air, he appeared not to notice. She couldn't seem to feel the cold either. Nor did the medic.

The husband was still staring at his hands, shaking.

Regan exchanged a knowing frown with Wickham as she reached for her handcuffs. Two strides later, the distinctive whine of a cardiac defibrillator charging filled the night.

And then, "*Clear!*"

A dull thud followed.

The shocks had begun. Even if Danielle made it, there was no hope for her baby. If that knife hadn't killed it, the electrical jolts would. Judging by the panic on the husband's face as he shot to his feet, Sergeant Blessing had figured it out.

"Wait!"

The neighbor grabbed Blessing's right arm. Jasik leapt through the open side of the slider and pinned Blessing's left.

"Charging to three hundred."

Blessing thrashed, nearly knocking both his captors to the ground. "Goddamn it! The *baby*—"

"Clear!"

Jasik regained his hold and drove Blessing to his knees, sealing the sergeant's shins to the ground as the paramedics ripped through the final steps of ECG protocol. As they hit three hundred sixty joules—for the third agonizing time—Blessing accepted the inescapable. His wife and child were dead.

He slumped into the snow as Jasik and the neighbor loosened their grips. A soft keening filled the night, laying waste to every one of Regan's meticulously honed defenses.

Her eyes burned. Her heart followed.

She pulled herself together and tossed her handcuffs to Jasik, her unspoken order clear. *Get it over with.*

Jasik caught the cuffs neatly and bent down.

That was as far as he got.

One moment the lanky MP was behind Sergeant Blessing, pushing him to his knees; the next, Blessing had twisted about, bashing his forehead into Jasik's skull.

A sharp grunt filled the air.

Regan caught the flash of blackened metal as Blessing ripped the 9mm from Jasik's holster. She lunged across the remaining three feet of snow, launching herself at Blessing as the weapon's barrel swung up.

She was too late.

The 9mm's retort reverberated through Regan as she and Blessing smashed into the slider.

To continue reading ***Blind Edge***
CLICK HERE

MEET THE AUTHOR

CANDACE IRVING is the daughter of a librarian and a retired US Navy chief. Candace grew up in the Philippines, Germany, and all over the United States. Her senior year of high school, she enlisted in the US Army. Following basic training, she transferred to the Navy's ROTC program at the University of Texas-Austin. While at UT, she spent a summer in Washington, DC, as a Congressional Intern. She also worked security for the UT Police.

BA in Political Science in hand, Candace was commissioned as an ensign in the US Navy and sent to Surface Warfare Officer's School to learn to drive warships. From there, she followed her father to sea.

Candace is married to her favorite soldier, a former US Army Combat Engineer. They live in the American Midwest, where the Army/Navy football game is avidly watched and argued over every year.

Go Navy; Beat Army!

Candace also writes military romantic suspense under the name Candace Irvin—without the "g"!

Email Candace at www.CandaceIrving.com

or connect via:

bookbub.com/profile/candace-irving
facebook.com/CandaceIrvingBooks
twitter.com/candace_irving
goodreads.com/Candace_Irving

ALSO BY CANDACE IRVING

Deception Point Military Detective Thrillers:

AIMPOINT

Has an elite explosives expert turned terrorist? Army Detective Regan Chase is ordered to use her budding relationship with his housemate —John Garrison—to find out. But John is hiding something too. Has the war-weary Special Forces captain been turned as well? As Regan's investigation deepens, lines are crossed—personal and professional. Even if Regan succeeds in thwarting a horrific bombing on German soil, what will the fallout do to her career?

A Deception Point Military Detective Thriller: A Regan Chase Novella & Book 1 in the series

BLIND EDGE

Army Detective Regan Chase responds to a series of murders and suicides brought on by the violent hallucinations plaguing a Special Forces A-Team—a team led by Regan's ex, John Garrison. Regan quickly clashes with an unforgiving, uncooperative and dangerously secretive John—and an even more secretive US Army. What really happened during that Afghan cave mission? As Regan pushes for answers, the murders and suicides continue to mount. By the time the Army comes clean, it may be too late. Regan's death warrant has already been signed—by John's hands.

A Deception Point Military Detective Thriller: Book 2

BACKBLAST

Army Detective Regan Chase just solved the most horrific case of her career. The terrorist responsible refuses to speak to anyone but her. The claim? There's a traitor in the Army. With the stakes critical, Regan heads for the government's newest classified interrogation site: A US Navy warship at sea. There, Regan uncovers a second, deadlier, terror plot that leads all the way to a US embassy—and beyond. Once again, Regan's on the verge of losing her life—and another far more valuable to her than her own...

A Deception Point Military Detective Thriller: Book 3

CHOKEPOINT

When a US Navy captain is brutally murdered, NCIS Special Agent Mira Ellis investigates. As Mira follows the killer to a ship hijacked at sea, the ties to her own past multiply. Mira doesn't know who to trust—including her partner. A decorated, former Navy SEAL of Saudi descent, Sam Riyad lied to an Army investigator during a terror case and undermined the mission of a Special Forces major. Whose side is Riyad really on? The fate of the Navy—and the world—depends on the answer.

A Deception Point Military Detective Thriller: Book 4

~More Deception Point Detective Thrillers Coming Soon~

Hidden Valor Military Veteran Suspense:

THE GARBAGE MAN

Former Army detective Kate Holland spent years hiding from the world—and herself. Now a small-town cop, the past catches up when a fellow vet is left along a backroad...in pieces. Years earlier, Kate spent eleven hours as a POW. Her Silver Star write-up says she killed eleven terrorists to avoid staying longer. But Kate has no memory of the deaths. And now, bizarre clues are cropping up. Is Kate finally losing her grip on reality? As the murders multiply, Kate must confront her demons...even as she finds herself in the killer's crosshairs.

A Hidden Valor Military Veteran Suspense: Book 1

IN THE NAME OF

Kate Holland finally remembers her eleven hours as a POW in Afghanistan. She wishes she didn't. PTSD raging, Kate's ready to turn in her badge with the Braxton PD. But the wife of a Muslim US Army soldier was stabbed and left to burn in a field, and Kate's boss has turned to her. Kate suspects an honor killing...until another soldier's wife is found in the next town, also stabbed and burned. When a third wife is murdered, Kate uncovers a connection to a local doctor. But the doc is not all she appears to be. Worse, Kate's nightmares and her case have begun to clash. The fallout is deadly as Kate's lured back to where it all began.

A Hidden Valor Military Veteran Suspense: Book 2

BENEATH THE BONES

When skeletal remains are unearthed on a sandbar amid the Arkansas River, Deputy Kate Holland's world is rocked again. The bones belong to a soldier once stationed at a nearby National Guard post. The more Kate digs into the murdered soldier's life, the more connections she discovers between the victim, an old family friend...and her own father. Fresh bodies are turning up too. Will the clues her father missed all those years ago lead to the deaths of every officer on the Braxton police force—including Kate's?

A Hidden Valor Military Veteran Suspense: Book 3

~More Hidden Valor Books Coming Soon~

COPYRIGHT

eBook ISBN: 978-1-952413-26-1

Paperback ISBN: 978-1-952413-30-8

Hardcover ISBN: 978-1-952413-31-5

IN THE NAME OF

This first edition was published by Blind Edge Press in 2021.

This is a work of fiction. The characters in this book do not exist outside the author's imagination. Any resemblance to actual persons, living or dead, is purely coincidental. All incidents in this book were invented by the author for the sole purpose of entertainment.

CPSIA information can be obtained
at www.ICGtesting.com
Printed in the USA
LVHW030020141222
735142LV00001B/66

9 781952 413308